The Charm School

"Miss Peabody," Ryan said, "I came in person because any other way would fail to do justice to the incredibly generous offer you made me."

She pressed her nail-bitten fingers into a steeple. "Then you will take me? I'm going to Rio on your ship?"

"No." He said it swiftly to kill the blooming hope on her face. "It is not that you are lacking in any way," he hastened to add. "The fault is with me, and with my ship and crew. The *Swan* is a working vessel filled with working men. We could never live up to the standards of such a genteel lady as yourself."

She flinched, looking down and to the side. Submissive, defeated. Ryan had the feeling he had drowned a kitten, and the feeling made him angry.

"I should think you'd let me be the judge of that," she ventured timidly.

He gestured across the yard toward the house. "Nothing on the *Silver Swan* can compare to this. You cannot trade paradise for months in cramped quarters in the company of seamen."

"I can, if only you will let me."

Praise for Susan Wiggs's *The Lightkeeper*:
"...captivating sense of place, one that creates an atmospheric energy from start to finish."
—*Publishers Weekly*

The Charm School

Susan Wiggs

MIRA

ISBN 1-55166-491-7

THE CHARM SCHOOL

Copyright © 1999 by Susan Wiggs.

Look us up on-line at: http://www.mirabooks.com

Printed in U.S.A.

To the most charming group of people I know:
LIBRARIANS.

You probably don't remember my name, but you saw me every week. I was the quiet child with the long pigtails and the insatiable appetite for Beverly Cleary, Carol Ryrie Brink and Louise Fitzhugh. I was the one you had to tap on the shoulder at closing time, because I was still sitting on a stool in the stacks, poring over Ramona's latest adventures or sniffling as I read Anne Frank's diary. I was the little girl with the huge wire basket on the front of her bike— for lugging home a stack of books that weighed more than she did.

I never thought to thank you back then, but I didn't understand how very much all those hours, and all those books, and all your patience meant to me or to the writer I would become. But I understand now. So this book is dedicated to you, to all of you, in gratitude for bringing books and readers together.

Thanks to the usual suspects: Joyce, Alice, Christina, Betty and Barb. Also to Jill, Kristin and Debbie, who make this business *much* less isolating.

Thanks also to my editors, Dianne Moggy and Amy Moore-Benson, who helped to shape this work with sensitivity and finesse. Special thanks to Marcy Posner and Robert Gottlieb, whose enthusiasm never flags.

The passages from Hans Christian Andersen's *The Ugly Duckling* (translated from the Danish by Jean Herscholt) are drawn from copy number 1990 of the 2500 Limited Editions Club, copyright 1942 for the George Macy Companies, Inc. The author humbly acknowledges her debt to the wisdom of the great storyteller, who wrote that

"Being born in a duck yard does not matter, if only you are hatched from a swan's egg."

Part One

~~~~~~~~~~~

The Ugly Duckling

"What nice little children you do have, mother," said the old duck with the rag around her leg. "They are all pretty except that one. He didn't come out so well. It's a pity you can't hatch him again."

And the poor duckling who had been the last one out of his egg, and who looked so ugly, was pecked and pushed about and made fun of by the ducks, and the chickens as well. "He's too big," said they all. The turkey gobbler, who thought himself an emperor because he was born wearing spurs, puffed up like a ship under full sail and bore down upon him, gobbling and gobbling until he was red in the face. The poor duckling did not know where he dared stand or where he dared walk. He was so sad because he was so desperately ugly, and because he was the laughingstock of the whole barnyard.

When morning came, the wild ducks flew up to have a look at the duckling. "What sort of creature are you?" they asked, as the duckling turned in all directions, bowing his best to them all. "You are terribly ugly," they told him, "but that's nothing to us so long as you don't marry into our family."

—Hans Christian Andersen,
The Ugly Duckling (1843)

One

> The real offense, as she ultimately perceived, was
> her having a mind of her own at all.
>
> —Henry James,
> *The Portrait of a Lady*

Boston, October 1851

Being invisible did have its advantages. Isadora Dudley Peabody knew no one would notice her, not even if the gleaming ballroom floor decided to open up and swallow her. It wouldn't happen, of course. Disappearing in the middle of a crowded room was bold indeed, and Isadora didn't have a bold bone in her body.

Her mind was a different matter altogether.

She surrendered the urge to disappear, relegating it to the land of impossible things—a vast continent in Isadora's world. Impossible things...a smile that was not forced, a compliment that was not barbed, a dream that was not punctured by the cruel thorn of disappointment.

She pressed herself back in a half-domed alcove window. A sneeze tickled her nose. Whipping out a handkerchief, she stifled it. But still she heard the gossip. The old biddies. Couldn't they find someone else to talk about?

"She's the black sheep of the family in more ways than one," whispered a scandalized voice. "She is so different from the rest of the Peabodys. So dark and ill-favored, while her brothers and sisters are all fair as mayflowers."

"Even her father's fortune failed to buy her a husband," came the reply.

"It'll take more than money—"

Isadora let the held-back sneeze erupt. Then, her hiding place betrayed, she left the alcove. The startled speakers—two of her mother's friends—made a great show of fluttering their fans and clearing their throats.

Adjusting her spectacles, Isadora pretended she hadn't heard. It shouldn't hurt so much. By now she should be used to the humiliation. But she wasn't, God help her, she wasn't. Particularly not tonight at a party to honor her younger sister's engagement. Celebrating Arabella's good fortune only served to magnify Isadora's disgraceful state.

Her corset itched. A rash had broken out between her breasts where the whalebone busk pressed against her sternum. It took a great deal of self-control to keep her hands demurely folded in front of her as she waited in agony for some reluctant, grimly smiling gentleman to come calling for a dance.

Except that they seldom came. No young man wanted to partner an ungainly, whey-faced spinster who was too shy to carry on a normal conversation—and too bored with banal social chatter to try very hard.

And so she stood against the block-painted wall, garnering no more attention than her mother's japanned highboy. The sounds of laughter, conversation and clinking glasses added a charming undertone to the music played by the twelve-piece ensemble. Unnoticed, she glanced across the central foyer toward her father's business study.

Escape beckoned.

In the darkened study, perhaps Isadora could compose herself and—heaven preserve her—wedge a hand down into her corset for a much-needed scratch.

She started toward the entranceway of the ballroom and paused beneath the carved federal walnut arch. She was almost there. She had only to slip across the foyer and down the corridor, and no one would be the wiser. No one would miss her.

Isadora fixed her mind on escape, skirting a group of her brothers' Harvard friends. She scurried past a knot of her father's cronies from the Somerset Club and was nearly thwarted by a gaggle of giggling debutantes. Moving into the foyer, she had to squeeze past a gilt cherub mirror and a graceful Boston fern in a pot with four legs.

One step, then another. Invisible. She was invisible; she could fly like a bird, slither like a snake. She pictured herself lithe and graceful, fleet of foot, causing no more stir than a breeze as she disappeared into nothingness, into freedom—

Deep in one of her fantasies, she forgot about her bow, which stuck out like a duck tail festooned with trailing ribbons.

She heard a scraping sound and turned in time to see that a ribbon had tangled around one of the legs of the fern pot. Time seemed to slow, and she saw the whole sequence as if through a wall of water. She reached for the curling ribbon a second too late. It went taut, upending the large plant. The alabaster pot shattered against the marble floor.

The abrupt movement and the explosion of sound caused everyone to freeze for precisely three seconds. Then all gazes turned to Isadora. The Harvard men. Her mother's friends. Gentlemen of commerce and ladies of society. Trapped by their stares, she stood as motionless—and as doomed—as a prisoner before a firing squad.

"Oh, Dora." As usual, Isadora's elder sister Lucinda took charge. "What a catastrophe, and right in the middle of Arabella's party, too. Here, let me untangle you." A moment later a housemaid appeared with a broom and dust shovel. A moment after that, the ensemble started playing again.

The recovery took only seconds, but to Isadora it spanned an eternity as long as her spinsterhood. Within that eternity, she heard the censorious murmurs, the titters of amusement and the throat-clearings of disapproval that had dogged her entire painful adolescence. Dear heaven, she had to get away from here.

But how did one escape from one's own life?

"Thank you, Lucinda," she said dutifully. "How clumsy of me."

Lucinda didn't deny it, but with brisk movements she brushed off Isadora and smiled up at her. "No harm done, dearest. It will take more than a dropped plant to ruin the evening. All is well."

She meant it, she really did, Isadora realized without rancor. Lucinda, the eldest of the Peabody offspring, was as blond and willowy as Botticelli's Venus. She'd married the richest mill owner in Framingham, moved to a brick-and-marble palace in the green hills, and every other year in the spring, like a prize brood mare, she brought forth a perfect pink-and-white baby.

Isadora forced herself to return her sister's smile. What an odd picture they must make, she thought. Lucinda, who had the looks of a Dresden china doll and Isadora, who looked as if she had an appetite for Dresden German sausage.

Her moment of infamy over, Isadora finally escaped to the study. It was the classic counting-room of a Boston merchant, appointed with finely carved furniture, books bound in tooled leather, and a goodly supply of spirits and tobacco. Breathing in the familiar smells with a sigh of relief, she shut her eyes and nearly melted against the walnut paneling.

"Heave to, girl, you look a bit tangled in your rigging," said a friendly voice. "Something foul-hook you?"

She opened her eyes to see a gentleman sitting in a Rutherford wing chair, an enameled snuffbox in one hand and a cup of cider-and-cream punch in the other.

"Mr. Easterbrook." Isadora came to attention. "How do you do?"

She imagined she could hear Abel Easterbrook's joints creak with rheumatism as he levered himself up and bowed, but his smile, framed by silver side-whiskers, radiated warmth. "I'm in fine trim, Miss Isadora." He seated himself heavily against the coffee-colored leather. "Fine trim, indeed. And yourself?"

I'm still madly in love with your son. Horrified at the thought, she bit back the words. One social blunder per hour should suffice even her.

"Though I've committed foul murder—" she gestured ruefully at the open door, indicating the Boston fern being carried off to the dust bin "—I am quite well, thank you, though the autumn weather has given me a case of the grippe. Did your ship arrive?" She knew Mr. Easterbrook's largest bark was expected in and that he was anxious about it.

He lifted his cup. "She did indeed. Found a berth at harbor tonight, and she's set to discharge cargo tomorrow. Broke records, she did." He dropped his voice to a conspiratorial whisper. "The *Silver Swan* grossed ninety thousand dollars in 190 days."

Isadora gasped, genuinely impressed, for matters of business interested her. "Heavens be, that is quite an achievement."

"I daresay it is. I have the new skipper to thank." Easterbrook toyed with the chain of the money scales on the gateleg table by his chair. Isadora liked Abel Easterbrook because he treated her more like a business associate than a young—or not so very young—lady. She liked him because he had fathered Chad Easterbrook, the most perfect man ever created. Neither of which she would admit on pain of death.

"A new captain?" she inquired politely.

"He's a brash Southerner. A Virginia gent, name of Calhoun. Had such impressive sailing credentials that I hired him on the spot. I judge a man by the cut of his jib, and Calhoun seemed well clewed up."

She smiled, picturing a grizzled old ship captain. Only

a man as conservative as Abel would call his employee "brash."

He took out a handkerchief and buffed his snuffbox until it shone. It was painted with the Easterbrook shipping emblem—a silver swan on a field of blue. "He's still aboard the *Swan* tonight, settling the sailors' bills. Hope to have a new sailing plan from him before the week is out. Next run is to Rio de Janeiro."

"Congratulations," said Isadora. "You've had a marvelous success."

Abel Easterbrook beamed. "Quite so." He lifted his cup in salute. "To you, Miss Isadora. Thank you for keeping an old salt company. And to my speedy new skipper, Mr. Ryan Calhoun."

He barely had time to take a sip when a footman came in and discreetly handed him a note. Abel excused himself and left the study, grumbling about a business that couldn't run without him.

Isadora hung back, savoring her solitude, and mulled over Mr. Easterbrook's news. Ryan Calhoun. A brash Virginia gent. Isadora wasn't brash in the least, though sometimes she wished she were.

She used the moment of privacy to adjust her corset, wishing she knew a curse word or two to describe the whalebone-and-buckram prison. On impulse, she picked up a dagger-shaped letter opener from the desk. Unable to resist the urge, she inserted the letter opener down the bodice of her gown to scratch at the rash that had formed there.

As she eased her discomfort, she chanced to look into the oval mirror hanging on the wall behind her father's desk.

Peering over the thick lenses of her rimless spectacles,

she saw herself for exactly what she was. Her hair was the color of a mud puddle. Her eyes lacked the pure clear blue so prized by her parents and so evident in her siblings. She had none of the gifts of laughter and beauty her brothers and sisters possessed in such abundance. Instead, she wore a sullen expression, and her nose was red from the sniffles.

If the Peabodys were a family that believed in magic—and being proper Bostonians they most certainly were not—they would call Isadora a changeling child: dark where the others were fair, pallid where the others were fashionably pale, round where the others were angular, tall where the others were petite.

The unforgiving mirror reflected a discontented creature in matronly black bombazine stretched over a bone-crushing corset. At her mother's insistence, she wore her hair in a Psyche knot, for the Grecian mode—a topknot with streamers of cascading tendrils—was considered the height of fashion. The problem was, her long, unruly hair stuck out in all directions, and the delicate tendrils resembled fat sausage curls. She made the very picture of youth drying up like a fig on the shelf. The image filled her with such an immense self-loathing and shame that she wanted to do something desperate.

But what? *What?* Could she not even think of an imaginative way to banish her own misery?

Enough, she told herself, giving her bodice a last good scratch with the letter opener. As she did so, the door to the study blew open, and a fresh wave of revelers poured into the foyer. They brought with them the crisp smell of autumn and gales of cultured conversation.

Too late, Isadora realized the guests could see straight into the office. She froze, the letter opener still stuck halfway down the front of her. Loud male laughter boomed from the foyer. "Good God, Izzie," said her brother Quentin, standing amid a group of his friends from Harvard. "Is this your imitation of fair Juliet?"

Too mortified to speak, she managed to extract the letter opener. It dropped with a thud on the carpet. Swept up on a wave of hilarity, Quentin and his friends headed for the ballroom.

Isadora stared down at the dagger on the floor. She wanted to die. She really wanted to die. But then she saw him—the one person who could lift her out of her wretched melancholy.

Chad Easterbrook.

With long, fluid strides he followed Quentin's group to the ballroom, heading for the refreshment table to help himself to frothy cider punch. Immediately, several ladies in pastel gowns managed to sidle near him. Praying her faux pas had not been observed by Chad, Isadora returned to the ballroom.

Chad Easterbrook. His name sang through her mind. His image lived in her heart. His smile haunted her dreams. He moved with effortless grace, black hair gleaming, tailored clothes artlessly stylish. When she looked at Chad, she saw all that she wanted personified in one extraordinary package of charm, wit and sophistication. He wasn't merely handsome to look at; the quality went deeper than that. People wanted to be near him. It was as if their lives became brighter, warmer, more colorful simply by virtue of knowing him. His ideal male beauty was the sort the Pre-Raphaelite painters strove to depict. His charm held the romantic appeal of a drawing room suitor; he beguiled his listeners with low-voiced witticisms and languorous laughter.

Isadora pushed her spectacles down her nose and stared, wanting him with such fierceness that her itching busk flared into a fiery ache. If only...she thought. If only he could look into her soul and see all she had to offer him.

But it was hard for a man to look into a woman's soul when he had to see past bombazine and buckram and worst of all, a painful shell of bashfulness. The few times he'd deigned to speak to her, he'd asked her to relay a message to Arabella, whose hand in marriage he'd narrowly lost to Robert Hallowell III.

Still, she wished things could be different, that for once she could be the pretty one, the popular one—to see what it was like. To dance one time with Chad Easterbrook, to feel his arms around her, to know the intimacy of a private smile.

He and his cronies alternated between spirited bursts of laughter and dramatic whispers of conspiracy. Then, one by one, each young man paired himself off with a lady for the next dance. The tune was "Sail We Away" set to an irresistible rhythm and new enough to pique the interest of even the most blasé socialite.

Incredibly, Chad Easterbrook emerged from the group with no partner. He set down his crystal cup of punch and started walking toward Isadora. She watched, enraptured, as he crossed the room. She forgot to breathe as he stopped and bowed in gallant fashion, lamplight flicking blue tones in his hair.

"I don't suppose, Miss Peabody," he said in his melodic voice, "you'd consider doing me an enormous favor."

She glanced over her shoulder and spied nothing but her father's moose head hunting trophy from Maine. Her face aflame, she turned back to Chad. "Me?" she said, her voice breaking.

With a patient smile, he nodded.

She felt faint with amazement. "You're addressing me?"

"Unless that moose bears the name Miss Peabody, I believe I am." He spoke with the lazy, sardonic inflection that characterized longtime Harvard club men. "Come, Miss Isadora. Don't leave me in suspense any longer. Don't make me beg."

Could he possibly want to dance with her? That had to be it. Chad Easterbrook wanted to dance with her. "I...I'd be delighted," she managed to choke out. Oddly, she experienced the exchange as if she were an observer outside her body. The dowdy spinster and the dashing scholar. If the miracle weren't happening right before her very eyes, she'd never believe it.

Bowing, he offered his hand. Isadora took it, glad for the moleskin gloves her mother insisted she wear, for that way Chad would never know how icy and clammy her palms were.

Since he stood a few inches shorter, she hunched her shoulders a bit, breathless with surprise and delight. So this is what it feels like, she thought, letting the melody enter her veins like fine wine. This is what a dream come true feels like.

Chad's attention lifted her lighter than air; she felt more graceful than a swan on still water. Finally, finally she had broken through his indifference. Finally he was going to dance with her.

But instead of leading her out onto the parquet floor, he brought her into the domed alcove that had been her refuge at the start of the ball. Ye powers, an assignation?

Was that what he wanted? She almost laughed aloud with delight.

A gold-fringed drape concealed them. Moist-eyed, tingling all over, she nearly burst with expectancy as she pushed down her spectacles and watched him. "Yes, Chad? What was it you wanted?"

He began rummaging in the pocket of his waistcoat. "This will take only a moment of your time.... Let's see, I had it here somewhere...."

A watch on a chain slipped out of his pocket. In addition to the watch, he held a small gold ring with a blue topaz stone in it. Praise be, was he going to ask her to marry him? For the first time in her life, Isadora understood a lady's need for a fan, for she had broken out in a copious sweat.

"I'd like you to take this." He pressed the ring into her hand.

"Oh, Chad." Her heart brimmed over with happiness. "I don't know what to say."

"Say you'll do it." His smile was vague, his eyes restless as he pulled the curtain aside and scanned the crowd.

Her finger was too thick for the dainty ring. "Of course I will, but—"

"She's there, in that lavender dress." Putting one hand on Isadora's shoulder, he leaned out of the alcove and pointed. "Lydia Haven. She's dancing with Foster Candy. I took her ring as a prank and she's so cross with me, she won't allow me near her to give it back. Do tell her I'm sorry...."

Isadora didn't hear the rest over the rush of blood in her ears. Through a blur of humiliation she saw Lydia Haven, ravishing in her lilac gown, tipping back her head as she laughed at a jest made by her dancing partner.

"You want me," she managed to say, "to deliver Miss Haven's ring to her?"

"That's it exactly, there's a girl." With his hand tucked into the small of her back, he steered her out of the alcove.

The hard busk dug into her breastbone as she resisted him. "Mr. Easterbrook," she said.

"Yes?"

She yearned to hurl the ring right into his excessively handsome face. Instead, she did something worse. Something much, much worse.

She looked him in the eye and said, "As you wish."

"I knew I could count on you, Izzie my girl." He gestured at the crowd. "Oh, look, you'll have to hurry. The set's ended."

Hating herself, she marched off to do as he asked. She handed the ring back to its owner. Lydia gave her a lovely smile and said, "Why, thank you, Dora. I thought you were going to steal Chad clean away from me." She and her friends giggled, each peal of mirth a lethal dagger. "Look at you in your black," Lydia continued, fingering the gros grain ribbon trim on Isadora's skirt. "What are you mourning, dear?"

The death of good manners, Isadora thought, but she was too mortified to speak. Pursued by female titters, she tried to beat a hasty retreat. But her way was blocked by a blond woman with a belled pointe skirt and an ivory-and-lace fan. The lady smiled tentatively, as if she were about to offer a greeting.

Isadora curtsied, hoping the flaming blush in her cheeks would subside. Only the stiff corset held her upright as she brushed past the woman. Had it not been for the merciless undergarment, she would have crumpled from pure shame. She had to get away, and quickly.

To her horror, she heard someone calling to her. "Dear, dear Isadora," sang Mrs. Robert Hallowell Jr. The mother of Arabella's intended, she beamed with the bright dazzle of social triumph. "Aren't we fetching tonight?"

"Some of us are," Isadora said in an undertone.

"How happy you must be to see your younger sister become a bride. Why, soon it will be just yourself and your dear, dear parents, all alone in this house. Won't that be cozy?"

"We shall be cozy indeed," she said to Mrs. Hallowell, "and how terribly kind of you to point it out."

"Come along," the older lady said. "We must raise a toast to the betrothal."

No, dear God, no, she could not face them all now. Isadora had never been adept at concealing her feelings; her family would know immediately that she was upset, would question her in their unbearably well-intentioned way, and she would fall to pieces before them.

"Isadora, didn't you hear me? You must come join the family circle. And where have your brothers got to?" Mrs. Hallowell waved her gloved hand impatiently.

Someone grasped Isadora's arm. Startled, she gave a little cry and drew back to find herself looking at the blond woman she'd practically trampled while trying to escape the ballroom.

Perfect curls. A mature, deeply beautiful face. Eyes full of sympathy. One look into those eyes confirmed what Isadora had suspected—the woman had witnessed Isadora's grinding humiliation.

"May I...help you?" Isadora asked.

"Why, yes, as a matter of fact." The woman turned to Mrs. Hallowell. "I'm feeling the tiniest bit faint, Hester. Isadora has been so kind as to offer me the refuge of her chamber for a small rest."

Mrs. Hallowell's eyes narrowed. "But Lily, we were going to toast the new family circle."

"I'm sure our guest's comfort takes precedence over a toast," Isadora murmured. Weak with gratitude, she led the woman up the stairs to her large, airy chamber and shut the door, smashing her backside against it for emphasis. "Thank you," she said softly.

The woman waved away her thanks as she turned up the flame of a gaslight. "My name is Mrs. Lily Raines Calhoun," she said.

Isadora detected a soft Southern accent in Lily's voice. "How do you do? You're visiting from out of town?"

"Indeed I am. I come from Virginia, though I've recently returned from three years on the Continent. The Hallowells were kind enough to invite me to your family's party."

"I hope you're having a pleasant time." Strains of music and a round of applause wafted up from the ballroom. Arabella and her handsome fiancé would be the center of attention now, surrounded by Lucinda and Quentin and Bronson and their parents, bursting with pride. Isadora suppressed the urge to clap her hands over her ears.

"As a matter of fact, I'm not. I've been hoping to have a word with Mr. Abel Easterbrook."

"Oh, dear. I'm afraid he's been called away from the party on business."

Lily peeled off her gloves and lifted a crystal vial of rose water. "May I?"

"Of course."

She sprinkled the fragrant water on her wrists. "I suppose I shall have to wait, then. I am no stranger to waiting." She lowered her head, the gaslight touching a delicate profile, a face haunted by doubt. "I'm actually looking for Ryan Calhoun. As it turns out, he's run off to sea aboard an Easterbrook vessel."

Isadora's problem with Chad faded quickly to pettiness. Here was a woman who had traveled across the Atlantic to see her husband—only to find him missing.

"Dear heaven, Mrs. Calhoun, I'm so sorry," she said, crossing the room to take the lady's hands. "I—what did you say his name was?"

"Ryan. Ryan Michael Calhoun."

"What a marvelous coincidence," Isadora said, hugely pleased to feel a sudden sense of purpose. "You needn't bother with Mr. Easterbrook at all. I can take you directly to Ryan Calhoun. Tonight, if you wish."

"What?"

"I know exactly where he is, Mrs. Calhoun."

Two

Now our ship is arrived
And anchored in the Sound.
We'll drink a health to the whores
That does our ship surround.

Then into the boat they get
And alongside they came.
"Waterman, call my husband,
For I'm damned if I know his name."

—"A Man of War Song"
(traditional)

"What did you say your name was, sugar-pie?" Ryan Calhoun asked the woman in his lap. She and the others had arrived in bumboats even before the *Silver Swan* had moored. The harbor lovelies hadn't waited for the docking; they did their most brisk business swarming aboard a ship that had dropped anchor after being at sea for months.

Thus, the *Swan* had found its berth courtesy of a harried harbor pilot, with a half-dozen bawds accompanying him.

"Sugar-pie suits me just fine," she said with a moist-lipped laugh, then fed him a generous gulp of rum from the engraved silver flask he'd bought in Havana.

He raised no objection when the whore slipped the costly flask into the top of her worsted-silk stocking. Nothing could dampen Ryan's spirits tonight. Dressed in his favorite lime-green waistcoat—with no shirt underneath—he sat on the high deck of the fastest bark in Boston; his crew reveled wildly as the moon rose over the harbor, and a vast quantity of sweet liquor boiled through his veins. Life for Ryan Calhoun was good indeed.

"'S'all yours, sugar-pie," he said agreeably. "'S'all yours."

"Aye-aye, skipper," she said with a giggle.

He leaned forward so that his face was almost buried in her cleavage. Then he shut his eyes, his gently spinning head echoing the constant motion of the ship at sea, the ship that had been his home for the past nine months. What better life had a man but this? he wondered—a successful voyage, a well-endowed woman encumbered with nothing so inconvenient as a mind of her own, and a bottle of sugary Jamaican rum.

He breathed deeply of the soft, faintly sweaty flesh. Female musk. There was no more evocative substance the world over. So what if this woman had no name, so what if she was coarse, so what if she stole from him? She possessed the only thing worth having. It would take a better man than Ryan to quibble with Nature herself. Showing unsteady reverence, he kissed one breast, then the other, pressing his mouth into the softness pushed up by an artfully inadequate corset.

"Ooh, skipper." Unblushing, she brought one long leg around his midsection. "I came here for more than teasing."

He opened his eyes and blinked up into her painted, fleshy face. She had few qualities that properly belonged to a lady but for the shape, the name and that precious essence. He wondered if he was still sober enough to stagger off to his stateroom with her.

Leaning back in the deck chair, he could see into the gangway leading to the orlop deck. A man and woman in a hammock swayed with a familiar rhythm, the woman's legs bare to the hams and hanging over the sides of the webbed sling. Another couple slept atop a coil of rope, a bottle cradled between them. Amidships, Chips and Luigi Conti made music with mouth harp and whistle while Journey, the steward, pounded out a rhythm on a skin drum. Dancing couples reeled and laughed, bumping into barrels and crates. Someone had unlatched the hen coop, and a few biddies ran around the deck in hilarious confusion.

Something distant and sober inside Ryan suddenly came to attention. For once in his misbegotten life, he'd succeeded. And not in a small way, but in a way all the world would notice. He'd made a voyage in record time; he'd delivered a fortune to the ship's owner.

If only his father had lived, perhaps he would have acknowledged Ryan's achievement. That would have been a first.

Ryan felt a peculiar thickness in his throat. He'd succeeded. He wished he could freeze this moment in his heart and keep it there forever. He wished he had someone besides a nameless prostitute to share it with.

He banished the darkness and resolved to enjoy his triumph.

"A toast!" he roared, holding the woman's clasped hand aloft like a prize-fighter. "To the *Swan,* and to all her brave crew!"

"To us!" the men bellowed, clinking mugs.

Ryan aimed a crooked grin at his companion, who had begun squirming suggestively in his lap. "Sugar-pie, my legs are going numb."

She screeched with laughter. "I hope that don't affect the rest of you."

"We'll see when we get to the stateroom."

Her hips ground down on him. "Who needs the stateroom?"

He had a fleeting thought of privacy, but the rum— and the whore's sly fingers—coaxed a dark, desire-filled laugh from him. With slow, teasing movements he plunged his hand beneath her skirts. He found the stolen flask but passed it right over in pursuit of richer treasures.

No doubt the puritanical Mr. Easterbrook would be appalled to see such revelry on his ship, but Ryan banished the last of his scruples. No proper Bostonian would show up now. Anyone who strayed to the docks at this time of night deserved what he saw.

"I feel quite wicked being out so late," Isadora confessed to Lily Raines Calhoun. She leaned back against the burgundy leather seat of the hooded clarence. Her father, who always demanded the best, had had the carriage fitted with a curved glass, like a show window, in the front. Lily and Isadora sat side by side on the rear seat, watching the city through the glass.

A waning moon cast the State House dome in pale gray; misty orbs of gaslight glowed along State Street, and shadows haunted side streets and Merchants' Row.

"Your driver looked a mite startled when we told him we wanted to go to the harbor," Lily remarked. "I do hope this won't cause trouble with your family."

"Believe me, Mrs. Calhoun, since the age of fourteen, I've done nothing but cause trouble for my family."

Lily turned, the light on her face flickering from pale to gold in the swinging glow of the carriage lantern. "Whatever can you mean?"

Isadora toyed idly with the strings of her lace cap. "Until I was fourteen, I lived with a maiden aunt in Salem. I only saw my family once in a great while." She thought back to the long, dreamy years with Aunt Button when nothing mattered more than spending a few hours reading a wonderful book. "It was an arrangement that suited all of us very well indeed. But when my great aunt died, I had to return to the house on Beacon Hill. I'm afraid I've been a trial to them ever since."

"I can't imagine you a trial," Lily said.

"Yes, you can," Isadora replied with gentle censure. "You're too kind to say so. A plain spinster, awkward in conversation, clumsy on the dance floor—I'm a trial, especially to the Peabodys."

"We all have our own unique gifts. It is incumbent upon the larger society to discover them."

"And if they do not?"

Lily Calhoun turned on the seat so that she was facing Isadora. The shifting lamplight glazed her face with fire. Very deliberately, with her dainty gloved hands, she reached out and removed Isadora's small rectangular-lensed spectacles, letting them dangle from the black silk ribbon around her neck.

"Why then, my dear Miss Peabody," she said in her lazy, lovely drawl, "they aren't seeing you at all."

It was something so like Aunt Button would have said that Isadora felt a sudden lump in her throat.

"They are the Peabodys of Beacon Hill." Isadora used her haughtiest accent, coaxing a smile from Lily. "They see the world as they think it should be seen."

"Perhaps you're in the wrong world, then."

"It's the only one I know, Mrs. Calhoun." Isadora turned a rueful smile out the window. A newcomer—and a Southerner at that—couldn't understand. In families like the Peabodys', nothing changed, ever. It was the sacred mission of each generation of Peabodys to carry on exactly as their parents had before them, and so on until the end of time.

Misfits like Isadora were culled from the herd. Put off somewhere until weariness and middle age rendered them harmless. In old age, they could actually become useful as Aunt Button had. They could watch over the misfits of succeeding generations.

There had to be something else, Isadora often thought. But what? She yearned to fly away free, to escape. But what she wished to escape was her own life, and that was the one thing she couldn't get away from.

She wanted to slap herself for even thinking in such bleak terms. Willfully she pulled her mind away from depressing thoughts and turned back to her companion.

Lily Calhoun stared straight ahead, her front teeth worrying her lower lip. "I'd best warn you about

Ryan," she said. "He's the black sheep of his family, though I've never cared for that term."

Isadora's interest was piqued. Perhaps she and this Ryan Calhoun had something in common. "Is he a constant trial?"

"A trial? My dear, he could charm a pearl from an oyster."

Isadora's interest waned. She had nothing in common with a charming person.

"I had hoped that coming north would instill in him a sense of responsibility. Instead, the first thing he did upon leaving Virginia was to set his manservant free."

"He had a slave?" Distaste coiled in Isadora's belly.

Lily nodded. "He and Journey were like brothers."

"And he freed his 'brother.'"

"He did indeed."

"Bravo," Isadora said decisively.

"Abolitionist?" Lily asked.

"I am."

"Now we know what topics of conversation we must avoid if we're to be friends." Lily paused, then added, "It's strange being here in the company of Yankees. Most of you regard me as a half-educated Southern slavemistress."

"I doubt that. Beacon Hill's best families have made their fortunes milling cotton grown by slave labor. It's considered gauche to bring the topic up—though that's never stopped me from opposing it."

The clarence lurched around the corner to India Street. Like reaching fingers, the darkened wharves projected out into Town Cove and Boston Harbor. The masts and spars of clipper ships, brigs, sloops and schooners rose against the night sky.

"Oh, my." Lily gazed out at the dazzle of anchor lamps on black water. "It's finally real to me. My Ryan really did run away to sea."

"Mr. Easterbrook was most pleased with the job he did." Isadora felt the urge to defend Ryan Calhoun, a man who'd had the courage to free a slave. "He made a voyage in record time. I understand the next run is to Rio."

To Isadora, Rio de Janeiro was more than a place on a map. She and Aunt Button used to read stories of distant places. Rio had been a particular favorite, famous for its exotic carnivals. They had stayed up late, imagining the hot smell of roasting coffee and the sound of Latin tenors and samba music. When Aunt Button was too ill to see anymore, Isadora would sit and read aloud to her for hours. One of the last books they'd read together took place in Rio.

As they neared the berths of Easterbrook Wharf, Isadora reached for the speaking tube to alert the driver. She looked forward to meeting this man who pleased Abel Easterbrook and earned a fortune, this man who freed slaves. A black sheep who had succeeded so soundly in his chosen profession would be an inspiration to her.

Perhaps he was in his aft stateroom, resting after the fruitful voyage. Or perhaps he sat at the checkered counting table, doling out sailors' bills to the common seamen. Perhaps—

The sound of shattering glass caused the horses to shy. While the driver subdued them, Isadora leaned over the running board and looked out.

The *Silver Swan* ran more than its anchor lamps. Bright Japanese lanterns swayed from her spars, halyards and outriggers, illuminating the decks. Every once in a while, someone set off a fireblossom that soared skyward with a whistle, then made a starburst of yellow sulfur light.

When the coach rolled to a halt, Isadora didn't wait for the driver to open the door. She descended on her own, lurching a little when she landed.

Lily held back for the driver, then alighted like a butterfly on a flower. The tinny sound of pipes and the thud of a drum issued from the high decks of the bark.

"Carriage ho!" someone shouted, then loosed a braying laugh.

"Where away?" yelled another voice.

"Fine on the starboard quarter!" A shadowed shape came to the rail. Isadora tugged self-consciously at the knotted strings of her cap and patted her lacquered sausage curls.

"More ladies! More ladies!" shouted a rum-roughened voice. "Welcome aboard!"

More ladies?

Isadora straightened her shoulders and offered her arm to Lily. "I suppose we should board, then."

Lily pressed her mouth into a flat line, and Isadora wondered what could be passing through her mind. The prodigal husband was supposed to humble himself and come home. Not force the wife to come to him.

"Come spare us a favor, loveys," yelled the rum voice. "We just swallowed anchor after three seasons at sea!"

Lily paused. "I would suggest that you go back to the carriage. This will not be pleasant."

"Nonsense. It was my idea to bring you here. If you're going, I'm going." Isadora took Lily firmly by the arm. They went aboard via the slanting gangplank, steadying themselves with the rope rails. The music's tempo grew stronger; so did the laughter—and the syrupy stench of rum.

Isadora frowned in confusion. Mr. Easterbrook had implied that Ryan Calhoun was a skilled and disciplined skipper. Surely he would not allow—

"Oh, dear Lord above." Lily stopped on the midships deck. Her grip on Isadora's arm tightened.

The whole deck resembled a Hogarth painting—the lowest of the low, engaged in the lowest of pursuits. The screeching whistle was piped by a sailor with a mustache. A Negro man with a skin drum and another with a mouth harp accompanied him.

Isadora fumbled with her spectacles. Even in her imagination she could not have conjured up such a scene: jack-tars in loose trousers and striped shirts dancing with bare-legged women who kissed them in public. Chickens running willy-nilly around the deck. A huge bald man with a ring of gold gleaming in one ear stood drinking directly from an unbunged barrel, upended and balanced upon his bare shoulder.

She brought her shocked gaze in a full circle around the brightly lit deck, and at the last she found herself gaping at an extraordinary man. Like a king on a throne, he sat upon a big armless chair. Backlit by burning torches, the laughing man appeared almost inhumanly handsome with a long fall of fiery red hair flowing over his broad shoulders and framing his chiseled face. He wore a garish green waistcoat that left too much of his brawny arms and chest uncovered. Draped across his lap lay a woman whose bosoms spilled from her bodice. His left arm supported her generous girth; the other—heavens be—was plunged deep beneath the tattered folds of her skirts and petticoats.

Shocking as that sight proved to be, Isadora felt her attention captured by the man's face and demeanor. He had not yet noticed them, for he was preoccupied with the woman. There was something darkly compelling about the way he kept his concentration riveted upon the lady, regarding her with total absorption as if he meant to lose himself in her.

The man with the drum began to beat a tattoo that curiously resembled the nervous warning of a rattle snake.

Finally the red-haired man looked up, raising his face from its fleshy pillow and peering over the woman's bosoms. He studied Isadora for a moment; then, dismissing her, he moved his gaze to Lily. Giving a lopsided, beatific grin, he said in a smooth Virginia drawl, "Hello, Mother."

Three

Why not seize the pleasure at once? How often is
happiness destroyed by preparation, foolish
preparation!

—Jane Austen,
(1798)

The music stopped. Ryan felt the whore shift on his lap
as she twisted to see the newcomers. She scowled bleary
eyed at the tall woman with the corkscrew curls poking
out from the rim of a bonnet. "The fat one's your
mother?"

"No." With as much poise as he could muster, he set
the woman on deck and stood up, pressing the backs of
his knees against the chair to steady himself. Chips, the
carpenter, had the presence of mind to step forward and
lead the whore away, pacifying her with a fresh flask.

Ryan did his best to straighten out his crooked grin.
"Mother, what an unexpected surprise."

"I clearly am," Lily said.

Drunk as he was, Ryan read the disappointment in her

face. It pulled down the corners of her mouth, made her hesitate for a heartbreakingly long moment before she reached out and embraced him.

He reeked of rum and cheap perfume. He pulled back quickly, not wanting to taint his mother. Nothing had changed since the last time he'd seen her, not really. At their parting, they had been standing together at Albion Landing in the south reaches of Chesapeake Bay. She'd warned him that eschewing the University of Virginia and going north to Harvard would demand more from him, far more than he could possibly imagine. Possibly more than he had within him.

Drunk or sober, he was doomed to disappoint his mother, no matter what he did. He regretted being so public about it. He gestured toward the high aft deck. "Come to the stateroom. We can talk there—"

"What in the name of Saint Elmo's fire is going on?" demanded a furious voice.

Ryan blinked his bleary eyes and groaned. Abel Easterbrook. Just what he needed. For the first time, apprehension touched his spine with ice. Tonight's revels had put his whole mission in jeopardy. He and Journey were so close to their goal. One more voyage, and they'd have the money they needed. Now, thanks to his lack of restraint, he might have put the next voyage in doubt.

Fixing yet another lopsided smile on his face, he hid his thoughts and bowed to greet his employer. The sweetness of rum pushed ominously at the back of his throat. He swallowed hard, hoping he wouldn't disgrace himself even more than he already had. "I was conducting a small celebration in honor of our safe return, sir." He exaggerated the enunciation of each word, hoping the long, slurred vowels would simply be attributed to his Southern upbringing rather than all that rum. "I thought a bit of levity would be good for company morale."

"You're not paid to think." Easterbrook's stormy gaze swept the decks, taking in the half-clad couples crumpled in the shadows, the men clustered eagerly around the keg, the chickens poking through spilled crumbs. "I am shocked. Shocked, I say. Small celebration indeed."

"It is, sir. You see, where I come from..." Ryan paused. He'd made up so many lies to get Easterbrook to hire him that he had to stop for a moment to recall them. "Uh, aboard the *Twyla* of famous memory, it was considered a grievous error to send the crew ashore sober. There was the danger, you see, that the men would take landlubber jobs and wouldn't sign on for the next voyage."

With a grand gesture, he encompassed the deck, littered with motley drunkards and coarse bawds. "These are the men who have given the *Silver Swan* her place in the record books. They have earned their reward." He caught the eye of Ralph Izard, the chief mate. At his skipper's pleading look, Izard clapped his hands, sending people lurching and stumbling belowdecks.

Ryan stepped back with a gallant point of his booted foot. "Mr. Easterbrook, allow me to introduce my mother, Mrs. Lily Raines Calhoun and her companion—" He broke off, eyeing the dark-clad woman in the spectacles. She stood with gloved hands clasped tightly as if praying for his immortal soul.

If she knew Ryan Calhoun at all, she'd realize her efforts were for naught. He was doomed. It would take more than a lady's fervent prayers to save him.

Easterbrook bowed over Lily's extended hand. Then he turned to the other woman. "Shiver my timbers, Miss Isadora. What in the name of Davy Jones are you doing here?"

"You know each other?" Ryan staggered against a hatch coaming, putting out a hand to catch himself.

"I was summoned from a social gathering at her father's home, damn your eyes. I have no idea what she's doing here."

The woman called Miss Isadora cleared her throat. "Well, I thought—that is, Mrs. Calhoun happened to ask about her...*son,* and since you'd mentioned that he was here with the *Swan* I thought, er, that is, Mrs. Calhoun was a guest at our party tonight, as were you, sir. Only she was a guest of the Hallowells—the groom's family, you see. She seemed so eager to locate Mr.—er, Captain Calhoun, so I deemed it reasonable to suppose we would find him aboard."

Ryan wondered if the lady had been at the rum, so garbled was her explanation. He eyed her downward sloping shoulders, her twisting, praying hands. Christ, the woman was terrified.

"Mr. Easterbrook." Lily's voice slid like warm molasses into the conversation. "Miss Peabody was kind enough to conduct me here when she learned I was looking for my son."

The timbre of her voice coaxed a puppy-dog smile from the old codger. Lily Raines Calhoun had that way about her. She was a sorceress with her voice, her accent, her intimate inflections. With the softest of comments, she had the power to mesmerize her listeners. Only Ryan could discern the steel beneath the gossamer silk of her voice. Especially when she said the words "my son."

He was in trouble. He was in terrible trouble.

And as always, he didn't give a damn.

"And now, thanks to you," Lily continued, sending a lovely, supplicating smile at Abel Easterbrook, "I have found him. Perhaps you would be so gallant as to drive us home, Mr. Easterbrook."

"It would be my honor," Easterbrook said. "I can conclude my business in a moment or two." He turned to Ryan. "I was shanghaied from a dancing party by my houseman. It seems Rivera is being sought by the police for questioning." Clasping his hands behind his waist like an admiral, Easterbrook paced in agitation. "Police are on the trot for runaway slaves these days."

During Ryan's absence, the Fugitive Slave Law had gone into effect, making it illegal to abet or harbor runaways. "Rivera's not involved in that," he said quickly. "He's got more games than a ship has rats, but none of them involve fugitives."

"Then where in Hades is he?"

"I'm afraid Rivera didn't return with us. He married a woman in Havana and wouldn't leave her." There was, of course, much more to the story—a duel, a bribe, a furious father, a forced marriage—but Ryan knew better than to overexplain the matter, particularly in mixed company.

"Well, he's a criminal and good riddance," Abel said.

"He was a mighty fine interpreter," Ryan reminded him, struggling to think past the fog of rum in his brain. "The best we had."

"So now I am liable for his debts, and I have no

Spanish interpreter for future voyages. Well done indeed, Captain."

The woman called Isadora Peabody whispered something in a nervous breath.

"What's that?" Abel demanded grumpily.

"I speak Spanish." Miss Isadora looked appalled that she had actually dared to utter a word. Staring at the planks, she added, "Also French, Italian and Portuguese. My great aunt tutored me in languages, and then at Mount Holyoke Seminary I continued—" She broke off, clearing her throat. "My, I do go on. Forgive me. What I mean to say is, if you have documents that need translating, I could perhaps help."

"Thank you for the offer, my dear. But I could never prevail upon a lady." Easterbrook swung back to Ryan again. "You, sir, are an irredeemable dandy-cock and worse."

Ryan tried his best to bear the insult with proper stoic contrition. But he couldn't help it. When he opened his mouth, laughter burst out. It took several tries to stop. Finally he found a handkerchief and wiped his eyes. "Mr. Easterbrook, forgive me. I hope you'll understand that this small festive occasion is the only amusement we've had in a hundred eighty days, and that you'll—"

"Calhoun?"

"Yes, sir?"

"Shut up, Calhoun."

"Sir," the Peabody woman said, "I realize this is only my opinion, but earlier this evening you spoke of Mr. Calhoun's prodigious talent for running a fast, profitable ship."

Ryan squared his shoulders. "Ma'am," he said unsteadily, "I don't know who the hell you are, but you're a fine judge of character."

She eyed him suspiciously, then cut her gaze away—in fright or in disgust, he couldn't tell.

Easterbrook cleared his throat. "I will grant you this. You have made a difficult voyage in record time. You have added a fortune to the company coffers. And so I am trying to convince myself to give you a second chance. Tuesday at five o'clock I shall come here to discuss a new sailing plan. At that time, I expect you to have a new translator in place and the *Swan*'s cargo discharged, her papers in order and a new cargo lined up for the winter ice run to Rio de Janeiro."

Ryan had no idea how he would accomplish all that in such a short time. But he needed the post, needed to skipper another command. More desperately than anyone could imagine. He wished the seriousness of his cause had occurred to him before the harbor bawds had swarmed aboard.

All his life he'd been borne along by personal charm, good looks and a general lack of respect for convention. Those shallow virtues weren't enough anymore. Now he had to dig deeper and see if he had what it took to succeed. And so he nodded smartly. "You will have it. You can count on me."

"Don't disappoint me, Calhoun."

"I shan't, sir."

Easterbrook tossed him a suspicious glare. Then he cocked out both arms. "Allow me, ladies."

Ryan sagged against the deck chair, allowing himself a long, slow sigh of relief. If he could survive both his mother and his employer tonight, how hard could tomorrow be?

* * *

It was impossible, Isadora decided the next day as she stood in the parlor of her parents' Beacon Hill mansion. Impossible to believe he still might want her.

She sneezed explosively, clapping a handkerchief to her nose and cursing the persistent grippe that plagued her. Then she looked down for the hundredth time at the hastily dashed-off note that had been delivered this morning. From Chad Easterbrook.

After the sting of her humiliation the night before, the invitation soothed her like a balm. Suddenly the world didn't look so bleak; suddenly the colors of autumn she spied out her window glowed with stunning vibrance. It was a perfect day, with the russet leaves swirling in the breeze and Squire Pickering's hawthorn hedge ablaze with sunset colors. Asters and mums and unexpected bursts of late-blooming roses decked the long, narrow, tiered garden in the back.

She sneezed again. A pity the colorful season plagued her this way.

Chad Easterbrook's note affected her in the same manner the autumn colors adorned the landscape. He turned her drab world bright. Judging by their conversation the night before, she had no reason to hope that he would show her favor. But oh, she hoped. Hoped until she ached with it. Perhaps this time would be different. This time, doing his bidding would endear her to him.

She had to believe that. She had to believe there was an end to her loneliness. That something—some*one*— could fill the well of emptiness inside her. And that someone was Chad Easterbrook.

She sighed, holding herself very stiff and straight so that the busk of her corset wouldn't stab into her. Closing her eyes, she allowed herself a small smile of triumph. Chad wanted her to participate in the afternoon's diversion—a croquet match on Kimball Green.

She pictured the scene: Chad and his crowd wearing dress whites and assembled on the green for croquet. She glowed at the thought of being one of the happy group as they spent a lazy afternoon in laughter and sunshine. Thanks to Chad, she would soon be a part of his charmed world.

Lovingly, a smile playing about her lips, she folded his note and tucked it in the most romantic spot she could think of—beneath her busk.

It itched.

The memory of the ball reared in her mind. She pictured herself stumbling to help Chad with his romantic entanglement. Making a spectacle of herself by knocking over the plant. Being seen scratching her chest with a letter opener. Stammering an excuse to Mrs. Hallowell. Rushing off to find Ryan Calhoun at the harbor.

The thought of the red-headed Virginian, his lap draped with a half-clad woman and his belly full of rum, brought an unexpected twitch of disgust to Isadora's mouth. No matter how deeply she humiliated herself, she had never sunk to that level.

She had finally met someone who was more of a disgrace than she was.

He would never know what a comfort he was to her.

She straightened her shoulders. Today would be different, she thought, holding back a sneeze. Today she'd redeem herself from last night's fiasco.

First, a dress. Though she had absolutely no sense of fashion, she knew better than to wear black to a croquet match. She plucked up her skirts and hurried to her chambers, opening the walnut clothes press and peering inside.

Dear heavens. When had she managed to amass such a collection of black, brown and gray? She had black gowns with black lace. Black gowns with brown piping. Black gowns with gray eyelet. But there—off to one side. It was an ecru tea gown made for some awkward, forgotten social occasion. The dress was just the thing for an afternoon of croquet.

She rang for Thankful, and the maid arrived in a trice, setting her feather duster on the bed. "Well, it's different, miss, and that's a fact," Thankful said, picking up the pale India cotton dress.

"Do you think it's too different from my usual style?" Isadora asked.

"Yes, it is." With the brisk efficiency that had served her—and the Peabody family—well for three decades, Thankful took up her stay hook and freed Isadora from the black day gown. Then she held up the new dress. "Let's see if we can make this fit."

Isadora obediently put up her hands, and Thankful dropped the gown over her head, saying, "You know, your sister Arabella always looked so lovely in this color. The veriest picture, she was—" Thankful unapologetically put her knee in the middle of Isadora's back and tugged hard "—stepping out with Lord knows how many gentleman callers...."

Isadora clutched the bedpost to steady herself as the maid struggled with the closures on the gown. She stopped listening to Thankful's chatter. She'd heard the stories many times—Lucinda's social triumphs, the duel that had almost erupted between two of Arabella's suitors, Quentin's habit of stepping out with a different

young lady every night, Bronson's liaisons with the best
girls in Boston....

As the maid prattled on and performed the punishing
ritual of forcing the dress to contain her, Isadora tried
not to wince. She had often wondered why a lady's garments must hurt. Corsets strangled, shoes pinched, ornamental combs dug into delicate scalps and society said
"Ahh," and made admiring noises. It had always been
a puzzle to her.

"Thankful," she said, "I think the stays are as tight
as they need be."

"One more twist, there we are," the maid said. "I
declare, you should follow the example of your mother
and sisters, miss. They never seem to mind sacrificing a
bit of comfort for fashion."

Isadora didn't argue. The maid, like everyone else in
the world, simply could not understand what had happened with the middle daughter of Boston's leading couple. She was the product of the same careful breeding
that had given Beacon Hill her gorgeous sisters and gallant brothers. Yet Isadora was nothing like them. Not
even close.

"There you are," Thankful pronounced, stepping
back and wiping the sweat from her brow. "Will there
be anything else, miss?"

"No, thank you." Isadora smoothed her hands down
over the skirt, feeling better already. A pretty gown was
the thing to win Chad's attention.

She picked up a small hand mirror on a side table. By
holding it out in front of her, she could admire the dress
in individual pieces—high, puffy sleeves, ribbed panel,
taut bodice, full skirts.

Setting aside the mirror, she noticed Thankful had left

behind her feather duster. Rather than ring for the maid again, Isadora decided to take it to her. Hurrying along to the servants' back stairway, she didn't realize until it was almost too late that Thankful and the kitchen maid, Tilly, were gossiping in the stair.

"...thought I was going to have to call you to help truss her up," Thankful was saying, a chuckle in her voice.

"I'm glad you didn't summon me," Tilly replied. "I would have been consumed by the giggles."

"And that dress. Wait 'til you see. She looks like a mishap in a sail-making factory."

Isadora froze. Ordinarily she was quite awkward and given to noisy retreats, but not this time. This time, she felt as small as a mouse as she gripped the smooth-turned railing and made her way up the stairs. This time, her feet—as mortified as the rest of her—made not a sound.

Not a sound as she climbed up the stairs, walking slowly though she wanted to run to escape the hissing laughter wafting up from the landing. Not a sound as she moved along the carpeted hallway, not a sound as she pushed open the door to Arabella's chamber, not a sound as she stood on the looped round rug in front of the cheval glass.

And then, looking at herself in the tall mirror, she made a sound. A sob.

The cut of the dress widened her figure to epic proportions. The pale linen washed her of all color save for the hot flags of shame that burned in her cheeks. Hanks of hair slipped from her Psyche knot, and the sausage curls on either side of her face grew wet and droopy as her tears soaked into them.

What had she been thinking, dressing this way? Who would ever want such a creature as this abomination in the mirror?

She returned to her own room and opened the French doors, walking out onto the balcony into the middle of an autumn day so glorious that its beauty mocked her.

She looked over the edge of the balustrade. It was a long way down. If she should happen to trip, if she should happen to fall, who would miss her?

She stood teetering on the brink, feeling a peculiar darkness close around her. How seductive it was, the idea that her misery could end so swiftly. So permanently. And so dramatically, with Chad Easterbrook's note tucked close to her heart.

But in the end, she turned away, as cowardly of her own impulses as she was of everything else that required a backbone.

How long, she wondered, had she despised herself? She knew she hadn't come to her unhappy state of self-loathing quickly or without deliberation. It had taken all of her endlessly long maiden years to reach it.

Sinful, Isadora told herself. And self-indulgent to feel this terrible. But then, she was a sinful creature. Every dark and unattractive impulse resided within her—sloth, envy, covetousness, yearning. Desire. She was guilty of all that and more.

From the time she left her great aunt's house, she had been taught that a young lady must be pretty and popular. An accident of birth had placed her smack in the middle of two gorgeous sisters and two perfect brothers. How wonderful life must seem to them, how thrilling to awaken each day and know that it would be a pleasant one.

Isadora knew what happiness felt like. She had been happy once. She had been happy with Aunt Button.

She closed her eyes, thinking back to the days of her youth. When Isadora was five, Aunt Button came down from Salem. Strong-willed as a military general, she had no use for pretty things, and that included pretty great-nieces. She amazed Isadora by being more taken with her conversation and interests than with the charm and beauty of the others. She whisked her off to Salem and the Peabodys barely noticed.

Aunt Button and Isadora had a jolly time there—Isadora became better educated than any boy. Aunt Button taught her that there was nothing unseemly about this. Isadora's appearance simply didn't matter to her. Nor did it matter to Isadora.

Until the day Aunt Button died and Isadora was forced to return to the Beacon Hill mansion of her parents.

She would never forget the look on her mother's face when she walked in the door. Her words were simple: "And here is Isadora, back with us again." But it was the expression on her face that lived in Isadora's heart and shaped all the days and months and endless years that came after.

The bright, untidy fourteen-year-old had no idea how to transform herself into a society belle. She knew too much Greek, Latin, Hebrew and mathematics to be pop-ular and cared too much about social responsibility to be trusted.

So here she stood, dying by inches. Shriveling like a prune in the pantry, plain and colorless and feeling more desperate than ever. She wished her parents would leave her to her books and studies, but they kept thrusting her out into society where she gasped like a beached fish.

And by shoving her before the shipping heirs and Harvard princelings, they had inadvertently sparked a dream in Isadora—the dream of Chad Easterbrook. It was absurd, really, to yearn for such a perfect specimen of manhood, but she couldn't help herself. She kept thinking that if she tried hard enough, she might one day come to mean something to him.

Picking up a button hook, she strained her arms to reach the back. Yanking at one of the buttons, she heard a tearing sound, but she didn't care. She would never wear this abominable dress again.

When she had stripped down to her chemise, she remembered Chad's note—slightly damp—tucked between her breasts.

"Oh, Aunt Button," she whispered to the empty room. "What shall I do? What can possibly save me now?"

She wanted to burn the note. She should burn it. But in the end she did something much, much better. She did exactly what her Aunt Button would have done: she gave in to her strengths, such as they were.

Walking purposefully to the writing desk by the window, she dipped a quill and composed a note of her own.

Four

A tough but nervous, tenacious but restless race
[the Yankees]; materially ambitious.... A race
whose typical member is eternally torn between a
passion for righteousness and a desire to get on
in the world.

—Samuel Eliot Morison,
Maritime History of Massachusetts

"This collar itches," Journey complained. "This
waistcoat chafes in my armpits."

"Stop whining," said Ryan. "I have a headache the
size of Atlantis and I've got no idea what we're doing
here."

"Wasting time, when we should be trying to save
your sorry white backside," Journey observed, running
a long finger around the neckline of his boiled collar.
"These shoes pinch," he added.

Ryan whirled on him, seeing stars from the sudden
movement. But after a few seconds he focused and saw

that yes, he really was here, halfway up Beacon Hill at the Belknap intersection, on a mission so incredibly foolish he wondered if he might still be drunk from the night before.

"It's not *my* backside that needs saving," he said.

Journey, who was magnificently tall, looked down his nose at Ryan, who was also tall but not magnificently so. "Then explain why I had to be the one to run your creditors off this morning."

"What creditors?" Ryan demanded. "And how the devil did they find me?"

"Our arrival was announced at a party in one of these very strongholds," Journey declared, gesturing. The solid brick mansions huddled shoulder to shoulder, a united front against the encroachment of riffraff. The staid facades of the houses and clipped greens of Boston Common stood in implacable denial that anything so upsetting as poverty existed in the world.

Ryan had come here often in his Harvard days. He'd attended stuffy essay readings and anemic musicales in this rarefied neighborhood. But when, foolishly, he tried to seek friendship based on something deeper than wealth or athletic prowess, he encountered a deep-rooted snobbery that raked over his senses like the holystone over a ship's deck.

"This morning's creditors were Mr. deLauncey of Harvard Trust and his associate, Mr. Keith," Journey explained. "Apparently their generosity ends when a man leaves Harvard."

Ryan trudged on. "And on top of everything, my mother decides to come back from Europe."

"Uh-huh. And you know what else? She's coming to Rio with us," Journey said.

Ryan stopped again, reeling. Disbelief pounded harder than his headache. *"What?"*

"She and her maid, Fayette, signed on as passengers. She wants to go see your aunt in Rio."

"Excellent. I've always dreamed of spending weeks at sea in the company of my mother." With slow, plodding steps he continued walking. He loved his mother, he always had, but the two of them inhabited different worlds. Lily Raines Calhoun was like a hothouse gardenia—beautiful, delicate and overpowering when she was in full bloom.

She had no inkling of what he planned for this voyage and why it was so important. He hoped like hell she wouldn't interfere.

"Do you suppose your mother will tell Mr. Easterbrook that you lied about your skipper's credentials?" Journey ventured.

Ryan glowered at him. "You're making my headache worse. And the money he made off me should stop any inquiries."

A black-lacquered coach rumbled past, the muscular team straining up the red brickwork slope. It felt strange to tread these streets, this place of pretense. The inhabitants pushed hard at the wheels of commerce, yet their wealth was inherited, built solidly on the backs of the opium and slave trades. Not so different from his own father, Ryan reflected, though rather than trafficking in slaves he had merely owned them.

Ryan was considered a traitor to his class for enrolling in the radical Yankee institution known as Harvard. When he'd been dismissed from the university, he'd never thought to return to Beacon Hill again. Certainly he didn't think he'd be welcome, having disgraced himself by running away to sea.

"I don't know why you're doing this," Journey grumbled. "You should have written the plaguey female a note and said no thank you to her offer."

Ryan scanned the discreet brass plaques identifying each house they passed. Greenwood, Appleton, Kimball, Lowell...they were known as Boston's First Families, and they were a clannish lot.

"Some things, my dear Journey, demand a personal reply," he explained. "Besides, I'm curious about this plaguey female, as you call Miss Isadora Peabody." He patted the letter in his waistcoat pocket. "What sort of woman would make me such an outrageous offer?"

Journey grinned, his teeth flashing in his deep brown face. "You must have impressed the bloomers off her, Captain."

"A frightening thought."

They walked along a brutally trimmed hedgerow, coming to an intimidating Palladian manse near the corner of Chestnut and Beacon Streets. The Peabody home. Ryan had known some Peabodys in college—Quentin and Bronson. Relations of some sort?

He stood back, getting a crick in his neck as he looked up at the towering house. The glaring sun stabbed into his brain, reviving his headache. "I suppose we can assume," he said to Journey, "that she did not make this offer because she is in need of money."

"Probably not." Journey tugged at the shining black wrought iron gate-pull. He let them both in and they crossed a rigorously disciplined garden, Grecian in flavor, with a shiny silver gazing ball on a pedestal in the middle of a box hedge maze.

The door knocker depicted Neptune with cheeks puffed out and a frown on his face. Ryan lifted the handle. Before he knocked, Journey said, "A question, Skipper."

"What is it?"

"Have you found a translator for the next voyage?"

Ryan sighed, his head still pounding, the taste of rum old and sticky in the back of his throat. "My friend, it was all I could do this morning to find the floor beneath my bunk."

Journey studied him, brown eyes probing with a depth that had been plumbed by years of friendship. "Why do you drink like that, honey?" he asked softly. "Why do you drink until you make yourself crazy?"

Ryan rapped smartly with the knocker. "Because it's easier than staying sane," he muttered. His life, he reflected, wasn't supposed to turn out like this. He was supposed to be sitting on his front porch sipping a mint julep while a mute servant waved a punkah fan over his head. Instead, he'd become a sea captain in charge of a shockingly motley crew. A Southern man committed to a cause that had virtually destroyed his family.

The door swung open on silent hinges. Ryan found himself greeted by a butler in a plain broadcloth suit. The little gent appeared to be well familiar with the trappings of the socially acceptable, for in one brief glance he took in the expensive cut of Ryan's suit and deemed it adequate.

"Yes, sir?" he asked.

Ryan bowed from the waist. "I am Ryan Calhoun, here to see Miss Peabody, if you please."

The butler stepped back, allowing him to enter. He and Journey stood upon a plush Turkey carpet of red and violet. A gilt mirror adorned one wall, and in the corner was a plant stand without a plant on it.

"I shall see if Miss Arabella is at home," the butler said.

The name didn't sound familiar to Ryan, nor to Journey, judging by the jab he gave Ryan with his elbow.

"That would be Miss Isadora, would it not?" Ryan said.

The butler allowed his eyes to widen—whether at Ryan's Southern drawl or at the mention of Miss Isadora, he couldn't tell.

"You are here to see Miss Isadora?"

Ryan smiled patiently. "That's correct. Is she at home?"

"I..." The diminutive man cleared his throat. "I shall inquire. If you like, you may wait in the parlor." He gestured. "Your man can go around to the servants' entrance in the rear."

Ryan expected the error. "This is Mr. Journey Calhoun, and he isn't a servant, but my business partner."

The calm, self-possessed man seemed to be unraveling by inches. He cracked the knuckles of his left hand. "I...I see. Would you please excuse me?"

"By all means." *You officious little snot,* he added silently as the butler scurried away.

"You should have sent me around the back," Journey said. "The food and conversation's better, anyway."

"You're no servant, damn it." Ryan strolled boldly into the ornate parlor. A chandelier glistening with cut crystal droplets lorded over an arrangement of expensive furniture and objets d'art. A Revere tea service and an array of sparkling cut glass decanters graced a sideboard.

"Didn't mean to sound ungrateful," Journey said.

"You re-charted your entire life so I wouldn't be a servant." He leaned his elbow on the blue-and-gilt fireplace mantel, a slender Meissen vase in the center.

"That's true," Ryan said at length. "That's for damned sure. And don't think for a minute I regret it."

A peculiar feeling washed over Ryan. He loved this man, loved him with a ferocity he'd never felt for his own brother. He and Journey had come up together, from sassy rough-and-tumble seven year olds to the men they were now.

The fact that one had been master and the other a slave hadn't interfered in the friendship—at least, not at first.

Ryan checked his appearance in a gilt-framed mirror. Considering the night he'd had, he looked remarkably well put together, his red hair recently cut by Timothy Datty, the cabin boy. His collar and sky-blue frock coat were crisp and clean, thanks to Luigi Conti, the sail maker who was particular about such things.

He had been seven years old and formally dressed the first day Journey had been brought to him, he recalled. Father had made him wait in the hot summer parlor of Albion, and precisely at noon, Purdy had brought in a little boy with a skinny neck and huge eyes.

"This be my nephew Journey," Purdy had said, her gaze cutting down and to the side in the manner of most slaves. "He's a real good boy, ain't you, Journey? A real good boy."

And Journey had surprised Ryan. Instead of the meek, deferential countenance bred and beaten into the house servants and field hands, he looked Ryan directly in the eye and spoke in a high, clear voice: "I'm the best boy there is."

That had been the beginning. The lazy, hot growing-up years had been a time of turbulence balanced with moments of exquisitely sweet tranquillity. They played and fought together, went fishing and boating on Mockjack Bay together. Ryan slept in a mahogany four-poster bed, Journey on a straw pallet on the floor; but more often than not, when Purdy brought breakfast in the morning, she'd find them both splayed out in the big bed. When Ryan went to church, Journey waited in the carriage outside. When Journey wanted to learn to read and cipher, Ryan taught him in secret, by the light of a tallow stub cribbed from the kitchen.

When Journey's father was sold to pay off the debts of Ryan's father, Ryan wept and raged with him.

By the time the boys turned sixteen, Journey was married and a father himself. Ryan had seduced a number of local girls, and debutantes from all the best families had begun to notice him.

Life would have gone on in this vein except for two extraordinary things. First, Ryan elected to attend Harvard, Yankee radicals and all. And second, he insisted on bringing Journey with him.

Journey had fought him every inch of the way. He adored his wife and children, who lived at a neighboring plantation. But Ryan was insistent, even lordly about it. No proper gentleman matriculated at a university without his manservant. It was Journey's duty to go. He had no choice.

Ryan had a plan. He couldn't even tell Journey, because the slave's wrath and grief had to be convincing.

Ryan smiled into the mirror, remembering the day he crossed the Mason Dixon line and gave Journey his freedom. Journey had held the manumission papers to his chest, unable to speak as the tears rolled down his face.

Now their shipping enterprise had brought them one step closer to their ultimate goal—to buy Journey's wife and babies, bring them north and set them free.

"Got to be something wrong with her," Journey said, startling Ryan out of his remembrances.

"Wrong with who?"

"The plaguey woman." Journey's gaze tracked along one wall that was entirely covered by shelf after shelf of books. "Why would a body want to leave a house like this?"

"There must be something about this life she can't abide," Ryan whispered, thinking of his own reasons for leaving Albion. "Maybe we should ask—"

"Miss Peabody will receive you in the garden," the butler said from the doorway. "This way, please."

Ryan and Journey followed him along a tall, narrow corridor hung with portraits. The family tree, Ryan assumed, noting that each subject seemed to be extraordinarily handsome. Either the painters were expert flatterers or this clan had been bred for show.

They passed through a glassed-in verandah and then emerged onto a clipped and sculpted yard. Paradise in miniature, Ryan thought, noting the vine pergolas and pruned yew trees, At the far end stood a gazebo with a domed roof and open sides. In the middle sat a woman in black, her head bent as she read a thick book in her lap.

"Miss Peabody?" Ryan said.

She looked up, blinking owlishly as if she had come from a dark place into the light. A pair of spectacles sat low on her nose, and she seemed to see better by peering over the top of the lenses.

"Yes." Her voice squeaked, and she cleared her throat. "Yes," she said again. "Captain Calhoun. I am indeed pleased that you've come."

He stood before her, watching her hands, expecting her to extend one for his kiss. Instead, she clutched the book very hard, displaying fingernails that had been bitten ragged. She had, of all things, the indirect, cowed look of a slave. As if she feared she might be beaten at any moment.

Discomfited by the thought, he opted for a formal bow from the waist. "This is Mr. Journey Calhoun, my associate and steward of the *Swan*."

She clutched the book tighter. "Oh! I was expecting a note, not two grown men! I'm—um—pleased to meet you."

Ryan had never met a more socially gauche woman in his life. He dared not look at Journey, for if their gazes met, they would surely dishonor her with a fit of sniggering.

She cleared her throat again and used one finger to push her spectacles up the bridge of her nose. Said nose was red and swollen; either she was unwell or the book had moved her to tears.

She sneezed violently into a crumpled handkerchief. Unwell, Ryan decided.

She tucked the handkerchief up her sleeve. "My apologies. It is the grippe, I fear."

"Do you suffer from it often?"

"Constantly, Captain. Except in the springtime. Then it is the hay fever that plagues me, though I can seldom tell the difference between the two ailments—" She broke off, looking horrified. "Forgive me for going on about such a disagreeable subject."

"I find nothing disagreeable about discussing you, Miss Peabody," Ryan said, forcing his gallantry to its limits. He was here to refuse her offer, so he might as well do it politely.

She finally seemed to remember the book she was holding. "Pardon me," she said, shutting the tome and setting it on the marble table beside her.

He turned his head to see its title. The symbols on the cover looked only vaguely familiar; he had made a point of sleeping through the classics at university.

"Ptolemy," she said.

"In the original Greek," he guessed.

"Oh, indeed. I wouldn't want to read Ptolemy any other way. He has such a distinctive authority in the original."

"I couldn't agree with you more," Ryan said. He could hear a chuckle starting in Journey's throat. "I take it you have a facility with languages."

"Yes, yes, I do. I was fortunate to have been tutored by my late great aunt, who was quite the scholar in her day, and I also attended Mount Holyoke. I am conversant in Spanish, French, Italian and Portuguese and have a reading knowledge of Latin, Greek and Hebrew."

She was probably more knowledgeable than the majority of Harvard graduates, Ryan guessed. Curious. Why would her wealthy parents allow a girl such latitude?

"Miss Peabody," he said, "I came in person because any other way would fail to do justice to the incredibly generous offer you made me."

She pressed her nail-bitten fingers into a steeple.

"Then you will take me? I'm going to Rio on your ship?"

"No." He said it swiftly to kill the blooming hope on her face. "It is not that you are lacking in any way," he hastened to add. "The fault is with me, and with my ship and crew. The *Swan* is a working vessel filled with working men. We could never live up to the standards of such a genteel lady as yourself."

She flinched, looking down and to the side. Submissive, defeated. Ryan had the feeling he had drowned a kitten, and the feeling made him angry.

"I should think you'd let me be the judge of that," she ventured timidly.

He gestured across the yard toward the house. "Nothing on the *Silver Swan* can compare to this. You cannot trade paradise for months in cramped quarters in the company of seamen."

"I can, if only you will let me."

What an irritating, intractable thing she was. Ryan paced the deck of the gazebo. "Ma'am, you seem to think your service as a translator is all that is required of you on this voyage. Rivera, our former translator, was also an able navigator."

"Celestial or instrumental?" she asked.

"Both," he fired back.

"Fine. I am versed in both. I've studied the Bowditch and have taken courses in spherical trigonometry." Her timidity fell away as she spoke.

A low whistle came from Journey, who stood in the yard near the gazebo.

"I don't use Bowditch," Ryan said, struggling to hide his surprise.

"There's no need. The position can be figured without it," she agreed.

In truth, the trigonometric formulas were all black magic to Ryan, but he wasn't about to admit it to this smug female. "So you understand a thing or two about navigation. That does not qualify you for this venture."

"I daresay I know more than a thing or two."

She lifted her chin in defiance. *Defiance.* Ryan imagined her on his ship, defying his orders.

"What's the proper position for the royal yard?"

"Thirty-six degrees to the larboard beam...until you reach the equator. Then it changes to starboard."

He turned his back to hide his amazement, looking out at the lawn as he asked, "Then tell me how to haul out into the stream."

"You reef the studding sail gear."

He refused to look at Journey, knowing he'd find him grinning from ear to ear. "And what about the chafing gear?"

"That's simple," she retorted. "You put it on and leave it there."

"I concede, Miss Peabody, that you have startled and impressed me with your knowledge. But understanding the finer points of seamanship requires more than—"

"Good God, Calhoun, it really is you," called a voice from the verandah.

Miss Peabody made an uncomfortable little whimper in her throat. Ryan shaded his eyes as a party of white-clad young people came hurrying toward him.

He recognized the men from his Harvard days: Quentin Peabody, famous for his tennis serve and infamous for his phenomenal stomach, which held vast quantities of liquor. His brother Bronson, so attractive he was almost pretty, was deeply studious and well-liked. Foster Candy, a braying ass of a fellow—or a veritable hog when it came to wallowing in the gossip pit—and Robert Hallowell whose only memorable quality was his family's wealth. And finally Chad Easterbrook, Abel's son and heir. He was graced with a godlike handsomeness and a frighteningly vacant mind.

They arrived in a tumble of laughter and introductions, and Ryan made the acquaintance of the ladies— Lydia Haven and Isadora's sister, Arabella, who resembled a fashion doll in a dressmaker's shop.

"What a pleasure to see you, Calhoun," Quentin declared in the lazy, academic drawl of the longtime university man. "You made quite the stir when you lit out from Harvard, old chap. Quite the stir."

"People at Harvard are easily stirred." Ryan gestured at Journey. "I'd like you all to make the acquaintance of my business partner, Mr. Journey Calhoun."

They just stared. Then Foster stepped forward, bowing from the waist. "The pleasure is ours," he shouted, enunciating each word carefully. "I am sure."

Journey grinned. "I'm African, sir. Not deaf."

Their laughter had a nervous edge, but Quentin managed to turn the attention from Journey to Isadora. She sat like a statue, her face pale, her eyes cast down. The liveliness that had animated her moments ago had vanished.

"Do my eyes deceive me?" Quentin asked with a gamin chuckle, "Or is it true? Is my sister actually to be found in conversation with a gentleman rather than with her nose in a book?"

The others laughed. Isadora managed a tight, uncomfortable smile.

"Oh, do stop," Arabella protested prettily, shaking a white lace fan. "Can't you see you're embarrassing poor Izzie?"

Isadora responded by sneezing violently into her handkerchief.

"Bless you," Chad Easterbrook murmured automatically.

She sent him a tremulous smile, shy and curiously sweet. Judging by Chad's expression, he had no appreciation of what was immediately apparent to anyone with half a brain—the poor girl was quite thoroughly in love with him.

"How was your croquet match?" she asked softly, her voice wavering a little.

"Oh, capital," Chad said. Offhandedly he added, "Though you were missed, of course."

"Yes, indeed." Lydia Haven brushed out a flounce in her white dress. "You certainly were. It is always so amusing to have you around, Izzie."

"Thank you. But...as I was compelled to inform Chad, I'm unwell. I'm...ah..." She sneezed again, pressing the rumpled handkerchief to her reddened nose.

"What can be keeping the refreshments?" Bronson wondered aloud. "I asked for lemonade to be served out here. I'll go inquire."

The women gathered in the gazebo, and the men wandered away, Foster and Robert lighting their pipes. They fell into conversation, none of it terribly interesting. Ryan realized he'd had a better time discussing navigation with Isadora. He listened with only one ear to the men's talk. Until Foster addressed him directly.

"I'm told—though, of course, I have no experience

of this—that as soon as a gentleman leaves the college, he finds himself in quite a calamity.''

Ryan lifted one eyebrow. ''I've done all right.''

''But isn't it true that all your tailors and gaming friends, so generous to Harvard men, are apt to call in their markers?'' Foster persisted, his eyes narrowing with slyness. ''Perhaps not. Perhaps they sent their dun notes to your dear mama.''

Ryan flexed his fist and took a step toward him. Journey planted himself in his path. ''Easy, Skipper,'' he said quietly. ''Remember why we came here. Remember what's important.''

Ryan took a deep breath. He had to stay focused on the business venture.

He ignored the talk until Isadora's name came up.

''There's a family joke, you know,'' said Quentin in a low voice, ''that our parents had to tie a codfish cake around Izzie's neck to get the cat to play with her.''

Foster Candy made a choked sound of amusement. ''There, old stick, I daresay I'd charge a steeper price than a fish cake!''

''Lemonade,'' Bronson called, helping the butler wheel a wooden cart across the lawn.

The refreshments arrived and the talk started up again, but the drink tasted bitter to Ryan. As he stood back and watched the laughing, white-clad croquet party and Isadora sitting like a black crow on her stool, he wished he had never come here.

''She lives in hell,'' he muttered to Journey.

''There are many kinds of hell. Some worse than others.''

Ryan knew Journey was thinking of his family, still in bondage in Virginia, their only hope of freedom rest-

ing with the fortunes of the *Silver Swan*. Yet Isadora
Peabody suffered in her own way; that was apparent
enough. While Southern families institutionalized their
inhumanity, claiming a moral right to keep slaves and
justifying it in the oddest of fashions, this proper Yankee
society had its own subtle brand of torture.

It was a calculated cruelty, razor sharp, aimed at the
most vulnerable. Miss Isadora had no defenses against
the biting cleverness of her croquet-playing, lemonade-
drinking peers. Timid socially, yet gifted with a fierce
intellect, she was regarded as an aberration. Different
and not to be trusted.

She was regarded as "poor Izzie." But already Ryan
realized she was "not-so-dumb Dora."

Chad Easterbrook, vast in his mental absence, clearly
had no notion that she worshiped him. Perhaps, then, it
was the perfect match, Ryan mused cynically, leaning
against a pergola and watching as Isadora sneezed yet
again, and Chad blessed her and she gazed up at him as
if he'd offered her the moon on a platter. He was capable
of only selfish thought, and she suffered from an excess
of thoughtfulness. Between the two of them they made
a whole person. Possibly even an interesting person.

Except that it was clear to Ryan that they were not a
couple. Lydia Haven commandeered the young man's
attention with all the determination of a battle chief leading a charge. He was hers, following her across the lawn
like a trained spaniel and leaving Isadora to snuffle un-
graciously into her handkerchief.

"We should go," Ryan said. "Miss Peabody," he
continued, taking her hand and bowing, lifting it to his
lips. "Your offer was more than kind, and for that I
thank you. Good day."

"But we haven't—you can't—"

Feeling terrible, he left her stammering. He heard one of the other young women sigh. He and Journey found their own way out and Ryan was relieved to leave the stifling atmosphere of the Peabody mansion behind.

"Are you thinking what I'm thinking?" Journey asked.

"Don't you dare suggest it," Ryan said, adding in his best Boston accent, "old chap."

"But she speaks six languages—"

"No."

"She's miserable here—"

"No."

"She's a hell of a lot more interesting than the ladies you brought aboard last ni—"

"Damn it," Ryan almost shouted, *"no."*

Isadora refused to take no for an answer. So what if Ryan Calhoun turned out to be as shallow and mocking as Quentin and his friends? He had something she wanted—a way out of Boston. And she was determined to get it.

As she waited in the brick-fronted Merchants' Exchange offices of Abel Easterbrook, she allowed herself a brief, satisfying moment of gloating. Though he didn't know it, Captain Calhoun himself had given her the key to obtaining the post.

"Ahoy, Miss Isadora!" Abel opened the door to his inner chamber and greeted her with a bewhiskered smile. "Welcome aboard."

"I shan't keep you long, sir, for I know you're busy." She seated herself in the chair he held for her. Lithographs of ships and lighthouses graced the braddedleather walls of the office and stacks of ledger books filled the shelves. She folded her gloved hands, inhaling the scent of ink and tobacco and paper—the scent of commerce.

"You have a marvelous office," she said, shaking her head briefly when Abel offered her a cup of sherry.

"It's been in the family for three generations," he said. "One day it'll all be Chad's."

A thrill shot down her spine. If Abel agreed to her plan, she could finally win Chad's esteem. By the time Chad took over the company, Isadora intended to be indispensable to the enterprise. With her knowledge of the business, she would be a great asset to Chad. Perhaps a great enough asset to be his wi—

She cut the thought short. One step at a time, she told herself. "Have you had a chance to consider my proposal, sir?"

He tamped his pipe on a tray. "I have, Miss Isadora. Your credentials are copper-bottomed, unimpeachable. However, what you ask is impossible. I cannot allow you to sign on as a member of the crew of the *Silver Swan*."

She kept her chin steady despite the urge to crumple in defeat. "May I ask why?"

"It's not a woman's place—"

"Ah, but it is." She relaxed, pleased that she had prepared herself for this argument. "The *Fairacre* has not only a woman bo'sun, but the cook is a female as well."

"The cook is the skipper's wife," he argued.

"She wasn't when she signed on," Isadora replied.

"I rest my case. I can't let you be bound away with a shipload of jack-tars. God forbid you should come back married to one of them."

She smiled at the irony. "Believe me, Mr. Easterbrook, there is no chance of any sort of...entanglement." She thought of the ripe, laughing woman Ryan Calhoun had held in his lap the night she'd met him. If that sort was his preference, he wouldn't look twice at Isadora. "And did you know," she continued, "that the *Pandora* has three women aboard—and that she grossed a hundred thousand last year?"

"All right, I'll concede that some crews include females. But Calhoun's a loose cannon. You saw him the other night—he'll give you the devil to pay and no pitch hot."

"That is precisely why you need me. I alone know how important the Rio voyage is to you. I can be your eyes and ears on that ship, Mr. Easterbrook. I can make regular reports about Captain Calhoun's behavior and the way he conducts his affairs."

A crack appeared in his reluctance. "Wouldn't mind having a barnacle on the hull for this voyage," he admitted. "But it wouldn't be right to send a lady like you. He might shame you."

"His mother will be there as a passenger—"

"He'll probably humiliate her, as well."

"Sir, I assure you, Mrs. Calhoun and I can look after our own reputations. The one who needs looking after is Captain Calhoun."

"This is headed for rocky shoals, I can feel it."

"Not at all. It will be smooth sailing, and I intend to see to it for your sake. Use the man's skill as a skipper, but don't let him scuttle your reputation as a leader in commerce."

Her words made great headway into the kindly old

man's pride. Feeling herself close to victory, she said, "Mr. Easterbrook, you have ever been a visionary, on the leading edge of modern business. Engaging my services is the next logical step."

Five

First ponder, then dare.

—Helmuth von Moltke
(attributed)

"C-can I h-help you, ma'am?" a young boy asked Isadora.

She turned on the dock to look at him. "Is this the *Silver Swan*?" Isadora asked.

The lad—a wiry, nervous boy of perhaps fifteen—nodded jerkily. "Yes'm." He snatched off his tarpaulin seaman's cap. "Tim-Timothy Datty, at your service."

"I am looking for Captain Calhoun."

"H-he's aboard, but—"

"Good. I was hoping he would be." She headed toward the gangway, stepping around the dock where brawny-shouldered stevedores were discharging the cargo. She tried not to stare but couldn't help herself.

In contrast to the fitted frock coats, silk hats and chicken-skin gloves of drawing-room gentlemen, the men of the wharf wore loose trousers, shirts and neck-erchiefs fastened with slip-ties. Crude expressions, spo-ken in a variety of foreign accents, filled the air. She could not fathom the meaning of *poodle faking* but she felt certain she didn't want to know.

"M-ma'am." Timothy Datty trotted alongside her. "C-c-captain's not ''

"You needn't stop what you're doing to accompany me," she said. "I know the way."

He pressed his mouth shut, waving his hands. There was something earnest and appealing about the boy. A pity about his stutter. Elocution lessons and special read-ings might help, but she didn't suggest it for fear of embarrassing him. Besides, she was in a hurry to see Ryan Calhoun.

She wondered if he would be surprised to see her. With a shiver of anticipation, she remembered the way he'd taken his leave of her after their meeting. He had crossed the lawn, looking as masterful and dignified as a young prince, and bowed over her hand. Even Lydia Haven had dragged her attention away from Chad long enough to notice the gallant gesture.

Isadora held Ryan Calhoun's boldness in quiet fasci-nation. While she shrinkingly obeyed the rules of her parents and society, Mr. Calhoun flouted convention and took his own path. Perhaps his very lack of protocol would make him see the sense in her plan, then.

One of the stevedores struck up a bawdy song in Por-tuguese, the strong, operatic voice ringing across the wa-terfront. Women's body parts sounded so much more poetic in Portuguese, Isadora observed, trying her best not to blush. She headed up to the main deck and then climbed to the...she consulted her memory as she progressed. The afterdeck—yes, that was it—reached by means of a gangway and companion ladder.

She had burned the gaslight late the night before, studying a tome of nautical terms. At their meeting in the garden, Captain Calhoun had nearly exhausted her supply of knowledge, and she had stocked up on more. A deceptive practice, yes, but Isadora was desperate.

She could hear young Timothy Datty shouting to her from the dock far below, but with the singing stevedore and the screech of lifting gear, she couldn't hear him. And why was he jumping up and down and waving his arms?

The deserted main deck had been cleared of crates and barrels, though a few remnants of the revelry remained—stray chicken feathers, a broken bottle, a spent cigar. She tucked away her apprehension and made her way to the captain's stateroom, finding the door slightly ajar. Within, she could hear a faint thumping sound.

Clearing her throat, she knocked at the door. "Captain Calhoun, are you there?"

"Al...almost..." His voice sounded ragged, and he let out a gasp and a moan.

He was ill! Dear heaven, he might be dying in there. She pushed the door open and marched inside. "I'm here, Captain. Do you need any help?"

"I—oh, for Christ's sake." The crude words came from within a draped alcove.

"What the hell's going on?" asked a female voice, also behind the drapes.

Isadora stopped in her tracks, frozen like a hunted rabbit. Heavens be, he was with a woman. *In flagrante delicto.* That must have been what Timothy had been trying to tell her. She willed herself to flee, willed her feet to turn toward the door, but she was too horrified to obey even common sense.

A hand, and then a head, appeared through the drapes. Isadora recognized the woman from the night of the party, the one with yellow hair and red lips and huge—

"I'm so sorry," Isadora managed to whisper.

"Not half as sorry as me," the woman said in a coarse voice. She exited from the bed, pushing her feet into a pair of slippers and tugging up her bodice as she clumped to the door. "Don't summon me again unless you have time for me," she called over her shoulder, then left in a huff.

Isadora knew she should follow, but horror held her rooted. She looked anywhere but at the bunk, trying to distract herself by cataloguing the details of her surroundings, but all appeared as a blur; she couldn't concentrate.

"You are like a bad rash," Ryan Calhoun said, coming out of the bed and jerking the curtain shut. "You won't go away." Grumbling peevishly, he pulled on a tall boot.

Isadora caught her breath. Seeing a gentleman with his shirt open at the throat, its tails loose over his trousers, his hair in tousled disarray, was a new experience to her. She even forgot to be insulted.

He yanked on the second boot and scowled at her. "Miss Peabody, I paid you the honor of a personal visit to tell you why I cannot bring you along on the voyage. So why are you here?"

"Because I need you," she blurted, letting out her breath in a rush. Mortified, she cleared her throat, composing herself. "I mean, I was hoping you would see the sense in engaging my services as translator so that I wouldn't have to prevail on Mr. Easterbrook.''

"You didn't."

"I'm afraid you left me no choice." She took a folded letter from her reticule and handed it to him. "Your refusal compelled me to take matters into my own hands."

Almost viciously, he broke the waxen seal on the letter. Angling the cream stock paper toward the light, he read it.

Trying not to fidget, Isadora looked around the room. The cabin resembled a merchant's office and parlor in miniature. A long table aft was curved slightly to echo the fantail shape of the stern. Benches flanked the table, and in the middle rested a tray of crystal decanters clad in silver filigree. There was also a small writing desk with an industrious array of cubbyholes, and a tiny door leading, she supposed, to the water closet. A squat sea chest with an intimidating-looking lock rested near the upholstered aft bench. The stern windows, of leaded bottle-bottom glass, glittered with the afternoon light.

The light, though weak, fell kindly over Ryan Calhoun, illuminating his negligent pose, his rumpled clothing and the frown that deepened with every word he read.

And even scowling, Isadora couldn't help but notice, he was an uncommon man. Some might even say beautiful in the classical sense, the wave of reddish hair almost Grecian, the height of his cheekbones and brow unmistakably patrician. Judging by the tight fit of his trousers beneath the trailing broadcloth shirt, the lady he'd been entertaining had every right to be resentful of the interruption.

"So you brought pressure to bear on Abel," said Ryan, catching her staring at him. "Charming."

"I dislike the implication of that. I merely presented my point of view and he agreed." She prayed silently that Ryan Calhoun would never learn that her offer included spying on him. "Mr. Easterbrook is a man of commerce—a very successful one, as you well know. He was more than happy to approve my position."

"And what does his son think of this, Miss Peabody?" A harsh cruelty edged Ryan Calhoun's voice. "What does Chad think, or does he think at all? I'm not quite certain he knows how."

She swallowed, finding her throat suddenly parched. "It was Abel's decision. I'm sure I have no idea what Chad thinks."

"How can you bear to be away from the gallant Chad for so long? Have you thought about that?"

She flinched. No one was supposed to know about her secret adoration of Chad Easterbrook. No one. How had this rude, blunt man guessed?

Ryan crushed the letter in his fist. "I won't have it."

Her first instinct was to flee. Not this time, she told herself. She straightened her shoulders, summoning her determination and rallying her courage. "I'm afraid you have no choice."

He tossed the letter toward a bin beside the desk. It swirled around the rim, then went in. "If I have to use my dying breath to do it, I'll prove to you that you're not cut out for life at sea, Isadora Peabody." He went to the door and held it open with mock gallantry. "Take that thought to bed with you tonight."

Isadora took no pride in her methods of persuasion, and Captain Calhoun's reaction wasn't all she had wished for, but indeed she had won.

Standing in the parlor as she awaited her visitors, she closed her eyes and pictured the ship that would soon be her home for the next six months. Tall masts, sails as light and billowy as the very clouds, a sleek hull cutting a foamy white wake...it was a cosmos unto itself, a world of its own.

The *Silver Swan*. The very name evoked images of exotic wonder. She imagined herself swept into a strange and fabulous world, leaving behind this place where she had never fit in.

"You certainly look pleased with yourself, Isadora," her mother said, gliding into the summer parlor. "Dare I hope you're actually looking forward to having company?"

Isadora opened her eyes, the images in her mind vanishing like dust before a chill wind. "I suppose I am, Mother."

Sophia Cabot Peabody flickered her fan before her face. "That's a welcome change. Perhaps I can also count on you to attend Mrs. Fuller's reading party."

"No, Mother. After my dissertation at the last gathering, I doubt I'll be welcome there again."

As a social activity, reading parties were all the rage. The erudite of Louisberg Square and Beacon Hill gathered to exchange ideas, cultivate friendships and sometimes even romance.

"Do you wonder?" Sophia asked, her voice tinged with equal measures of affection and exasperation. "You cannot truly think that Dr. Channing actually meant for you to argue with his theory about the nature of human emotion."

"How could I not? How absurd to claim women are so helplessly governed by their hearts that their heads empty right into them. His lectures are supposed to spark discussion."

"But you're not supposed to prove him wrong."

"If he is, why not prove it?" Isadora countered. "The inventor of a theory should be able to defend it. Dr. Channing was simply put out because he could not answer my challenges."

"Put out is stating it mildly." Sophia straightened a fold of Isadora's black dress. "I suppose the fault is mine for letting you live all those years in Salem. Your great aunt failed to instill in you the most fundamental lessons. Yes, a woman might be much smarter than a man. But if she dares to show it, she becomes a pariah."

Isadora squeezed her mother's hand. "Then I am destined to be a pariah. I have no judgment for this sort of thing. How was I to know he wasn't looking for a challenge?"

Sophia smiled wryly. "No man is, my dear. No man." Her smile widened as she looked past Isadora. "Not even your father," she murmured, crossing the room to her husband.

Isadora watched her parents fondly, yet aware of the distance that had always lain between them. She could see the mutual respect they had for one another, could feel the affection they shared, yet she had no clue about the nature of their love. Was there passion? She couldn't tell. To the outside observer, they were two excessively handsome people, gifted in commerce and conversation, certain of their place in the world. But passion? Did they know of such a thing? Did they care?

Thankful tapped discreetly on the parlor door. "Your guests have arrived."

Isadora's mouth went dry. This was it, then. The moment she had been waiting for and dreading. She needed her parents' blessing on this venture.

"How delightful," Sophia said, completely ignorant of the true purpose of the meeting. She had assumed it to be merely a social call. "Do show them in."

Like a dazzle of sunshine, Lily Raines Calhoun flowed into the room. "Mr. and Mrs. Peabody. Miss Peabody. How kind of you to receive us on such short notice."

Ryan entered behind her, looking even more appealing than he had the day before. He wore a well-tailored suit of clothes, though his waistcoat and cravat startled the eye. The cravat was a blinding royal blue, the waistcoat busy with a print of yellow banana fruit and exotic flowers.

He moved with a rolling gait, the unmistakable aspect of a man of the sea. From the corner of her eye, Isadora could see her father studying Ryan Calhoun, assessing him.

"Here is my son, Ryan," Lily said, her graceful hand drawing him forward. He bent first over Sophia's fingers, then Isadora's. She thanked heaven for the black moleskin fingerless mitts she wore, for there was something searingly intimate about the gesture, and at least the fabric protected her from direct contact with his lips.

When Captain Calhoun looked up at her, his face was full of cruel-edged mockery. Isadora forced herself to hold her gaze steady. He was not going to make this easy for her. Very well. She would endure him.

She felt a familiar tickle at the back of her nose. Tak-

ing out a handkerchief with the lightning speed of a cavalier drawing a rapier, she stopped the sneeze in time.

Lily smiled at her. "Bless you, my dear."

She said "Mah dee-ah" in the nicest way. As if she
actually meant it. Isadora sensed she'd find an ally in
Lily Calhoun.

Once they were all settled on the burgundy-striped
chaise, the settee and the wing chairs before the hearth,
Thankful served strong coffee laced with cream, and tea
cakes heavy with honey and hazelnuts.

"And what is the name of your place in Virginia
again?" Sophia asked sweetly.

Isadora held herself very still and secretly bit her
tongue. Her mother knew more about the Calhoun family than Lily herself, no doubt. A number of not-so-
discreet inquiries had informed her about the lavish plantation on Mockjack Bay, Virginia. Once it was established that the Calhoun family possessed only slightly
less social status than the Lord Above, Sophia decided
they were the right sort of people.

"Our place is called Albion. When my husband died,
his elder son Hunter inherited it. Hunter is my stepson,
and Ryan's half brother."

Isadora watched Ryan's face carefully. A half brother.
Did the two get along? Probably not, she decided, recalling Lily's anecdote about Ryan disgracing himself
by choosing Harvard over Virginia tradition.

He winked at her. *Winked.*

Heavens be, what was he up to now?

She pursed her lips and stared straight ahead, fighting
a blush. Her mother and sisters were famous wits in
conversation, but Isadora had never acquired the knack.
She had no idea what to say to a man who winked at

her. When she spoke her mind, she was considered offensive. When she echoed someone else's opinion, she was denounced as boring. So whenever possible, she held her tongue and let her mind wander.

She knew she shouldn't succumb to fantasy, but the murmurs of conversation lulled her, and before she knew it, she was a Southern belle at a place called Albion, where the sun always shone and the workers sang glad praises to the sky and the air was filled with birdsong and the scent of magnolias. Dressed in tulle flounces from a Paris couturier, she waited on the verandah while her favorite suitor galloped up on a white horse.

"Hello, Chad," she would greet him demurely... except the man on the horse wasn't Chad. He had flame-colored hair, a crooked grin, a provocative wink and... heavens be. What was Ryan Calhoun doing in the middle of her fantasy?

"...wouldn't you say so, Isadora?" her mother was asking.

Jolted out of her reverie, Isadora nodded vigorously, having no idea what she was agreeing to. "Indeed I would, Mother."

Ryan scowled at her.

"That is," she hastened to add, "except that I also wouldn't."

Ryan rolled his eyes. What a hen-wit he must think her. She said, "And what do you think, Mr. Calhoun?"

"I think that sea voyages are dangerously unhealthy, particularly for a lady of delicate constitution," he said. "If I may be permitted to agree with my hostess," he added gallantly, inclining his head toward Sophia.

Isadora sent him a dagger glare. Didn't he remember what Mr. Easterbrook's letter said? Either he took Isadora along, or his position would be downgraded from skipper to second mate.

"I have been touring the Continent for years," Lily said. "I've sailed from Gibraltar to Athens and suffered absolutely no ill health at all other than the usual *mal de mer*. Mr. and Mrs. Peabody, I was so hoping you would permit Isadora to go."

Grateful for the support, Isadora perched on the edge of her seat. "You have always said that travel enhances a person's character, Papa," she reminded her father.

"It's been so long since I've seen my dear sister," Lily said. "Rose is the widow of a Brazilian planter. She lives in a magnificent villa high in the forested hills overlooking Guanabara Bay. I've promised her for years that I'd visit." She lifted her cup to her lips and took and unhurried sip. "Isadora would be such an asset to the voyage. Ryan needs her expertise as a translator, but if she spoke not a word other than English, I would beg to have her along as my guest and my companion."

"Did I say I needed her?" Ryan asked with a laconic half grin. "I don't recall that."

"Mother, I simply must go," Isadora said in a rush, deciding not to dignify his insolent remark with a reply. "I know how deeply I would grieve were I deprived of my own dear sisters' company." She managed to say this with a sincere expression.

"Mr. Peabody," Sophia said, addressing her husband formally, "what say you?" She framed it as a question, though Isadora knew she had already made up her mind.

"Well, most certainly I approve," Papa assured her. "You know how I feel about broadening our daughters' experiences."

"Does Miss Isadora need broadening?" Ryan Calhoun asked, the very picture of innocence. He stared at her, daring her to crumple before his insults. "Where?"

"Perhaps I need to learn to pity those with feeble minds," she snapped, surprised to feel anger rather than humiliation, and further surprised that the anger felt... rather good.

"Sailing a ship is an unusual vocation for a Harvard man," Mr. Peabody observed, ignoring the heated exchange. "Particularly for such a young man. Don't most sailors spend years working their way up to skipper?"

"Indeed they do, sir. I was fortunate to win my first command early." He savored a sip of his coffee. "I grew up on Mockjack Bay, with a view straight out to the Atlantic. I'd sit for hours on the end of our dock, watching the ships come and go, stowing away on the short runs to neighboring farms."

"I couldn't get him to do a blessed thing," Lily said with fond exasperation. "He and Journey even built a lookout in the top of a tree by the water. After I discovered he'd been stowing away on the local barges, I decided to let him follow his heart. He learned seamanship from Captain Hastings himself of the frigate *Carlota*."

"When I discovered Mr. Easterbrook was looking for a skipper, I decided it was Providence itself drawing me back to the sea," Ryan said. "None of my schooling could take that desire from me."

Isadora felt her anger melting into something else as she studied him. He looked so romantic in his colorful, finely cut clothes that fit his trim form so well. He had one arm draped over the back of a chair, a thick lock of hair adorning his brow. He might have been a poet, though he lacked the pallor and thinness of a man of letters. No, Ryan Calhoun was too vigorous and too vibrant to toil in private with paper and pen.

A sea captain. Isadora realized that she was looking at a man who had become what he was born to be.

What a gift that was. Few people ever achieved that.

She refused even to contemplate what she was born to be. Maiden daughter, keeping her elderly parents company. When her beautiful nieces and nephews were old enough, she might serve as their tutor or chaperon.

The very thought made her shudder.

She lifted her chin. She was going on a sea voyage. Like it or not, Ryan Calhoun was going to save her from a fate of obscure mediocrity.

But as he looked across the room at her, there was nothing but mocking laughter in his eyes as he said, "And as for your schooling, Miss Peabody, I pray you are prepared for its hard lessons."

Part Two

The Bird of Passage

"You don't understand me," said the duckling. "I think I'd better go out into the wide world."

"Do you think this is the whole world?" the mother duck asked. "Why, it extends on and on, clear across to the other side of the garden and right on into the parson's field, though that is farther than I have ever been."

"Say there, comrade," the wild geese said to the duckling, "you're so ugly that we have taken a fancy to you. Come with us and be a bird of passage."

—Hans Christian Andersen,
The Ugly Duckling (1843)

Six

I have seen old ships sail like swans asleep.

—Herman James Elroy Flecker,
The Old Ships

Everything was in order, from the perfectly packed traveling box—specially designed to fit the carriages of Brazil—to the dove gray bonnet Thankful had tied with a precise bow beneath Isadora's chin. The bootblacked surface of her traveling trunk shone in the morning sun. She had a detachable pocket inside her black silk pongee skirts filled with paper money as well as gold and silver coins in the common currency of the high seas, pounds sterling.

Porters, stevedores, deckhands and passengers crowded the waterfront area, for at least nine ships would clear Boston harbor this day. Passersby paused to study the Peabody clan, and their expressions formed uncensored maps of their thoughts. They took in the silver dignity of the parents, the golden beauty of the brothers and sisters, then dismissed Isadora as a poor relation.

She hardened herself against the stares. Soon she would be gone from here, gone to a place she could only imagine, a place she and Aunt Button had found in their cozy nights by the fire in Salem. Her only regret was that Chad had not come to say goodbye.

Finally she saw it—the *Silver Swan*. The stately bark still held open its cargo hatches, taking on freight with rampant speed. The sight of the ship and the knowledge that the wind was in the right quarter for departure, filled her with excitement.

She nearly burst with anticipation. There was no chance of that, however. Thankful had been merciless in lacing her corset. The busk pressed like a restraining hand against her breastbone. Isadora wondered how, on shipboard, she would dress herself in stays each day, but she didn't dare voice her fears aloud. She didn't want to do or say anything to give her family second thoughts about letting her go.

Perhaps she would simply sleep in her stays.

A boatswain's whistle pierced the air. "I should go aboard," she said.

"Indeed." Clearing his throat, her father turned to the porter who brought her things along in a large, creaky barrow. "You have everything you need—plenty of books—be certain you read the Emerson and send me your thoughts on it."

"Of course, Papa. On the ship's manifest I am listed—to my shame—as an idler. So I expect I'll have plenty of time for reading."

"Being an idler simply means you don't take a turn standing watch," Bronson said, taking her hand and squeezing it. "For that you can be grateful. The schedule sounds quite grueling for a common sailor."

"There is nothing common about our Izzie," Quentin declared.

"Behave yourself at Harvard, Quentin," she said.

"What, and ruin my reputation?"

"Oh, Izzie." Arabella hugged her. "And to think, when you return, I shall be a married lady!"

"I'll bring you a special wedding gift. Something terribly exotic, I should think. A live parrot? A mango tree?"

Lucinda held the baby while her two toddlers clung to her skirts. "Dora, what an adventure. I never thought, of all of us, you would be the one to go sailing off to distant shores."

Finally Isadora found herself facing her mother, and a world of memories and emotions swirled through her. Her mother loved her, of that she had no doubt, yet she was haunted by the pervasive feeling that she was a disappointment to this proud, handsome woman. That nothing she could do would ever please her entirely.

Except maybe disappear.

"I'll write, Mother," she promised dutifully.

"So shall I. And I want you to tell me everything that happens to you. Everything." To Isadora's astonishment, Sophia violated the dignity of the moment by bursting—oh so briefly—into sobs.

Her father snapped to attention as though someone had shoved a sword into his back. Within seconds, all three men were thrusting handkerchiefs at Sophia. Within a few more seconds, she had dried her face and was fussing with the ribbons of Isadora's bonnet. "I wish you'd agreed to take Thankful along," she said, not even acknowledging her outburst. "Remember to wear your hooded burnouse and stay out of the sun and the wind. They are so deleterious to one's health and countenance.''

''Yes, Mother. Goodbye, Mother. Goodbye, everyone.'' In spite of her eagerness to go, Isadora held a thick grief in her throat as she dispensed hugs to all and accepted sloppy, adoring kisses from her small niece and nephew. Then she turned away.

The stevedores paraded up and down gangways with barrels and crates in tow. Journey and some of the crewmen were present, shouting orders. She guessed that the man with the thin, mournful face and the whistle was Ralph Izard, the chief mate, and she recognized Timothy Datty, the boy who had tried so hard to stop her from humiliating herself.

He would soon learn the futility of that.

She turned to look at her family one last time, using a finger to inch her spectacles down so she could see over the blasted things. Gilded by a dazzle of morning light, the Peabody clan stood on the wharf as if posing for a portrait. Lucinda held the baby in her arms while the two elder children waved sweetly. Arabella and Sophia linked arms while the men formed a tall backdrop for the lace-clad ladies and children. Dear heaven, if there were a painter alive who could capture such magnificent beauty, he had not yet done so. And he should, really. It was truly the most perfect family ever.

Especially now, Isadora thought wryly.

She lifted her hand in a final farewell. And then she turned away, keeping her chin high and her gaze to the sky as she boarded the *Silver Swan.*

She knew better than to expect any sort of civilized welcome here. This was a working vessel, its entire purpose to make money. The decks swarmed with running sailors and porters, customs officers and agents and others she did not recognize. What a marvel it all was to her, the hogsheads and bundles that entered the belly of the ship in an endless parade, the eager agility of the sailors scrambling up through the rigging, readying her for the voyage.

The very idea of all these goods being sent to distant places captivated her. When something went abroad, did the experience change it in some fundamental way? Would that bolt of Framingham broadcloth somehow be transformed into something vibrant, something its creator had never imagined? Would the giant blocks of Vermont mountain ice, wrapped in a thick insulation of straw and burlap, be used to cool foodstuffs no Vermonter had ever dreamed of tasting?

She heard a clucking sound. A swaying stack of crates came lurching toward her. She could only see the cutoff duck trousers and bare feet of its bearer. When the column leaned precariously, she quickly stepped forward and pressed her hand against the top crate. "Careful, there," she said.

"Thank you." A head peeked out from behind the crates, showing a friendly, gap-toothed grin and a wizened African face. "Wouldn't want to spill our dinner before we even set sail." He had a vaguely melodic accent, light inflections lifting his words.

She peered over the top of her spectacles. "The chickens, you mean," she said awkwardly.

"Some are layers, some will be for the stew pot."

Keeping a hand on the crates, Isadora moved along the deck with the little African man. "You must be the cook, then."

"Aye. Samuel Liotta from Jamaica, but they call me

the Doctor, and so shall you. You must be the lady idler.''

"I will be serving as Captain Calhoun's interpreter and clerk. My name is Isadora Dudley Peabody."

"Welcome aboard, Missy," the cook said brightly.

She helped him set down the crates. Peering into the pen, she discovered a small goat and a piglet.

"Alfredo and the pig, I calls them. One for milk, one for meat." He dusted his hands on a canvas apron. "Come, then. Time to meet more members of the crew."

The cook had, for whatever reason, decided to take her under his wing. With considerably better manners than she expected from a seaman, he introduced her to her shipmates.

Ralph Izard served as chief mate, which put him in charge of just about everything. As he rushed past, he had no time to talk, but he smiled cordially enough. She noted a certain sad resignation in his eyes.

William Click, the second mate, spoke with a Cockney accent and wore a short-handled quirt in a hip holster at his side. Chips, the carpenter, was tall and skinny; Luigi Conti, the Italian sail maker, was tiny, with merry eyes and a huge black mustache. Gerald Craven, the jibboom man with tattooed arms and a gold hoop earring, gave her a curt greeting, then hastened off to help Timothy haul down a tangle in the rigging.

Isadora brought her carpetbag to her assigned quarters. Here, she would spend her last night in Boston, and in the morning they would sail with the tide.

According to the Doctor, the *Silver Swan* was an unusual vessel. Sloop-rigged in order to carry less sail and thus a smaller crew, she had been built for a sea captain who insisted on traveling with his wife and four children. That accounted for the grandeur of the captain's stateroom and for the snugness of the two side staterooms, which had once housed the children. Lily Calhoun and her maid would occupy one of the rooms, Isadora the other.

She found a single bunk, too short to accommodate her height, a single portal to let in the daylight and a single washstand with a lavatory and chamber pot. The cabin had the austere air of a monk's cell, and she found that she rather liked the feel of it.

Lily and Fayette greeted her cheerily when they arrived. She accompanied them to their cabin, which was larger, with two boxlike bunks and a sitting area below the portal.

"Are you terribly excited?" Lily asked, helping her maid with a stubborn latch on a case.

"I hardly slept a wink all night."

"It's a little frightening, isn't it?" Lily asked.

"It's a *lot* frightening," Fayette said, casting a suspicious glance at the door. "Only time I ever went somewhere with Mr. Ryan in charge was a day of fishing. We ended up in the middle of Mockjack Bay in a skiff, and he didn't have *no* idea how to get back. No idea at all."

Lily caught Isadora's eye. "I believe Ryan was nine years old at the time."

"He and that Journey. Always trouble." Fayette shook her head mournfully and began filling a drawer under the bunk.

Lily smiled wistfully. "He was always a willful boy."

"You spoiled him, and no mistake," Fayette muttered.

"I suppose I did. His father paid him so little attention. I was Jared's second wife," she explained to Isadora. "With his first, he had Hunter, and Ryan seemed almost an afterthought. Jared wore me as an ornament on his arm, but he hadn't the first idea what to do with a boy like Ryan." She bit her lip. "Oh, dear. I mustn't speak ill of the dead."

Fayette chuckled. "Sweetie, that ain't nothing we ain't all thought of." She glanced up at Isadora. "Beware the man who values you for your pretty face."

"It's not a worry that plagues me," Isadora said wryly, pushing her spectacles up the bridge of her nose. "And surely love grew with familiarity."

"You are so very young, my dear," said Lily. "As young as I was when I was raising Ryan. He grew up wild and free, and I fear I indulged his every whim, trying to make up for his father. Ryan was attractive, impulsive and charismatic, and he knew how to get what he wanted—from everyone but his father."

"There's always been a hole in that boy's life," Fayette said. "But it ain't your place to patch it up. Let him find his own way, Miz Lily."

Isadora felt a prickle of discomfort. People in her family never spoke of such intimate matters, particularly not with the servants.

"I think I shall go out on deck," she said. "I don't want to miss a thing." She left the cabin and returned to deck, finding a spot beside an aft companion ladder where she seemed to be out of the way.

Captain Calhoun was in his stateroom with a shipping agent. She could hear them speaking, but couldn't make out their words. She contented herself with watching the work go on, exchanging a word or two with the crewmen as they passed. She couldn't believe how swiftly the hours had gone by as she made the acquaintance of the men who would be her only company for months on end.

Oddly, she didn't feel as ill at ease with the sailors as she did in social situations on dry land. For the first time, Isadora started to believe that she might actually achieve something on this voyage. What it was, she couldn't be certain, but she dared to hope that when Chad Easterbrook found out how well she had discharged her duties aboard the *Silver Swan,* he'd be very proud indeed.

Then, as if her fervent hope had conjured him, Chad Easterbrook boarded the ship along with his father.

Isadora bustled forward to greet them, nearly tripping over her hem in her haste.

"Mr. Easterbrook!" she said to Abel. And then to Chad: "Mr. Easterbrook!"

"How about that, they have the same name," Ryan Calhoun observed, coming out of his stateroom. He still wore his shore clothes, and rather grand ones at that— kelly green breeches and a yellow silk waistcoat. He also still wore his insolent expression, his clear-eyed gaze promising a rough time for the clerk he didn't want.

Isadora turned away from him, fixing a welcoming smile on her face for the newcomers. Together, Chad and Abel made a dazzling pair. Abel's shock of white hair contrasted sharply with Chad's dark Byronian curls, and they both wore long, caped coats of charcoal wool.

Like the hero of her favorite novel, Chad strode across the deck, his flinty gaze held aloft as he surveyed the final preparations. Sadly, the unfortunate movement of a yardarm tackle spoiled the effect. The large length of wood swung out on its way up the mast, catching him in the midsection—or perhaps lower.

Making a terrible *oof* sound, he doubled over, clutching his father's shoulder.

"Have to watch your step on deck, son," Abel said with gruff concern. "One eye for the ship, and one for yourself."

Isadora came up short, almost quivering to stay the impulse of reaching for Chad, of actually touching him. "Oh, Mr. Easterbrook," she said. "Are you all right?"

He straightened up and nodded, his nostrils pinching as he inhaled deeply. "Quite...quite," he said with a decided lack of conviction.

She caught Ryan studying her with a discomfiting keenness. "Perhaps," he drawled, "you should go ashore and visit your tender mercies upon *him.*"

She sniffed. "I'm needed here. I'll not shirk my duties."

"I shall remember that, Miss Peabody."

The laconic promise in his eyes created an odd havoc in her. Flustered, she hoped the brim of her fanned silk bonnet concealed her blush. Dipping a brief, formal curtsy, she said, "How pleasant to have this chance to say farewell," measuring each word and taking care to address the elder Easterbrook as well as the younger.

"We wish you fair winds and a safe voyage," Abel said, his kindly face crinkling with good humor. He nudged Chad with his elbow. "Don't we, son?"

"We do indeed." Debonair as a fairy-tale prince, Chad bowed from the waist. "Safe winds and a fair voyage."

Isadora savored the gentle warmth he inspired in her. "I shall write a letter daily, telling you of all my adventures." She caught a merry, conspiratorial look from Abel; they had agreed that each letter would contain a private report on the conduct of the skipper and crew. She took an awkward step back, praying no yardarm would sweep her away. "I know you and Captain Calhoun have business to discuss, so if you'll excuse me..." She took another step back. *Kiss me goodbye,* her heart begged him. *Kiss me goodbye.*

But of course, the mad fantasy had no place on a deck aswarm with sailors. She lifted her gloved hand and offered a lame wave. And then it happened. Chad looked at her, and he smiled a smile that promised so much more than a kiss.... Someday, please God, someday.

Awash with pleasure, she hurried away, getting her foot tangled in the hem of her dress, then almost stumbling. But she didn't. She caught herself and stood leaning against the pinrail, thinking of Chad and how perhaps this voyage would transform her in his eyes.

Father and son finished their conference with Ryan and returned to the wharves. She watched them until they were mere specks in the distance, one light head, one dark, finally blending in with the crowd.

"And now," said a voice behind her, "one question remains."

Startled, Isadora turned, knocking her glasses askew with the abrupt motion.

The chief mate shouted orders, and the second mate repeated them. A rush of running feet pounded the decks.

"And what remains, Captain Calhoun?" Self-conscious, she straightened the spectacles.

"To assure myself that you aren't having second thoughts." He stepped toward her, took her hand and

gave a gallant, mocking bow that made her insides churn
with nervousness. A light breeze lifted the fringe of hair
that showed beneath his cap, and the afternoon sunlight
put a sparkle in his eyes.

She narrowed her eyes in suspicion. "Why would I
be having second thoughts?"

He stared straight into her eyes, and she had the
strangest feeling that he could see inside her to the matters that whirled through her mind. "Most women do,"
he said.

Seven

I must go
Where the fleet of stars is anchored and the young
Star captains glow.

—Herman James Elroy Flecker,
The Dying Patriot

"You know what's curious?" Ryan asked, standing back from the captain's table and watching Journey expertly pour the claret.

"Your taste in neck cloths?" Journey ventured, looking askance at the hibiscus-and-lime paisley cravat Ryan had donned for supper.

Ryan ignored him. "When I was in school, I could no more remember a Latin declension than the table of the elements. Yet on this ship I can keep every fact and figure as keenly in my mind as if God himself whispered them into my ear. Why do you suppose that is?"

"Maybe because Latin declensions don't help you deal with dishonest stevedores."

Ryan vividly recalled the endless hours of stumbling through lessons at Albion. "Why can't I learn something simply for learning's sake?"

"You're starting to sound like your daddy."

A chill slid through him. It was true. He recalled all those humiliating times he'd stood before Jared Calhoun, squirming inside while his father quizzed him mercilessly about Horace and the gospel and the price of tobacco in Richmond.

If you constantly have your head in the stars, his father used to demand, *how are you going to keep your feet firmly on the ground?*

"There's no need, if I go to sea," Ryan murmured.

"What's that?"

Ryan shook his head. "Nothing. You know, I keep the stars up here, too." He touched his temple. "Ever since we were lads, I've been able to read the stars as easily as most boys read their scripture."

Journey put a cut glass stopper in the crystal decanter. The *Silver Swan*'s previous skipper had been a man of excellent taste and terrible business practices. When Abel Easterbrook discovered the extent of his cheating, he'd had the man hauled off in chains, leaving behind a salon full of his ill-gotten gains. Ryan had inherited comfortable quarters indeed.

Built into the wall of the cabin, invisible behind a false panel and snug against the hull itself, was the purser's till, a safekeep of steel with a combination lock. Other than Abel himself, only Ryan knew the combination. When he sold the cargo in Rio, he'd receive payment in pounds sterling. It would all go into the till, never to be opened until Abel did the honors once they returned.

"I remember," Journey said, "when we were lads we'd climb to our lookout on a clear night and navigate our way to the Spanish main."

Ryan smiled, picturing the two of them lying side by side on the rough wooden planks of their tree house, hands clasped behind their heads, gazes turned to heaven. The breeze had stirred the poplar leaves, but to the boys' ears it was the shush of the great deep Atlantic rushing past the hull of their ship. Their destination was a place he and Journey had conjured up from their imaginations. They had built it on their own boyish dreams, endowing the perfect island with everything a boy could want: gumdrop trees, geysers that spewed sarsaparilla, crystal clear freshwater pools for swimming. A pond in which the fish leaped for joy, grabbing right onto the end of their fishing poles. No chores, no schoolroom, no lessons, no stern tutor or disapproving papa, no mammy with a hickory rod.

"Did we ever actually reach that place?" Ryan checked the buttons of his cuffs. "I don't remember."

Journey set down the salt cellars, a thoughtful, distant expression on his face. "We're still looking, Skipper. We're still looking."

A light knock sounded at the door, and in came his mother, attended by Fayette, her maid. He greeted the ladies with the Southern gallantry that had been bred into his very bones: a courtly bow, a charming smile, a sweep of his arm toward the table.

Then he spied Miss Isadora Peabody standing uncertainly in the companionway. A twinge of exasperation nagged at him. If she felt awkward, it was her own doing. She had used her influence with Abel to muscle her way aboard this ship. Ryan had resolved to use his position as skipper to make her regret it.

"You're a crew member," he said. "You'd best eat in the galley with the men." He started to close the door.

"Oh, Ryan, for heaven's sake," his mother said, grabbing the door before it slammed. "Miss Peabody is my companion. I won't hear of her eating hard tack and ale in the galley."

"Truly," Miss Peabody murmured, "if the captain orders me to go elsewhere, then I must obey."

"But *I'm* the mother," Lily said smugly. She elbowed Ryan aside. "Come in, and we shall celebrate our last night before departure."

Isadora didn't look at Ryan as she edged into the stateroom. He couldn't quite bring himself to banish her. The painfully arranged hair, the trussed-up style of her black dress, the way she squinted behind her spectacles caused him to feel an unaccustomed tug of...of what? Annoyance, yes, and something perhaps akin to pity.

He tried to figure out why his mind kept clinging to thoughts of her. He'd always been a man who attracted pretty women, and Miss Peabody was not pretty. He enjoyed the charm of female company, yet she was not charming. He liked the inanity of lighthearted conversation, yet she was neither inane nor lighthearted.

So why did she plague him?

Perhaps it was the secrets she guarded within the hazel-and-gold depths of her eyes. In spite of himself, he wanted to know what thoughts hovered there, what ideas. What hopes and dreams.

Of course, he didn't want to hear about her misguided passion for Chad Easterbrook, but other things about her—who she was and what she wanted, what she loved and hated, what surprised her, what delighted her, what angered her.

Immediately he pulled back. The only reason he wanted to discover her inner being was so that he could control her, keep her in line and keep her out of his affairs.

He treated her with a perfect parody of courtesy. "Our first night aboard the *Swan*," he declared. "We must drink a toast."

"I don't drink strong spirits." Her voice was quick and nervous.

"Then I assure you, we'll only serve weak ones," Ryan said. A warning look from his mother stopped him from going on.

"Have you any Cochituate water?" she inquired.

"No, I don't have any Co-kit-tuate water," he said, unable to resist mimicking her prissy accent. "This is a sea voyage, not a temperance crusade."

He and Journey helped the ladies to their seats around the captain's table. Once they were under way, formal meals like tonight's supper would be rare, so Ryan intended to enjoy this one, Miss Peabody notwithstanding.

As Journey poured wine from the decanter, Fayette caught his eye. "I best get to the galley," the maid said, fixing him with a censorious glare. "I don't hold with no wine-drinking."

Journey set his hands on his hips. "Girl, you've known me all my life. Don't be looking at me like I got some disease."

"Maybe you do, Journey-boy," Fayette said in a tone Ryan recognized from his boyhood. "You all uppity now."

The moment could have crackled with tension, but

Journey laughed easily. "No, ma'am, I'm like any other man."

"Hmph." She made a fuss over spreading Lily's napkin in her lap. "Uppity."

"All men are, Fayette," Lily said. "Every last one of them."

Ryan knew, when news of Journey's freedom had reached Albion, some of the field hands had threatened to revolt. The very idea that one of their own was now living as a free man had inflamed them. Lily, newly widowed and ready to set sail for England, had postponed her trip in order to quell the hot tempers and improve living conditions for the workers.

Isadora Peabody watched the exchange, her face draining to a pasty white. Lily laid her hand over Isadora's. "You'll have to excuse us, my dear. We're family, every last one of us, and we shouldn't be performing like this in front of company."

"Oh, dear. I'm not company. I'm an 'idler,'" Miss Peabody declared.

For some reason, everyone laughed, and the tension eased as Fayette took Journey aside and the two of them went up on deck.

"He *is* your steward," Lily said. "Do you think he should stay?"

"Let them go, Mama. There are things they can speak of only to one another."

"They've not seen each other in a great while. What can she possibly tell him?"

He sighed, feeling Miss Peabody's gaze on him. "Mama, I've always considered myself a blood brother to Journey, but I've never lived in that skin. Fayette has." Ryan ached for the man who had been his only steady friend since they were boys. He ached for Delilah, the wife Journey missed so much that sometimes Ryan heard him weeping at night, fiercely, sobbing between his clenched teeth. But when morning came, Journey always faced the day with ready strength, boldly committed to their enterprise.

If this present voyage went well, Journey would be reunited with Delilah and their children inside a year. It was the only thing that mattered in Ryan's life.

The Doctor and Timothy Datty arrived with supper on a two-handled platter. The last meal before setting sail was always lavish—roasted turkey, warm fresh bread, leeks and carrots and a good red wine from the Languedoc. They spoke of the heading they would take out of Boston harbor; of Lily's long tour of the Continent; of fabled Rio and of the aunt Ryan had never met. Or rather, Ryan and his mother spoke while Isadora listened with rapt attention. Aunt Rose had married a Brazilian coffee planter and lived in a lofty castle as grand as any storybook fortress. She and Lily had not seen one another in twenty years.

After supper, Lily excused herself to retire for the night. Ryan accompanied her and Isadora out into the companionway. Isadora hesitated in the low arched doorway and cast a glance through the hatchway where the night sky shone with silver stars.

Lily paused at the door to her cabin. "It's early yet. Ryan, why don't you take Miss Isadora on a turn around the deck?"

It was all he could do to keep from groaning aloud. "A turn on deck?" he echoed. "This is not a pleasure cruise." And his feelings for his clerk were anything but pleasant.

Isadora blinked rapidly, eyeing the open sky. Then she said, "Um, I suppose...I—" She held her hands clasped tightly across her middle. "Captain Calhoun, I am in your service, and I know quite well that you are most certainly not obliged to squire me around."

"And you are not obliged to accept my squiring." He felt a twinge of exasperation. He caught a warning glance from his mother. "But there is no law on land or sea that outlaws an evening stroll."

She looked outside again, her yearning palpable. The woman was as easy to read as an amateur card cheat. "No, there is not."

Lily murmured a good-night and went to her quarters.

Resigned, he cocked his arm out at the elbow. "Shall we?"

She nodded but didn't take his arm, preceding him up the companion ladder. Her crinolines and tight laced-up boots made the going chancey. She hesitated midway up the ladder. It was too dark to see what the trouble was; then Ryan heard a quiet ripping sound and an "Oh, dear."

"Are you all right?" he asked.

"I seem to have stepped on the hem of my petticoat. I'll just...just...oh, *dear!*"

She fell backward, slamming into Ryan. He reeled against an upright stanchion. The air left him in a *whoosh* and for a few seconds he couldn't breathe. Reflexively he'd flung his arms around her midsection when they'd collided. He hung on, marveling at the taut, hard shell of her corsets. Christ, how did the woman breathe?

"Oh heavens," she said in a small, mortified whisper. "I've squashed you flat."

"I'm fine," he said quickly, setting her on her feet.

She tottered a little, then grabbed the side of the ladder. "Captain Calhoun, I am terribly sorry."

She was so meek, so humble. This was the perfect opportunity to swath himself in the mantle of righteous anger, to declare her entirely unsuited to her duties and send her ashore. She'd offer no argument now.

But he studied the downward angle of her head, the shoulders sloping in defeat, and he thought of her in the garden that day, a dark weed amid the flowers of Beacon Hill, the spinster pining for a shipping heir, and realized that, with a word, he could squash *her* flat.

"Try holding your skirts up out of the way," he suggested brusquely. "And tomorrow, wear fewer petticoats. And do lose the iron maiden."

"I beg your pardon?"

"Iron maiden. That damned corset."

She took hold of the ladder again. Ryan stood on alert, ready to catch her in case she came crashing down. She didn't. She scrambled up and waited topside for him to follow.

When they emerged onto the deck, a brilliant night greeted them. The southerly breeze sang lightly through the shrouds.

"Everything's battened down and shipshape," Gerald Craven said, his bald head gleaming in the starlight as he made his way toward the galley. "I took care of that stowage problem."

"Excellent, Mr. Craven."

"I understand badly stowed cargo and ballast can create a problem of balance," Isadora said as Craven left.

Ryan was amazed she knew even the first thing about ballast. "You've been reading again."

"Charles Dana. He explains why it's so hazardous to have the cargo poorly stowed. In heavy seas, anything left out on deck could come loose and damage the ship—or the crew. In the hold, cargo rolling around could unbalance her."

When she spoke of things she'd learned in books, she shed some of her awkwardness. As she stood holding the rail, he could see the strength of her grip on the varnished wood, the set of her shoulders as she faced outward from the darkened harbor. She wanted this voyage, wanted it badly. He didn't have to ask her why. He knew. Thinking of her parents and siblings and the way the Peabody family functioned, he knew.

He wished she'd find another ship to make her escape on.

She pushed her glasses down her nose and lifted her gaze to the sky. "I love the autumn constellations," she said. "Is it the cold, do you think, that gives them such clarity?"

"Perhaps. Why do you wear the spectacles if you're always having to peer over them in order to see?" Ryan asked, impertinent and not caring that he was.

"My mother feared my eyes had gone weak from too much reading, so she insisted on the spectacles. To be honest, I think I see better without them."

He bit his tongue to avoid saying something insulting about her mother. "So we're off with the tide," he said, changing the subject.

"I thought they'd never finish loading the cargo. I don't think I've ever seen so much ice."

"White gold. Our success depends on getting it quickly to harbor in Rio. If the consignees are happy and I negotiate a nice cargo for home, the entire voyage should make Mr. Easterbrook happy.''

"I'm curious.'' She turned to face him. The glow from the binnacle lamps flickered over her rounded cheeks, the lenses of her spectacles. "You are so very ambitious, so very set on earning a fortune at this.''

"Surely that doesn't offend your Yankee sensibilities,'' he said. This voyage, for Ryan, had many more complicated reasons, but he was quite clear on what he would do with the earnings.

"Heavens, no. But you must admit it's unusual for a Southern gentleman to become a Yankee skipper.''

He was disgruntled at the way she had commandeered a place on the ship, yet curious all the same. "May I say something quite personal?''

"Can I stop you?''

"No.''

"Then go on.''

"Miss Peabody, I think we're both the black sheep of our families. I because I refuse to build my fortune on the backs of slaves, and you because you...'' Damn. He'd talked himself into a corner now.

"Because I'm the plain spinster in a family of beautiful and popular socialites,'' she finished for him. "You are quite correct, Captain Calhoun.'' She started to walk away.

He caught her arm. "Do not put words in my mouth. That's not what I meant.''

She stared at his hand on her arm for so long that he felt awkward and released her. "I see. Then what, pray, did you mean?''

"Simply that... Oh, hell. Are you always this sensitive?''

"Yes. It is one of my great failings." She looked toward the bow. They could see the silhouettes of Journey and Fayette there, shadows against the lights along the shore. They stood with their heads bent close, deep in conversation.

"They're speaking of home," Ryan explained. "Fayette can tell him things...no one else can possibly know."

"Why would he want to hear news of the place where he was in bondage?" she asked.

Ryan hesitated, then decided there was no harm in telling her. "Because he left a part of himself behind."

"What do you mean?"

"His wife and children. They belong to our neighbors, the Beaumonts."

Her gasp ended on a quiet, heartfelt sob. "Dear lord," she said. "Then freedom for him is exile."

"It was a hard choice to make." Ryan remembered how he'd lain awake night after night, agonizing as the day of his departure for Harvard drew closer. "If I freed him, he would never be able to see his family again. But if he remained a slave, he'd live as half a man, bound to me for all his days, and his children after him."

Miss Isadora Dudley Peabody burst into tears.

Discomfited, Ryan groped in his pocket and found a clean handkerchief. "I take it you have strong feelings on the issue of slavery?"

"That's precisely it. I thought I did, but until this moment I never quite grasped what it means. You did the right thing." She blew her nose audibly, then crushed the handkerchief in her fist. "I'll launder it for you," she promised.

He almost smiled, but stopped himself. He didn't need

anyone's approval, let alone the admiration of this prissy Boston woman. They were worlds apart; it was simply the circumscribed closeness of shipboard life that gave the illusion of intimacy.

"I had best retire," Isadora said. "I know I shan't sleep a wink, but I promised myself I would try."

She started toward the companion ladder. Her feet, enclosed in the flimsy little boots with high, wobbling heels, moved uncertainly over the deck. The shoes, he decided, would have to go. So would the Beacon Hill matron costume. The voluminous black-and-gray skirts and petticoats, the rigid shell of the corset, all the trappings of propriety had no place on a working ship. Her damned hair alone was a problem, too, since she insisted in scraping it all up into a knot on her head and then letting those curls trail down in the front. So the hair, too, he decided. She'd have to change that along with the dress and the shoes.

He smiled at the image. Getting the very proper Miss Peabody to slap about on deck like a barefoot sailor would prove a challenge indeed.

Ryan had always enjoyed a challenge.

Eight

You know how often we have longed for a sea
voyage, as the fulfillment of all our dreams of
poetry and romance, the realization of our highest
conceptions of free, joyous existence.... Let me
assure you, my dears...that going to sea is not at
all the thing that we have taken it to be.

—Harriet Beecher Stowe,
Sunny Memories of Foreign Lands

Isadora dreamed of a pack of wolves snapping at her
from all sides, chewing the heels off her shoes, ripping
her petticoats to shreds. Rudely stirred from sleep by a
piercing whistle, she lay in her bunk at dawn and knew
the wolves in her dream were actually misgivings.

She inhaled air so damp it seemed to drench her lungs.
Her back ached from lying huddled in a cramped space
in the dark. Last night's turkey and claret sat ill in her
stomach, and when she rose to avail herself of the cham-
berpot—that in itself a disgusting operation she endured
only by scrunching her eyes shut tight and refusing to

think of it—she smacked her head on a beam so hard she saw stars.

Sitting on the edge of the bunk, she rubbed her head and peered out the woefully tiny portal. Indeed, they had left their berth in the harbor and were now at anchor; they'd be headed out to sea any moment.

The night before, she'd managed to struggle out of her corset and had slept in her chemise. She eyed the garment—a Corset Amazone that her mother had ordered specially from Freebodys—with loathing. The great fallacy of the corset was that it did not sheer off fullness; it merely displaced it to uncomfortable locales. Captain Calhoun had not been far wrong in calling it an iron maiden, after a medieval torture device.

Resigned, she stood up to don the corset. A sharp pain shot up her leg, stealing her breath. She sank back to the bunk, holding out her left ankle. It resembled a great sausage, swollen and discolored. Gingerly she touched the bruise, wincing at the pain. She must have injured herself when she fell off the ladder—directly onto Captain Calhoun.

This is not a pleasure cruise. His sarcastic words, uttered the night before, still rang in her ears.

Dear lord, had she ever actually thought she belonged on this voyage?

People had told Isadora all her life that she was foolish. Now, at last, she was fulfilling the prophecy. What possible business did she have on a ship, living among men of dubious repute and bound for the pirate-infested waters of the south Atlantic?

Gritting her teeth, she struggled through the ordeal of getting dressed, her conviction hardening with each moment. She was Isadora Dudley Peabody of the Beacon

Hill Peabodys. She should be home reading a book or embroidering slipper tops, perhaps drinking tepid coffee from a china cup. Not bumping around in a tiny cabin trying to tie her own stays and bring order to her wild, waist-length hair.

Perhaps, she thought, her urgent fingers grappling with stay wires and corset hooks, there was still time to turn away, to back out. If she hurried, she could get herself on a lighter boat or launch; surely there were any number of skiffs plying back and forth across Boston harbor.

Yes, that was the thing to do. That was precisely it. She looped her hair a few times and stabbed it into place with some pins, rammed on her bonnet and spectacles and hastened out of the cabin. Pain blazed from her ankle, but she forced herself to keep a steady gait. A wall of sea-fresh air greeted her in the companionway. Through the hatch, she could see men running to and fro, their faces intense as they discharged their duties, their voices raised in jolly song:

"All hands on board!
Farewell to friends!
'Tis the signal for unmooring
We're bound across the ocean blue,
Heave your anchor to the bow,
And we'll think on those girls when we're far, far away,
And we'll think on those girls when we're far, far away."

Ryan Calhoun stood on deck and once again Isadora was struck by the dazzling male beauty that emanated like sunlight from him. He was sipping from an enameled metal mug and speaking with a customs official. They referred to a mass of scrolled papers strewn across the navigators' desk. Though she hated to interrupt, she knew she had to act fast to get herself back home where she belonged.

Home? The house on Beacon Hill? When had she ever belonged there?

She thrust aside the questions. Though she might be a misfit in her own life, she was even more out of place here on this ship, where men in rope-belted trousers scrambled up rigging and masts and swore even when they knew a lady was around.

"Captain Calhoun," she said, puffing a little as she hoisted herself up the companion ladder to the next deck. She hobbled along on her injured ankle. "Captain, I must speak to you of a—"

"Ah, Miss Peabody." Ryan nodded brusquely at her. Then, rude as Foster Candy, he turned back to the port official. "I've already furnished three copies of the manifest, sir. As to that claim form, I—"

She bobbed an awkward curtsy. "Captain, a moment of your time—"

"Allow me to introduce Mr. Dickie Warbass of the Customs Office," he said, not even looking at her.

"How do you do." Another hasty curtsy. "Begging your pardon, Captain, but I must—"

"This is the one, right here." He thrust a document into her hands. "Mr. Warbass and I have been searching for half an hour for some form in Portuguese."

She frowned down at the paper. "But Captain, I—"

"What does it say?" he asked. "I apologize for our haste, but Mr. Warbass has other duties to attend to this morning and we mustn't keep him."

"You have a launch?" she asked the official.

"Of course."

She breathed a sigh of relief. Mr. Warbass could take her off the ship. Back to her mother and father and their baffled but familiar affection. Back to her brothers and sisters, so perfect and humorous that the world worshiped at their feet. Back to pining for Chad Easterbrook, praying he'd notice her. Back to the whirl of a society that did not welcome her.

Troublesome thoughts, for certain, but not nearly so troublesome as the idea of making a rough sea voyage in the company of strangers to a foreign land. She couldn't believe she'd actually come this far.

She felt as if she were tumbling out of control through unknown waters, like a barnacle pried forcibly from the dock.

She inched her spectacles down her nose and peered over the rims to read the document. "It's a copy of the consignment agreement with a firm called Ferraro and Son. Is that what you had in mind, Captain?"

He pointed to a space at the bottom. "My signature goes here, I presume?"

"Yes, and you're welcome," she said pointedly.

"Welcome to what?"

She shut her eyes until patience returned. "Never mind. The date as well. And a mark…a seal of note."

"I've got that right here." Warbass produced a brass seal.

While they worked on the documents, Isadora's attention wandered to the activity on the ship. Responding like clockwork soldiers to the shouted orders of the chief mate, the crew sent up the topgallant sails and courses,

the royals and flying jib. They moved with athletic lithe-
ness and a surety of their place in the world.

Favoring her injured ankle, she leaned her head back,
growing dizzy from the view of the masts swaying high
overhead. Then something—the heel of her shoe, perhaps—hooked into a coil of line. She wheeled her arms,
grabbing at anything, finding a web of rope nearby. The
moment she clutched it, a series of knots along the rail
came loose, unraveling like a row of knitting being
pulled apart.

Luigi, the sail maker, roared an Italian obscenity and
dove for the reeling line. Mortified, Isadora pressed her
palms to her burning cheeks.

"Miss Peabody?" Captain Calhoun's voice was a
low, deadly murmur near her ear.

A chill rippled down her spine. "I'm sorry, I—"

"Do you suppose you could create another disaster?
It's half past seven and you've only created one so far."

The stinging heat of tears blinded her. She willed them
away. "I don't find that amusing, Captain."

"Nor does Mr. Conti." He gestured at the still-
screaming Italian. "Would you mind feeding the kitten?" His voice was falsely soft, falsely calm.

She wrinkled her forehead in bafflement. "Feed
the...?"

"Kitten. She's in my quarters. Hasn't been well since
I took her aboard. There's milk in one of the decanters.
Perhaps a little of that and some sardines."

"You have a kitten aboard, and you want me to feed
her."

"Yes."

"I don't believe that's part of my duties."

"If you don't go feed the damned cat now," he said,

that silky Southern voice rising with each word, "you'll be picking oakum for the next six months." He seemed to grow in stature as the threat exploded from him. He really was a tall man, startlingly so. Rarely had she met a man taller than she, but here was one. A very angry one.

"Very well," she said, refusing to flinch before his temper. Ankle smarting, she headed aft, determined to dispense with the task and return in time to escape in Mr. Warbass's launch.

Muttering under her breath, she stepped into the dim chamber. Being alone in Captain Calhoun's private quarters made her feel inappropriately intrusive. Recalling the first time she'd come here, she glanced at the shrouded bunk and shuddered. He was a profligate, a womanizer. She should be glad she was leaving.

"Here, kitty," she called softly. As her gaze darted here and there, she realized she wasn't looking for a cat. She was looking at the things that made up Ryan Calhoun's world. A stack of books—novels and monographs and sailing manuals. A logbook and ledger on the desk. A small oval of porcelain bearing the likeness of his mother. A sampler stitched with the saying Fine Words Butter No Parsnips.

From the kneehole of the desk came a faint mewing sound. Isadora got down on her hands and knees, huffing a little as her corset squeezed her, and made a coaxing motion with her hand. "There you are."

A small, sleek body shot past her to a dark corner under the stern windows. Staying low, Isadora followed. "Come out, you little scamp. Come and eat. I can't believe he could forget to feed you this morning."

She had nearly reached the cat when it tried to squeeze

itself into a gap in the paneling. With a frown, she slid the panel aside. She saw, with some surprise, a large, steel money safe. The sight sent a nervous chill down her back, and she glanced guiltily over her shoulder. She should not be here. But now the cat was stuck inside.

"Here, kitty," she said, wiggling her fingers. "Oh, do come out."

The tiny cat poked forth a wary pink nose, then its small gray head, then its skinny body. Isadora took it gently beneath the middle and draped it over her arm. Trustingly, the cat relaxed like a fur stole. Nearly shaking with relief, Isadora slid the panel shut. She found the milk and sardines and, wrinkling her nose in distaste, created a horribly unappetizing mass in a small tray on the stern bench.

The cat settled down to eat with great delicacy.

Outside, a whistle sounded again and something bumped heavily into the hull. Quickly, Isadora went back to the deck.

Just in time to see Ryan Calhoun waving farewell to Mr. Warbass, whose launch was headed into port.

"He left!" she said in dismay.

"He did," Ryan agreed.

"But I wanted to—"

"Captain, the navigator's ready for our coordinates," said Mr. Click, the second mate. "I've entered them into the deck log."

"Excuse me." Ryan Calhoun walked away from her.

Before she could protest, a grinding sound rumbled through the air. She saw men turning around the capstan, bringing in the great anchors from fore and aft. The ship rolled a little, wallowed and settled like a duck laying an egg. More shouts, more running about.

Dear God, she was leaving. Leaving against her will. She was as much a prisoner as a pirate's captive. She didn't know whether to scream or weep.

And then, high above, a wonder occurred.

With a great, unearthly *whoosh,* the wind filled the sails.

It was not an event she could have imagined or guessed at by watching from shore or looking at prints or paintings. The seamed canvas pulsed with a life of its own, much as the wings of a great bird took on their life from both the bird and from the wind that went underneath them and lifted. A burgeoning. A blossoming.

By holding a rail and leaning back, she could gaze up and see nothing but white canvas and blue sky, their contrast sharp and so intense it made the eyes smart. Then she looked ahead at the sea rolling out before the bow and almost wept with the beauty of it. Glassy swells rose before the ship as the *Swan* pulled into the main trades. The sensation of speed was so acute that Isadora heard a stream of laughter. Pure, clear laughter.

And to her amazement, she realized that the glad sound was coming from her. It sprang from the depths of a joy she had never known before.

When had she ever, ever laughed like this?

She passed the first hour of the voyage in this rapturous state, simply standing with her hand gripping a shroud while the men went about their duties and the sea swept them into its vast embrace.

She'd had no idea it would be intoxicating. She grew dizzy as she inhaled the salt tang, tinged with resin and tar. The blood seemed to pulse faster in her veins, giving her a heady feeling of possibility. She inhaled deeply, wincing when her corset stopped her from filling her lungs to the brim. Tomorrow, perhaps, she would wear the garment a notch looser. For what did it matter if she relaxed a bit? This was her adventure. She had no one to impress so long as she performed her duties. After the voyage she would never see these people again.

She watched the gap between ship and shore grow to a huge gulf. Perhaps this was a little like dying, the departed no longer visible to the others, yet both still existed, only in different worlds.

The very thought opened her to something she had forbidden herself to do for a long time. She began to feel hope again. To yearn. She had always been good at dreaming, but what she had never done before was believe a dream could actually come true. She believed now. The wonder of setting sail created possibilities she had never considered before.

Finally, she sensed a presence nearby and turned. There stood Captain Calhoun, looking handsome and windblown in clothing far different from his shore togs. He had on trousers of well-worn, glove-soft fabric that hugged his hips in a way that was positively indecent. In contrast, his shirt blew loose around the chest and shoulders, lending him a piratical air.

Her resentment over the cat came rolling back at her. "Something else, Captain?" She was surprised—and rather proud—of her caustic tone.

"I don't know what you mean."

She forced her gaze away from the amazing trousers. "No dogs to feed? Perhaps the resident hamster or vole?"

Sunlight glinted in his eyes, but he didn't smile. "No

vole," he said. "No hamster. The rats will fend for themselves."

"Then perhaps there's something that actually requires my skills."

"Ah." His gaze swept over her with lazy insolence. "You have skills?"

Isadora looked at his intent face, the blue eyes, the wind-reddened cheeks. She refused to rise to his baiting. "You have no idea what I'm capable of, Captain. None at all."

Standing in the cockpit with William Click, who was taking a turn at the helm, Ryan kept a weather eye on Isadora Peabody. Her first day at sea was a marvel to her. She reveled in the wind and waves, conversing with the sailors with far less bashfulness than she'd exhibited earlier, and even joining in a small task or two—tying off a ratline, fastening the anchor hitch.

When he saw her handling the sails or letting go the brails, he felt a stab of chagrin. He wanted her to suffer, not flourish. He wanted her to learn her place, not make a place for herself on shipboard.

Yet every so often she would lift her face to the wind and close her eyes. A look of rapture would come over her, and in spite of himself, he could feel a strange, unwanted affinity for her. He felt the same sentiment under sail. Only a true lover of the sea could relate to the chest-tightening, ecstatic sense of anticipation.

Christ. The woman even robbed *that* joy from him by learning to love what he had always loved.

"How's your mother doing, Captain?" asked Click.

"The seasickness is at her. And her maid, too. I expected as much." Ryan had checked on Lily and Fayette frequently, cracking open the door to their cabin to find them both lying green-lipped and limp upon their berths, Fayette praying softly and Lily staring miserably out the small portal. Isadora had offered to attend to them, but they declined, preferring to keep their misery private.

"The new one doesn't seem at all affected by it," Click observed, nodding in Isadora's direction. She stood like a figurehead with her face pointed into the wind, taking bracing gulps of sea air. "Odd bird, ain't she?"

Ryan studied the second mate, with his bitten-off ear and leather vest with the rabbit's foot in the pocket and a juju bag full of bat bones on a string around his neck. "You would know, Mr. Click. You would know."

He charted the coordinates and observed the changing of the first watch. The Doctor served dinner, which Ryan ate standing up—scouse, hasty pudding and salt beef, a fresh apple and a healthy squeeze of lime juice.

Then, drawn by an impulse of deviltry, he went to the bow where Isadora stood. Her bonnet—the silly gray one he disliked—had blown off and bounced against her back with each breath of the wind. Her light-brown hair had been plucked from its topknot, and yard-long streamers tangled idly in the breeze. She seemed oblivious to her dishevelment as she watched the progress of the ship.

"Have you eaten?" he asked without greeting her.

"I had half an apple for my dinner, and it was quite enough, thank you. I don't want to risk getting seasick." She pursed her lips in prissy superiority.

"Eat something," Ryan said intractably. "That's an order."

She sniffed, poking her nose into the air. "Your orders are foolish. Last time you gave me an order, you missed your chance to get rid of me.''

A lead weight sank slowly in Ryan's gut. "Do tell."

"I was going to go back to Boston in Mr. Warbass's launch, but you sent me on that foolish errand about the cat—"

"You kept getting underfoot—"

"—and by the time I was finished, the launch had left."

The lead weight of regret hit bottom. "Next time you decide to abandon ship, remind me not to stop you."

"Remind yourself not to be so rude," she returned.

An idea struck him. "We'll be hailing ships all through the next several days. I'll put you on one that's headed back into Boston."

She gave that superior-sounding sniff again. "You're too late. I've decided to stay. You see, I realized what the problem was." Her tone reminded him of a schoolmarm's lecture. "The upheaval before a voyage upsets even a seasoned traveler. It's an enormous undertaking, leaving one's home and becoming a part of a tiny universe here in the middle of the sea. Anyone with a half-decent imagination is bound to have misgivings."

She stared directly at him, and said, "I suppose I should thank you. This voyage is going to be an adventure I should not like to miss. It was rude of you to order me about, but since it had such happy consequences, I forgive you."

"Don't forgive me."

"Why not?"

"Because I didn't apologize, you goose!"

"Well!" Indignation huffed from her.

They stood in discomfiting silence for a time, listening

to the song of the wind through the shrouds, the rhythmic creak of timber and the surge of saltwater past the hull. Seating herself on a lashed crate, she took out a steel-tipped pen and wrote something on the paper secured to the marbled board she held.

"What are you writing?" Ryan asked.

"Blinding rush of blue. It's the most perfect phrase to describe the way the sea races past the hull."

"A letter home, then?"

"It's…um…private."

She shouldn't have said that. He snatched the letter from her. "There's no privacy on shipboard."

"Captain!"

He would have given it back, but he kept remembering her words to Chad Easterbrook. *I shall write a letter daily, telling you of all my adventures.*

Ryan glanced down at the board. She had a fine, legible hand.

"Dear Mr. Easterbrook…" He didn't have to read further. She was writing to the upright, insufferable Chad Easterbrook. What the hell had he ever done to earn such constancy?

"Give that back," she said, standing up, raising her voice.

Ryan told himself this was none of his affair. He told himself he shouldn't feel a hot stab of irritation that this Yankee spinster had given her admiration and esteem to Chad Easterbrook.

"Not until you let me count the ways you love him," Ryan teased. "For truly, he is a man of many facets. At least two." He glanced at the page again and read further. Instead of the breathless schoolgirl phrases he expected to find, the contents of the note shocked him completely.

...main stateroom is in an untidy state, and there is a steel money safe secreted under the banquette...

Fury made the words melt before his eyes. "Ah. Never let it be said you're not thorough, my dear Witch of the Wave. But then, shouldn't you be listed on the manifest as *spy* rather than clerk or translator?"

"Give that back," she said again, reaching for the letter.

The wind rattled the paper and then plucked it from his fingers. "Oops," he said.

"How dare you," she snapped, stepping forward, the pen clenched in her fist.

"It was an accident." He widened his eyes in innocence.

She heaved an exasperated sigh. "I shall only write another."

"That's how you did it, then," he said, glaring at her. "You got Abel to send you on this voyage by promising to monitor my every move."

"You can hardly blame him. He didn't find you in a trustworthy...state that first night."

"He found me hopelessly drunk and in the process of seducing a half-naked wench. Did you write that down, hm?"

"I—"

"Suppose I report to you each time I take a piss. Will you be writing that, too?"

She squinted at him, then pushed down her eyeglasses and peered over the top of them. "You are the rudest man I have ever met."

"Sugar, if you think that was rude, hang on to your bloomers, because I intend to get a lot worse."

Ryan stood back, watching her. When she wasn't squinting, her eyes were quite remarkable, gold-flecked and strangely compelling. "Why do you look over the top of those spectacles in order to see?"

"Because everything up close is blurred when I look through them." She snapped her mouth shut and blanched.

"Perfect," said Ryan. Before she could stop him, he yanked the glasses off her, taking a few strands of hair along with them.

She emitted an audible gasp, and, oddly, the sound excited him, for it reminded him of the startled inhalation of a woman who had been aroused. Of course, in this case the only thing he had aroused was her anger.

"Give those back."

He dropped the spectacles overboard. "Oops."

She gaped at him. "You...you...brute. Cad. Troglodyte. Goth." She exhausted her supply of insults, and still he remained unmoved.

"I'm afraid it's too late."

"That was my only pair."

"Then I guess you won't be making any more of your sneaky little reports," he snarled.

"I'll do as I please. I'll write what I choose."

"No, you won't. I am the captain of this ship. On land, that doesn't mean much. But aboard the *Swan* it is everything. My word is law. My acts are unimpeachable."

"Am I supposed to be impressed by this?"

"I rather hoped you would be."

"Well, I'm not."

"A pity. I guess I'll have to find some other way to impress you."

"Don't bother," she snapped. "Nothing will work." She turned on her heel, wobbling slightly with the motion. Her dignity, he could tell, was hanging by a thread. "Good day, Captain Calhoun," she said over her shoulder, then made her way down to her quarters.

Nine

I can see the Lady has a genius for ruling, whilst
I have a genius for not being ruled.

—Jane Welsh Carlyle
(1845)

"Is there anything I can do for you?" Isadora asked
the next day, cracking open the door to Lily's chamber.
She stepped back as the odor of sickness hit her. Lily
and Fayette lay limp upon their bunks, their eyes staring
dully at nothing.

Without waiting for an answer, Isadora helped herself
to the cotton bib apron hanging on a wall hook and got
to work. During the last years of Aunt Button's life, she
had taken charge of nursing her, and the experience of
caring for another human being gratified her. Willingly,
she embraced the task.

She emptied the chamber pot and aired the bedclothes.
She dispensed sponge baths, helped the women put on
clean nightgowns and removed the others to launder

them. She worked with fierce purpose, grateful for the activity. If she let herself be idle for even a few moments, she would burst with fury at Ryan Calhoun. At least the labor gave her some outlet for the angry energy coursing through her.

Holding the basket of clothes and linens in front of her, she tapped her foot on the galley floor. The Doctor glanced up. "Aye, miss, what can I do for you?"

"I should like a vat of hot water and some lye soap for washing. Please."

He considered this a moment. Then he nodded. "I'll put a kettle on—but it's sea water, you understand. We don't use the fresh for laundry."

"I understand." Within moments she was kneeling on deck, her sleeves rolled up and her elbows sticking out as she vigorously scrubbed the garments up and down a ridged washboard. She had never once in her life done laundry, and the task proved harder than it looked. The water kept sloshing all over her lap. She splashed herself in the face, and her eyes stung from the soap. As usual, her hair wouldn't stay in its knot, and long strands fell forward to dip into the vat. By the time she finished, she was nearly as wet as the clothes.

Yet oddly, she wasn't concerned with her appearance. Back in Boston, someone was always correcting her posture, tidying her hair, evening out the drape of her dress. The men of the *Swan* did not seem to care in the least what she wore or what her hair looked like. It was quite liberating and, she supposed, quite wicked, to enjoy such an unconventional attitude.

With an exaggerated swagger, Ryan Calhoun strolled near, exquisitely dressed in popinjay attire, for earlier in the day they had hailed a British frigate. He insisted that a skipper must look prosperous to be perceived as a worthy merchant. Isadora suspected he merely liked to dress in fancy attire because he was vain.

Still, he had done some trading—Ipswich cotton for Glasgow wool—and made a nice profit. To the disgusting hilarity of the men, Ryan had offered to throw in Isadora for free.

She studied him furtively now, this man who seemed determined to make her regret this voyage. A froth of Irish lace adorned his neck, spilling out over a peacock blue waistcoat of figured silk. His expertly creased trousers were tucked into boots that gleamed with fresh polish.

Criminal, she thought resentfully. It was criminal that a man should look so comely in the middle of the ocean. Only Ryan Calhoun could wear such loud colors and make them seem brighter and richer. What a vain and self-centered man he was, to look so fine when she looked so…damp.

He lingered on the deck and watched her until she said, "Haven't you anything better to do? Perhaps someone has a pocket watch or some books or other valuables that need to be pitched overboard."

He chuckled. It infuriated her that he had such a charming laugh. She wished his laughter could sound as obnoxious as he truly was.

"I'm intrigued, Miss Peabody. Isn't that Fayette's calico dress?"

"It is. She and your mother are unwell. I have decided to look after them."

"Why?"

"To keep myself from killing you," she said between her teeth, increasing her vigor with the washboard.

"Ah. Still vexed about the spectacles?" He lifted one eyebrow, just so. "Good. Think about that next time you decide to record my misdeeds aboard the ship."

"You should not have jettisoned my eyeglasses." Isadora would not admit, on pain of death, that she did not miss the eyeglasses at all. Wearing them had been a great bother. They had never worked properly. She was always having to find a way to peer over or under the lenses. Without them, she could see much better.

A fact she refused to divulge to Ryan Calhoun.

"That is one thing you must learn about me, Miss Peabody," he said. "I am a creature of impulse. I almost never think before I act."

"An impressive quality, I'm sure." She could not begin to explain how offensive his action had been. Regardless of whether they worked or not, the spectacles belonged to her. They were personal, perhaps as much a part as her brown hair and hazel eyes. She felt naked without them. They were a symbol of her identity, and he had taken that away.

An unwanted inner voice told her she used to hide behind them. She hushed the inner voice. It was not up to Ryan Calhoun to drag her out of hiding.

She lifted the heavy lump of sodden fabric out of the tub and slapped it on the deck. Picking up the tub, she staggered toward the rail to empty it. The weight of it unbalanced her, and she lurched forward. The tub sloshed over, a fount of gray wash water exploding upward and drenching Ryan Calhoun from head to toe.

His stylishly cut red hair. His exquisite lace neck cloth. His silken turquoise waistcoat. His creased trousers and gleaming boots.

Isadora stood back, blinking and aghast. Then a satisfying sense of justice settled over her. "Oops," she said.

She expected fury from him, but he surprised her. He threw back his head and roared with laughter.

What a singular way to cope with a humiliating mishap, she thought, puzzled by his mirth. She studied his tanned, wet throat and curling long hair and strong white teeth and dancing eyes. He was so quick to laugh at his own expense.

"Touché, Miss Peabody. Touché."

"The pleasure was mine, I'm sure," she said. She had the most inexplicable urge to smile at him. Determinedly she kept her face blank, her mouth grim.

He whistled as he strolled down the deck, water squishing from his boots. Isadora stared after him, intrigued. The seamen on duty stared, too, elbowing each other and whispering.

Papa had warned her that travel by sailing ship meant days of tedium.

Papa, for the first time in his life, was wrong.

One morning at sunrise, after the changing of the watch, Ryan was walking the starboard rail when he came across the sail maker crouched on deck with Isadora.

Despite living in tiny quarters with a minimum of amenities, she clung to her lubberly fashion of wearing a tightly bound gray or black dress, a bonnet and that idiotic knotted coiffure. Yet the wind, far more persistent even than Isadora's stubbornness, plucked long strands of hair from her bonnet and swirled them in the sun until the exposure made her hair glisten with gold highlights.

Between Luigi and Isadora lay a pile of ropes and

pulleys. "This," the sail maker said, holding it out to her, "is a heaving line. You throw it with a monkey's fist, like so." He demonstrated. Then Isadora took a turn with it, beaming when she succeeded.

"And this one?" She held up a decorated knot.

"A cat's-paw. And this one, see, it's got a knot to hold a line on a gangway, this is a Turk's head."

She took up the next one. "What do you call this back splice?"

"A dog's cock," Luigi said matter-of-factly.

Miss Isadora dropped it as if it had burned her. "Ye powers."

Laughing to himself, Ryan approached them. "A lesson in your sea-going jargon?" he inquired.

Luigi winked, twitching his mustache. "The lady, she is a fast learner."

"Then perhaps one day you'll tell her how we refer to heaving in a line a bit."

She stood up. "And what would the answer to that one be?"

"If the back splice makes you blush, I don't think you're ready to hear." Goaded by one of his famous impulses, Ryan cocked out his arm. "I was about to take the morning longitude sights and thought you might like to join me."

He told himself he'd invited her as a small reward. She had been performing the exhausting task of nursing his mother and Fayette. She'd earned a little civil conversation.

She eyed him suspiciously. Over the past several days they had circled one another with cautious interest. Ryan could never be certain what she would do next, this "idler" he'd taken on to do the translating and clerical work. As the crew settled into the predictable rhythms of life under sail, there was a subtle, indefinable difference in the air about them.

Ignorant of social graces, these rough sailors, these sons of Neptune simply accepted her. Ryan had expected them to defer to her, to behave differently in her presence, but instead, they took it upon themselves to initiate her into their way of life.

One day she might be seated on a crate with Luigi, mending sail with a big hooked needle. The next might find her laughing as Gerald Craven, the jibboom man, taught her to play a tune on the Portuguese accordion. In the galley, she showed the Doctor how to make fudge. Once, Ryan came out of the chart room to find her holding Chips's hand in her lap. The sight gave Ryan a sudden hot sting of annoyance until he realized she was picking a splinter out of the carpenter's hand.

She made friends of them. This willful young woman from Beacon Hill, who came from people who wouldn't deign to let a boy like Timothy Datty black their boots, had suddenly taken on a different role aboard the *Silver Swan*. She wanted to know about Luigi's impressive array of tattoos and what each one meant. She asked after Gerald Craven's children, knowing they had come down with the measles shortly before the *Swan* set sail. She conversed readily and easily with Chips, ordinarily a quiet man who contented himself with his hand-carving. The Doctor let her dry her stockings in his galley, a privilege he wouldn't afford Ryan. And even William Click, the unpopular second mate, was wont to sit with her of an evening, smoking his pipe and listening as she read from one of the many books she had brought.

"How are my mother and Fayette today?" Ryan asked as they made their way toward the chart room.

"Little better, I fear. I managed to get them to sip some broth, but they are both still reluctant to leave their beds."

"Some folks never get their sea legs," he said, then eyed Isadora, noting the way long trails of hair had been plucked from their pins. "You don't suffer the *mal de mer*. What is your secret, Miss Peabody?"

"I've learned to be very cautious about what I eat."

He narrowed his eyes, studying her. Were her cheeks less round? Did he detect dark circles under her eyes? "You'll fall ill of weakness," he warned her. "You'll waste away."

She laughed softly; she seemed to laugh far more readily at sea than on land. "I daresay I've a long way to go before facing that calamity, Captain." She took a deep breath of the morning air. "Indeed, my health is much improved aboard this ship. I've not sneezed or sniffled since we left Boston."

It was true, he realized with a start. The watery eyes, the reddened nose, the explosive sneezes—he'd seen none of them lately.

Ralph Izard stood on the foredeck, turning to greet them as they approached. "I think we can bring up the sea anchor, skipper," he said to Ryan. "Seas've calmed a good bit since last night."

"We've dropped anchor?" Isadora asked with a frown.

"A sea anchor," Izard explained. "We used a drogue thrown overboard to keep the bow to the direction of the sea." He indicated the windlass. "I was about to bring it up."

"May I?" she asked, her face lighting up.

Izard glanced at Ryan, who shrugged. "Mind your fingers—we don't want them pinched by the rope."

Mr. Izard gave her a handspike and showed her how to insert it into the body of the windlass cylinder. Positioning herself behind the foremast, she began to work the apparatus. Slowly the thick rope, wet and hung with seaweed, began to emerge from the water.

"Steady now," Izard said. "Keep her steady, and the rope will coil around it all of itself. Shall I give you a hand?"

"Don't you dare," she said, her voice strained. "I can do this." Grinding away at the windlass, she made a very strange sailor—though her full skirts and landlubber shoes impeded her progress. A long, rolling wave lifted the bow at a sharp slant.

"Careful," Ryan said. "Chips lifted out some of the planks to get at the dry rot, and—"

"Oh!" The heel of her shoe caught in a crevice between some of the missing boards. The next happened so quickly Ryan was powerless to stop it. Her feet came out from under her, and she let go of the handspikes. The rope spun wildly on the spool, winding her hair around it along with the twisted line. A second later, she lay against the foremast, bound there by her own hair. Her face had paled to a pasty white.

"Miss Peabody!" Ryan dropped to his knees. "Are you hurt?"

"No, but...it pulls at my scalp. Can you free me?"

"It does too hurt," he snapped, making a few tentative attempts at untangling her. "You were dragged by the hair and your head slammed against the mast. So quit trying to be valiant and admit it hurts like hell."

She bit her lip. "It hurts like...the dickens."

"That's harsh," Izard muttered.

Each time Ryan moved the windlass, it pulled at her hair. Frustrated, he called for Journey, who came running, his broad bare feet slapping on the deck.

"Good job, honey," he said, clearly impressed. "We haven't ever had someone get tangled up in the windlass before."

"I should like to get up now," Isadora said.

The sailors who were off watch came to see what was the matter. So did Luigi and Chips. William arrived shortly as well, and everyone gathered around the capstan to witness the woman with a yard of hair tangled in the gears and rope.

Isadora Peabody's cheeks turned red. "If you don't mind, I should like to get up," she said again.

"Any ideas?" Ryan asked the men.

"We could cut the line."

"It's as thick as a man's wrist. That would take all day, and we'd be billed for destroying the line."

"Dismantle the knight-heads of the windlass and slide the hair and the rope off the side?"

"I just repaired that," Chips objected. "Took me half a day. The man who touches it dies."

"Unwind it the opposite way."

"I tried that. It pulls. She'll lose her whole scalp."

Ryan and Journey looked at one another. Journey's gaze flicked to the sheathed midshipman's dirk Ryan wore in his belt. They had the same thought at the same time.

"Miss Peabody." Ryan went down on one knee. "Close your eyes."

"What in heaven's name are you doing?" Her voice rose, quavering with distrust.

"Getting you out of this fix. Now, close your eyes."

Isadora knew she was disobeying a direct order, but she didn't care. The men began to murmur among themselves, and so she opened her eyes.

Just in time to see Ryan unsheath a thin-bladed knife. She screamed, scrambling back as far as the entanglement would permit, her hair pulling viciously at her scalp. The blade flashed in the sunlight, then came down with a thunk. She waited to feel a rush of blood, but instead she sprang free of the coil.

She sprawled on the deck, her face inches from the skipper's booted foot. "You've gone mad, haven't you?" she said in a shaky voice. "I've heard of this— men gone too long at sea lose their grasp on sanity, and—eek!" She put her hand to her head, where her hair should have been. Then she looked at the windlass. Her hair. Still caught in the coils of rope. But it was no longer attached to her head.

"My hair!" she cried. "You've cut off my hair."

The crewmen slunk away, clearly loath to interfere.

Ryan Calhoun squatted down. Without looking at her, he lifted the hem of her skirt. "Christ, no wonder you bumble about the decks. You've got on at least five petticoats."

"How dare you?"

"I'm the skipper, that's how." He grasped her by the ankle and began to unlace her high-heeled boot. "This," he said through his teeth as he tugged it off, "is the cause of your troubles." He cast her shoe overboard and grabbed the other foot.

"Stop that," Isadora cried, trying to wrench away from him. "Stop that, I say!"

He held her ankle in a ruthless grip as he removed the other shoe. She flinched, for he pressed his thumb hard where she'd injured herself the first day at sea.

"I've watched you stumble around the ship until I was sure you'd topple overboard. No more." He pitched the shoe over the rail.

She put both hands to her head, feeling the barren place where he'd hacked off her hair. "Dear heaven," she whispered, "what have you done?"

He met her shocked gaze with a steely stare. "It's only hair," he said. "It'll grow back."

She sat immobile, too stunned to do anything but gape like a codfish. It was some dreadful Samson-and-Delilah scenario in reverse. What sin had she committed, what god had she angered, that Ryan Calhoun would visit this calamity upon her? To think she had left behind her home, her family and all she held dear for this terrible misadventure.

She dropped her hands into her lap. A fresh wind blew tendrils of her newly cropped locks against her cheeks and neck. She shivered from the light, cool breath of the breeze on her neck. Her feet, covered by only thin black stockings, felt shockingly bare.

"What—" She stopped and swallowed, feeling the awful press of tears in her eyes. No. She would not cry. She took a deep breath and tried again. "What have I ever done to make you hate me so?"

He shook his head. "Miss Peabody, I don't hate you. Whatever gave you that impression?"

"To begin with, you threw my spectacles overboard."

"Do you miss them?"

She hesitated. In truth, she barely noticed the lack. "That is beside the point," she said. "They belonged to me, as did my shoes. As did my hair. You had no right."

"On the contrary, Miss Peabody. I have every right."

"Ah, yes. How could I forget? You are master of this ship. Your word is law. I wouldn't be surprised if you appointed yourself lord high executioner."

He caught her in his angry stare. "Don't tempt me."

"You have robbed me of my spectacles, my shoes and my hair."

"You're better off barefoot. Those heeled things you wore made you as useless as tits on a fish."

The image made her shudder. "Why does cruelty come so easily to you?" she asked softly. "Doesn't that scare you sometimes? It would scare me."

"Everything scares you, Miss Peabody." With that, he straightened up and walked away, casually slipping his knife back into its hip sheath.

She drew her knees up to her chest and dropped her head onto them. She would not cry. She would not cry.

"B-begging your p-pardon, miss," someone said.

She lifted her head. "Timothy."

"I have some sk-skill at barbering," he said in an explosive rush. He showed her a slender pair of scissors. "If you like, I'll make a straighter job of the skipper's handiwork."

"Very well." She surprised herself by agreeing and following him into the deserted galley. The deck felt hard and alien beneath her stockinged feet. "Do what you can."

He moved behind her and gently lifted the hacked off strands away from the nape of her neck. She heard a deft *snip-snipping* sound as he set to work.

"Timothy."

"Y-yes, miss?"

"May I ask you something?"

"C-course."

"Did all the men on deck witness this incident?"

"They did, miss."

"And did it not occur to any of you to intervene? To stop the captain from abusing me?"

"I didn't see no ab-abusing, miss." He smoothed his hand over her hair. Her head and scalp felt light as if a great tugging weight had been removed. "See, miss, on the last sail, Rivera lost a finger on the capstan. I expect the sk-skipper, he—he acted right quick so's nothing like that would happen to you."

She fell silent and sat still as Timothy finished her hair. He stood in front of her, scrutinizing his work, evening things out here and there, then nodding with satisfaction.

"See, miss, the skipper, he ain't a bad man. He's—"

"Walking in on you before you say something foolish," Ryan interrupted, stepping into the galley.

"Y-yes, sir!" Closing the scissors, Timothy straightened up and hurried out.

Isadora regarded him stonily. He was going to apologize. She was not going to accept.

"Mr. Datty did a yeoman's job on that hair." He blinked, then narrowed his eyes keenly as if something startled him. His mouth curved subtly up at the corners. "He did indeed." He held up a very small shaving mirror.

She had a vague impression of a cloud of unkempt curls, an unhappy face flushed with anger. She pushed the mirror away.

She felt naked without the long tangle of hair that had cloaked her for as long as she could remember. The hair was her shield, her covering. What would stand between her and the world now?

"You seem determined to see me shorn of dignity," she said.

"Quite the opposite," he said in his maddening drawl. "I would say there is more dignity in a woman who walks with ease and confidence rather than tottering around on tall-heeled shoes."

"And when did your opinion matter?" she demanded.

He took a step toward her and went down on one knee so that their faces were level. She felt an odd jolt of...something. Fear? No, for there was no urgency to get away from him. On the contrary, his stance before her, his expression and the way his hands came to rest on her shoulders made her want to stay exactly where she was.

She had no idea why this reaction came over her, particularly in the midst of her rage. But there was something compelling in the way he waited, not answering her question but simply watching her.

Determined not to let him stare her down, she studied him, trying to discern some clue as to why he insisted on tormenting her. He had the sort of face one would describe as boyishly handsome, a face that would probably still be handsome even when he reached fourscore years of age. A finely drawn mouth that smiled too readily. Dimples that softened the chiseled effect of his nose and cheekbones. Eyes that crinkled at the corners and that had in their depths the strangest combination of mischief and pathos.

There was, in her heart, a heat she had never felt before. A *knowing*. Here was a person who had the power to stir her blood. And this was not, she knew instinctively, a good thing.

"Well?" she prompted, telling herself such thoughts were fanciful, ridiculous. He was someone whose actions she must report to his employer.

He kept his hands on her shoulders even though she wished he'd move them. "Miss Peabody, I know you'll be disappointed to hear this, but my opinion matters. Everything I think, say, do, or wish matters. That is the nature of being the captain."

She sniffed. "So you will use your power to make me miserable."

He smiled, his face softly lit with infuriating sympathy. "Miss Peabody."

She glared at him.

"Isadora. May I call you Isadora?"

"Why ask permission? You're the captain, the despot, the most high admiral of the ocean sea."

"Not the ocean. This ship." Very slowly, deliberately, almost insolently he let his hands skim across her shoulders and trail down her arms. "Isadora, you surely don't need me to make you miserable. You're doing a fine job of that on your own."

She caught her breath in fury and surprise. "How dare you?"

He laughed, his hands cradling her elbows. "Because I have nothing to lose, Isadora. Not a damned thing to lose."

Despite his laughter, she heard pain in his voice, saw it in his eyes. She had never met such a maddening, interesting, complex individual.

"What do you mean by that?"

"You despise me already, sugar. So it doesn't seem to matter what I do."

"Your mother is a woman of such admirable manners. I find it surprising that she raised a man who would say such a thing. Particularly after hacking off a lady's hair with a sabre."

"It was a midshipman's dirk."

"It was the height of rudeness."

"We're talking in circles here, Isadora. We've been over this. I'm not going to apologize. And you're not going to be miserable any longer. You were supposed to leave that unhappy mode of life behind when we left Boston."

"Unhappy? How dare you suggest I am unhappy?"

He let out a sigh of exasperation. "My dear, you are unhappy to the last inch of your shadow. I fear this state is so familiar to you that you no longer recognize it as unhappiness." Finally he did the unthinkable. He moved his hands to cover hers, making an insistent circular motion with his thumbs in her palms. "What I want you to know is that you don't have to live like that, Isadora. At least, not while you sail under my ensign."

She had a strange urge to shut her eyes and simply feel the sensation of his thumbs rubbing her. His fingertips were sinfully warm and leathery from work, so different from the clammy clutches of men forced to partner her at Boston dance parties.

She made herself sit very still, eyes wide open as she fought the inexplicable slow warmth that filled her, beginning with the tips of her fingers and flowing through her body, settling in its more unmentionable places. "I really don't think," she began, then had to pause and moisten her lips before going on, "I don't think you need concern yourself with my happiness or lack thereof.''

"I'm the skipper. Every aspect of every crewman's life concerns me.'' He let go of one hand and cradled her cheek in his palm.

She was too startled to pull back.

"Even if it were not for that,'' he continued, "I would care, Isadora. I don't have many good qualities, but I do care.''

"I...I...'' She swallowed, then gave up trying to speak.

"Be safe,'' he said. "That's what today was about. Wear your clothes and fix your hair for comfort, not confinement. No one would look askance at you if you entered the galley for supper without all this frippery.'' To punctuate his statement, he ran his hand across the ornate worked trim around her throat. "We're simple men of the sea, not ballroom snobs on Beacon Hill.''

He stood, leaving her feeling curiously bereft, and went toward the door. "I shall see you on deck.''

"Wait!''

He turned back with an eagerness that startled her. "Yes?''

"You forgot your mirror.'' She picked it up and held the palm-sized glass out to him.

"So I did.'' He took it from her with a wink. "You'd not like to see me after shaving without a mirror. Not a pretty sight.''

She sat very still after he left, listening to the creak of the timber and the rush of the water past the hull.

Whiskers or no, she thought, Ryan Calhoun would *always* be a pretty sight.

Ten

Woman stock is rising in the market.

—Lydia Maria Child,
Letter (1856)

Ryan stared into the little mirror with fierce concentration as he drew a straight razor along the side of his jaw. The ship plunged into a trough, causing him to list to one side. He felt the subtle bite of the blade in his chin and swore.

But it was no less than he deserved, he decided. Isadora Peabody's words still haunted him: *Why does cruelty come so easily to you?*

He'd wanted to deny it, but the truth was, thoughtlessness did seem to come naturally to him. It had ever been that way with Ryan and women. He was all too willing to partake of their physical charms, but the involvement always ended there. The minute he started to care about them in a deeper way, he made it his business to push them away with careless, cutting words.

Isadora, of course, was the first one he'd actually attacked.

"Have a towel, Skipper." Journey tossed him one.

Ryan pressed it to his chin. "You're my steward. You should be doing this."

"I'm busy," Journey said distractedly.

Ryan stopped the bleeding and lathered up again to finish shaving. "Did you take the morning readings?"

"I did. I'm reckoning our position now." Journey gazed intently at the papers on the table in front of him. He had a gift for the logarithms of navigation, figuring in his head with lightning quickness. He gave the task his total attention, yet with his left hand, he fingered the small pouch he wore on a leather strap around his neck. The pendant lay against his heart. Toying with it was a habit, an unconscious tic. Delilah, the wife he'd left behind, had given him the pouch. Inside was a tiny love knot fashioned from a lock of her hair.

Ryan's gut twisted with impatience and urgency. It wasn't right, it wasn't natural for a family to be separated like this. He recalled the morning he and Journey had left to go north. They had stopped at Bonterre, the neighboring plantation where Delilah lived.

Ryan had waited in the open carriage while Journey dropped to the ground near the slave quarters. An anguished smile had strained his face as Delilah came running out of one of the cabins, a toddler held against her hip and her thin cotton dress outlining the ripe shape of her pregnancy. Putting Ruthie down, she'd placed her arms around her husband's neck, then risen on tiptoe to kiss him solemnly. And then she'd said something Ryan would never forget, something he wasn't supposed to hear. But her words had been imprinted on his heart forever. "Honey," Journey's wife had said, "Life don't work right when you're not around."

Ryan swore at the pain from that memory. He finished shaving and wiped his face, then went out on deck, leaving Journey to his navigational figuring.

A balmy day greeted Ryan. With a sweep of his gaze he read the wind and the sea; this was *his* gift. Marble-hard swells rose beneath a brisk wind from the west. They would cover a good distance today.

"Morning, Captain." Ralph Izard bent over the deck, securing a new winch, for Ryan had decided to add an extra lifeboat as a safety measure. Izard's face, chapped and furred with the beginnings of a beard, crinkled as he smiled briefly. "A fair wind, eh?"

"So it seems, Mr. Izard." He indicated the tall leather-bound journal under the chief mate's arm. "Is everything in order?"

"Aye, though I think we took on too little ballast," he replied. "And maybe too many victuals."

Ryan ignored the comment about the ballast. It would only be a problem in the heaviest of seas, and even then, his skilled crew could navigate an ugly storm. He didn't much like paying for ballast, preferring to stoke the hold with paying cargo. Happily, the huge blocks of Vermont ice fulfilled that function.

"I'll pay what it takes for the victuals," he said. A lot of skippers cut corners by laying in inferior food in skimpy quantities for their sailors. Ryan knew better than to test their loyalty by taxing their stomachs. "A well-fed sailor is a happy sailor."

"As you say, skipper. You'll hear no back-slack from a crew that's got its mouth stuffed with ladyfingers." He winked, looking wise and world-weary at the same time.

Ryan moved on, though he thought about Ralph Izard for a moment. He liked the chief mate; Izard was his prime minister, boatswain, sailing-master and quartermaster all at once, and he excelled at what he did.

And he alone knew what no one else had guessed.

Ryan's first record-breaking voyage had been a fluke.

It wasn't his skill as a skipper that had brought the *Swan* to harbor so profitably, but a combination of good weather and blind beginner's luck. Izard was well aware of this. He had never spoken of it, though the knowledge always hung between him and Ryan—unuttered yet undeniable.

He climbed the companion stair to the foredeck. A startling sight greeted him.

Isadora Peabody bent over a pair of deck chairs, tucking an olive-colored blanket around his mother and Fayette. The two women looked wasted and wan, still miserable with the sea sickness. Yet, finally, after Ryan had tried for days to coax them from their beds, they'd come on deck.

Isadora appeared different today. What was left of her hair was tied back carelessly with a ribbon, a few curls escaping to twine around her face. The sun, increasingly strong as they traveled farther and farther south, brought out a warm gold color in some of the strands. Her stiff brown dress appeared less cumbersome. Maybe she'd heeded his advice and left off a couple of those petticoats.

He knew he wouldn't be asking her.

He stepped onto the deck, moving past the chicken coop. "Morning, ladies."

Isadora straightened, her face hardening to a mask of indifference.

He scowled at her in annoyance. He wanted to ask her if she still wanted to be stuck to the windlass by her hair. God knew she deserved it.

"Hello, Ryan," his mother said.

"Mama." He bent and kissed Lily's cheek. "It's good to see you both out in the air."

"Isadora convinced us. Since we couldn't feel much worse, we agreed to sit on deck for a while."

"I'll see if your tea is ready," Isadora said, moving past Ryan.

He caught a whiff of the soap she used—something clean and herbal—and he didn't realize he was staring after her until his mother said, "So what exactly did you do to the poor girl?"

"What makes you think I did anything at all? Did she tell you—"

"She didn't say a word, Ryan. I honestly don't think she's the sort of lady to tell tales out of school."

Fayette chuckled knowingly. "Didn't have to say a thing. But she shows up wearing parlor scuffs and her hair badly shorn, and we guessed you had something to do with it."

Ryan sat on a coil of rope and took out the Turk's head he was braiding, adding to the ornamental knot strand by strand. "She's a babe in arms when it comes to sailing. Stumbled around on her high heels and got her hair caught in the apparatus." He blew out his breath in exasperation. "We had…words."

Lily shook her head. "Oh, Ryan."

Something deep inside him recoiled at her tone of voice. He'd heard it all his life. "Oh, Ryan" stood for a wealth of defects and disappointments. Each and every one of them richly deserved. Some things would never

change. She would be "Oh, Ryan-ing" him until he was
an old man.

"You of all people know my imperfections, Mama,"
he said. "Did you think I was taking Miss Peabody on
a pleasure cruise?"

Lily studied him solemnly, her expression loving yet
wary. "It could be, you know."

"A pleasure cruise?" He snorted. "Such a thing as
pleasure has been outlawed in Boston."

"According to the navigation log, we are presently a
very long way from Boston," Isadora said, arriving with
a wooden tray.

Ryan stood, chagrined that she had overheard his
comment. "And how far are we from pleasure?" he
couldn't resist asking.

"Everything was very pleasant indeed," she said,
"until a few moments ago." She handed Lily and Fayette each a thick china mug. "I added a touch of lemon
and honey. If that agrees with you, we'll try some broth
and bread later."

He glared at her, but instead of feeling contempt, he
caught himself wondering what she was like under all
that black-and-brown armor. Did her impressive height
come from long legs? Were her breasts full and round,
crested with dusky rose peaks? Was her skin soft and
smooth to the touch...? Christ. He'd been too long at
sea.

"I hope you find the morning...*pleasant*, ladies,"
Ryan said, exaggerating his drawl and his formal bow.
"For me, duty calls."

A few days later, below the jibboom, he found that
someone had repaired the rigging. He picked up the

broad web of rope, noting the precision of the knots.

"I'll finish that now," Isadora said.

Wordlessly, he handed it to her. Damn. The woman *was* like a bad rash. She wouldn't go away. Everywhere he turned, he nearly collided with her.

"Luigi showed me how to do the mending," she explained, though Ryan hadn't asked.

"It's a useful skill," he admitted. What he didn't admit was that he had noticed her growing camaraderie with each member of the crew. Each one seemed drawn to her, if not charmed by her then at least engaged enough by her natural curiosity to share something with her—a skill, a tidbit of sea lore, a useful turn of phrase. He didn't know why this was so, but it was. Probably because he was as small-minded and immature as his mother claimed.

He cleared his throat. "Thank you for looking after my mother and Fayette."

For the first time in days, she regarded him directly. She had nice eyes, he realized, now that they weren't peering over the unneeded thick-lensed spectacles. The color shifted between warm brown and vibrant green.

He couldn't remember the last time he'd admired a woman's irises.

"It's my pleasure to look after them," Isadora said.

She was that sort of person, he realized. One who understood human need and derived satisfaction from tending to it. One who would make a wonderful mother.

A scowl darkened his brow. She had set her cap for Chad Easterbrook, who had no idea what sort of mother she would make. He had no idea what sort of person she was, for that matter.

"Captain Calhoun?" she said.

"Since I've decided to address you as Isadora, I think you should call me Ryan," he said.

"It won't matter. Because what I was going to say is that it's clear we don't get along." Her hands tightened on the rope. "I bullied my way onto your ship and I refuse to be sorry for that. You, in turn, have been bullying me since we set sail, and you're not sorry, either."

"When you state it that way—"

"I think it would be better for all concerned if you and I simply stayed out of one another's way, don't you?"

For some reason, he chose that particular moment to remember the way he'd touched her in the galley. She'd struck him as so alone and bereft that he hadn't been able to help himself. He'd rested his hands on her shoulders, then stroked her arms, and her softness had pleased him. He'd touched her face—this very face that now watched him impassively—and had been terrified that she was going to cry.

No, this woman wasn't a weeper. That much was clear.

"You think we should steer clear of each other."

"As much as possible, given the fact that we're confined to this ship."

"I see." He knew she was right. She was absolutely right. He hated how right she was. "I will agree to this request, but on one condition."

"What is that, Cap—Ryan?"

"That you keep yourself safe. No tottering around on inappropriate shoes, no testing the waters like an old salt, nothing of the sort."

"I'm not accustomed to following orders," she said.

"Yes, you are. You've followed every order and dictate of Beacon Hill society all your life."

She caught her breath as if he'd struck her. "You see what I mean?" She shook out the knot. "We must begin our campaign of mutual indifference at once."

He sent her a mocking smile, hiding a sense of loss he hadn't expected to feel. "As you wish."

But as the days passed, he found it impossible not to notice her. In fact, his attention sought her out the way a tongue seeks out a sore tooth. He saw her seated on the foredeck with Timothy Datty, patiently repeating sounds and words with him to break his habit of stuttering. At sunup, she and the Doctor were wont to be found at the aft balcony, their lines cast out to troll for fish. Sometimes she helped Luigi with his sail making, insisting that he drill her in lessons to improve her command of Italian.

The common seamen soon learned she was game for more active duties. On a balmy Wednesday morning, Ryan looked up to see her balanced in the shrouds and bent over a yardarm as she helped Gerald reefing a sail.

His heart galloping in his chest, Ryan sounded the whistle and bellowed, "Come down from there, Miss Peabody."

"I'm busy," she said.

"That's an order."

"You ordered me to ignore you, so that is what I shall do."

And Ryan Calhoun, who knew better, released a lengthy stream of colorful invective in an obnoxiously loud voice.

Isadora looked across the web of rigging at Gerald.

"Did you hear something? Or was it merely a great gust of wind?"

Ryan stalked off. In driving Isadora away, holding her at arm's length, he had propelled her toward the others. Judging by her behavior in Boston, he'd formed the idea that she was a solitary sort, not one to seek company when a good book lay at hand. Now she enjoyed being around people. She liked to talk and loved to listen. And judging by the reaction of the crew, she was damned good at it.

Even William Click, the moody and secretive second mate, warmed to her. He showed her how to man the pulleys to bring water up from the sea, and sometimes they knelt side by side on the midships deck, doing their laundry. And Ralph Izard, generally circumspect about his personal life, often gave her a turn at the helm as he stood by, sharing his memories of his boyhood in New York City.

Day by day, man by man, she was becoming their friend, their confidante, their shipmate. She was coming to know them in a way Ryan, as the captain, never could. By virtue of his role, he couldn't speak to Timothy Datty of the farm he'd left in Rhode Island, to Gerald Craven of his recent trip to New Orleans. Ryan had to hold himself apart from the crew, but Isadora seemed to blossom in their midst.

On quiet evenings after the supper hour, he would spy her skylarking with the men on the open main deck. She openly and good-humoredly despaired of her skill as a dancer, so the men were determined to teach her to curtsey and dance like an accomplished lady. At first Ryan tried not to pay attention, but lately she seemed to speak louder and laugh more frequently than she had before. She was becoming hard to ignore.

Chips had carved her a serviceable recorder flute. Before long, she joined in the makeshift ensemble consisting of Journey with his skin drum, Luigi with his fiddle and Gerald with his hornpipes. The music they made was so merry that even his mother and Fayette came above to sit beneath their blankets and tap their feet, trying to forget their persistent misery.

At least having his mother on deck gave him an excuse to draw close to the festivities. He greeted the ladies and Lily held on to his hand. "When will I ever get my sea legs?" she asked.

"You should be over the sickness by now."

"I'm trying, Ryan. Really I am. We both are. Isadora brings us broth and bread, sometimes even a bit of egg and biscuit. She is an angel, I tell you. Purely an angel."

Ryan shot a furtive glance at the "angel." She held the recorder to her lips, eyes dancing as she picked out the melody of "The Bo'sun's Wife." Her slippered foot tapped on the oaken deck. The lowering sun burnished the loose curls of her hair. But Ryan's gaze kept wandering to her mouth. Full and moist, her lips circled the mouthpiece of the recorder, and at the corners they turned up slightly as if in amusement.

He watched those lips and the way her nimble fingers played over the openings, making music. Unexpected heat rushed through him, and his thoughts wandered to dark, forbidden places scented by a woman's musky perfume. He imagined, with startling vividness, the brush of bare silken skin and the softness of smiling lips beneath his own.

Ryan shifted uncomfortably from foot to foot, trying

to reel in his thoughts and feeling a tight discomfort in his trousers. When he realized what was happening to him, he muttered something about taking a sounding, and then he walked away.

Damn it.

He missed her.

Eleven

Aboard at a ship's helm,
A young steerman steering with care.

—Walt Whitman,
Aboard at a Ship's Helm

"Tell me about your family, Journey," Isadora said.

Seated across from her at the galley table, he looked up from mending a shirt. The soft blue fabric lay draped over his bony knees, and a faraway expression clouded his gaze.

She didn't have long to wonder where he had been in his daydream. He said, "I haven't seen my Delilah or my babies in four years."

Isadora felt each quiet, simple word like a velvet-gloved blow. She'd always known that slavery was an inhuman, unjust institution, but her conviction sprang from reading pamphlets and essays penned by educated men and women.

By contrast, Journey's presence, his dignity, his quiet despair, illustrated the point with brutal clarity.

"Does it disturb you to talk about them?" she asked.

"Not any more than not talking about them." He stabbed his needle into the seam of the shirt, a sturdy broadcloth garment commonly worn by all the crewmen.

Almost all, she reflected, shifting uncomfortably on the bench. Now that they had entered southern climes, she hadn't suffered from the grippe in days. Yet her corset chafed more than ever. The soft broadcloth would feel wonderful.

Knowing her mother would call for smelling salts at the very thought of her daughter lowering her standards of dress, Isadora had removed one layer of petticoats. She felt wicked doing so, but much more comfortable. Each day, her attitude relaxed a little more. Her confidence grew a little stronger. It was a wonder, after so many years of trying to press herself into society's mold, to suddenly suspect that the problem was with the mold, not with her.

Now, seventy-three miles north of the equator and a little east of St. Paul's Rocks, she made up her mind to shed another layer or two.

"Then tell me about your family, do," she urged Journey, feeling petty for dwelling on her own discomfort.

He went back to sewing, and his expression relaxed into the dreaminess she'd glimpsed earlier. "Delilah and me, we met at Sunday meeting. She was a sassy thing, always two steps from trouble. But nobody minded, 'cause she sang like a lark in church and had the face of an angel."

He smiled, and Isadora wondered what it would be like to have a man smile that way at the thought of her. When he pictured Delilah as an angel, did he mean it literally, with a halo and wings, or was it the love in his heart that gilded her with a special aura?

She savored the fanciful thought. How singular it was to be a shipmate, she thought suddenly. How easy it was to get involved in their concerns. She found life under sail so absorbing that she ceased thinking about Chad Easterbrook for days on end. She'd added almost nothing to the letter she'd been composing to him, which she intended to send the next time they hailed a ship. Her reports to Abel were perfunctory. Aside from personally attacking her at every turn, Ryan's behavior had been disgustingly exemplary.

"So you met in church," she prompted Journey, eager for the rest of his story.

His polished, narrow face softened with memory. "Mr. Jared—that was Ryan's father—always wanted me to marry up with a girl from Albion, but after I met Dee, I wouldn't hear of it, even though I could only see her on Sundays—on account of her living at another place."

Isadora understood what he wouldn't say. Intermarriage among the slaves of the same plantation insured that a new generation of laborers would come along. The very idea was so outrageous that she could hardly comprehend it.

"So you were permitted to marry," she ventured.

One corner of Journey's mouth lifted. "Ma'am, one of these days you should ask Ryan how we were 'permitted' to marry."

She didn't ask Ryan anything these days. They were both being stubborn about staying out of each other's way. She was determined that he would be first to breach the silence.

"We married up when I was sixteen. Dee was fifteen,

near as we can tell." He sewed swiftly, the needle stabbing into the fabric and emerging with a deft rhythm.

He spoke so casually that Isadora took a moment to realize that slaves weren't told their birthdays. Of course, she thought. A birthday would humanize a slave, and the system depended on keeping them on the level of chattel or livestock.

"Then the girls came along—first Ruthie and then Celeste. Ruthie, she's the prettiest baby in the whole wide world, and no mistake. Celeste, too, I reckon," he hastened to add. "But I ain't never seen Celeste. Ain't never seen my baby girl."

He pulled his large hand from beneath the fabric. A dark pearl of blood glistened on the tip of his finger. He put it briefly in his mouth, then removed it to say, "Excuse me, miss. Best go clean this up before I ruin the shirt."

Ain't never seen my baby girl.

His words haunted the galley like mournful ghosts. After he stepped outside, Isadora walked over to the table and picked up his work. The seam was perfect, with stitches so fine she could barely see them. She ran her hand over the fabric, and somehow she knew that Dee—a woman she didn't know and would never meet—would give her very soul to mend this shirt.

When the *Silver Swan* lay-to a few miles north of the line, a full-moon calm settled over the bark. Yet the seas were rough with Atlantic combers that had been gathering muscle for thousands of miles, all the way from the coast of Africa. Lily and Fayette, who had enjoyed a few days of comfort, descended again in seasick misery to their cabin.

Isadora, Ryan observed from his splay-legged stance at the helm, seemed to be getting on better than ever. She spent a lot of time on deck or in the galley or chart room, absorbing knowledge and sailor lore like a sea sponge. She moved less awkwardly around the decks, having learned to steady herself with one hand on the rail or rigging.

She haunted him, appearing out of nowhere and pretending he wasn't there. As they approached the equator, Ryan stood at the helm once again. He saw her making her way aft, clearly unaware of his proximity.

She paused to stoop down and scoop up the cat, draping it over one arm and stroking its fur. The new assurance in her movements and posture made a dramatic difference in the way she appeared. Her clothes were not so fussy and fine as those she'd worn in the Beacon Hill drawing room of her parents. Her short hair spilled untidily around her neck and shoulders.

Yet for all her dishevelment, she looked...different. She carried herself with a new posture and attitude. He found that he preferred a woman in tatters and bare feet who would look him square in the eye to a humble, perfectly groomed female who shrank timidly from the slightest slant of a glance.

He was annoyed at her for ignoring him, but at least he respected her.

At the moment she stood unguarded, pausing to lift her face to the summery sky filled with the lofty billows of high clouds. Lately she hadn't bothered with bonnet or parasol and she seemed not to notice the effect the wind and sun were having. Her pale skin had taken on a honeyed hue; her hair bore streaks of gold. It was a look Ryan knew her strait-laced mother would term *common*.

Yet he had another word for it.

A high-pitched squeal pierced the air, startling both Isadora and Ryan. She dropped the cat, who scampered under a bumboat. Looking aft, Ryan spied the Doctor with the pig held under one arm, a broad, curved knife in his other hand.

"Heavenly days," Isadora murmured, rushing past Ryan. "He's going to slaughter Lydia."

Ryan followed her. "Lydia? You call the pig Lydia?"

She ignored him. "Doctor! Oh, Doctor, please stop, do!" she called down the decks.

The cook turned. "What is it, Miss?"

"You can't—you mustn't kill the pig."

The Doctor glanced at Ryan. "Porker's all fatted up. I figured it's time. Skipper?"

Ryan looked at the snuffling, struggling creature under the cook's arm. He looked at the horror and grief on Isadora's face. "I suppose we could grant the beast a reprieve," he said offhandedly. "We're decently close to Rio, and stores are good."

"But—"

"Leave go, Doctor. She grieved for three days over that last chicken you stewed. I can't abide a whining woman."

The next day Ryan spied Isadora shading her eyes to watch Click and Craven tarring the mainmast. The men swung in saddles, their bare legs and bare chests smudged with tar. They paused in their work to wave at her and, grinning, she waved back.

It wasn't proper, Ryan thought, her seeing barechested men wherever she turned.

Ducking under a shroud, she didn't notice him until she was almost upon him.

"Oh," she said, "Captain Calhoun."

"I thought I'd take a turn at the helm." He spoke with elaborate indifference.

She eyed him nervously, as if she did not quite trust him—or herself with him. "I wanted to be topside when we cross the equator. Will you say when?"

He was ridiculously happy to oblige. Perhaps that was the virtue of Isadora. Perhaps that was why the crew indulged her whims. Her wide-eyed curiosity about everything relieved the monotony of the long days at sea.

"Mr. Datty, at the helm, sir," he called to Timothy.

"Aye, sir." The boy arrived with a sharp salute that amused Ryan.

He gave the helm to Timothy and his free hand to Isadora. She hesitated, eyeing his hand as if it were a venomous serpent.

"It's made of flesh and blood like any other man's," he said lightly, hiding his annoyance. Color misted her cheeks, and he laughed. "Unless that's precisely the problem."

Almost defiantly, she put her hand in his. Hers felt...surprising. Yes, that was it. Women of her station were supposed to have soft, moist skin. Isadora, by contrast, had a sturdy grip and...calluses.

"You take your lessons in sail making and seamanship seriously, I gather," he said, leading the way to a companion ladder and reaching to help her up.

"I take everything seriously, Captain."

"I noticed. Why is that, Isadora?" They came to the bow of the ship and he turned to study her.

"I have no idea."

"There!" Ryan said suddenly, shading his eyes. "There it is!"

"There what is?"

"The equator." He took out his spyglass and handed it to her.

She closed one eye and peered through it. "What am I looking for?"

"The equator. Isn't that what you came here to see?"

"See? But—"

"Keep looking." Furtively, Ryan plucked a hair from his head. On the pretext of adjusting the focus, he held the hair crosswise over the lens. "Now can you see it? The equator?"

"Why, yes," she crowed, clearly elated. "I do believe I can." Her mouth curved into a smile that had a disquieting effect on him. "How fascinating. And isn't that an elephant walking along the line?"

He took the spyglass from her and put it away. "I was fairly certain you wouldn't fall for that."

She regarded him with her usual prim disapproval, though her eyes still danced with humor. "I am not in the habit of 'falling' for things, Captain. I've no idea why you would attempt such a prank with me."

"To see you smile. You don't do it often enough, and you should."

She regarded him somberly. "Why should I?"

"Because..." Ryan began to feel foolish. "Because I order you to, and I'm the captain."

She rewarded him with a grin. "Then I suppose I have no choice."

He grinned back. "No, ma'am, I don't guess you do." He leaned back against a timber head. "We're about nine hundred miles out from Rio."

"It sounds like an unbearably large number." She shaded her eyes and gazed at the nothingness that surrounded them.

"The briny blue. As far as the eye can see. That's why I like the crew to get along."

"They seem to. Even Mr. Click has been quiet this past week. When do you think we'll make Rio?"

"Within the week. There's a premium of a hundred dollars a day for each day under average for the whole trip." He reached up, running his hand along an awning. "This looks good. Is it new?"

"I doused it with salt water," she said, meeting his puzzled gaze. "Luigi says it prevents mildew."

"So it does," Ryan said, and though they spoke of mundane matters, he felt a beat of emotion that had nothing to do with awnings or deadlines or anything but the woman standing with him on his ship.

This was new to him. *She* was new to him. In the past he'd been drawn to women whose beauty outweighed their brains, whose idle chatter rang louder than their common sense—in short, women who didn't make him see himself for what he was—a spoiled, shallow young man who hadn't grasped the importance of social conscience until it was too late. He used to prefer women who didn't challenge him to be more than he was. But not anymore. He wasn't certain exactly when or why it had happened, but at some point he had started to feel something soft and new for Isadora Peabody.

"Look," he said, nervous with the sensations churning in his gut, "I realize we haven't been getting on—"

"Not for lack of *my* trying."

He gritted his teeth to stifle a retort. "Don't ruin my graciousness by being infuriating."

"I was not—"

"Only because I'm stopping you. Now, hush up and listen. I was angry about the way you made yourself a part of this enterprise. You used your connections with Abel Easterbrook to your advantage."

"It's no more than men of commerce do."

"Damn it," he burst out, "you are the hardest person to offer an apology to."

She flinched at his language. "Is that what this is? An apology?"

"Yes, damn it," he shouted.

"Well, it's not working."

"Not for lack of *my* trying," he said, mimicking her.

"Steady there, miss," Chips cautioned Isadora. "Keep one hand in the rigging no matter what, and make sure your feet stay balanced in the ratlines."

Though she had climbed only a few feet off the deck, Isadora felt vulnerable, particularly when the ship crested a swell and listed a little. Yet despite her uncertainty, she felt proud and excited. The Isadora who had left Boston Harbor would never have dared to climb a ship's rigging. But since the men of the *Swan* had decided to teach her the ways of the sea, she had dared a hundred new things and her confidence grew every day.

"What the devil—?" Ryan Calhoun hurried over, a scowl on his face. "Damn it, Chips, you can't let the lady go aloft."

"It's not his fault, Captain," Isadora said hastily. "I

insisted. I heard a rumor that Cape Frio is near and I wanted to see it.''

The truth was, she wanted to see everything. For her, the voyage had grown and burgeoned into a journey of self-discovery. She had no idea what she would find at the end. All she knew was that she felt more at home aboard this ship than she ever had in the middle of her own life in blessedly distant Boston.

''Come down from there this instant,'' Ryan said, his voice harsh with command. He stood leaning against the capstan, looking unconsciously appealing as well as commanding.

Isadora couldn't stop the wave of warmth that engulfed her. Though he couldn't know it, he had everything to do with her newfound sense of belonging. The way she looked or spoke or comported herself mattered not at all to Ryan Calhoun. He treated her no better and no worse than his crew of seamen. Thanks to him, she'd learned to endure a flash of male temper, to understand teasing and joking, to see humor in situations that used to appall the old Isadora.

The amusing part was that he seemed to have no idea how good this was for her. She smiled bravely down at him. Climbing the spanker rigging had seemed such a grand idea when she'd first thought of it. Chips scrambled around like a monkey, making it look so simple. Yet now that she had begun her ascent, she began to regret it.

''Don't make me order you down,'' Ryan said furiously.

She quickly made up her mind. Pride demanded that she stay her course.

Since crossing the equator several days earlier, they

had gone back to avoiding one another. Let him save his roguish charm for girls with empty heads and full bosoms. Isadora was not about to be taken in by him.

"I'm going to continue, Mr. Pole," she said to Chips.

The ship's carpenter sent Ryan a helpless look. "Opposite hand and foot every time, miss, there's the way. Opposite hand and foot."

"Damn it, I'll keelhaul you, Pole," Ryan shouted. "Don't think I won't."

"You won't." Chips failed to suppress a grin. "I have to help the lady. It's her first time, you know."

Isadora tried not to smile as she grasped the rigging in one hand and raised her opposite foot to the next ratline. Her blowing skirts made the going awkward, and it was immodest in the extreme to climb in this manner, but she couldn't help herself. She hungered for a sight of the wild, exotic land they had sailed so fast and so far to find.

"I can see your drawers," Ryan Calhoun called loudly.

She nearly let go. Only a keen sense of self-preservation kept her hanging on. "A gentleman would not look. And he certainly wouldn't make a comment."

"Who would ever mistake me for a gentleman?"

The rigging bowed out in the opposite direction and Isadora realized he was climbing, too. In three quick hauls, he had hoisted himself into the ratlines and was facing her through the web of rope.

"Since you insist on making this climb," he said, "I'll do it with you so I can save you if you start to fall."

"If I start to fall," she said ruefully, "there'll be no saving me." She nearly laughed at the expression on his face. "Don't worry. I do not plan to fall. And you really don't have to climb with me."

"You'd rather have me stand on deck below you, looking up your skirts with the rest of them?"

Her hands gripped the line with a vengeance. "I shall not answer that insolent question." Without further ado, she continued upward, as she had seen the seamen do so often. The climb was harder than it looked, for the loose ropes tended to bow this way and that with the sway of the ship.

She tried her best to ignore Ryan Calhoun. When they were halfway up the topmast, Isadora made the mistake of looking down.

"Dear God," she whispered.

"It's a long way down, isn't it?" he said pleasantly.

She ignored him. The deck appeared tiny, dotted with doll-size crates and hatches and coils. Due to the slant of the ship, she knew if she climbed any farther, she'd be out over open water.

The wind whistled through her hair and the sun warmed her face. Lord, but it was hot. Sweat soaked her in places she dared not mention, and a blister had formed on the palm of her right hand.

This was a terrible, foolish idea. Why had she wanted to climb the rigging today?

"A bit higher," Ryan urged her, his voice insolent and teasing. "Up here, where the ratlines are set too close together, we call this the ladies' ladder. You'd think it was made for you."

She hated that he could see her fright. Setting her sights aloft, she continued to climb. The blister on her hand burst and then stung with sweat and grime from the rope. Far below, the sea resembled blue marble, veined in purest white, intimidating as a snake pit as it foamed and seethed around the ship.

Oh, please, she thought helplessly. *Let me survive this and I'll never try anything adventurous again.*

Her gaze tracked the arrow-straight wake of the *Swan,* then found the horizon to the south. What she saw gave her such a jolt that she nearly let go of the rigging.

"Steady there," Ryan said, climbing up beside her. "You're finally getting a good view of Brazil."

"It's astonishing," she said, forgetting to be mad at him. "The mountains are so beautiful—they look as though they're draped in green velvet."

"There's Corcovado, and the tallest ones are called 'Dedos de Deus,'" Ryan said, indicating a row of five sharp peaks nudging the shoreline. The rich emerald green, set against the clear blue sky, created a picture so intense that Isadora's eyes smarted.

"The Fingers of God," she translated.

"The nearest mountain town is Petropolis. In the summer, every *carioca* worth his salt moves up there for cooler weather and to get away from the yellow jack."

She shuddered. "The yellow fever, you mean." It was a terrible killer, she'd read, particularly virulent among Yankees who had no resistance to the disease. "It's hard to imagine such a plague on a land so beautiful."

She kept her gaze on the horizon, enthralled with the view, until her hands trembled with the effort of holding herself aloft. "Captain," she said suddenly. "Look there—to the northeast."

He glanced back over his shoulder and studied the sky. The distant clouds had a peculiar bruised quality. A yellowish caste tinged the light coming from that quadrant, and as she held on, Isadora noticed the heavi-

ness of the seas. "There's a storm coming, isn't there?"
she asked.

"Uh-huh. A squall."

A shriek swirled up from the deck. "What in the name
of heaven are you doing?"

Startled, Isadora lost her hold on the rigging. For a
split second she hung weightless, flying free, doomed.
Then, with a joint-twisting jolt, she stopped falling. Ryan
had reached through the rigging and held her by the
wrists, the cords in his neck standing out with the strain.

"I suggest," he said between his teeth, "that you grab
hold of the ropes. *Now.*"

She obeyed mechanically, her hands quicker than her
mind. Another blister, this one on her left hand, burst as
she took hold of the rigging.

"Get down from there this instant," Lily called, her
voice strident with fear. "Both of you."

"Thank you," Isadora said, staring with gratitude and
incredulity at Ryan. "Truly, you saved my life."

"I don't appreciate having to save lives," he grumbled, starting to climb down. "Don't scare me like that
again."

Something in his voice gave her pause. With an unaccustomed prickle in her throat, she climbed down,
groping carefully with each foot and then following it
with the opposite hand. Her palms stung, but she didn't
care. The sensation of falling, and then of having Ryan
catch her, had been extraordinary. Mere fright didn't begin to cover it.

"Did you get hurt?" he asked.

"No." She sent him a tremulous smile. "I've never
scared anyone before. Not in that way, I mean."

"Then in what way?"

She fixed her eyes on each successive rung of the rigging and spoke from a place she had always kept private. "I suppose I was quite frightening to the young men who were sent to dance with me at parties."

He gave a derisive snort. "Then those young men were more yellow than greasy dogs."

She didn't want platitudes from him; she didn't expect sympathy. "They never knew what to say to me, nor I to them, so it was awkward all around. As I said, frightening." She felt her foot strike the planks of the deck and breathed a sigh of relief.

"Land sakes, child," Lily scolded fiercely. "What were you thinking? You could have been killed."

"And would have been if you'd shrieked a mite louder, Mama," Ryan said.

"I couldn't help myself. I generally shriek when a disaster is at hand."

"No harm done." Isadora felt suddenly as awkward as she had with the reluctant suitors of Boston. High in the rigging, looking across the vast sea at a land of such mystical beauty, she had felt like a different person. Now, with the solid oak deck swaying beneath her feet, she was herself again—ungainly, tongue-tied Isadora. She'd bared too much of herself up there. Ryan knew things she'd never told another soul.

Without daring to look at him, she said, "I'm afraid I've got some blisters. I'd best tend to them in the galley."

She hurried away, but the wind carried Lily's voice: "I know you weren't happy with this arrangement, Ryan, but must you try to get rid of her by throwing her overboard?"

Twelve

A capital ship for an ocean trip
Was the *Walloping Window Blind*—
No gale that blew dismayed her crew
Or troubled the captain's mind.
The man at the wheel was taught to feel
Contempt for the wildest blow.
And it often appeared, when the weather had
    cleared,
That he'd been in his bunk below.

— Charles Edward Carryl,
    Davy and the Goblin: A Nautical Ballad

The disaster came so swiftly and so completely that there was, Ryan conceded, a certain poetry in its magnificence. He'd felt the ominous heavy air when he and Isadora had been up on the mast. Though he had focused his attention on her to an alarming—and surprising—degree, a detached practical part of him had seen the power of the coming storm.

The untrained eye might have noted the darkish underbellies of the clouds. The optimistic sailor might have heeded the proximity of Rio and thought that perhaps they'd reach safe harbor before the violent squall struck.

Ryan knew better. A wind gall, luminous in its strange halo on the edge of a cloud, promised heavy rains to windward. He'd concealed his reaction from Isadora and his mother, but the moment he'd broken free of them he had convened the watch and sent them rushing about, battening the ship for a storm.

It struck within the hour, a long wall of wind and heavy seas pitching in from the far Atlantic. A swell hit the ship with such force that her timbers reverberated stem to stern, the vibrations driving up into the legs of those on deck. Gale winds plucked at the shrouds like a clumsy musician playing a badly strung fiddle.

Ryan and Izard met in the chart room. The chief mate's eyes said what his voice would not—Ryan's beginner's luck had run out. Here was the storm that would test his true mettle as a skipper.

"We'll heave to and make her fast," Ryan said.

Izard didn't argue. He merely nodded. An open hatchway let in a gust of wind that swept the charts off the slant-topped table. Wordlessly Izard stowed the charts and turned down the lantern.

As the ship plunged into its inevitable roll, Ryan passed Journey in the companionway. "Check on the women," he said tersely. "Tell them to keep to their quarters."

Though a chilling dread seized him, he couldn't deny the tingle and spark of excitement that churned through him as he rushed out to the deck. Acres of foam surrounded the ship.

He shouldn't like this, but God help him, he did. He desired the sea as he desired a woman's body. The sea was his mistress, one with the power to heal, nurture, love, torture...or destroy at her caprice. Like a woman, she was dark, mysterious, unpredictable— impossible to skim over the surface; a man had to plunge in and sink deep.

"Heave," he ordered. "Heave and sink her."

The men didn't need to be told twice. With a rusty whir of the hawse pipe, the heavy-weather anchors spun out and plummeted downward.

Scrolling waves rose higher and higher, and the *Swan* climbed helplessly to a foaming peak, then dove with breathtaking speed into the trough. Ryan stood in the cockpit with the second mate, both men mute with awe.

"We'll be swamped," Click promised him.

"I've got Craven and Pole manning the pumps." Ryan heard a grinding sound, and regarded the cables while the stern fishtailed helplessly. "We've got to run before it," he shouted.

"We'll be lost for sure," Click bellowed back. "We might have to jettison our cargo to boot!"

A crushing sense of defeat pressed at Ryan. Christ, not the cargo. The storm had grown mythically ugly, with the seething seas and the smoky clouds a vision of hell. He took a deep breath and bellowed the order past his own reluctance. "Up anchor, and take a double reef in the mains'l for hoisting!"

He knew in his gut it would take more men than he had to navigate the yawing ship through the gale. He refused to let himself think of disaster. Refused to think about his shame if he had to turn the ship over to the underwriters.

Timothy Datty came running, the wind blowing his feet out from under him. "My fault, skipper," he said. "I fouled a rope."

"Can you fix it?"

"Aye, sir!" the boy shouted.

"Carry on, then." Ryan wrestled with the tiller and Timothy went aloft. He reefed the topsails. Luigi set the staysails, and the ship raced before the wind, sweeping up and down the swells, on no set course save that determined by the unrelenting storm.

Datty was in the process of hoisting the mainsail, precariously balanced on the lee yardarm. He reached over to fasten the earring, a short length of rope used to lash the upper corners of the sail to the yardarm.

At that moment a wave struck the ship, a huge slap of water so thick and deep that Ryan felt himself start to drown as the sea gushed over him. Instinctively he hung on to the tiller, opening his eyes to slits and seeing nothing but green water rushing past.

He was under deep. Perhaps the ship had turned. His lungs nearly burst, and when he was about to surrender to the urge to let go, the water slid away like the seas before Moses.

Drawing in a frantic breath, he became aware of two things—

Timothy Datty had fallen from the yardarm.

And in defiance of orders, Isadora Peabody had appeared on deck.

Lightning blazed near the ship. Ryan swore, pounding across the deck, trying to center himself under Datty. The youth hung from the earring, suspended from the jackstay. His slender body swung like the clapper of a bell, back and forth with the violent pitch of the ship.

Ryan didn't stop to think. He grabbed a coil of rope and a gaff hook and started to climb. As he went up the rigging, he saw Isadora pitch in like a seasoned tar, helping Izard wrestle the tiller and taking physical risks, disobeying all good caution, flouting his command.

He had no time to grow angry at her. The storm swept him up in its teeth and he felt like the prey of a wolf that shook him, trying to break his neck. He hung on, his gaze never leaving Timothy. Any moment now the boy might lose his grasp, might fall into the house-high swells, never to be seen again.

I won't let you fall. Ryan closed the vow into his heart as he climbed. Securing himself in the footrope under the yardarm, he tossed out the rope. Time and time again the wind snatched it away. The end of the rope flashed by too quickly. Impossible to grab it. Timothy's face, running clear with rainwater and spume, was the greenish white of a marble slab.

His eyes rolled; his lips moved in mindless, hopeless prayer.

Ryan felt himself losing the boy. He shouted encouragement, screamed at the lad to hang on, but the wind stole his words.

He suspected Timothy wasn't listening, anyway. He could see the slender hands frozen around the earring line. The lad was weakening. If he let go to grab the thrown line, he'd fall for sure.

"Here," said a voice near Ryan, practically in his ear.

Incredulous, he looked through the rigging and saw Isadora, passing him the end of the rope. "Secure this to the yardarm and swing out and grab him."

It was an insane idea. Datty hung too far out toward the end of the yardarm to reach. But if Ryan did as she

said, if he swung out as the ship pitched leeward, he
might be able to grab the boy.

"You want to see us *both* die, don't you?" he
shouted, but even as he did, he grasped the rope and
lashed it to the yardarm.

On the deck below, Ralph and Journey held the other
end of the line to rein him in after he pulled Timothy to
safety. That was all the thought he would allow. Anything more and he'd talk himself out of it.

He watched the swells and waited until the ship
pitched toward Timothy. Then, with a last look at Isadora—wet face, plastered hair, wide, terrified eyes—he
pushed off from the foot rope.

The sensation of soaring was, for the briefest of moments, an ecstasy and a wonderment he hadn't expected.
The next moment he felt nothing. The sea rose up at
him. He'd miscalculated the distance. He was going to
miss Timothy altogether. He might even sweep the boy
away for good.

"Again," Isadora screamed. "You must try again!"

He belled out and then swung back.

And Timothy dangled right in front of him.

Ryan saw his own arm as if it were a stranger's. Out
it came, wrapping around Timothy's slender form. He
felt the *whoosh* of lungs emptying, and he could not have
said if it was he or the boy who had made the sound.

His legs and chest burned as, with a heated whir, he
slid down the rope and smacked, bruised but safe, into
Journey and Ralph. Timothy sprawled on the deck, flex-
ing his hands and shuddering.

As nimble as any seaman, Isadora descended from the
rigging. Ryan dragged her to a hatch and all but stuffed
her down a companion ladder, too furious to speak.

Then he braced himself. Until today, the sea had been his fair-weather friend. Now, retribution was at hand, and God knew, he deserved it. He was a careless man, sometimes even cruel in his carelessness. With hardly a thought for the consequences, he had ripped Journey from his family, offering little more than a wish and a prayer of reuniting them. He had lied through his teeth to gain command of the *Swan*. Now they would all die because of it.

He expected the storm to destroy him and the ship and cargo and crew. But instead, as quickly as it had whipped up, the squall skirled away to the northeast, leaving high seas and a brooding sky in its aftermath.

Ryan stood with Journey on the deck. "It's over."

"We survived," Journey said.

"We did better than that," Izard pointed out, joining them at the rail. He started to laugh with pure joy. "I took a reading. We're less than ten miles out of Rio."

Isadora sat in the galley, a rough green blanket draped around her shoulders and a mug of tepid tea cradled between her hands. Shaken and cautious, the Doctor had allowed a small fire in the stove to heat water for tea. She took a sip, glancing over the rim at Timothy Datty. Someone had put dry trousers and a shirt on him; now he lay fast asleep upon a bench, knees drawn up and hands cradling his cheek.

He looked exhausted by his ordeal and impossibly, achingly young. In the hollow of his lap, the ship's cat slept. Setting her mug in a holder, Isadora stood and covered Timothy with the green blanket. Some impulse compelled her to put out a hand, brush the salt-stiffened, spikey hair away from his pale brow.

In that moment, she knew this lad was more than a shipmate to her. Dear God, they'd almost lost him.

"Get into some dry clothes," said a voice from the doorway. "I don't want you catching a chill."

Yanked out of the sentimental moment, she turned to scowl at Ryan Calhoun. "I'm not at all cold. We're in the tropics, remember?"

He tossed his head, damp hair sprinkling his shirt. It, like his trousers, was dry. He came into the galley, stopping in front of her, standing so close she could feel the heat from his body. She tried to step back, but he'd cornered her against the table. "Very well," he said. "That wet dress gives us all an intriguing view of your smallclothes, so you might as well entertain us."

She folded her arms protectively across her chest. "Only someone like you would find a storm at sea entertaining."

"Someone like me," he said, running his thumb down the inside of her arm until she batted his hand away. "And exactly which someone am I like?"

"Like...like the very devil," she blurted out.

"Do tell," he said, touching her other arm so that she unfolded that one, too. "I've been called many things, but not the devil."

She knew she should find his nearness and the impudence of his touch offensive, but God help her, she didn't. For some reason the gentle, insistent up-and-down motion of his hand soothed her, made it difficult to think. "Like Lucifer, you have a great capacity for strength and goodness. Yet you use your power to tease and torment me."

"Is that what this is?" he asked with a delighted chuckle. "Teasing? Tormenting?"

"Why do you find this so amusing?" she asked, starting to feel light-headed and strange.

"Because I came here to thank you for your help during the storm and you've completely misconstrued my intent."

She kept staring at his mouth. He was so much taller than she, that her eyes were level with his mouth. He had a wonderful, chiseled shape to his lips, and he smiled more easily than anyone she'd ever met.

"Then you're...welcome. But you needn't thank me."

His hand lifted and the side of his finger slipped beneath her chin, bringing her gaze up to his. "True. In fact, you're far more deserving of..."

For some reason, her eyes seemed to want to drift shut. And her mouth, her mouth wanted to...

"Deserving of what?" she asked faintly, her whisper barely audible above the noise of the dissipating storm.

He pressed closer. She felt herself lean into him, and then, swearing between his clenched teeth, he stepped back. "You're far more deserving of a lecture on safety," he said. "I ordered you to stay in your quarters, and you deliberately violated that."

Mortified by the sense of forbidden intimacy that had surrounded her only moments ago, Isadora ducked beneath his arm and hurried to the door. "I didn't hear any argument from you when you were up that yardarm," she said.

"Then be sure to note that in your report to Mr. Easterbrook." His insolent, ice-blue stare fastened on her bodice. He was trying to intimidate her, she thought. And, as she fled from the galley, she conceded that it was working.

* * *

They were obliged to wear ship and stand off from shore until the heavy seas abated. Ryan used the time to prepare for a grand entrance to Rio.

On his previous trip to the Caribbean, he'd learned that in a seaport, appearances were everything. He represented the ship's interests to port authorities, shipping agents and consignees. To get the highest prices for his cargo, a skipper had to appear prosperous and well-groomed from stem to stern. Fortunately, the *Swan* was a fine-looking vessel, the crewmen diligent in their swabbing and polishing. The storm had caused only minor damage. The bark would look like a proud bird as she sailed into harbor.

Ryan kept the crew busy scrubbing down the decks and smoothing them with the holystone, polishing the brass, checking the sails and awnings for spots of mildew. Even the women pitched in, his mother pulling things from the linen locker while Fayette strung them along a line on the afterdeck. Isadora made reparations to the storm-battered hen coop and then—hugely amusing the crew—groomed the goat with a silver-backed hairbrush.

He tried to figure out what it was about her that so fascinated and infuriated him. They always seemed to rub one another the wrong way, even when things started out pleasantly enough. One moment they were laughing at a shared joke; the next they were grousing at each other over the most minor of issues. And sometimes he found himself—of all the damn fool things—pressing her into a dark corner and wondering what secrets she hid beneath her voluminous skirts.

He had always taken pride in his ability to understand

the female of the species. He thought he knew what women wanted, what they needed, what they expected. And, until Isadora, he had been able to provide it with reliable regularity.

But this one, this intelligent, vexing, interesting female, did not seem to be taken by any of the usual charms. She didn't care for fashion, though she clung to the restrictive modes of Beacon Hill out of habit. She was immune to flattery, for she neither trusted nor believed a compliment sent her way. She took no delight in the usual ladylike pursuits of needlework and gossip, finding more pleasure in perusing the Bowditch with Ralph Izard or conducting elocution lessons for Timothy Datty. To look at her, he'd never have guessed she had the strength to endure the storm, yet the hardships only made her quicker and more assured than she'd ever been on dry land. Worst of all, she was impervious to the unexpected mist of heat that pervaded the atmosphere whenever they found themselves alone together. He had no idea where his unwanted urge to be close to her came from. He meant to intimidate her, humiliate her, make her sorry she'd forced her presence on him, yet his plan kept misfiring. He kept catching himself enjoying the closeness far too much...and wanting far more than was good for both of them.

He was insatiably curious about her. She gave tirelessly to others, but what did she want for herself? He should ask her, and he would, if she'd ever deign to speak to him again after yesterday's scene in the galley.

"There now, don't you look a sight." Journey came into the stateroom. "What is that color you're wearing today—mango?"

Ryan plucked at his silken cravat, admiring the peach-blush shade of it. "One of my favorite colors."

"Goes well with the lime green sash."

Ryan ignored the wry censure in his voice. His steward favored somber colors and a dignified manner, but that didn't suit Ryan. "There's a reason for this," he said.

"Yes. Horrible personal taste, for one."

"So you say. But picture Ferraro's cold storage plant. Hundreds of workers swarming about, dozens of skippers with ice to sell. Who will they remember next season—a black-clad downeast Puritan, or the dashing Captain Calhoun?"

Journey turned his hands palms-out and took a step back. "Never mind, then. Commerce before taste, always."

"Captain!" Timothy rapped smartly at the door. "P-pilot's here!"

Ryan strode out to the main deck. The harbor pilot had come over in a launch and boarded. Dark-skinned, a battered hat clutched beneath his arm, he was staring drop-jawed at Lily, who had come out with Fayette and Isadora to observe the arrival.

"I guess he found something prettier than you," Journey said.

Lily wore a dress of lavender and lace, complete with a wide-brimmed picnic bonnet and a ruffle-edged parasol. Ryan had seen flower arrangements less elaborate than his mother.

Fayette stood dutifully behind her mistress, though the maid's wide-eyed gaze devoured the busy harbor with tall ships moving in and out, pilot boats and launches scooting to and fro.

And then there was Isadora, already shrinking into herself, he observed with annoyance. Now that they were about to go ashore, she was reverting to the gawky, timid creature he'd met in Boston. She kept her shoulders hunched and her eyes cast down, though she darted an occasional glance toward Sugar Loaf, the massive up-ended rock that marked the harbor. She had trussed herself up in an ugly brown dress he hadn't seen south of the tenth parallel and her hair, which had begun to look somewhat better than squirrel fur, had disappeared into an odd black-and-brown bonnet.

At least, Ryan mused, landfall had not leached the healthy color from her face and she hadn't coughed or sneezed in weeks.

With a gracious smile, he strode toward the pilot. "*Senhor,* welcome aboard the *Swan.*"

"Oh, my," Lily murmured, admiring his shore togs with a proud maternal head-to-toe glance. "My baby boy is too handsome for words, isn't he, Isadora?"

Isadora gave him a quick look, then ducked her head. "As you say, there are no words."

At that moment, the shoreline forts fired a salute. Ryan raised his arms to acknowledge the courtesy.

The pilot tore his gaze from Lily long enough to offer Ryan a bow and a gap-toothed smile. Ryan gestured at the wharves. "How much to bring us in to a berth?"

"Forty pound sterling, senhor. In now, and later out."

Ryan clutched at his heart. "Did you hear that, Mr. Izard? Just when I thought we'd make landfall without incident, I'm attacked by a pirate."

"*Senhor,* I do not understand. I offer a service at a fair price—"

"Fifteen pounds sterling and not a farthing more," Ryan said.

The man sent a wounded look heavenward and released a long string of Portuguese lamentation.

Ryan waited patiently for his counteroffer, but instead, Isadora cleared her throat. "Captain Calhoun, the poor man said he has five daughters, and his mother-in-law has come to die in his house. I really do think the proper thing to do is to meet his price."

The Brazilian clearly saw Isadora as the weak spot, and addressed his next prayerful stream of speech to her.

She listened, enraptured. "He says a lesser pilot would risk grounding a ship of this size," she warned. "Forty pounds is nothing compared to the many thousands you stand to lose if you allow a lesser pilot to run you aground. He's absolutely right. He—"

"Twenty, and that's my final offer," Ryan snapped.

"Thirty," the man countered.

"Done," Ryan declared before Isadora could intervene again.

The Brazilian's face lit up with a brilliant smile, and he hurried off to work.

Ryan whirled on Isadora, lowering his voice to a furious mutter. "Don't ever do that again."

"I am your translator."

"Then translate. Don't advise me on what to pay."

"But five daughters and a dying mother-in-law? The ten extra pounds would mean the world to the poor man."

"Poor, hah. The old salt's a bachelor who lives on his boat. The extra money goes to keep him in women, cigars, and *curaçao*."

"How do you know that?" she demanded.

"It's my business to know that. Now, the next time there's any translating to be done, you give it to me word for word—without any of your back-slack."

He stalked away, feeling strangely invigorated by the spat. That was the odd thing about knowing Isadora. Sparring with her was far more fun than polite conversation with a dozen other misses.

Lily hired a coach to take them up into the hills where her sister lived. While Fayette oversaw the masses of traveling trunks, Lily wafted a fan in front of her face. The smells of roasting coffee and burning sugar cane filled the air.

In preparation for landing, Isadora had read a traveler's guide and studied the engravings to learn the lay of the land. But no travelogue or sketch could have prepared her for Rio. She stood in a thrall of amazement, observing the busy, glittering paradise: a mountain called Corcovado, shaped like a man bending over and draped in emerald silk. The Sugar Loaf rock, massive and gleaming like pure marble in the hot sun. Botafogo, a sparkling diamond necklace that collared the turquoise bay. Overlooking all this splendor was a dazzling white edifice she recognized as Laranjeras Palace.

Dear Lord Almighty, Isadora thought. I have died and ascended to paradise. She almost believed the fanciful thought, except for the rivulets of sweat that trickled unbearably down her back and between her breasts.

"Ah, here's our coach," Lily exclaimed. "I cannot believe I'm nearly there. I can hardly bear the anticipation."

Isadora studied the coach with a twinge of suspicion. All but buried beneath a pyramid of luggage, the conveyance looked as if it might collapse at any moment. "Do you think we'll be safe in that?" she asked.

"Of course. It's the way all people of fashion travel. Have you got everything you need?"

"Yes, but I should stay here," Isadora protested. "Captain Calhoun might need help translating—"

"Not today," Ryan said, striding along the waterfront. He retained his seaman's rolling gate, though he wore beautifully cut shore togs—tight black trousers and a full, blousy white shirt, with a tangerine-colored waistcoat.

He was with a dark, slender man of indeterminate race—he had the close-curled hair of an African, yet his skin was rich cinnamon in tone.

"Edison Carneros, at your service," he said, his bow like that of a matador before a cheering crowd. When he straightened, he looked directly at Fayette.

Isadora felt the heat sizzle between them. That was the only way she could explain it. The moment their gazes connected, the two experienced a leap of knowing. Isadora glanced at Ryan to see if he, too, had sensed the sudden, undeniable interest.

"He's an agent of my consignee," Ryan explained, clearly oblivious to Fayette's reaction to Carneros. "Since he speaks excellent English, I'll have no need of a translator." His grin was dazzling, his eyes dancing.

"Why, son, you certainly look pleased with yourself," Lily observed.

"The ice cargo," Carneros said. "It is in a most excellent condition. Yours is the first ice of the season to arrive." He fashioned his brown face into a mournful look that failed to disguise his glee. "He will rob me blind, making me pay such a sum for the ice."

Ryan laughed. "You'll earn it back. Senhor Ferraro is no fool. He knows what it's worth to be the first to fill his plant."

The coach driver helped Lily in, and Ryan offered Isadora his hand. He'd not been pleased with her first live translation with the harbor pilot. Clearly this was his way of showing it—by handling her as if she were a stranger.

The rejection was harsh simply because he was so charming about it. He kept one hand on hers, the other pressed to the small of her back. She knew with mortified certainty that he would feel the dampness of her sweat.

"What do you think of Rio?" he asked as she stepped up to the footboard. His tone was dismissive; he didn't care about her answer.

What she wanted to tell him was that it was astonishing, magical, enchanting. A paradise she had seen only in dreams. "It's very attractive," she said tersely.

He handed her up and she seated herself beside Lily under the colorful fringed awning.

"Fayette," called Lily, "are you coming?"

The maid mumbled, "Yes'm." But she never stopped staring at Carneros, nor did he take his eyes off her as he helped her into the coach. A magnetic energy seemed to charge the air around the pretty dark-skinned maid and the slender, debonair agent.

"Go with God," Carneros said softly, addressing all the ladies but not taking his eyes off Fayette. "Until we meet again—farewell."

The coach lurched, then started up the dusty road.

"Really, Fayette," Lily said in a scolding voice that failed to mask her indulgence. "We're not an hour in port and you're flirting already. What am I to do with you?''

"Don't know, ma'am," Fayette said vaguely, leaning against a corner awning pole with a distant look on her face. "I surely don't know." She sighed sweetly and lifted one hand in farewell. Carneros returned the gesture, but Ryan had already turned away.

Isadora directed her attention to the scenery. She spied the *mercado* in the distance, pinwheels of color and sound, bright sunshades stretched over mounds of melons and pineapples and fruits she had never seen before. They passed busy *bodegas* and a church with an airy song coming from the choir, and a flock of nuns moving down the street. Black-skinned servants and laundresses with baskets balanced on their heads passed in droves up and down the road.

"There's too much of it," she said. "It's so hard to take it all in."

"You have three glorious weeks here before setting sail again," Lily said. "You should make it a point to see a new sight each day. That's something we learned while touring the Continent, isn't it, Fayette? Something new each and every day. Fayette? You haven't heard a word I've said."

"No, ma'am," the maid said dreamily.

When the road wound around a hill they came to a cluster of houses. The dwellings, set into the side of the hill, were pink-and-white confections of dusty pastel plaster. On all of the verges, seemingly in every rock and crevice, something grew: fuschia, bougainvillea, crimson and white poinsettia.

The coach went on into a thick forest, but it was like no forest Isadora had ever seen. The trees grew immeasurably tall; they had thick glistening leaves and some blossomed with mysterious huge yellow-tongued flowers. Lush ferns carpeted the floor. Birds, the same green and yellow as the foliage, swooped here and there, and somewhere close by, a secret spring trickled.

She leaned back against the seat and trembled, simply trembled, for she felt as if she had landed in the middle of a dream, and she was terrified of waking up.

Yet when the coach ground to a halt on the crushed seashell drive of a vast pink villa, she dared to believe it was real.

The driver gave a whistle. A herd of houseboys swarmed over the carriage, helping them out and chattering away in a charming patois as they liberated the luggage. Isadora was delighted and challenged by the language. How different it was from her textbook Portuguese. The rapid, colorful slang barely gave the nod to the formal mother tongue.

She caught the eye of one of the boys and smiled pleasantly, greeting him in her best Portuguese.

He and his friends giggled uncontrollably.

Lily asked, "What did you say to them?"

"I hope I said it's a pleasure to be here, but the way they're giggling, I can't be certain." She found the boys enchanting. She could not be certain of their race. They were not black in the way Journey and the Doctor were, but neither were they Anglo. Their faces and bare legs were the color of the *caffe com leche* the port authorities had served at the landing.

She found it interesting that their race was indeterminate—and that it did not seem to matter in the least.

A high-pitched squeal issued from a colonnaded walkway leading from the main house. Lily became alert like a hound on the scent. She whirled around and answered the squeal with one of her own.

"Rose! Oh, my darling Rose!"

The two women fell into each other's arms with such heartfelt emotion that Isadora and Fayette held hands and gulped back tears as they watched.

The two sisters made an entrancing pair. Lily was as pale and delicate as her namesake, and Rose was as bold and vibrant as hers. She wore an extraordinary garment—a tiered skirt that showed her shapely ankles and bare feet. Her blouse was cut low in the neck. Isadora could tell for certain that Rose wore no corsets and petticoats under the loose, light costume.

When Lily made the introductions, Rose embraced both Fayette and Isadora in turn. "Welcome to my home," she declared. A touch of Virginia still accented her words, but her speech also had the rhythmic cadences of Brazil. She laughed at their stares and plucked playfully at Lily's multilayered skirts. "We dress for the weather at Villa do Cielo, and so must you. Were it not for the hot-blooded nature of our menfolk, we would probably go about in the nude."

Isadora stifled a gasp. Yet lightning did not strike simply because a woman mentioned something earthy. She decided she liked Rose very much indeed.

As Rose led the way under the blossom-draped colonnade, she looked up and saw that each flower was a perfect orchid.

Isadora knew she was going to enjoy Rio.

Thirteen

Be good and you will be lonesome.

—Mark Twain,
Following the Equator

Hot, sweet and languid—those were the dominant impressions Ryan had of Rio. After concluding his preliminary business with Ferraro's agent, he arranged for the cargo to be discharged. Luigi, who spoke his native tongue with the team of Italian stevedores, had matters well in hand.

Before hiring a rig to convey him to his aunt's in Tijuca, Ryan stood at the loud, busy waterfront and felt himself slowly fill up with a splendid feeling so rare that at first he couldn't identify it. But it had a name—pride.

Pride that he had done something of consequence, and done it so well that even strangers on the wharves had learned who he was. Captain Calhoun, who carried a tiny crew and too much sail. Captain Calhoun, who had won a bonus for coming in days before his due date.

The wharf rats learned his identity as quickly as the shipping agents and local merchants. "I have the finest diamonds for sale," hissed a smiling young man with oily hair and restless hands. "Come and see my selection."

Ryan cheerfully declined the suspicious offer, only to find the oily merchant replaced by a soft-hipped whore. "You have been long time at sea," she purred, running her tongue around her lips in a gesture that should be outlawed. "I make you happy, happy today."

"Card game?" another man asked. "Faro or dice?"

Ryan grinned from ear to ear. He hadn't even gotten paid yet.

And then, because a sudden hollowness opened up inside him, he held out his arm to the whore and asked, "What's your name, sugar-pie?"

In the end, he realized he'd never even heard it. All he remembered was the ripeness of her, the intoxicating musk, the way her soft body opened to him, the way he sank into her. Yet the act had a disturbingly mechanical nature. He pleasured her, yes, but in a curiously detached fashion. And, in a curiously detached fashion, he found his own pleasure as well, and paid her handsomely for the encounter.

Late that afternoon, he emerged from the brothel with a head muzzy from drink, a body sated by sex and a jumble of confusing thoughts and misgivings. He had been offered contraband riches, sex, gambling, strong drink. At one time such things had been all he desired in life and he would have happily accepted. Yet now such pleasures held only faint allure for him. Instead, he went out to look at the teeming market and terraced hills and pastel palaces of Rio, and one thought tugged at

him: none of this meant anything unless he had someone
to share it with.

Someone who looked at the world with wide-eyed
wonder. Someone who drank in new sights and sounds
with a passion belied by her sober mien. Someone who
took a new experience and clasped it to her breast like
a precious treasure.

"The coach is ready," Journey said, coming toward
Ryan. "What the matter?" He peered at him. "You look
sick."

"Maybe. In my mind," Ryan said, and he walked
toward the carriage.

His Aunt Rose made an embarrassing fuss over him,
exclaiming at his height, his handsomeness, the clarity
of his cerulean eyes, the glossiness of his auburn hair.

Lily looked on, indulging her for a few moments before saying, "He's my son, Rose dear. Not a show
horse."

"You should see me when I'm sober," he said, swaying a little.

"Of course." Rose hugged him. She smelled pleasantly of coffee and flowers. He hoped it masked his own
less pleasant scent of liquor and cheap perfume. "Forgive me, Ryan. I wasn't blessed with children of my
own, so I must do all my mothering when I can."

"And you do it with a natural grace," he assured her,
smiling despite a pounding headache. "Where is Isadora?"

Lily and Rose exchanged a knowing glance. Ryan
cursed himself for letting his eagerness show.

Isadora came down the carved cypress stairwell, uncertainty evident in her stiff posture. "I—I apologize for keeping everyone waiting—"

"Nonsense, my dear," Rose interrupted. "We keep no schedules at Villa do Cielo."

"House of the sky," Isadora softly translated. "What an enchanting image."

"Now that we're all together," said Rose, "let us go in to supper." She led the way across the arched foyer. Lily linked arms with her, and Ryan was confronted with the prospect of partnering Isadora.

He found the notion absurdly appealing.

He cocked out his elbow. "Shall we go?"

She sent him that startled, I-can't-believe-you're-being-nice-to-me look that gratified him even as it broke his heart. Had no one ever shown this poor woman a bit of courtesy?

She wrinkled her nose and pruned her lips in disapproval. "Captain Calhoun, what sort of business were you conducting?"

He didn't feel ashamed, exactly. Sheepish, perhaps. "I took care of a...personal affair as well."

"So I gather."

"It was a long voyage, Isadora. It's not natural for a man to...do without."

"I'm certain I wouldn't know anything about that."

"I'm trying to explain myself so you can include it in your report to Easterbrook."

"Why, how dare—" She stopped as his mother and Aunt Rose came into view.

He pressed his arm against her until she took it. "Thank you, Captain," she murmured.

"Now that we're ashore, you should call me Ryan."

"I couldn't possibly."

He gestured at his mother and aunt who crossed the patio ahead of them. "The other ladies do."

"Your ladies of the night, I presume," she said tartly.

"That would be 'ladies of the afternoon,'" he explained. "And for the record, there was only one. You *are* keeping score, are you not?"

She made a strange wheezing sound, but couldn't seem to get a word out.

"I meant my mother and aunt," he said, taking pity on her. "*They* call me by my given name."

"They're related to you."

He winked at Isadora. "That can be arranged."

Her gaze darted away. "You shouldn't tease."

Maybe I wasn't. The idea was too absurd and too startling to voice aloud, yet the instant it occurred to him, it sent down roots that reached deep inside to a tender place in his heart. It was the oddest notion that had ever occurred to him. Isadora Peabody? The prim, bashful Yankee who dreamed of Chad Easterbrook?

Ryan had clearly been too long at sea.

Isadora had no appetite for supper, though the meal was both delicious and exotic. There was avocado seasoned with vinegar, yams and beefsteak and two kinds of wine, melon and guava and lemony ice shaved from the large block Ryan had brought his aunt as a gift.

Yet for all the bounty, Isadora could only pick at her food. She felt jumpy and out of sorts, and she wasn't sure why. Eagerness, she decided, studying the ochre walls of the dining room, the arched doorway and windows with their carved wooden screens. That, and a decided enchantment with this strange new place, with the fragrance of orchids and tamarind trees and the strains of soft guitar music that came from the servants' wing.

And disillusionment with Ryan. The moment he'd reached shore, he'd gone looking for a woman, which he had made a point of explaining to her without apology.

"There's so much to see," Lily declared. "And in such a short time."

"It doesn't have to be short," Rose said. "You could stay with me."

"Here?"

"Of course. What is there at Albion for you?"

Lily took a sip of her wine. "Albion is my home. It's where I raised my son and buried my husband. My stepson has two children I barely know. I spent too long on the Continent. I can't stay away forever."

Ryan eyed her keenly. "Father's dead and I'll never live at Albion again, Mama. I think Aunt Rose has a fine idea. Let Hunter have Albion. He never needed us anyway."

Hunter. Isadora tried to picture the stepbrother—older, of course. Dissolute, with a big red nose from drinking all those mint juleps on the porch while his slaves worked themselves to death in the fields.

"What are his children like?" Rose asked.

"I hardly know—they were both in leading strings when I left. The boy's name is Theodore and his sister is Belinda. Hunter's wife—her name is Lacey—didn't welcome my attention." A wistful expression softened Lily's face. "I would have liked to be a grandmama." The expression vanished as she drilled Ryan with a stare. "Perhaps one day someone of my own flesh and blood will oblige me."

Ryan laughed. "I know I performed a small miracle in getting us here so fast, but even I would have trouble having a baby."

Rose burst out laughing. Her sister merely shook her head. "Whatever shall I do with the boy?"

Isadora took a very small bite of melon, chewed it carefully and swallowed. She prayed they would not see the hot blush that stained her cheeks.

"We've embarrassed our guest with all this bawdy talk," Rose said. "Shame on us."

"No, really—"

"Nonsense, my dear. Let us move on to politer topics." She folded her unfashionably sunbrowned arms on the table. "You are a most intelligent young lady. Lily was telling me you've a gift for languages."

Isadora shook her head. "If the conversation I heard at the wharves today was any indication, I am no expert."

"She's being modest," Ryan said. "She's the best interpreter I've ever heard."

She blinked. After her performance with the harbor pilot, she hadn't expected praise.

"Is that so?" Rose asked, lifting a dark eyebrow.

"It is," he said, upending his wine goblet.

Isadora felt a soft shock of pleasure. Praise from Ryan Calhoun should not feel so good, but Lord help her, it did. She knew pride was a vanity, yet his compliment warmed her like the wine she was drinking.

"You have," Rose observed, "a most remarkable smile."

Isadora immediately pressed her mouth into a flat line. Ryan had probably given her a compliment because he felt guilty about his behavior.

"I'm sorry, I shouldn't have said anything," Rose commented. "But that smile—it quite transforms you. And the cut of your hair is quite...revolutionary. I simply adore it. Perhaps I shall get mine cut short, too."

Isadora had no idea what to say. Lily rescued her by turning the subject back to Albion and people they knew years before. Isadora sampled her lemon ice and listened, enjoying the stories of these lovely strangers while barefooted servants waited on them.

A low churring sound came through the arched windows, startling her. Noting her widened eyes, Rose said, "That noise you're hearing is a taramin—a nocturnal monkey. He's a pet of sorts. Shy, but he'll come around for a taste of fruit or honey from the kitchen."

"I'd love to see him."

"Ryan, show Isadora out to the patio," Rose said.

"No, really," Isadora began, quickly changing her mind. Rose's suggestion bore a nightmarish resemblance to the well-meaning matchmakers of Boston, forever trying to pair her up with mortified young men. "It's not nec—"

"I don't mind." Ryan pushed his chair from the table. She searched his face to see if he wore the look of those doomed suitors.

"You can stop in the kitchen for a pail of food," Rose suggested. "The monkey is sure to be prowling about the garden."

Torches illuminated the stone-paved area which formed the heart of the villa. Low arches flanked the patio, and one side had no wall but a wrought iron fence and a huge, unusual tree with a twisted trunk that resembled straining sinew and branches that grew almost horizontally out from it.

The scent of flowers weighted the night air, the odor so thick and exotic that Isadora felt woozy simply breathing it. She stopped in front of the burbling fountain in the center of the patio and stood very still, inhaling deeply, feeling the essence of the night pour through her, bringing parts of her to life that had been sleeping since before she could remember, sleeping so soundly that until this moment she didn't know they existed.

"Are you ill?" Ryan asked, breaking in on her ecstatic reveries.

She opened her eyes. "No. Why do you ask?"

"You looked a little...peaked," he said. "A little dizzy."

"If I'm dizzy it's not due to illness," she said, flushing. "It's because this place is so wonderful—the smells and sounds and the very feel of the air—it makes me...tingle," she explained, then flushed again. "For want of a better word."

"Tingle," he repeated, an amused quirk lifting the side of his mouth.

"What I mean is that this environment gives me a sense of vitality I've not felt before. Does it have that effect on you, Captain Calhoun?"

He studied her with a frank and probing scrutiny that made her uncomfortable. And without moving his gaze from her, he said, "I do believe I feel that tingling effect, Isadora."

"Now you're teasing me," she said, but the night was too perfect to feel angry about it.

He held out his hand to her. "Oddly, I'm not. Shall we go in search of this elusive creature?"

When she touched his hand, the tingling sensation heightened. She hadn't expected that. Perhaps it was something she'd eaten—all the fruit had tasted so exotic. She felt light on her feet and graceful, probably a trick of equilibrium, since she had been so long at sea.

They walked to the end of the path, finding a sundial sitting in the gloom.

"How do you call a monkey?" Ryan asked.

"I have no idea. I've never even seen a monkey."

He rattled the pail of fruit and made a smooching sound with his mouth. Isadora laughed. "That's your monkey call?"

He winked at her. "Can you do any better?"

She pursed her lips and tried to emulate the churring sound they'd heard in the dining room.

"I don't know how the monkey feels," Ryan said with a chuckle, "but you've certainly got my attention."

She laughed again, wondering if it was the perfumed garden air, the wine she'd drunk, or sheer madness that made everything seem so delightfully funny.

"Ah, Isadora. If your laughter doesn't tempt the little rodent, I don't know what will." He propped one foot on a garden bench made of tiled masonry. The negligently elegant pose looked wonderful on him. "You have the prettiest laugh I've ever heard."

"And you, sir, have the glibbest tongue."

He grinned. "Talked my way onto the *Swan*."

"I have often wondered. How did you manage that?"

"I won't say. You already find me despicable enough."

"I don't find you despicable," she protested. "Just...exasperating."

"Ah, exasperating. Does this mean I'm rising in your esteem?"

"At least it's a feeling you can understand," she said, "because you find me equally exasperating."

He fixed her with an unreadable stare. "I was with a woman this afternoon."

"I know that. I'm not stupid."

"Were you shocked?" he asked.

"Was it worth it?" she countered.

"Are you going to report me?"

"That depends."

"On what?"

"On why you did it." She bit her lip. "Besides...the explanation you gave me earlier."

"To shock you? And perhaps...hell, I don't know. It's not...what you think. I came away feeling empty. It's hard to explain."

"Then why do you do it?"

"Because I'm a bad man."

She shook her head. "I think you're actually a good man with some very bad habits."

He propped an elbow on his knee and gave her a dazzling smile. "Isadora—" He broke off and grabbed her hand, holding on tight. "He's coming," he muttered in a low voice.

"The monkey?" she whispered.

He nodded. They waited, straining to hear. A distant night bird called and another, even more distant, answered. Closer in, the bushes rustled with a furtive sound.

Isadora kept her grip on Ryan's hand. She liked holding his hand. His bore calluses of hard work and a comfortable dry warmth. She couldn't help but note the size—she had large hands for a woman but his were much bigger, swallowing hers so her fingers nestled safely inside. Safe. That was the way she felt with Ryan Calhoun. Safe, as if nothing in the world could harm her so long as she kept hold of his hand.

It was a fanciful notion. An un-Isadoralike notion. Yet it rang through her with a strange resonance.

Safe with him. When had she ever been unsafe? Physically—never. She had lived the sheltered life of the daughter of one of Boston's first families. But in other ways her peril was constant. She could not even walk into her parents' drawing room without feeling as if she were in danger of drowning.

It occurred to her that she hadn't experienced the drowning sensation since she had left Boston. Not even in the deadliest moments of the great storm.

"There, see?" Ryan whispered, his lips so close to her ear. She shivered with the warm vibration.

Ye powers. Here she sat in a perfumed garden, holding hands with a man while he whispered in her ear. Her fevered imagination had, of course, conjured this moment many times. But the man in her daydream had always been Chad Easterbrook. And in her daydream, the moment had never, ever felt this delicious.

"I don't see it," she whispered back. She told herself no romance heated this moment. They shared only a mutual curiosity in what the exotic night would bring, a mutual anticipation of learning the secrets of the forest.

"A tiny shadow. It's there."

He did the most extraordinary thing. With a restrained gentleness so poignant it made her chest ache, he touched her cheek in order to turn her head toward the low shrubbery border. His touch nearly shattered her, for not since Aunt Button had someone caressed her with such tenderness. Yet this surpassed even Aunt Button's affection, for this sent shivers radiating outward along her limbs and stirring up a strange pool of heat somewhere deep inside her.

"Do you see it now?" he whispered.

She forced herself to concentrate. "Heavens he. I think I do," she said, mouthing the words, barely speaking them.

A tiny creature, furtive as a thief, darted out of the bushes and snatched up a chunk of papaya.

"He is so little," she whispered, "Like a wizened old man."

The monkey crouched over its find, stuffing its mouth greedily until it could hold no more. Then, grasping a piece of plantain in its tiny paw, it made off into the shadowy night forest.

Isadora felt a welling of wonder and joy in her chest. She could not have erased the smile on her face if she'd tried, but she didn't try. She turned to Ryan, realizing that even though the creature was gone, he still kept his lips close to hers, still cradled her cheek in his large, warm hand.

"How wonderful," she said. "I can't believe we saw such an amazing creature."

"You," he said with laughter in his voice, "are a very hard woman to impress."

"What do you mean?" She was amazed she could even get the words out, for his other hand let go of hers and slipped, as furtive as the night creature they had come to see, around her waist, holding her lightly but firmly.

Men had touched her there to dance with her, but they had been different. They'd all had the aspect of wooden soldiers forced in front of a firing squad. But Ryan...

dear Lord, she could only think of him as Ryan now...he gave her the impression he actually wanted to be here, wanted to touch her.

He smiled gently, the faint torchlight softening his features. "What I mean is I've crossed oceans and battled storms to bring you here, and you've taken it all in stride. I haven't seen you so perfectly enraptured, not once, until you saw the little fellow come stealing out of the forest."

That's not what has me so perfectly enraptured. The thought—and the utter truth of it—startled her. She nearly blurted the words aloud.

But at the last moment, she stopped herself. Because she didn't trust herself, didn't trust her heart. Didn't trust Ryan not to break it.

"I suppose," she said softly, with a touch of irony, "I seem terribly worldly and sophisticated."

"Far too worldly and sophisticated for the likes of a Virginia farm boy turned sailor," he said.

Still touching her. Holding her. His gaze a lodestone she could not look away from.

She managed a wobbly smile at his statement. "Farm boy? Judging by what your mother has told me of Albion, you grew up in a world of unimaginable wealth."

"I never found what I wanted in that world," he said.

She moistened her lips, tasting the fruit she had eaten earlier and finding herself strangely hungry again, empty and yearning for... "What is it you're looking for?" she heard herself ask. "What do you want?"

He chuckled low in his throat, and the sound sent a thrill through her. "Those are two different questions, Isadora." Though she didn't think it possible, he leaned even closer, so that the warmth of his breath and the fruity scent of the rum drink he'd imbibed mingled with her own shallow inhalations.

He was close. So close. She'd never been this close to a man before.

"Do...you have...two different answers?" she managed to force out.

"Only one at the moment. Only one."

The hand at her waist tightened. She had the most inexplicable urge to touch him as well, for her hands lay clenched in her lap and she wanted to put them somewhere else. Wanted to put them on him.

Her fingers reached up, lightly coming to rest against the wall of his chest.

His swift intake of breath was a sound of surprise— but not one of outrage.

"Which one?" she asked, still unable to believe that she, Isadora Dudley Peabody, was in the middle of this splendid garden, in the middle of this splendid moment, in the arms of this splendid man.

"What I want," he said, and the words sounded tense and strained. "Ask me what I want, Isadora."

"What do you want?"

"I'll only answer if you promise you'll believe me."

"If I—"

"Promise, Isadora. Say you'll trust my answer."

"I'll trust your answer."

He smiled, and once again she heard that silken chuckle that did such odd and unsettling things to her. "What I want," he said, "is to kiss you."

"Liar," she said automatically.

"You promised you'd believe me."

"Because I thought for once you'd tell me the truth."

"You know what your problem is?"

"You?"

"No. It's that you talk too damned much. I suppose I could swear on King James's Bible that I want to kiss you, but there's a better way to convince you."

The smoldering look in his eyes astonished her, held her mesmerized. "How is that?"

"Like this, love. Like this."

And then it happened. Slowly. Each passing second an endless heartbeat of time, and she experienced it all, reveled and immersed herself in it. The way he bent his head ever so slightly, for unlike most men, he was taller than she. The way his thumb skimmed lightly, searchingly, across the crest of her cheekbone then rode downward, brushing at a spot on the side of her throat that pulsed with a heat she had never felt before. The way his other hand at her waist drew her closer, tighter.

And then his lips. The lips she had watched, day after day, with increasing fascination and bafflement. The lips that had sneered at her, sworn at her, laughed and shouted and smiled at her. He didn't plaster her with his kiss; he merely tasted her, at first barely touching her mouth with his own.

Back and forth, slowly, subtly, he moved his head, sharing the merest hint of himself, the briefest brush of pressure. Overwhelmed by the sensations, she let her eyes drift shut and heard a strange, whimpering sound escape her. As of their own accord, her fists clenched into the fabric of his shirt.

Closer. She wanted to be closer. She wanted to taste more of him, to feel the pressure of his mouth on hers. But he simply kept brushing her lips, holding her gently as if she were fragile, breakable. The hand at her waist moved, a minor shift, barely noticeable, except that she felt his thumb graze the underside of her breast, could feel his touch even through the stiff buckram of her corset. She felt a surging and singing inside, things she had read about in the romantic novels she was not supposed to see until she was married, but read in secret anyway. And, oh, this was so much better. She wanted so much more than this moment, yet she was terrified that it might end.

She had an overwhelming urge to lean toward him, to press into his embrace, to crush her mouth against his. But she didn't dare. Didn't know how. Didn't trust him to accept her.

It was an act of supreme self-control, then, to hold herself rigid, unmoving, disbelieving.

And finally it was over. From the time he had begun to kiss her until the moment it ended, an eternity had passed. The world had changed color, tilted on its axis. Yet when Ryan Calhoun drew back from her and regarded her solemnly for several long moments, he looked exactly the same: handsome, relaxed, assured.

And she was a perfect mess inside.

"I won't apologize," he said easily, "although a gentleman would. I'm not sorry that happened." He stood, his lithe grace never more apparent, and helped her to her feet. She went like a marionette on a string, wooden and stiff, jerky in her movements.

"We'd best get inside. They'll want to hear all about the monkey."

"What monkey?" she asked stupidly.

Fourteen

O bed! O bed! Delicious bed!
That heaven upon earth to the weary head.

—Thomas Hood
(1841)

Ryan awoke the next day and stared for a long time at the plaster-and-timber ceiling of his large, airy room in the villa. "I still can't believe I did that," he said aloud, though there was no one to hear.

He had taken Isadora Peabody in his arms. He had kissed her.

In the past, flouting convention had been a way of life for him. But Isadora, milled like the straightest of spars by convention, made him understand that he was not immune to censure. That things he did could cause profound effects.

What fool notion had possessed him? It was not that he regretted kissing her—he simply didn't have the conscience for that. What he regretted was her reaction. She had been so startled, so vulnerable that he knew she was in danger of letting the kiss mean far too much to her.

This could signal a disaster. This could change everything between them, just when they had begun to move toward an accord. With Isadora, he had a relationship he'd never thought possible with a woman. He had a true friendship. Trust. Mutual respect. Equal footing. Delight in shared interests.

Perhaps she would even quit making those infernal reports to Abel.

He had probably destroyed it all by kissing her. So long as they were friends, he couldn't harm her. But if he dared to move into her heart, he would strip away all her defenses, open her to a hurt she didn't deserve. She was too fragile for a rogue like him.

He crushed his eyes shut against the glaring morning sunlight. Damn it.

Goddamn it all to hell.

There were girls aplenty for kissing. But there was only one Isadora.

He remembered her stiff posture, her shocked expression last night. She had been outraged in every cell of her body. He knew it. Could feel it emanating from her.

But when she had softened in his arms, when she had moistened her lips and timidly touched him, he'd forgotten who she was. Forgotten she was born and bred of the Beacon Hill elite. Forgotten she and her kind looked down on Southerners, particularly those who moved in the company of pirates and cutthroats. Forgotten that her heart belonged to Chad Easterbrook whether the upright bit of plant life deserved her or not.

Ryan of all people understood what it was like to want something you couldn't have. To want it with all your heart and soul. To want it with a passion that made nothing else matter. He should respect that in Isadora.

He got up and bathed in the cool water from the basin at the washstand, using a spicy scented soap, then cleaning his teeth with a tooth powder that tasted like anise. He thought of the long, laughing conversations they shared. The bickering and bantering. The quiet moments reading books. The satisfaction of taking a sounding on shipboard and finding that their figures agreed. That was the Isadora he wanted back. He had to return to the place they were before he had stepped over the line, to the friendship, the camaraderie, the respect.

But even as he thought it, he knew he would keep pushing her. He *liked* seeing her unbend, liked making her laugh, and hell, he liked seeing her get mad.

He was through pretending he was a gentleman. She knew better than that, anyway. She knew damned well that he was a groping mass of male desire. No more pretending, then. No more standing aside while she dreamed of Chad Easterbrook.

Ryan was moving in for a good time.

Isadora's nightmare began when she awoke. It started with a maid barely more than four feet tall. Scolding like a jungle parrot, she blustered into the room and started ordering Isadora around in a musical Brazilian patois.

"My name is Angelica. You can have your coffee and *churro* while I do your hair. And for the riding today, you may not wear that strange *norteamericano* gown. I have brought something much, much better...."

"What riding?" Isadora managed to ask. "I don't know how to ride."

"That is no matter. The *burro* knows what to do. All you have to do is sit. A monkey can sit."

"I am certainly not going to ride a jackass. Truly, I cannot—" Isadora almost choked on her fried bread. "What in heaven's name is that?"

Angelica laughed, her face jolly and appealing despite the sad state of her teeth. "It is your costume for riding."

"I won't do it. I won't put that on."

"Senhora Peabody, you are not going to insult your hostess by refusing, are you?"

"I'm afraid I shall have to."

"I'm afraid I cannot let you."

The argument went on, but the diminutive servant proved the stronger, and by eight o'clock Isadora stood in the courtyard, dubiously eyeing a sleepy looking burro. She felt utterly ridiculous—Angelica had made her put on a strange, wide-legged split skirt that barely covered her shins. "Like the *gauchos* wear," the maid had declared, buttoning the back of a loose white blouse.

She felt completely naked. Yet without her corset and longcloth petticoats, she detected a comfort and ease that was alien to her. Well, she thought. If Rose insisted on riding a mule for a bit this morning, she could oblige.

But it wasn't Rose who came out to greet her in the courtyard.

It was Ryan.

After all their days together on shipboard, Isadora told herself, she should be used to his startling handsomeness, but she wasn't. Freshly dressed in fitted dark breeches and a blousy white shirt, he looked more outrageously attractive than ever.

She couldn't help herself. She kept thinking of last

night. It changed everything. Last night he had kissed her—too intimately to be dismissed as a friendly gesture, too lightly to be construed as true passion.

His regrets had come almost instantly, she recalled. He'd hastened to return to the house, and the rest of the evening he'd studiously avoided her while regaling his aunt with tales of his adventures at sea.

Isadora had somehow managed to endure the evening by sitting stiffly, her back rigid, nodding when spoken to and pleading fatigue far earlier than she should have, then disappearing into her chamber. She would have been able to get through today if she didn't have to see Ryan. The longer she spent away from him, the more she could convince herself that their embrace had been a figment of her imagination.

But now she had to look him in the eye by the dazzling light of day. All the feelings he had stirred in her— the warmth, the yearning, the frustration, the ecstasy— had barely cooled and in fact heated anew when he came near.

She angled the flat brim of her straw hat over her eyes. "Was this your idea?"

"Good morning to you, too," he said cheerfully.

Clearly, the night before hadn't affected him at all. He was back to being the friendly, unconventional Ryan she'd known from the start.

"I don't ride, you know," she said.

"Before you boarded the *Swan,* you didn't sail, either," he replied.

"But there was a point to sailing. I have no idea what the point of riding an ass is."

"Ah, you'll see." He grinned and went over to one of the burros. "Do you know how to mount it?"

She felt a blush splotching her neck and cheeks. "How difficult can it be?"

"I'll hold its head and you get on." He reached for the bridle. The animal bit at him, large yellow teeth snapping loudly. Ryan pulled his hand out of harm's way. "This must be a female."

"You are so amusing."

He managed to hold the beast and she surprised herself by swinging easily into the saddle. The animal was small and short-legged, so that helped, and once settled astride, she understood completely why she had been made to wear the gaucho pants.

After they were both mounted, she looked across the courtyard at Ryan and burst out laughing.

"What?"

"Your noble steed," she said. "What a picture you make. I should call you Don Quixote."

"You are so amusing," he said, mimicking her tone. "Come, Sancho. Our quest begins."

"Our quest for what?"

"You'll see." He patted his saddlebag, then kicked his heels into the burro's flanks. The little animal trotted forward, and Isadora's mount followed.

She enjoyed the ride too much. She loved seeing the countryside from the back of a plodding burro. Everything passed with delicious slowness. They rode two abreast on the gravelly mountain pathways, winding downward toward the city. The hot, dry sun felt good. The hat brim shaded her face, but she could feel the brush of heat on her bare arms and the backs of her hands.

She and Ryan spoke little as they descended the steep road to the heart of Rio. Isadora kept thinking of the

way Ryan had touched her, holding her as if she were
something fragile and fine, something he didn't want to
hurt yet couldn't let go.

Then she remembered that this was Ryan Calhoun.
He had probably learned the seductive manner of embracing a woman from his countless lovers, and he'd
honed it to a fine art. He had, in fact, come from the
arms of another woman as if it didn't matter whose embrace he shared. She was making a fanciful moment out
to be too big an affair. They were together in a scented
garden, coaxing an exotic animal out into the light, and
the moment had been no more than that.

That's all it was. That's all it could ever be. That's
all she dared to want it to be.

"You're living inside your head, Isadora," Ryan
called to her.

"What do you mean by that?"

He swept one arm out to encompass the view of the
harbor, the sparkling waters and the distant mountains.
"I've brought you to paradise and you're scowling.
What are you thinking about that makes you scowl?"

She felt the rash of a new blush. "Nothing. This is a
different mode of travel for me, and I'm not used to it."

"Well, try enjoying the scenery, and the travel won't
bother you so much."

He was right, she discovered. Rio was endlessly fascinating, from the Fountain of the Laundresses with its
chattering servants and energetic water boys stationed at
the spigots to the fashionable rua do Ouvidor, where
mysterious, bejeweled *donas* went about in curtained lit-
ters.

They visited the ship and watched the discharging of
the cargo. Ryan's next task was to check the inventory

against that of the consignee, then come to a reckoning
of a price.

"We'll sail back with more specie than any other ship
in Boston Harbor," Ryan declared. "A hundred thousand pounds sterling."

From anyone else, she would have dismissed it as an
idle boast.

They tethered their mules at the edge of the vast, busy
marketplace. Lusty voiced vendors hawked their wares
from beneath gaily colored awnings. Some chanted
rhymes or banged wooden clappers to get attention.
Mounds of fruit, flowers, fish, cloth and every sort of
small ware cluttered the market square.

Ryan took her hand. Isadora felt a twinge of pleasure
but immediately denied it. He had grabbed hold of her
because the crowd surged around him. Nothing more.

"Let's shop," he said.

"For what?" Her gaze took in a veritable banquet of
sights and sounds—the fruit, the coffee and vegetables,
hammered metals from the mountain mines, jerked beef
and cod, ungainly sacks of beans and rice, brilliantly
dyed cloth and bamboo cages with exotic birds.

"For everything," Ryan declared.

She couldn't help herself. She laughed with delight.
No matter how exasperating he could be, Ryan Calhoun
made everything fun.

The hours sped by as they walked through the market.
They ate melons, letting the juice dribble down their
chins. They sent a special fifty-pound sack of coffee to
the *Swan* to take back to the Peabodys as a gift and
bought a silver samovar for Arabella's wedding gift.
They picked out silver filigree earrings for Lily and

Rose, a tortoiseshell comb for Fayette and a fancy cigar for Journey.

Ryan bought something else from the jeweler, but tucked the small box away before Isadora could see what it was. Doubtless a trinket for one of his lady friends, she thought with a stab of jealousy.

What a calamity it was, finding that she was jealous of harborside whores.

She thrust away the disgusting thought. She would not let it mar her day. If she must fix her hopes on a man, she should be thinking of Chad rather than allowing her attention to stray to such an inappropriate man as Ryan Calhoun. Chad had held her heart for so long. She would not turn her back on him for the sake of an inconstant, swaggering sea captain.

She knew better than to believe she meant anything to Ryan. She told herself to concentrate on her goal to be an asset to the company. She was too smart to open herself to heartache over Ryan Calhoun.

Having settled that issue in her mind, she hurried toward a brightly painted puppet theater. She laughed at the antics of a pair of marionettes, translating the silly story for Ryan.

"They fight like cats and dogs," she said, pointing to the papier-mâché man and woman bobbing before the crowd, "and they've both gone off to a masquerade *fantasia,* each determined to find a more worthy love. And each discovers an exotic stranger."

The crowd guffawed and clapped as the puppets danced.

"Let me guess," Ryan said. "When they take off the masks, they discover they've been in love with each other all along."

"Of course."

"Just like in real life," he said with a chuckle.

He put his hand on the small of her back in order to steer her toward more vendors' stalls. They perused pyramids of papayas and mangos. Her body responded to his light touch before her mind could deny it. She felt the warmth, the flush of pleasure, and by the time she realized what she was feeling, it was too late to stop herself from reacting.

He stopped at a display of carnival masks.

"No," she said, guessing his intent.

"Yes." He bought a handful of feathered-and-gilt masks and a colorful fringed shawl. "For the lady," he explained.

"I don't need it."

"Which is precisely why you must have it." And he looped the shawl around behind her, using it as a sling to draw her closer and closer to him. She thought she might die of embarrassment.

Instead, something unexpected happened. She started to enjoy the moment. The vendor and his friends laughed and clapped with delight. Isadora put her hands over her head and pantomimed the style of a flamenco dancer. Her hat fell back and trailed on its strings. Ryan held out the shawl like a matador's cape and she charged him, grabbing the fabric from his grasp and teasing him with it.

When their pantomime was finished, Ryan bowed deeply. He took Isadora's hand and presented her to the crowd like a showman at the circus. She laughed long and loud, quite unable to believe that she, Isadora Peabody of Beacon Hill, was playing a street performer in the middle of the Brazilian *mercado*.

They were leaving the marketplace when a handsome tilbury rolled to a halt in the street by the burros. A slender, dignified man of middle years stepped out.

"Captain Calhoun?"

"At your service," Ryan said.

"Your chief mate said I'd find you at the *mercado*. I am Maurício Ferraro."

Ryan broke into a grin. "My elusive consignee!"

"Congratulations on a most successful run."

"Congratulations on being the first to fill your warehouse with ice," Ryan said with a conspiratorial wink. "May I present Miss Isadora Peabody."

"Charmed." The dark, smiling Brazilian took her hand and held it to his lips with excessive courtesy. "I was hoping you would join me and my family for supper tomorrow. You and your delightful lady friend."

Isadora was so stunned to hear herself referred to in such terms that she barely heard Ryan say "Mighty obliged," barely felt him steer her toward the burros and help her mount. Was that why everyone liked her? Because Ryan had shown her favor?

She didn't know what surprised her more—that Senhor Ferraro thought her delightful or that he assumed she was Ryan's lady. The rest of the day passed in a delicious blur of activity. They took their time going back to the villa, stopping every so often to take in the arresting beauty of the exotic city. Everywhere Isadora looked, she saw new wonders, from the lush floral growth in every alley and garden to the jagged distant mountains with their smooth granite faces plunging into Guanabara Bay.

"Why are we stopping here?" she asked.

He tethered the burros. "It's Ipanema," he said. "One of the most famous beaches in the world."

Indeed it was a remarkable place, populated by bathers in all shapes, sizes and colors. Parents relaxed in hinged wooden chairs shaded by giant parasols while children dug in the sand or chased balls or each other.

As they walked, they sank into the sugar-white, sugar-fine sand. Ryan stopped at a bench and bade her sit.

"I want to walk on the beach," she protested.

"So you shall." Without asking for permission or explaining himself, he knelt in front of her, grabbed her left ankle and removed her shoe and stocking.

She would have shrieked in protest but she was too shocked. By the time she found her tongue, both her feet were bare.

"Why did you do that?"

Calmly he removed his own shoes and socks. "It's too hard to walk in the sand in shoes."

"It's indecent."

He parked their shoes on the bench. "You're not going to start that again. I won't allow it." He grabbed her hand and pulled her to her feet. "Let's walk."

She took three steps in the warm sand and stopped. "Oh, dear."

"Now what's wrong?"

She looked down at her shockingly bare feet, buried to the arches in silken sand. "This is the most sinfully delicious sensation I've ever felt."

He laughed. "Oh, love. You *have* led a sheltered life."

They walked on, passing Sugar Loaf Rock. Beyond the rock, they found a deserted spot where cliffs towered over the shore and the waves stole onto the beach. Without hesitation, Ryan led her directly into the surf.

"We mustn't," she said. "This is—"

"Don't squeak and squawk at me, Isadora," he said with excessive patience. "It's so tiresome when you do that."

The surf was creamy and sinuous as it rushed to the shore, swirling around their ankles. "It's warm," Isadora exclaimed, "and I was wrong."

"About what?"

"*This* is the most sinfully delicious sensation I've ever felt."

"No," he said, pulling her against him. In that one movement she felt the multiple pressures of his thigh against hers, hip to hip, chest to breast. "*You* are."

Fifteen

Oh Lord! If you but knew what a brimstone of a
creature I am behind all this beautiful amiability!

—Jane Welsh Carlyle
(1836)

"Why are you scowling at me so?" Isadora asked,
holding the running strap of the carriage.

Ryan deepened his scowl, peering at her in the dim
light of the coach lamp that shone through the window.
"I was wondering if Senhor Ferraro will believe my supper companion was the same laughing, carefree girl he
met at the marketplace yesterday."

"Not all men put such stock in a person's appearance," she said, shifting her gaze out the window.

Ryan had a devilish urge to grab her, muss her hair
and clothes, to make her sorry she'd attempted to crawl
back into her proper Bostonian shell. She wore the
black-and-brown dress he'd hated from the start, the
drab skirts belled out over multiple crinolines. She'd

scraped her hair away from her face, though he was pleased to see the wavy stray locks retained a golden vibrance imparted by weeks of exposure to sun and sea.

But far more alarming than her sober mode of dress was her attitude. She had once again adopted a cowed and apologetic demeanor, holding her shoulders hunched and her chin lowered almost to her chest. This was the way Isadora Peabody of Beacon Hill had presented herself to the world: as a woman who had absolutely no sense of her own worth.

"You look as if you're dressed for a funeral wake," he grumbled.

She turned from the window, let her gaze flick over him, taking in the yellow waistcoat and turquoise jacket. "You more than make up for my lack of color."

"Could you at least try not to look as if you're on the way to the gallows?"

"I am not fond of social engagements. I never have been. You should have come without me tonight."

Somewhere along the way, life had taught her that social engagements were painful. She had learned to gird herself for the ordeal like a soldier arming for battle. A tough corset and a servile attitude became her shield and her sword. Once again, she'd bitten her fingernails ragged, a habit he'd hoped she'd conquered on shipboard.

Why do you do this? he wanted to ask her. But he didn't. Criticizing her lack of poise was dangerous. Because as soon as he let himself worry about her, he'd start to care, and that could be deadly, could distract him from his cause. He needed to marshal all his reckless nerve in order to do what had to be done about Journey's wife.

The coach delivered them to a fashionable address in

the Botafogo section of Rio. Turning in from the broad brickwork lane lined by carabba trees, they passed through a massive gate of wrought iron. Family crests bearing ships and lions hung from the bars of the gate. The conveyance followed a cobbled circular drive with a lighted fountain in the center.

The Ferraros' home was a multilevel mansion lit by torches ensconced in the walls. A houseman, smiling hugely, conducted them into a salon decked in gauzy draperies and carved wooden screens, potted palms in the corners. Turkish divans and ottomans overflowed with large, soft cushions. The atmosphere of luxury and sensuality enclosed them like a seductive embrace.

Ryan looked at Isadora to see how she was taking it all in. She was biting her nails, he saw with a heated rush of annoyance. He put his hand on hers. "You have such a sweet mouth, Isadora," he whispered. "I can think of a much better purpose for it than nail biting."

She slapped his hands away. "I wish you wouldn't speak to me in such a suggestive manner."

"Why not?"

"It's...improper. No, it's worse than that. It's insincere."

"How so?"

"I say so."

"And you would know." He cupped her blushing cheek in the palm of his hand, lightly rubbing his thumb over her bottom lip, marveling at how soft it was, remembering how it had tasted when he'd kissed her. "You are no expert on men, Isadora. And you're especially no expert on *me*."

She jerked away, blinking fast as if on the verge of

tears. "Captain Calhoun, I am not well suited to teasing."

The stark, honest hurt in her expression bothered him. Although she had no idea about the depths of his interest in her, she was right about one thing. Unless he could offer her something more than flirtation, he should keep his distance. Except that the flirtation was so damned fun.

"After yesterday, I thought our friendship had progressed to a toleration of teasing."

"Yesterday was…yesterday." Isadora made a turn around the room, gingerly exploring the rich surroundings. "It's not much like Boston, is it?"

"Do you disapprove?"

"Heavens, no. It all looks so wonderfully comfortable. Quite decadent."

"And decadence meets with your approval?"

"Senhor Calhoun! Senhorita Peabody!" Ferraro bustled into the room. He wore an elegant coat and trousers made of fine black fabric with a red sash around his middle. "Welcome to our home!"

At his side stood a plump, smiling woman in a flowing pale dress. "May I present my wife, Amalia." Though she was well past middle age and clearly no raving beauty, Doña Amalia's dark eyes shone with affection for her husband and welcome for her guests. Her affable look drew Ryan in, and he found himself warming to her instantly.

"Welcome to Rio," she said, holding out both hands to Isadora.

Maurício cocked his head to one side. "You are looking very formal, senhorita." He winked. "And the two of you—are you affianced?"

"Absolutely not!" she burst out.

Ryan was offended by her vehemence.

"An idle question," Maurício said. "Come now. We will cure that with some food and wine!"

The four of them went in to a supper of melon and shellfish, sherried mushrooms, a salad of fruit and greens, beefsteak and stewed vegetables and *goiabada* made of guavas and sugar. An array of wines and cordials accompanied each course.

"I have heard much of Boston," Amalia said, sprinkling shredded manioc root on her husband's salad. "Your native city is a great center of learning, yes?"

"Indeed it is," Isadora replied. "People from Boston place a high premium on education."

"And scholarship has always been important in your family?"

"Oh, yes. Though never quite so important as..." She caught herself, flushed and looked down at her plate. "As other things," she finished vaguely.

Ryan had an idea that those "other things" had to do with being witty and entertaining at parties, snagging the proper husband and resembling a silver-gilt ornament on a rich man's arm. He took a deep drink of wine, scowling into his goblet.

"How did you enjoy your sightseeing yesterday, senhorita?" Ferraro asked.

"I found it all quite stunning. Your city is so incredibly rich in things to see and do."

"Then you must do it all," Amalia insisted.

"I wish I could, but that would take a lifetime." She glanced at Ryan. "We have only a short time here, isn't that so, Captain?"

"Sadly, yes," Ryan said.

"I wish I could spend longer," Isadora said.

The Ferraros beamed. "That is Rio. Though your home might be elsewhere, Rio takes your heart, always." They joined hands, and Ryan found the gesture oddly touching, for it was so open and unconscious.

What would it be like, he wondered, to have that? To have someone you could reach out and touch, knowing she'd always be there? To have someone who knew without asking how you liked your salad?

An old yearning tugged at him, a wish he'd had for many years. It was a simple wish, really. He wanted to share his life with someone the way the Ferraros shared theirs. In his travels, he'd seen wonders beyond imagining, he'd faced moments of danger and triumph, but it all added up to nothing because there was no one to tell about it, no one to listen to his hopes and fears and dreams.

Ryan set down his empty goblet. Damn. He'd had too much wine.

"You must miss the familiarity of your home," Amalia said, motioning for a servant to refill Ryan's cup.

"Not too much." Isadora ducked her head guiltily. "I mean no disloyalty, but my life in Boston was quite settled and predictable. I imagine I could be away for years and find everything unchanged upon my return."

Amalia laughed. "Surely your friends and family would not want to be deprived of you for too long."

A blush misted Isadora's cheeks. "How very flattering to think there are those who would miss me."

"Of course there would be. Perhaps even a special gentleman—"

"Dear heaven, no," Isadora said, almost in a panic.

Her hand went to her bosom as if her heart were trying to pound its way out of the cage.

Senhor Ferraro laughed with delight. "When a lady protests so vehemently, it is always because of a special gentleman."

Isadora shut her eyes and smiled ruefully. "I am so unforgivably predictable."

Their hosts shared a knowing look.

Ryan slammed back his wine. Chad Easterbrook again. What did she see in that vacant-headed epiphyte?

With their cheery conversation and their pride in Rio, the Ferraros eventually put Isadora at her ease. At the end of the meal, Ferraro got Ryan's attention. "We must go outside for our cigars. Amalia will not abide the odor in the house." He bent and kissed his wife's hand. "Can you do without us for a few moments?"

"Of course. We'll enjoy our coffee together," Amalia said.

Ryan followed his host onto a verandah bordered by an ornate plaster balustrade.

"We should have no trouble getting you a cargo for Boston," Maurício said. "You are days ahead of the winter fleet."

"Mr. Ferraro, I'm glad you brought up the cargo. I know this isn't in the consignment agreement, but I won't accept anything produced by slave labor."

The merchant gave a low whistle. "That leaves out a lot of the best coffee in the world."

Ryan nodded. "It almost ruined me on my last run to Havana, but I managed to find a tobacco and sugar factor who represented nonslave interests."

"I can help you," Ferraro said after a moment. "I know a number of growers who employ paid labor."

Through the window they could see the ladies sipping their coffee and chatting. Ferraro lit the cigars and studied them through the threads of smoke. He probably had no idea that he was grinning like a lovestruck idiot at his wife.

Ryan took a shallow puff of his cigar. "You're a lucky man," he said. "Life is sweet for you."

"God has seen fit to bless me," he agreed, smiling even more as Amalia tipped back her head to laugh at something Isadora said. "I have the most beautiful wife in the world."

The heartfelt declaration resonated strangely through Ryan. Amalia Ferraro wasn't slender. She wasn't young. Her features were not arranged in any particularly breathtaking fashion. But Ryan had no doubt that in Ferraro's eyes, she was a gift from heaven.

"You're a man who enjoys his blessings," he said.

"And you are not?"

"I'm a man who has obligations," Ryan admitted. "The blessings—I can always hope—will follow."

Ferraro nodded. "That is something an impatient young man would say."

"You don't agree?"

Ferraro studied the ladies, Amalia in her flowing white and Isadora in her stiff black-and-brown dress. "What you, like most impatient young men, fail to understand is that sometimes the sweetest blessing of all is right before your eyes."

Isadora decided that Christmas in the tropics was vastly preferable to Christmas in Boston. The days lead- ing up to the feast day were warm and balmy, the people cheerful as they went about their chores and visits. In

Boston there would be caroling parties and sleigh rides and fevered preparations, and aside from seeing Chad at these functions, she gladly did without them.

Rose insisted that there was not much in the way of gift-giving in her household. On Three Kings Day people exchanged trinkets and fruits and nuts, perhaps a round of visits with neighbors and relatives and a parade of sail in the harbor.

Isadora felt an odd calm settle over her as she drifted through the days at Villa do Cielo. Ryan stayed busy with matters of commerce, seeing to the discharge and sale of his cargo and securing goods for the run back to Boston. Though she rarely saw him, she caught herself wondering about him often.

You are no expert on men, Isadora. And you're especially no expert on me. He had all but said she didn't know him, couldn't even begin to know him. She knew she should be ashamed of her curiosity about him. Yet when she did think of Ryan, she didn't experience the cold sweat and knotted stomach that thoughts of Chad inspired in her. Instead she felt...comfortable. Alive. And unafraid that the next step she took, the next word she uttered, would lead to disaster.

Very slowly she was coming to realize what was happening between her and Ryan.

Friendship.

The thought filled her heart with lightness. She had never had a friend before. Never, not once in her life. When she was small, she'd had Aunt Button. Her loving aunt had been a gift from heaven, but not specifically a friend. Isadora had made the acquaintance of other scholars at Mount Holyoke Seminary, but none had held out the hand of friendship. By the time she returned home to Beacon Hill, her favorite company consisted of books and political tracts and pamphlets.

Now she had a friend. What a singular notion. What a wonderful notion. She did not quite know what to do with the thought.

Every once in awhile, she was reminded that when Ryan touched her, when he looked at her in a certain way, when he spoke in a low whisper into her ear, she felt something deeper than friendship. She dwelled far too long on the day they had gone sightseeing in Rio. She remembered too clearly his kiss in the darkened garden, and the moment on the beach when he had embraced her. They had come together so naturally, as if embracing were the next logical step along the road they were traveling together.

Fortunately, reason had quickly returned. She had pulled away, he had turned away and the moment had ended without a lot of terrible awkwardness. She'd vowed afterward to avoid such encounters in the future. Ryan was her one true friend. She would not ruin that with impossible dreams of something that could never be.

Almost as a penance for her wayward thoughts, she had written Chad another long and copiously descriptive letter. She pictured him reading the missive she had labored over. She hoped her verbal sketch of the marionette show in the marketplace would coax a smile from him, that he would be moved by her description of a newborn babe left on the wheel at the Santa Casa de la Misericòrdia, that he would share her wonder at the fabulous hanging gardens around Rose's villa.

Along with the letter, she included a terse report to Abel about Ryan's progress with the cargo. She felt guilty doing so, but she had promised Abel. At least Ryan's business acumen was above reproach. She said so with honesty—and a touch of pride.

On New Year's Eve, Rose would host an annual masked ball. For two days beforehand, the tantalizing fragrances of roasting meat and baking bread drifted through the house. A great pavilion went up where the samba band would play and extra servants arrived from the village of Tijuca.

Isadora worked in the kitchen with Lily, Rose and some of the maids, fashioning a centerpiece of tiny confections of glazed cherries and pineapple. She'd never sat with housemaids and done menial work, but she loved the feminine chatter and the giggles, the beauty of the candied centerpiece they were creating, piece by lovely piece, taking shape as the women's conversation swirled around the long table of scrubbed pine.

"You must borrow one of my gowns from years past," Rose said to her sister and Isadora. "Each year, I order one specially made, so you'll have plenty to choose from."

Isadora bit her lip, remembering the dancing parties and soirees she had endured in Boston. How painful they were. These two beautiful sisters had no idea what it was like to stand in the shadows and overhear people discussing your complete failure in the marriage market. They had no idea what it was like to watch the man you love, silently praying he'd ask for a dance and then, when he didn't ask, to take yourself and your tears and your broken dreams to bed with you.

"I confess I've never been fond of parties," she forced herself to admit.

Lily and Rose exchanged a glance. "You've never

been fond of Boston parties,'' Lily corrected her. ''This will be different.''

Rose nodded vigorously. ''Everything in Rio is different.''

Isadora couldn't help smiling at her self-appointed *dueñas* who simply refused to look at her and see what she was. Instead they saw a pleasant companion, a fellow traveler, another pair of hands to work on the decorations. Not an ungainly, unmarriageable spinster.

''That's what I love about Rio,'' she said.

''Are you going to object to every layer,'' Lily demanded, ''or will you hush up and let us work?''

''But this costume's so...so...indecent,'' Isadora protested, fingering the thin silk of the tiered gypsy skirt Lily and Rose had put on her.

Rose let loose with a stream of dismissive laughter. ''My dear, you are in Rio, it is New Year's Eve and you're going to the masque in costume. You really have no choice.''

''Where are your scissors?'' Lily asked. ''I need to trim this ribbon.'' She looked around the room. ''Fayette is so much better at dressmaking than I. Where *is* the girl? She's been mooning about and wandering off for days.''

''Then you and I will make do,'' Rose said happily.

Isadora bit her lip. She had to force her gaze to stay level when she wanted to keep looking down to see that yes, it really was her in this full, tiered skirt of a color so brilliant she felt like one of the parrots in the jungle beyond the villa. Ankles bare and her feet strapped into sandals. A loose, scoop-necked blouse that showed a shocking inch of cleavage. Hair in a wild tumble, no combs or irons holding it in place.

"I'll be a laughingstock," she whispered.

Lily stepped in front of her, putting her hands on Isadora's shoulders. "Honey, they'll laugh only if you let them."

"I don't know what you mean."

"It's all to do with the way you carry yourself, the way you face the world." She reached around Isadora and tied on a black silk half mask. "Everything's an illusion. You're a gypsy woman, not Isadora Peabody. You're mysterious and alluring. Try swaying your hips, like so...."

"*Sway my hips?*" Isadora squawked.

And yet, with Rose on one side and Lily on the other, she followed their lead, feeling silly, then feeling nothing like Isadora. They were right, she conceded. Illusion was easy. Far easier than being herself.

"I must have been a gaucho in another life," Ryan declared, looking down in admiration at his flamboyant costume. "The women will love it."

Journey eyed the vermilion sash and the tight black knee breeches with the silver studs down the side seams. "Impressive. Especially when you add the hat." He tossed Ryan a flat-brimmed black hat sporting a scarlet plume. Ryan donned his half mask of black silk. "No one will ever recognize me now."

"Yes, there must be dozens of red-haired gauchos with a fondness for garish dress."

"Am I really garish?" Ryan asked, smoothing the eye-smarting sash.

"You are."

"Offensively so?"

Journey cracked a rare smile. "No, honey. I reckon you like the attention."

Ryan took a length of black silk and wound it around his head, pirate style, tucking away his bright coppery hair, then replacing the mask and hat. "And what will your costume be?"

Journey hesitated. Then he said, "I'll be going as a phantom. I'll be practically invisible."

Ryan's heart lurched, though he said nothing. Since the moment Journey had been ripped from his wife's arms, a vital part of him had been missing. Even while laboring over his navigation tables or caught up in the teeth of a storm at sea, he wasn't all there. Some part of him—the part that was laughter and ease and warmth— lay elsewhere. In Virginia. Toiling in the overheated kitchens of a white man's plantation.

As always, the thought made Ryan furious. "Soon, my friend," he vowed.

"What's that?"

"Soon. We'll get to Virginia soon."

Journey nodded. His face remained impassive, though his shoulders tensed. "Looks like we'll be ready to weigh anchor in a week. Ferraro must've liked you—he sold you an extra ton of coffee beans at a good price."

"It was Isadora he liked. We're going to set another record with this trip. Richest voyage on the Rio run."

Journey let out a long, cautious breath. "Price of a slave in Virginia hit an all-time high, according to the papers that Maine skipper brought from Savannah."

The words sounded strained and forced, and why not? Ryan wondered. He nearly choked on them himself. "I expect I'll negotiate a price we can live with."

Journey looked dubious. "And if you can't?"

"There's enough specie in the *Swan*'s safe hold to buy a whole army." Ryan felt tainted saying it. He was not a good man. He never had been, though he'd never stolen from another, never even considered it. But for the sake of getting Journey's wife and children to freedom, he would cross that line if need be.

"It's mighty risky, Ryan." Journey gave him another rare smile. "But when have we ever turned away from a risk?"

The coiled tension inside Ryan unwound a little. "Certainly not tonight. Come on, my friend. Let's go dancing."

Sixteen

To be ignorant of one's ignorance is the malady
of the ignorant.

—Amos Bronson Alcott,
"Table Talk"

As Ryan stepped onto the patio, he heard a chorus of
female screams. Perhaps Journey had been right, he reflected. Perhaps the color combinations of his costume
were a bit too...vivid.

The music stopped and the crowd fell back. Instantly
Ryan understood that the commotion was not for him.
A masked horseman rode into their midst upon a skittish
Andalusian mount. Laughing dangerously, he bore down
on a woman dressed in silver-and-gold skirts. She
screeched and ran from him—but not too quickly.

Lily rushed over to Ryan and clutched at his arm.
"That's Fayette."

"I know, Mama."

"I think you should do something."

"Why? That's Edison Carneros."

"Who? Oh, that lecherous character from the water-front."

"He's a good man, Mama." Ryan smiled down at her. She wore the tall comb-and-lace *mantilla* of a Spanish noblewoman and, as always, looked quite beautiful.

"Then why is he riding down my maid as if she's a fox to be hunted?"

"It must be love." Ryan couldn't suppress a grin. More than once he had observed Fayette and Edison meeting at the waterfront, disappearing into Carneros's office and then emerging much later with stars in their eyes and their clothing suspiciously mussed.

Fayette looked at Lily over her shoulder and hesitated. Carneros reached down and grasped her by the arm. She screeched again, though musical laughter underlay her alarm. Someone from the crowd gave her bare foot a boost, and she was heaved across the saddle of Edison's horse.

"Dear God, he's riding off with her!" Lily exclaimed.

"Looks that way."

As the romantic pair galloped out of the courtyard into the starry night, Ryan watched after them. Some of the ladies in the crowd waved lace-edged handkerchiefs, and the band started playing again.

"It's a...a carnival prank, isn't it?" Lily asked. "I mean, Rose tells me these things happen, all in the spirit of fun."

"I imagine they'll have fun, Mama."

She fell silent for several moments. The tinny melody of the band took over. Then she turned to him, her eyes unnaturally bright with an understanding he knew she wasn't ready to voice. "You're the one who should be having fun. Have I ever told you, son, that you are the most handsome man on earth?''

He laughed. ''I think I'd rather be the wisest. Maybe the richest.''

''Wisdom and riches. Your father had both. Yet he died miserable.''

Ryan blinked. This was the first time she had ever spoken so candidly of her marriage. ''Why do you say that?''

''Because even at the end, he didn't give in to the one thing that could have saved him.'' She sighed, staring off into the night, no doubt seeing a past that was invisible to Ryan. ''He should have taken the love I offered, but he never did, Ryan. Not ever.'' She waved a hand impatiently. ''How I do go on. It's the eve of a new year!''

The smile she gave him echoed the softness of the nights of his youth, when she used to sit by his bed and sing to him and Journey until they drifted, on the wings of her sweet voice, off to sleep. It never occurred to her that there was anything wrong with both boys sharing a bed, but only one having the right to grow up free. He hadn't known the truth then, but he realized it now. She considered the slaves her family. She simply hadn't known that they might want the freedom to choose.

He took her arm and escorted her onto the dance floor.

''Oh, don't dance with your old mother.'' She shooed him away, regal as she regained command of herself. ''There are too many wonderful girls waiting for you.''

Isadora couldn't quite understand how she had come to be here, in this airy patio, amid silky trumpet music and exotic food smells, dressed in something that felt as insubstantial as a nightgown.

Indeed, the moment seemed to belong to another person. It was as if the spirit of Rio had invaded her blood and bones, possessed her, transformed Isadora Dudley Peabody into someone completely different. A fanciful notion, but strangely accurate.

Though in truth it had been two lovely, relentless sisters who had possessed her.

Help me, she prayed silently, looking down at her scandalous gypsy costume. *This is surely a sin.*

Yet a part of her stood aside and observed that other ladies—perfectly proper wives of foreign ship's captains and coffee planters and politicians and Portuguese ministers—were garbed even more festively. And not only were they dancing and clapping to the music—they seemed to be enjoying it.

It struck Isadora that, despite the gypsy dress she wore, she occupied much the same position tonight as she did at the dancing parties and soirées her parents held in Boston. She stood on the side of the assembly, invisible, watching other people have a good time.

Across the open-air patio, she saw a broad-shouldered man slip from the shadows, stepping into a dazzle of colored light cast by an orange paper lantern.

Her breath caught. *Ryan.*

But Ryan as she had never seen him before. From the very first she had been startled by his flawless male beauty, though a certain careless flamboyance had kept him to a human level. As she grew to know him, she no longer dwelled upon his physical attributes, but came to enjoy the person he was.

Now the carelessness had given way to perfection. He

had dressed for the masquerade in tight black leather breeches with silver-studded outer seams, tucked into tall boots. A wide-sleeved red shirt gathered at the wrists, a half mask of black silk, an outrageous plumed hat and a slim, lethal-looking dress sword swinging at his side completed the costume.

He was the storybook cavalier who had performed feats of derring-do in the novels that used to keep her loneliness at bay. He was the bold hero whose sword-fights, described in fireside tales, had given her chills. He was every perfect fantasy she tried so hard not to dream about—but dreamed, anyway.

Heavens be, this was Ryan, she told herself, trying to quell the uncomfortable fluttering in her stomach. Ryan, who teased and gave commands and laughed in order to cover the strange darkness in his soul. Ryan, who strode across the patio, magnificently oblivious to the raft of beautiful girls who followed in his wake.

He went directly to the neighboring *patrao*'s daughter and bent gracefully over her lacy-gloved hand.

Isadora released an audible sigh as she watched him lead the giggling young woman out onto the tiled dance-floor, leaving behind a logjam of swooning ladies. She felt a peculiar agony in her heart. This was different from the ache of being ignored by Chad. *That* throbbed with the pain of futility, but the hurt of wanting Ryan was the hurt of a possibility being taken away.

Fanning herself with the painted fan that hung from a cord around her waist, she pressed herself against the wall to watch. Like a skilled physician, she attempted to discover the true nature of her ailment. Seeing Ryan like this—so handsome, so romantic—hurt her. Why?

Because she missed Chad, perhaps. Ryan revived all

her longing for the man she had wanted for years. He placed her squarely in the path of heartbreak again. Had she learned nothing from being trampled by a handsome man?

She resolved to stand aloof and try to enjoy the evening. The ache in her heart melted into a dull throb that was almost bearable when combined with the rhythmic thump of the music and the sinuous melody of the horns. Isadora did what she did best—she became invisible, retreated into her realm of the mind, with a wall of glass between herself and the real world, a safe place where she could watch unobserved.

Ryan danced with girl after girl, each one prettier than the last, prettier than Isadora's sisters, prettier than Lydia Haven. Isadora leaned against a vine-draped column, wondering what Chad was doing right now, wondering what Chad would look like in studded trousers of oiled leather that gleamed in the multicolored light.

And then the unthinkable happened. The dance ended and Ryan headed in her direction.

"Oh, no," she said, the words coming too easily. "I shan't fall into that trap again." She recalled the awful moment with Chad in Boston when she had been so certain he wanted to dance with her but all he really wanted was to send her on a fool's errand.

Ryan bowed before her, sweeping off the plumed hat. "May I have this dance, *senhorita?*"

"No," she said—too quickly.

He covered his heart with the hat. "You wound me to the quick. Why will you not dance with me?"

"Why do you care?"

"Because," he said with measured patience, "it's what people do at dancing parties."

"It's not what *I* do." Isadora drew herself up with exaggerated dignity. She'd rather be a wallflower than a spectacle. But she wanted to accept. She really did.

He stood silent for a moment. His gaze drifted from her face to her feet strapped into sandals. "Isadora Peabody, as I live and breathe."

"This is supposed to be a masquerade. I'm supposed to be a mystery lady."

"Oh, sugar-pie, you are that," he said gallantly. "The Isadora Peabody I know would never show her ankles like a sailor on shore leave."

"I'm not—that is, Isadora is not showing her ankles like a sailor on shore leave."

"But the mystery lady is."

She couldn't help herself. She giggled. *Giggled.* Isadora was quite certain she had never giggled before. "Perhaps," she admitted.

"And perhaps, being so mysterious, she would take a stroll with me in the garden."

Remembering what had happened during their last garden stroll, Isadora hesitated.

Ryan held out his hand. "Come with me, my mystery lady."

She got over her hesitation. Being in costume shielded her from the rigors of everyday propriety. She could be anyone she wanted tonight. A gypsy. A flamenco dancer. A pirate's lady.

A forbidden thrill shot up her spine as she took his hand.

"So I wonder," he said, leading her out between the colonnades, "why Isadora has avoided tonight's festivities."

"She's never been good at them," Isadora said.

"She's never been fond of standing at the edge of a dance floor and wishing she were up in her chamber reading a good book."

"Why does she always stand at the edge?"

"Because no one has ever brought her into the circle."

"The circle?"

"The charmed circle. It's an imaginary place, but it's very real, I assure you."

His hand, quite naturally, touched the nape of her neck beneath the heavy waves of her hair, rubbing her, making her feel strangely languorous. "Describe this place to me."

"Well, it is full of light and beauty and laughter." She leaned her head back a little, enjoying the tender massage of his hand on her neck.

"And Isadora has never been invited to this mythical place."

"Of course not." They came to a stone rampart overlooking Guanabara. The distant winking lights draped the bay like a necklace of luminous diamonds.

"Why not?" her cavalier asked, lowering his hand to the small of her back.

"Because she doesn't belong there."

"In whose opinion?"

"Not in anyone's opinion." She stared out at the stars mirrored in the water. "It's a fact, the way the world is, and it cannot be changed." Being behind the half mask gave her the courage of anonymity, false though it was. "She is awkward and socially gauche. Why would anyone in the charmed circle find me—er, find Isadora—pretty or amusing?"

She heard the hiss of his indrawn breath and dared to

look up into his eyes. Framed by the mask and gleaming with reflected light from the harbor, his regard appeared fierce. His fist gripped her upper arm, startling her.

"Because you are."

The conviction in his voice caught her, but she made herself laugh a gypsy's laugh. "You are too gallant for your own good, my cavalier. Isadora knows exactly who and what she is. After her adventures at sea, all her respectability will be gone. She has chapped skin and chopped-off hair. Her clothes don't fit properly anymore. She seems to be slowly sinking into a shocking state of nature."

He laughed, too, though the anger still churned in his eyes. Very deliberately, he put his hands on her shoulders and turned her to face him. His touch felt different—invasive, intimate, slightly dangerous. "Isadora is in big trouble, then."

In defiance of the balmy tropical night, a shiver touched the base of her spine. "Why do you say that?"

"Because she has a lot to learn." He took a step toward her, gripping her tighter.

She brought her hands up between them and fluttered her fan, beginning to feel amazingly natural in the role of coquette. "And who is going to teach her?"

"A famous cavalier." Before Isadora knew what was happening, he caught her in his embrace. "First, the dancing!"

"I don't dance," she blurted.

"But I do." With a whoop of sheer delight, he swept her around the open rampart in time with the sensual, percussive samba music that drifted from the patio. He wrapped his arm around her waist, hugging her so that she could feel his hips against hers. He led her in a circle, holding her so snugly that she had no choice but to follow the sweeping motion. These were dance steps that would horrify Beacon Hill society. Steps that should have made Isadora stumble clumsily, yet they didn't. She danced with abandon, a cavalier's lady who was fascinating and graceful and at ease—everything Isadora Dudley Peabody was not.

The melody ended and her brash cavalier brought her to sit upon the stone rampart overlooking Guanabara Bay.

"It's like a dream," she said, gazing out across the silver-studded black velvet view.

"Yes, it is," he agreed, but he was looking at her, not at the view.

For some reason that struck her as amusing and she laughed lightly, merrily, as if laughter were something she often did.

And in fact she did, when she was with Ryan.

No, not Ryan. She must not let herself think of him by name.

"Isadora," he began, clearly unaware of her game.

She shushed him immediately, still laughing, boldly pressing her fingers to his lips. She nearly stopped laughing when she touched his lips, for they felt firm and slightly moist and feeling them created a strange flood of disturbing warmth inside her.

"Isadora is not here."

He captured her hand, took it away from his mouth. "She's not?"

"No. And you must not use her name."

"Why not?"

"Because..." How could she explain it? "Because that would make the night real."

"And you don't want it to be real?"

She thought of the things in her life that were real—her family, the people she associated with in Boston, people who barely acknowledged her existence. "No," she said earnestly. "Not tonight. At the end of this voyage, I shall soon enough face what is real."

"You mean Isadora will face it," he corrected her.

"Yes."

"And what is real to Isadora?"

She paused, thinking. "The idea that she will serve her parents in their old age. And the rather pleasant prospect of helping to raise her nieces and nephews because her sisters are such good breeders. She will read great books and she'll be a faithful letter writer, though she will write many more letters than she will ever receive. But that's all right, for the reading and writing will fill her days. She has accepted the idea that she will never know passion, for no one feels passionate about Isadora—"

"What?"

"Passion. She'll never know it." She smiled, pleased that he had caught on. She had expected cynical teasing from him, but he kept surprising her. "So that is why you must keep reality at bay. You must let the night be magical."

He chuckled and squeezed his hand. "Sugar, don't you know?"

"Know what?"

"Every night is magical."

She laughed softly, loving the easy feel of it, loving the breeze through her hair and the way his loose shirt blew against his chest, outlining its shape. The sweetness of the moment washed through her, loosening her, warming her.

"You are never serious," she said.

"It's not permitted for a cavalier to be serious."

"What about Captain Calhoun?" she ventured. "Is *he* ever serious?"

"Only when it comes to serious matters."

"What sort of serious matters?"

"Matters of the heart," he said, lifting her hand and pressing it to his chest. "Matters of passion." With an earnestness she'd never seen in him before, he said, "Suppose I told you I want a certain young lady of Boston."

She took her hand away from his heart. He meant her? No, impossible. She forced her mind to consider the more reasonable possibilities. Lydia Haven, the beauty of Beacon Hill. Her sister Arabella, who was still desired even though she was engaged. A society belle, perhaps, or one of the women from the docks.

"Then why have you not courted her?" she inquired, trying to keep her humor up.

"She seemed too chilly and self-contained and far too intelligent to take a fellow like me seriously. And of course, she yearns for someone else altogether."

She narrowed her eyes. "Perhaps your Boston lady's coldness is a shield against getting hurt."

"Then I wish like hell she'd lower her defenses, for I would never hurt her."

"You wouldn't?" Her question came out as a whisper because suddenly she *knew*. It was insane, but his Boston lady was...

"Never."

"Then I wonder...what she is afraid of."

He moved closer to her on the stone rampart. "Take off the mask," he said.

"I'd rather not."

"I'd rather you did." He removed it and set it aside. The scented night breeze touched her face where the mask had been. "Why are you doing this?"

"Because I want to know exactly who you are when I kiss you."

Stunned, she could do nothing but sit and watch him remove his own half mask of black silk. And then he began.

It was not the sort of kiss he had given her before, the sweetly spontaneous one in the garden. Nor was it the kind of kiss she had always envisioned, aflame with heated passion. Instead he was careful, deliberate, almost clinical. He lifted a tendril of her hair that had drifted across her cheek and tucked it behind her ear. Then he took her face between both hands, skimming the pad of his thumb along her lower lip as if to prepare it for the touch of his mouth. One of his hands dropped, fingers playing over her throat and collarbone, so indecently exposed by the daring blouse. With an assurance Isadora could not possibly imagine ever feeling, he lowered the hand and let it curve around behind her so that he was embracing her, holding her close, their bodies touching, their lips getting closer and closer.

She made a feeble attempt to stop him, to stop the intimacy and the terrible overwhelming emotions welling up from a place inside her she had never explored until this moment. But she didn't want to stop him, not really. He was the most beautiful man in the world; she was plain Isadora Peabody, and she might never again get the chance to kiss someone like him.

Aching with the bleakness of that thought, which mingled painfully with her yearning, she closed her eyes.

And he kissed them. Her eyelids.

She was amazed.

And then he kissed her cheek and her temple and the side of her nose. And behind her left ear and—heavens be—her neck where a pulse leaped so frantically she feared she might swoon.

"You look..." he whispered, still kissing her there, up and down, oh so gently.

"Yes?" she prompted in a hoarse, alien voice. Dear God, maybe a miracle had occurred. Maybe he was going to say she looked pretty.

"You look...as if you're about to face a firing squad."

"Oh..." she said weakly, opening her eyes a little. "I'm sorry. I didn't mean—"

"Don't apologize. Just—if you possibly can—try to seem as if you're enjoying this."

"But I am," she said with great urgency. "Truly. I simply...this is a new activity for me and I don't quite know how to behave."

"What I'd like," he said wickedly, "is for you to *mis*behave."

"I'm certain I've been doing that ever since I set foot on your ship," she said, not even half joking.

"Then it's a start," he whispered, leaning close again. "It's a start."

And he began kissing her again, his leisurely exploration so maddening and frustrating she nearly screamed, for he seemed to be touching and kissing all of her except the parts that needed him the most. She bit her tongue to keep from telling him that. It would be too forward, too humiliating.

Too pathetic.

But then, his gently questing mouth strayed upward along her throat, and—almost by accident—she dropped her chin a little, and their lips met.

And the night changed color before her ecstatically closed eyes.

Ye powers, but his kiss felt good. He tasted of rum and sweet juice and some other ineffable flavor. His mouth—the beautiful mouth she had been caught staring at so many times—brushed hers and then increased its pressure and she was astonished at the soft texture of it, the lyrical shape and the way it fit perfectly against hers. She was so startled by the sensations flooding her that she let her jaw go slack, and then something even more astonishing occurred. His tongue slipped into her mouth.

She was certain it had to be an accident; surely it was an unnatural sin to do this…but…she liked it.

She would suffer eternal damnation for this; of that she had no doubt. But she liked it. She *loved* it. The sinuous slide of his tongue, in and then out, then back in when she surged involuntarily against him, needing and wanting more than she had ever dared to need or want before. Certain places on her body flared to life as if a torch had been touched to them—the tips of her breasts, unbound for the first time in her life. Between her legs in a spot whose existence she had trained herself to deny utterly. The pit of her stomach in which was born a fire that raged beyond quenching.

And then, far too quickly, it was over. He moved his hands to cup her shoulders, and drew back to look at her. "There," he said. "No worse than a firing squad, was it?"

She felt dazed, disoriented, as if she had awakened in a strange place. She blinked. "I wouldn't know. I've never faced a firing squad before."

"Then you'll have to trust me," he said with gentle laughter in his voice. "Poor you."

"Yes," she whispered, filled with the torpor and wistfulness of an awakening dreamer. "Poor me."

Seventeen

❧❧❧

Oh this is the place to live—a thought of winter
would never enter one's head.

—Diary of Susan Hathorn,
a sea captain's wife.
(1855)

Isadora awoke with a smile on her face and the knowledge that she had slept indecently late. Judging by the intense dazzle of sunlight on the plaster wall, it was pressing high noon.

The smile lingered. She knew she should feel guilty, for no one on Beacon Hill, or probably in Boston, or the entire United States for that matter, ever slept this late unless they were ill. Yet Isadora had no more viable excuse than the fact that she had been dancing with a man on a rampart at midnight, and soon after that she had kissed him.

A delicious shiver passed through her body, tingling unbearably until she grew restive and flushed with her thoughts. She got up and went to the washstand to bathe in the cool spring water, but the thoughts wouldn't leave her alone.

Heavens be. She—Isadora Dudley Peabody—had kissed a man last night.

It was not just any man. It was not just any kiss.

Ryan Calhoun. The most interesting, compelling person she had ever met. The only person who had ever tried to be her friend. But was he trying to be more than that?

She denied it instantly, her practical nature restoring itself. He had pursued her last night, had taken her to a private place and danced with her because they had been at a masquerade. A party where nothing was as it seemed.

In a way, the moments with Ryan were even less real than a dream. Last night stood apart from the rest of her life, glistening with the elusive light of promise and teasing her with the possibility of what might have been.

Trying to remember the kiss was like trying to repossess a wonderful dream after blazing wakefulness had intruded. She could recall what happened, but she could not recapture the magic. Each time she came close to reliving the sensation of his soft lips opening over hers, his nimble fingers skimming down her back, she became lost in a fog of embarrassment and desire that left her flushed and confused.

"I mustn't think of it," she told herself stoutly, scraping her hair into a pathetic topknot. The short locks wouldn't stay put, so she stabbed in more pins. She dressed herself in her familiar corset and berry-brown day dress, frowning at the way the usually crisp fabric hung in limp, pathetic folds.

No matter, she told herself. She had never been vain. She'd never had anything to be vain about. Particularly not now, with her inexpertly shorn hair and her face bleary and wan from staying up too late and dreaming too much the night before.

By the time she stepped out of her chamber into the colonnaded walkway, she felt as gauche and uncertain as she ever had at a Boston dancing party.

Ye powers. What on earth would she say to him?

She was spared from the immediate decision by Ryan himself. She had no sooner taken her place at the breakfast table than he came staggering into the *sala,* his hair badly combed and the contours of his face blurred by a growth of beard.

"Oh," he mumbled, his voice gravelly. "You're up."

She said nothing. He probably thought she was stunned speechless by the brilliance of his observation.

"Charming," his mother said, coming into the room with Rose at her side. Two servants arrived to pour the coffee and lay out platters of sweet bread and sliced fruit.

Ryan grunted rudely.

Isadora could scarcely believe this was the same man as the dashing gaucho who had romanced her last night. He added several spoonfuls of sugar to his *caffe com leche.* She preferred hers bitter. He dug into the chunks of fresh fruit and brioches; she picked at hers. The heat and humidity of the tropics had reduced her appetite dramatically. The one happy effect of the climate was that she hadn't been bothered by her persistent grippe and sneezing in many weeks.

As they ate, Lily kept glancing anxiously at the door. Each time a servant walked in, she froze, then relaxed.

"She's not coming back, Mother," Ryan said with quiet assurance.

"Did Fayette go somewhere?" Isadora asked.

Lily pressed her lips together as if keeping in a sob. Rose nodded gravely. "Last night she ran off with Edison Carneros."

Lily's chin quivered, but she looked directly at Isadora as she said, "I thought it was a prank, but I fear Fayette claimed her freedom last night."

"They probably went to settle at one of the *quilombos,* where fugitives go," Rose explained. "They're rough settlements, but that's generally where runaways hide."

"It's not the end of the world as you know it, Mama." Ryan sipped his coffee, then with more compassion, added, "He'll be good to her."

"She's my maid. She's always been my maid. Whatever shall I do?"

"You'll manage, Mama. You always do."

"I'm worried about Fayette. She has no idea what life is like."

"She was a slave, Mama. And you were a slave owner. *That* was what life was like for her. By running off with Edison, she freed you both. Don't you understand that?"

Lily's face paled to chalk white. "How dare you?"

"Somebody in this family had better dare. You've managed to wander through life without even saying the word *slave*. Without even thinking it. Servants, you call them. Maids. Field hands. Laundresses. But they were slaves. Property. Chattel. You owned them, body and soul."

"Ryan, what's happened to you? When did you become so harsh?"

"What's harsh, Mother, is the lash of a slave owner's whip."

Tears filled her eyes. "My maid has never felt the touch of a whip. I love Fayette."

"Then let her go, Mama. That's the only way to love her."

The tears overflowed then, coursing down her cheeks as her shoulders shook. "I'm so frightened. Everything's changing so fast."

"Some changes are long past due." Ryan found a handkerchief and Lily dried her cheeks with meticulous care.

Isadora blinked, astonished and elated. "I know you shall miss her, Lily. We all will. But it's for the best."

Lily took a nervous sip of her coffee. "A noble thought, but naive. Fayette was better off with me. She claimed to love Edison, but love can't fill an empty belly, nor keep the world at bay. The *quilombos* are horrid places. One of the housemaids told me that a runaway is in danger from the police, as well as from other fugitives."

"Can the slave patrols arrest her?" Isadora asked anxiously. The Fugitive Slave Law, that legislative abomination, had been in force in Boston for several months now. The law had created terror among the city's African people, free or not. Tension tore apart families, made neighbors distrust neighbors. She wondered if Brazil had a similar law.

"There is no extradition to the United States," Ryan said, leaning back laconically in his chair.

"But she could be forced into service here." Lily's

voice rang hollow with baffled hurt. "She is in more peril as a free woman than she ever was as my servant." She pushed back from the table, clearly too agitated to sit still. "There's an epidemic of yellow fever in the city. What if she falls ill? Or starves? Or is harmed by criminals? What if—"

"You can help by setting her free. Legally. I'll see that the papers are drawn up for you," Ryan said. "That way, she won't be considered a fugitive. Fayette is not a child. And she's not yours. She was never yours. Her will is hers and hers alone. So if she chooses to go off with Carneros, *your* only choice is to allow it." He rose from the table and gently kissed her on the cheek. "She knew the risks, and she chose freedom."

He went to the door. "I have to go to the city to see about her manumission papers." He bowed, the gallant gesture at odds with his unkempt appearance. "Ladies."

Isadora stared after him. He was the strangest man, rude as a longshoreman even as he helped free a slave woman. Capricious, that's what he was. He had probably already forgotten last night's embrace. How many times did the lesson have to be hammered into her? It was only a kiss, she told herself. She was far too old to romanticize a mere kiss, and far too proud to admit that it might mean more to her than it had to Ryan Calhoun.

She knew her heart shone in her eyes, knew Lily was watching her curiously, but she couldn't help herself. Last night had meant nothing to Ryan. He probably didn't remember it at all. Didn't remember dancing with her, holding her, kissing her until she saw stars.

She couldn't blame him, not really. What man alive would admit to kissing the spinster of Beacon Hill?

* * *

Ryan hoped his display of nonchalance had been convincing. He'd awakened the morning after the masquerade with a throbbing headache and a profound feeling of thwarted desire.

Thoughts of Isadora Peabody plagued him during the trek to the harbor and nagged at him when he was supposed to be concentrating on bribing an official for a *carta de alforria* for Fayette. He delivered the letter of liberty to Edison Carneros, who thanked him with tears in his eyes.

But once he returned to business, Ryan's thoughts wandered to Isadora again, when he should have been formulating the correct tonnage for ballast. He snapped at the men, made errors in his figuring and broke a half dozen pen nibs.

Journey shooed him off to his quarters, where he took the ship's cat in his lap, scowled out the stern windows at the *jangadas* plying to and fro and thought about Isadora some more.

He had no doubt he could rouse her ardor; she'd certainly responded eagerly enough. But it was a false emotion, one based on physical need. Ryan had no right to steal her heart.

He supposed he could make her forget all about Chad Easterbrook, given the time and temperament for seducing an inhibited woman. But Ryan occupied a precarious position, balanced uncertainly between unimaginable success and devastating failure. He had picked the worst possible time to pursue the daughter of Boston's most prominent family.

He should go on pretending the kiss had never happened.

But God. She kissed like an angel.

It was true, painfully true, and he had the experience to know the difference. Isadora's kiss brought back all the wonder and yearning and innocence and hope of youth. Her kiss reminded him of why the kiss was invented.

Yet he had learned to do without love in the past. His father had taught him that. Ryan decided to do what he had always done when his heart threatened to steer him toward a course of disaster. He'd throw himself into his work, spend the next week in feverish labor alongside the crew and avoid her until they set sail.

The voyage home was a different story; he didn't even want to think about that. Didn't want to think about seeing her relaxing on deck with a book or hauling in sheets alongside the men or fishing off the stern with the Doctor. Didn't want to think about her lying alone in her solitary berth, a single candle burning down to midnight while she dreamed of...what? Chad? Good God, not him. Ryan shouldn't know or care about Isadora's dreams.

For the next few days, he worked long and hard, sleeping on shipboard and taking his meals with other skippers on their vessels in the harbor. But shortly before they were to set sail, he knew he could no longer put off the trek to Tijuca. He went back up the mountainside to his aunt's villa.

"Hello, Mama," he said, finding her on the patio, looking serene and relaxed as she and her sister shelled beans into a carved wooden bowl. As he bent to kiss her cool cheek, he couldn't help admiring how adaptable Lily was. She switched roles from plantation mistress to world traveler to genteel houseguest with amazing ease. "I thought I'd find you packing your things."

Lily and Rose exchanged a glance, then his mother said, "Son, I've decided to stay with Rose."

"For how long?"

"Permanently," she said.

Ryan gave a low whistle. "But what about Albion?"

"That place hasn't been my home since Hunter inherited it. Now, don't scowl like that—Hunter has been a perfect angel, letting me know I have a home there for the rest of my life if I so choose." She set aside the bowl of beans. "Albion isn't my home anymore, nor my life. My travels on the Continent left me a changed woman. Seeing Rose again and losing Fayette only made the future that much clearer to me." She beamed at her sister. "My home is with my family, and these days, my family is Rose."

"I think that's fine, Mama," Ryan said, and he meant it. There was something both comforting and appropriate in the image of the two sisters gracefully growing old together in the middle of paradise.

"And you'll visit often, of course," she said, leaning forward anxiously in her chair.

"I will," he said, and he meant that, too.

"We'll be sending a crate down to the harbor," Rose said. "Lily and I picked out some fripperies for Isadora. She doesn't seem the sort to buy things for herself, so we took the liberty of choosing some mementos of her time with us."

"Where is she?" Ryan hoped his voice sounded nonchalant. "Packing?"

"Oh, I'm quite certain she's already done that. I believe she's gone exploring again," Lily said.

He narrowed his eyes. "Exploring?"

"She's been going off by herself constantly," Rose

said. "She insists on taking in as much sightseeing as she possibly can. I believe today's expedition was to sketch some of the local flora and fauna."

He felt a twinge of irritation. "She shouldn't go off by herself."

"There hasn't been anyone for her to go off with these past several days," Lily said pointedly.

"So were did she go today?" Ryan demanded.

"Into the rain forest. She wished to visit the Springs of Our Lady of Gloria do Outeiro."

"And she went alone."

Rose nodded. "The walk is not a demanding one. But I fear she didn't take anything to eat or drink with her." She patted a basket covered with a red embroidered napkin. "Angelica had this all fixed for her, and she forgot it."

Rose and Lily exchanged a glance that made Ryan think immediately of conspiracy. "Mama," he warned.

"Perhaps you could take her the basket," Lily suggested, all innocence.

Ryan swore under his breath. He should let her starve in the jungle.

But he knew damned well he wouldn't.

Isadora stopped to sketch an orchid she saw hanging from a huge, smooth-barked tree. Curling her feet under her, she sank to the spongey floor of the rain forest and studied the spray of deep pink blooms. According to her field guide, it was a moth orchid. The orchids and bromeliads intrigued her, for they seemed to be born of air and mist rather than earth and water, hanging from tree branches or liana vines as if they were butterflies that might take flight any moment.

She wished her quick pencil strokes could capture the lushness of the thick creamy petals. She longed for a palette that might do justice to the mysterious quality of the diffuse light that shone through the emerald forest.

If only she could uncork herself like a bottle and let the atmosphere pour in, become part of her. In Boston, nature had been kept at bay by concrete edifices and pruned hedgerows and fences. In Brazil the forest was an aggressive presence, spilling exuberantly through ravines and over walls, filling the cracks between rocks, sneaking across man-made pathways that, only the day before, had probably been clear.

The sheer abundance bombarded her senses. Flowers exploded like flames from shadowy places or rocky heights. Tumbling rapids knifed through rock and vegetation, an ice-blue blade slicing a path to the sea. Birds flew in hyacinth or yellow flocks beneath the high canopy formed by the trees.

Yet as overwhelmed as Isadora was with the splendor of the forest, she was gripped by a wistful ache to share her sense of discovery. Aunt Button would have loved this. But Aunt Button was gone. Isadora didn't know anyone else who would feel this awe and wonder. And that lack diminished it somehow, made it seem less important, less wondrous.

Ryan, she thought.

She shook off the impossible notion before it could depress her. Taking up her pencil again, she completed her drawing of the orchid. Perhaps she would write a chronicle of her days here and publish it. That way, kindred spirits—people totally unknown to her—could read her words and share her wonder.

But how could mere words possibly capture the almost painful thud of ecstasy she felt when she looked up at the dazzling sunlit green of the forest canopy? Words were such inadequate tools to convey her delirious rapture over something so beautiful that her eyes smarted with tears.

She finished sketching and walked on, trying to find a turn of phrase to describe that particular quality of light as it slanted down from impossibly blue skies through a faceted filter of leaves, ferns, mosses, epiphytes. As she hiked uphill, it occurred to her that she should feel winded with exertion, her legs weak from all the activity. But, oddly, that was not the case. She felt more fit and spry than ever before in her life.

Angelica, the maid who had befriended her the first day at Villa do Cielo, had told Isadora that if she climbed high enough she would find a great cataract where the spring was born from the earth. According to local wisdom, the water here was the sweetest and coldest in the mountains. The spring was so prized that the maker of Brazil's best *aguardiente* hired water carriers to bring down great casks on their shoulders. Today the path was deserted.

Before long the climb grew steeper and strewn with rocks. The liquid song of the rushing water beckoned her. She rounded a bend in the path, pushed aside the nodding fronds of a banana tree and knew she had almost reached the source.

Wet mossy rocks held a slick clear glow, brighter than diamonds. The trees and flowers growing along the verges swayed with the force of the torrent. The sounds of wind and water created a complex, elusive melody, filling her with a wild pleasure that she felt in every cell of her body.

The sense of imminent discovery held her in its thrall as she climbed on. Yet gradually she became aware of another sound, one nearly masked by the murmur of tumbling water and the rustle of leaves.

She stopped and looked behind her, suddenly apprehensive.

Her mind whirled with images of the dangerous creatures that lived in the rain forest. Vampire bats. Jaguars. Arrow poison frogs. Giant, ill-tempered sloths. Five-hundred-pound gorillas. Snakes that could squeeze the life out of a person.

She stepped off the path, setting her sketchbook down and grabbing a thick length of wood from the ground. Slimy creatures and frantic beetles scattered from the hollow it left in the fecund ground.

As she crouched in the shelter of a bush, her heart pounded painfully in her chest. Sweat trickled down her throat into the neckline of her dress. She wished she had listened to Angelica and gone native for today's outing. But native garb always reminded her too poignantly of her excursion to the market with Ryan, whom she was trying her best to forget.

The footsteps came closer. She thought of the warnings Angelica had given her when she'd started her forays into the wild. Native tribes lived in the forest; some of them were warlike or merely aggressively inquisitive. Rose had also warned her about the *quilombos,* bands of fugitive slaves that attacked first and asked questions later.

A shadow slipped over her—huge, forbidding, sinister. She acted without thinking. Using all her the strength, she brought the club crashing down.

Eighteen

And there is even a happiness
That makes the heart afraid.

—Thomas Hood
(1827)

Shaking from fear and exertion, Isadora looked at the stick in her hand, then down at the body on the ground. "Ye powers," she said, dropping to her knees. "Ryan."

He moaned, rubbing the back of his head. "I came here thinking you might be in danger," he said. "But it appears you're quite capable of defending yourself."

She dropped the stick, frowning. "Did I hurt you?"

"Am I bleeding?"

Gingerly she moved his hair aside. "I don't see any blood."

Bracing his hands behind him, he sat up, adjusting a canvas knapsack on his shoulders. "You got me at the thickest part of my skull," he said. "I suppose there's no harm done."

"I'm ever so sorry." But as she watched him lever himself to his feet and shake his head as if to clear it, her regret was tinged with wonder. Clubbing a man she believed to be an assailant was such an un-Isadoralike thing to do.

"I like knowing you can defend yourself. But next time, do me a favor and practice on a tree or something."

She suppressed a smile, feeling equal parts silly and sheepish. "Why would you think I'm in danger?"

A shadow passed over his eyes. They lost their usual sparkle and clarity, and as she often did, she sensed a depth in him he was reluctant to show. "You could get lost in here."

"I've kept to the path."

He took her hand. "So you have. As long as I've come this far, I might as well find this fabled spring or lagoon or whatever it is."

She felt a subtle thrill at the prospect of taking him on the trek with her. "Perhaps it's the fountain of youth."

"Just what I need. To be a boy again."

"You still are," she murmured, feeling an unexpected tenderness for him. They started up the path. She glanced at him sideways, liking the feel of her hand in his. "What was it like? Your boyhood?"

"Like any Virginia boyhood, I imagine. A big house, a distant father and an army of tutors."

"And a staff of slaves," she interjected. "Did it always strike you as unjust?" she couldn't resist asking. "When you were younger?"

"No. My father was a cold man, but not a harsh master. He never hired an overseer who was harsh, either.

So I didn't see the ugliest face of slavery when I was coming up. I never saw the flogging and torture. The starvation. The rape."

She winced.

"The very young don't often grasp subtle cruelties, and I suppose I was no different." He took a deep breath, studied a liana hanging over the path, then held it aside for her to pass under. "I guess the first time I understood what slavery really meant was when Journey married Delilah. After the ceremony, they were given an hour of privacy. Then they took Delilah away—she belongs to a neighbor—and I watched them say goodbye. I watched Journey, who was well over six feet tall even then, break down and cry. There's no way I could watch that and not feel the evil in my heart. So that was when I made up my mind."

She felt a thickness in her throat. "To set Journey free."

"Yes." He walked on, still holding her hand. "How much farther is it, anyway?"

"I'm not certain." Her nerves buzzed with apprehension. Since the morning after the masque, they had not seen each other. Perhaps he'd forgotten the kiss. She prayed that he had, for it was embarrassing to think of it now, in the harsh light of day. He probably kissed women all the time. She had seen him do so, the very first night she'd met him.

The trees towered like sentinels, their leathery leaves and buttressed trunks giving them the strange look of watchful giants. Slender vines, strong as rope, draped like cables from the abundant foliage. Tiger butterflies flitted from blossom to blossom. Long mosses festooned the branches like the beards of old men. Here and there, secreted in the crook of a tree, dangled another orchid or bromeliad, their aerial roots bristling from blossoms of amazing beauty.

As they neared the top of the climb, a flight of macaws passed over. The colorful birds swooped so close that Isadora could feel the whir of their wings. Toucans and parrots squabbled in the high branches.

But far more splendid than anything she'd seen so far was the waterfall. From a towering bluff of dark wet rock, the cataract hurled itself down into a deep, clear pool. Issuing forth a sound like thunder, the stream crashed with a violence that made her shiver. Yet where the falls plunged into the lagoon, the spray threw up rainbow arcs of light. The pervasive mist formed a layer of glitter, light as air, through the surrounding rocks and trees.

Isadora caught her breath, feeling delirious with pleasure as she inhaled the tingle of the mist in her nostrils.

"Well?" Ryan asked. "What do you think?"

"It's beautiful beyond words," she said. "I wish I could capture it in a letter or sketch to show people, but it's too big, too powerful for that."

"No letters then?" he asked, lifting an eyebrow.

"No letters, nor even a journal entry. I've been quite the delinquent lately." She held her breath, waiting for him to say something cutting about her reports to Abel.

"Let's go down near the water." He took her hand again. "Careful, it's slippery."

He found a spot on an outcropping of rock where the sun had penetrated the leafy canopy. Shrugging off his knapsack, he motioned for her to sit.

Isadora felt awkward as she spread her skirts and sank down. What a lot of trouble skirts and petticoats were for a woman who dared to do more than sit in a parlor or garden arbor.

"I brought lunch," he said.

She stared. "You planned this."

"Not exactly. In fact, I have a hundred other things I should be doing. But my dear aunt and mother had other plans for me."

Thank you, Rose and Lily.

They dined on sausage rolls and melon and they scooped water from the lagoon into their cupped hands. "It *is* sweet," Isadora exclaimed as droplets cascaded down the front of her. She didn't care about getting wet, not when the water was more pure than the air itself.

When they finished eating, Ryan took out a small greenish tube of tobacco that reminded her of a cheroot, or perhaps one of her father's cigars. "Now this," he said, "was not sent by my mother."

Striking a match on a rock, he lit it and smoked for a while, then held it out to her. "You smoke it like a cigar."

"I don't smoke cigars."

"It's not tobacco, but an herbal plant."

She sniffed the little swirl of gray-green smoke that came from it. "Ye powers, that's strong. What sort of herb?"

"Hemp. A common weed, really. Here. Inhale the smoke and hold it a moment. Like this." He drew on the thin cigar until its tip glowed an angry red. He closed his eyes, holding himself still for a moment, then he exhaled a cloud of bluish smoke.

Isadora draped her arms around her drawn-up knees. "And I should do this because...?"

"Because it's something new. Different. You will feel

the most interesting effects." He grinned. "Temporary, I assure you. I would never do anything permanent to you, Isadora." He offered the cigar again.

She hesitated. Soon she would be back in Boston, that world of stifling convention and proscribed rules. She'd never get this chance again. She took the proffered cheroot, touched the slightly moist end to her mouth, pursed her lips and sucked on it.

"Now *that*," Ryan said, still grinning, "is ladylike."

She spat out the smoke, wrinkling her nose at the sweetish herbal taste. "It's awful," she said. "When will I feel the effects?"

"You have to inhale the smoke along with a breath of air. Try again. Remember to hold it."

She put the cheroot in her mouth, going crosseyed as she peered down at the glowing tip.

Roaring with laughter, Ryan fell back on the rock.

She ignored him and inhaled deeper. Her lungs fought to expel the offensive substance, winning the battle as she blew it all out with a terrific cough. Her vision hopelessly blurred by tears, she made yet another attempt. Finally she succeeded in trapping the smoke inside her long enough to feel a distinct tingling sensation. Little shocks of torchlike warmth eddied up and down her arms, her legs, making her feel weightless and euphoric.

She tried several more inhalations, enjoying the perception that each moment seemed to spin out with honeyed slowness, watching the colors of the rainforest meld and blur upon the water and hearing the buzz and whir of the birds and insects grow loud in her ears.

Ryan watched her with increasing fascination. "You took to that quickly, Isadora."

She giggled. He was the only person in the world who

could make her giggle. "I am a quick study." She took a deep puff to demonstrate. "No wonder so many men smoke cigars."

He laughed again. "This is a bit different."

Suddenly the water in the lagoon looked too clear and cool to resist. She unbuttoned her shoes and rolled her stockings down, never stopping to wonder if she should.

"Oh, my," she murmured, swirling her bare toes in the water.

"Do you like it?"

"I believe I do."

As so many other moments with Ryan, this one stood apart from the rest of her life. This was a magical place, she concluded, filled with mystery and excitement. Though a part of her wished to stay here forever, she knew she would have to return to her previous existence very soon. Then she looked at Ryan and wondered if it was even possible to go back, unchanged, and fit into her former life.

He folded his arms behind his head, leaned back against a tree trunk and crossed his legs at the ankles. "Have you had a good time in Rio, Isadora?"

She felt silly and pleasant from the smoking. "Do you ask that of all your interpreters?"

"Of course," he said, deadly serious.

She inhaled more smoke, then handed it back to him. "I had better stop now."

"Why stop now?" he asked, inhaling to keep the red tip burning. "Are you afraid I might kiss you again?"

She blushed furiously, but the herb made her tongue loose. "Maybe I'm afraid you won't."

Each movement very deliberate, he set down the cheroot. With his gaze intent upon her, he got up and went to her side, quite unapologetically taking her face between his two hands and kissing her firmly on the mouth.

"If I'd known you were worried, I would have done something about it long ago." He removed his own shoes and socks and sat beside her on the rock, slowly kicking his feet back and forth. "How quickly do you suppose I can convince you to take a swim with me?"

"Here?" she asked, gesturing at the lagoon. Her hand floated very far away, not even a part of her. "Now?"

"Yes."

"I shall have to think about it. There. I've thought about it. Yes indeed, I should like to bathe here. There are only two problems."

"And what are they?"

"First, I have no bathing costume." She picked up the cheroot and took a worried puff. A nice floating calm wafted over her.

He stood and extended his hand, helping her up. "Isadora. Toreador-a. I adore-a you. You don't need a bathing costume. We're completely alone here."

She suspected some flaw in his logic, but she couldn't quite decide what it was. While she pondered this, he matter-of-factly unbuttoned her bodice and parted it, carefully pulling it off her shoulder.

"What was the other reason?" he asked. "You said there were two."

"Two what?"

"Reasons you can't bathe here. And the first reason was not valid."

"I've forgotten the second," she said with a loud burst of woozy laughter.

He reached around behind her with both hands. She

felt him unhooking the fastenings of her skirt. He smelled not unpleasantly of sweat, melon and smoke.

"What are you doing?"

"Taking your clothes off."

"Oh. Should you be doing that?"

"Sugar, I should have done this a long time ago."

"Oh," she said again, stepping out of her skirt as it pooled around her ankles. He grumbled and swore at the corset—"steel stays, for Christ's sake"—and cast it away with a flourish. Then off came her shift, camisole and bloomers.

"Ye powers," she said, puffing on the green cigar again. "I'm naked."

"Be patient, love." Ryan tore at his shirt and trousers. "In a moment, I will be, too."

Nineteen

Reproof on her lip, but a smile in her eye.

—Samuel Lover
(1836)

True to his word, he bared all while she smoked the cheroot down to ashes and gaped like a ninny. She had always known he was perfection itself. She saw immediately that it was true all over. He had the strong muscular body of a Greek athlete and skin that was tanned— except in certain areas—and smoothly unblemished.

She was quite familiar with his broad, bare chest due to the long days at sea, but his thighs and buttocks and manhood were a novelty to her inquisitive gaze. "Oh, my," she said.

"My indeed," he said, staring back. He took her hand. "Shall we?"

"Shall we what?"

In answer, he turned, still keeping hold of her hand, and jumped off the edge of the rock into the lagoon.

Isadora gasped at the cool silken shock of the water slipping over her. They went down, down, down, feet grazing the pebbled bottom and then they floated up, breaking the surface.

Isadora coughed violently, spewing out water. She flailed her arms, found Ryan and clung to him. "I remembered the other reason I shouldn't bathe," she said between coughs.

"And why is that?"

"I don't know how to swim."

He caught her against him, and she marveled at the feel of their flesh touching, sliding together, the water facilitating the movement. "Ah, Isadora. I adore a you. Hold on to me, and I'll show you." Kicking out, he towed her to shallow water where her feet could touch the bottom of the lagoon. She loved the feel of the water gliding over her. In the sunlit places it was warm and buoyant; in the cooler shadows the dark eddies gave her a delicious chill. She was Eve, she was a wood nymph, she was a natural creature, never bound by the tight corset stays of convention. Here she was in this natural world with a man who looked like a god teaching her to swim. It was all a fantastic dream—the colors too bright for the mortal world, the lagoon too beautiful for ordinary humans.

"Take my hands," he instructed her as they stood shoulder-deep in the water. "Let the current buoy you."

The gentle downstream flow lifted her. He showed her how to flutter her feet, then held her at the waist while she moved her arms. She stood grasping a liana vine while he demonstrated a dive beneath the surface. She tried it, keeping hold of the vine but plunging in, feeling as sleek and weightless as a fish. She opened her eyes to a blurred sunlit world, then drifted upward, laughing as she broke the surface.

He swam over to her. "You *are* a quick study. I've never taught anyone to swim before."

"You're not teaching me to swim, Ryan. You are teaching me to live." She leaned her head back, dipping in her hair, gazing up at the blue sky framed by towering branches and exotically shaped leaves. "In Boston, each day was the same. I got up, I had breakfast, I spent a few hours reading or writing correspondence. Sometimes there might be an invitation but it was always for more reading or conversation at someone else's house." She giggled. "It sounds so silly, yet what could be sillier than swimming naked in a lagoon in the middle of the jungle?"

She waved her hand absently in the crystalline water. "It's not that I dislike Boston," she said. "I think it's more that Boston dislikes me. Society favors women who are witty, charming and amusing."

He swam toward the cascade. "You are all of that. I never laughed so much as I do with you."

"But you're the only one." She experimented with her hands. If she paddled them away from her, she drifted backward. "All the young women who are socially successful in Boston are not merely witty and charming. They're also extremely pretty."

"So are you," he said.

She laughed. "Whatever it is that we smoked has made me quite drunk. But not nearly so drunk that I would believe that." He started to speak. She held up her hand. "I am untidy and ungainly, with no sense at all of how to dress or comport myself. I have a unique gift for making others feel awkward. I—"

He dove beneath the water and surfaced in front of her, so close she could see the way the myriad droplets magnified his pores. "You are absurd. Absurdly adorable. Isa-dorable. I wish I could make love to you."

She watched his face, his mouth, mesmerized. "I think you already are."

"Not with mere words, love. With my hands. My mouth. My body."

She drifted back, fascinated yet not frightened in the least. This was Ryan, after all. "You mustn't."

"I know that."

She thought for a moment. "Why mustn't you?"

"Because," he said with excessive patience, "you must keep yourself chaste and pure."

"Oh," she said. "For Chad?" She hadn't thought about him in days. At the moment she couldn't even recall what he looked like. "Chad. What sort of name is that, anyway? It sounds like a fish or perhaps a skin condition." She paddled on her back to the waterfall and let it beat upon her head. The water was cold; it created a delicious shiver when it mingled with the warmer water of the lagoon.

"I think you should do it anyway," she said suddenly.

"Do what?"

"Make love to me."

He started to laugh as if she'd made a joke. Then he narrowed his eyes in suspicion. "Why?"

"Because...I've never done it before. Like smoking the hemp leaves. It is my last day in Brazil. We are completely alone." She swam out from under the waterfall and looked at him directly. "No one ever need know."

He lunged through the water, pulled her toward him.

She studied his wet face, his slicked-back hair, his soft blue eyes as he guided her to calmer waters. A smile lifted one side of his mouth. "No one ever need know, eh?"

"No one's ever wanted to before, so you understand I'm curious."

"Curious. About what I'd do when—*if*—I were to make love to you."

"Yes."

He grinned wickedly. "I really like your question, Isadora." He moved back and swam in a slow, deliberate circle around her. "*If* I were going to make love to you, I would start by undressing you."

"You've already done that."

"Then I'm already making love to you."

She felt a jolt of awareness deep in her belly. "Oh, my. Then it's too late for honor?"

"It might be."

"Oh, my," she said again. "What would you do next?"

"I think perhaps I would start with your hand. You have very expressive hands so I thought I might—here— it's easier to show you." He grabbed her hand, held it gently in his. "I'm glad you stopped chewing your nails." He kept his gaze on her face as he slowly lifted her hand to his lips. "If I were going to make love to you, I would do this." He kissed one finger after the other, lavishing attention on each as if it were a sacred relic. No, a profane relic, for he was not at all reverent. He slipped a finger in his mouth and sucked at it, eliciting a gasp from her.

"Would that offend you if I did it?"

She felt light-headed, woozy from smoke and desire. "It would make me wonder what you'd do next."

"I'd pull you against me. Like this."

She found herself in his arms, bare breasts against bare chest, her mouth almost touching his.

"If we were actually making love," he said, "I would hope that you wouldn't be offended by this."

"By what?"

He shifted his hips.

"Oh!"

"That's merely an indication of how much I'd want you if we were making love."

"I'm feeling—that is, I would be feeling—some indications myself," she confessed.

"Very good. And then, of course, I'd kiss your lips. Like this." He lowered his head.

Ah. She was lost, lost in his kiss. She had the irrational yet undeniable feeling that every moment since she'd first laid eyes on him—dissolute, with a half-dressed doxy in his lap—had been moving her toward this encounter. She felt an upsurge of dizzying emotion, and she clung to him, digging her fingers into his bare shoulders, amazed to feel the silky ripple of muscle beneath her touch.

He lifted his mouth—his warm, sweet, soft mouth—from hers and whispered, "Oh, love, yes, if indeed we were making love, you would touch me like that. And I—" he kissed her again, slowly, lavishly, writing poetry with his tongue "—I would touch you like this."

He caressed her most private, most feminine places. Places she was forbidden even to put a name to or think about, but she thought about them now, about the trail of fire that blazed through her, unslaked by the cool water. She understood that she was addled from smoking the hemp leaves and so was he, yet she was glad. Grateful. Pleased that there was a substance that would make it all right for her to bathe naked with a naked man.

"And finally," he whispered in her ear while his hand still did those magical things, "finally I would have to bring you onto dry land so I could finish what I started."

"What you started..." she whispered.

His hand slid between her thighs. "I want to be where the water is."

Oh, my. This time she couldn't even find her voice, could only nod a mute, fascinated assent. Hand in hand they waded to the shore and fell back on the soft heap formed by her fallen petticoats.

"I knew these things were good for something," he said, then laughed, bracing himself on one arm to gaze at her. "Look at you, all wet and glistening." He bent and drew his tongue in a circle around each of her nipples. And she was too shocked and thrilled even to breathe. "You're a goddess, and if I happened to be making love to you for real, this would be a form of worship."

All her life she had been made to understand that she was unworthy. That no one—particularly no man—could possibly want her. Yet all those lessons—beaten into her not with a hickory cane but with the far more brutal cudgel of verbal logic—suddenly flowed away on a raft of sweet words from this laughing, red-haired man.

He had declared her a goddess. She reclined in an ecstasy of amazement as his lips drank the spring water from her breasts and shoulders and belly, as his fingers, probing with exquisite tenderness, parted her thighs to explore the damp folds of her womanhood.

"Shall I go on with my explanation?"

"What...explanation?" Rather than sobering up, she was growing dizzier and more intoxicated by the moment.

"Poor Isadora. Shall I continue?"

"Please...do."

Her breathy assent seemed to amuse him. He slid his fingers provocatively over her most sensitive spot. "The next thing I would do..."

She lifted her hips slightly, the motion far beyond the control of her will.

"...is kiss you right...here."

"No!"

"Ah, you know your part well. For I would expect from you a slight squawk of protest at this point."

"Protest?" Even as she spoke, her hips shifted under the delicate torture of his touch. "Of course there would be a protest. It's unnatural."

"What could be more natural than wanting to bring the ultimate pleasure to my goddess?"

"It's sinful."

"Have you seen it listed along with the seven deadly sins?"

"I don't even know what it's called."

"Then surely it doesn't exist." He slid his mouth down her neck and along her arm, up again and then down...lower, over her belly, sipping spring water from her navel. "So you have nothing to fear."

"We shall burn in hell."

"Not so." He nibbled her thigh. "We shall burn now."

His tongue traced the curve of her hipbone. And he gave her the deepest, most tender kiss she had never dared to imagine, and she had the most extraordinary reaction. As if she had drunk a great swallow of *curaçao*...only this was sweeter. As if she had inhaled a huge breath of herbal smoke...only this was lighter. As if she had dived into a spring of perfectly clear water...only this was more buoyant.

She had never flown like a bird, but that was how it felt. She had never burst into flames, but that was how it seemed. She had never seen stars with her eyes closed, but that was how it looked.

When the shattering sensations subsided, he made a leisurely meandering path of kisses northward. She felt stunned. And curiously, achingly incomplete.

"Ryan?" Her voice was a broken whisper.

"Mm?" He suckled soothingly at her breast.

"Is...is your...explanation over?"

"That depends."

"Depends on what?"

"On what you would expect from an encounter like this."

"I don't know what you mean."

"Well, if I were to make love to you, would you expect a fine physical release similar to the one you just experienced, or would you prefer a deeper, more spiritual joy?"

"You mean, there's a difference?"

He chuckled, his hand cupping her hip. "Oh, love. There is."

"I think," she said, winding her arms around his neck, "that I need a further explanation."

"It would take a far more serious commitment on your part. A sacrifice, you might call it."

"What sort of sacrifice?"

"Your heart and soul. Your will. Would you give them up? And your purity—well, I suppose you could say that's already gone. But your chastity. Technically speaking, that's still intact. Would you give that up?"

"For the spiritual joy you offer?" She shrugged. "Why not?"

"There's a more practical consideration. In an actual lovemaking situation, you would lose your virginity."

"Well, thank God. It has been an unwelcome encumbrance for far too long."

"Really?"

"Really."

"You're not concerned that, should you marry, a husband might expect an explanation?"

"I would have to tell him I was hopelessly seduced in the middle of the jungle by a pirate who mistook me for a goddess."

"That was no mistake."

Boldly she touched him. *There.* And smiled wickedly when he caught his breath. "Neither is this."

"Then you want it. The rest of the demonstration, that is."

"Yes." She could not get over the remarkable hardness of him. "Is this painful?" she asked.

"Not...in the way you'd think. It's quite...normal, I assure you."

"Then you should definitely continue. What would happen next?"

"Well, since we are about to take a step I never take lightly, I would kiss you some more." He did so, and now his kisses were more yielding and soft and moist than ever before, flavored with the forbidden essence of passion.

"And then," he whispered, his lips moving to her ear, "and then I would probably tell you that I love you."

Time stopped. Movement, heartbeat, wind, water. Everything stopped. Finally Isadora found her voice. "And would you mean it?"

"Probably not in the sense most ladies prefer. It would be a sort of 'If I don't have you now I'll explode' declaration. As opposed to the 'I will commit to you for life' declaration." He rippled his hand over her breasts. "And of course at this point such distinctions wouldn't matter much."

"I don't suppose they would," she conceded. But she could not deny that his words had carved out a small, ridiculous, hopeful spot in her heart. "Then what? What would happen next?"

"Hold on to me, and I'll show you."

She clung to his shoulders. She wondered if he realized he'd said the exact same words before teaching her to swim. He sank down, probing, pushing and in an age-old motion she'd never been taught but had always known, she raised her hips and wrapped her legs around him. There was a brief pressure, a flash of pain and between clenched teeth he said, "Ah, Christ, I'm sorry, I—"

"I'm not," she whispered, lost and loving it; lost in his embrace and loving the sensation of being covered by him, filled and possessed by him, their bodies sliding and straining together in a rhythm that was as natural to her as breathing, yet as new to her as the rainbow thrown up by the scintillating light through the waterfall. She could see it beyond his taut shoulders, could open her eyes and see a burst of sun-shot color, and it was a wonder to her, for it was the perfect wordless expression of the fantastic pleasure rising higher and higher within her, filling her chest, her throat, her flushed delighted face and finally coming out in the form of a sound she'd never heard before, a burst of awe and ecstasy, a single note that said, in one rush of joyful clamor, everything that she was feeling, everything that was inside her.

A moment later Ryan went motionless, arms braced and straining, face curiously intent as, for precisely one heartbeat he stared down at her. And in that brief pulse of time she became swiftly terrified, terrified that it was over, that this moment would end and the magic would disappear, taking the joy with it.

Yet it didn't happen that way. He spoke her name, no more, and she felt the startling rush of his release. A thrust, a ripple, a spasm. His eyelids lowered to half-mast and his expression mellowed to one of unfettered bliss. Finally he sank down slowly, very slowly, while the long dream stretched out like sunlight across the water, and the illusion was more real to her than life itself. She waited, feeling the pressure of his weight atop her, smelling his scent of spring water, then something dark, musky, evocative. Haunting.

And finally, he spoke. "Oh, Christ. What have I done?"

Even as he swore, he pulled away from her, pulled back, and for the first time since they'd dived into the lagoon, she felt her nakedness, felt ashamed.

"I wanted you to," she said in a small voice, snatching up her chemise and holding it like a shield in front of her. "A moment ago you looked at me and you saw a goddess. Now what do you see?"

"The biggest mistake of my life." He hid his gaze as he tugged on his smallclothes and trousers, negligently buttoning them. "I took shameless advantage of you. Made you inebriated and then seduced you."

"Ryan." Her voice rang crisply across the water, startling a flock of hyacinth macaws. "What precisely is your point?"

Without even looking at her, he handed her the corset. "I have no idea why women insist on wearing these contraptions."

She put it on, tugging absently at the front laces, feeling her hypersensitive breasts press against the top edge and wondering how he could so quickly dismiss her. She had experienced the greatest pleasure of her life, and he said it was all a mistake.

She thought suddenly of the whore he'd been with back in Boston. And the one in Rio that first day ashore. Of course. He took all such encounters quite casually.

"I think I understand," she said, stepping into her petticoats. The damp fabric held the faint scent of their love; she forced herself to ignore it. The blurred elation imparted by the smoking began to dissipate, mist driven back by a cold wind. "When you are inebriated, I'm a goddess. Then when you sober up, I'm a mistake."

He paused in dressing himself. Reaching out, he brushed his finger over her mortified cheek, once, so tenderly that she wanted to weep. "Ah, Isadora. *I'm* the one who made the mistake."

Part Three

The Bird of Winter

The winter grew cold—so bitterly cold that the duckling had to swim to and fro in the water to keep it from freezing over. But every night the hole in which he swam kept getting smaller and smaller. Then it froze so hard that the duckling had to paddle continuously to keep the crackling ice from closing in upon him. At last, too tired to move, he was frozen fast in the ice.

—Hans Christian Andersen,
The Ugly Duckling (1843)

Twenty

No coward soul is mine.

—Emily Brontë
(1846)

Ryan sat contemplating the largest fortune he'd ever seen in his life. In the glaring sunlight slanting through the stern windows of the captain's cabin, the stacks of pounds sterling glittered with eye-smarting brilliance.

At one time, this moment would have been one of triumph. He had earned far more than Easterbrook's margin had called for. Thanks to a fast trip on the brow of fair winds, he had accrued bonuses and premiums most sea captains only dreamed of.

He could not enjoy his success, though. Could not even look forward to setting sail. He could not do anything but think of Isadora.

He cringed, recalling the seductive interlude in the rain forest. He had truly hit bottom. On the pretext of protecting her, he'd followed her to the lagoon. On the pretext of introducing her to a new pleasure, he'd taught her to smoke hemp leaves. And on no particular pretext at all, he'd taken shameless advantage of her trust, her naivete and—God help them both—her state of helpless inebriation.

No matter that she'd wanted it, she was a proper lady of Boston who deserved a little restraint.

No matter that she'd asked for it, she was an innocent who didn't know the consequences of the act.

No matter that she'd enjoyed it, it would take an icon made of stone to be impervious to the pleasure they had found, the pleasure enhanced by the gentle lassitude of the drug combined with a setting that rivaled paradise.

Worst of all, far worse than taking advantage of a naive woman, was the fact that Ryan himself had done the unthinkable.

He had fallen in love.

He took a sullen sip of lemonade—everything else since his orgiastic consumption of spirits last night made his head pound—and scowled at the tally page in front of him.

How could he be so stupid? How could he lose his heart here, now, to a woman like Isadora? His future was a hazy dangerous cloud on the horizon. He couldn't drag her along this path with him. He was about to face his greatest ordeal yet—and he might have to violate every principle of maritime commerce in order to do it.

He had to free Journey's wife and children. He might well have to commit an act that could get him hanged. Everything depended on what happened in Virginia.

"My, my," Journey said from the doorway. "You do

look a mite glum for a man sitting in front of all that money."

Ryan felt a painful stab of affection as he regarded his lifelong friend. "I do, do I?" He picked up his pen and used the lever to fill the cartridge. "The notary left. I'm supposed to lock the specie in the till. Once I do that, only Abel Easterbrook can open it."

He signed his name to one of the papers and started putting the money into a coffer the size of a bread box.

"Sure is a lot of money," Journey remarked.

"Sure is," Ryan said. Money meant only one thing to Journey: reuniting with his family.

"But Delilah and my babies—"

"Will sail into Boston harbor with us." Ryan savored the expression on Journey's face. He might have lost his heart and with it, his chance to be anything but a memory to Isadora Peabody, but he would bring Journey and his family together no matter what the cost.

Even if it killed him.

"Cap...captain sent me to ask you to translate these." Timothy Datty set down a sheaf of papers sandwiched between marbled card stock.

Beneath a canvas awning, Isadora was seated in a deck chair. The *Swan* lay sixteen days out of Rio, and she had tried to avoid Ryan the entire time. He seemed to accept the arrangement with a certain sheepish relief.

He had been afraid she'd follow him around like a love-struck mooncalf. She could see that now, though it hurt. He should know better. Her practical nature had taken over. The extraordinary experience in the rain forest had been just that—an extraordinary, overwhelming, marvelous experience. An occurrence so perfect it could not, should not, ever be repeated. It was like finding a four-leafed clover or seeing a comet in the night sky: a once-in-a-lifetime phenomenon. She should count herself lucky for having lived that moment even once, for surely most people never knew such bliss. To wish for more was simply greedy. And futile.

She set aside the letter she was writing and smiled at Timothy. No point in condemning the lad simply because the skipper was a horse's backside.

"Thank you for bringing these," she said.

"You're...welcome." When he employed the breathing strategies she had taught him, Timothy rarely stuttered. He stood leaning against the pinrail, smiling and regarding her in a very curious way.

"Is there anything else you need?" she asked.

"Um...no. Just...did you like Rio?"

"Very much, thank you."

"I thought so."

"What makes you think so?"

"You seem...different, is all."

She smiled, knowing her smile was touched with sadness and knowing she was inches from tears. "Oh, I suppose I am different," she said, staring off into the empty distance. "I am indeed."

He withdrew and she looked at her hands. When had she stopped biting her nails? She had undergone a dramatic transformation on this voyage, and the changes manifested themselves in curious ways. She felt a certain sense of wonderment looking down at her hands with the nails neat and smooth, the skin tinged gold by the sun, the palms callused from working. Yet mingling with that wonderment was confusion and sometimes a wish to crawl back into her shell, hiding from the world as she did on Beacon Hill.

She set aside the letter in her lap. She had no idea what she had been writing or for whom she'd intended the missive. Ye powers, her brain had softened to cornmeal mush these days. She could not seem to concentrate on anything for very long.

Except for Ryan. Despite her resolve to be practical, she could think of him for uncounted hours without straying even once to other topics. It was quite awful, really, this sad obsession of hers. On some purely intellectual level she understood the reason for his constant presence. He was the first man to awaken her carnal desires, to show her physical pleasures she'd never imagined. Like an addict, she craved more of the ecstasy he'd shown her.

Fortunately for Isadora, she possessed a powerful reserve of common sense. Her will alone would protect her from making a fool of herself over an inconstant sea captain who probably couldn't wait to get her out of his life. Her will had given her the strength to flout convention and sign on aboard a merchant ship. Her will had given her the power to face the perils of life under sail. Surely she could fight a base and inappropriate attraction to Ryan Calhoun.

Though when, a few minutes later, he came strolling over to her as if summoned by her thoughts, she felt that powerful will falter. It was absurd, the way nature had favored him with such physical beauty and magnetic appeal. And the yearning ran deeper now, because she knew firsthand that the beauty and appeal extended over every square inch of his body.

Feeling hot and untidy, she shaded her eyes and tilted her head to look up at him. He could not have planned for the strong westerly wind to plaster his shirt to his damp chest so artfully, or for the sun to raise ruby-toned glints of light in his long, wavy hair, but one would think he had orchestrated the effect to taunt her.

Isadora smiled politely. "Good day, Captain Calhoun."

"Good day." He bowed from the waist, mocking her formality with a wink. He indicated the folio she held. "Thank you for taking on those translations. I thought we'd have done with paperwork once we left Rio, but it never seems to end."

"I don't mind doing my duty." She straightened the papers with a consciously officious air.

He didn't seem to be in a hurry to go. Instead, with an unreadable expression on his face, he sat cross-legged beside her on the deck. "Are you enjoying the voyage home, Isadora?"

"Thus far I am," she said.

"I'll need the *Swan*'s enrollment certificate copied again," he said, handing her a rolled document. "We'll be making port briefly in Virginia."

She took the official paper from him. "Virginia? We're going to call at Virginia?"

"Briefly." His jaw drew taut with tension.

"Do the men know of this?"

He glared at her. "If you persist in being insubordinate, I'll assign your duties to someone else."

The old Isadora would have flinched at his tone. But

she knew now how to face a man's anger; she knew it wouldn't kill her. "Virginia was not in the original sailing plan," she remarked.

"Damn it, woman," he burst out. "Just shut up and do your job."

"Aye-aye, *sir*." Unwilling to be intimidated, she put the enrollment certificate in her lap desk.

They sat in disgruntled silence for a time. Then he indicated the letter in her lap. "Writing to Chad again?"

She bristled at his astringent tone. "I—"

"Of course you are," he cut in, his voice quiet but sharp as a blade. "You promised to tell him of all your adventures abroad."

"I seem to recall I pledged to correspond—"

"What about the adventure at the waterfall, Isadora?"

Hearing the words spoken aloud created a havoc of emotions in her. It had been the most beautiful day of her life. But Ryan Calhoun seemed determined to make a mockery of it.

"Well?" he persisted. "Did you tell him about that?"

"How dare you."

"How dare I what? Finally make you speak of that day?"

"Don't make it my fault. *You've* been avoiding *me*. There is no need to speak of it," she said curtly. "It is over."

"I thought so, too," he said, and suddenly his voice lowered to a whisper. She could barely hear him above the creak of timber strained by wind-filled canvas. "But the more time goes by, the more I think about it."

She toyed with the black ribbon that bound the folio

together. "I see no point in dwelling on that day. You said it was a mistake, and you were correct."

"What about you? Was it a mistake for you, too?"

The direct question pushed her toward the brink. Could she unveil her feelings to him? Could she take that risk?

No. And the saddest part was, she had no idea what her feelings meant. Her emotions careened crazily, touching on yearning, lust, tenderness, melancholy. She never knew, when she opened her mouth to speak, whether she would laugh or cry. Regardless, he would not welcome them anymore than Chad Easterbrook ever had. So why tell him? Why open herself to that hurt?

Rather than hardening her to pain, all the countless wounds of the past only made her more vulnerable. So Isadora did the only thing she could. She gave him the practical explanation.

"We took a drug that made us do something very foolish."

"So you feel nothing now?"

"The only thing I feel is foolish." She was lying. She knew it even as she spoke. Even stone cold sober, she felt dizzy with passion each time she thought of him. But life had taught its hard lessons well. A handsome, charming man would bring nothing but heartache. She had to prove herself stronger than her desires.

"I'm certain it's the same for you," she added.

Without warning, he touched her cheek with the back of his hand. Lightly. His knuckles grazed her skin, leaving a trail of fire. The caress evoked other caresses, other moments. "You have no idea how it is with me, Isadora."

Something in his expression frightened her. The darkness. The intensity. Just when she thought she knew this man, he showed her another facet of himself. She pulled away, flinching from his disconcerting touch even when a part of her longed to settle her cheek into the cradle of his palm. "Then perhaps you should explain what you mean."

He dragged his fingers through his hair. "I can't give you anything, Isadora."

"I never asked for anything," she said.

He smiled, the expression shaded with a heartbreaking regret. "Oh, love, you have," he said.

"I don't understand."

"You expect everything. The moon. The stars. The planets and *their* moons. But you've chosen the wrong man. You've made the error of thinking I have something to offer."

She laughed, amazed that such a bitter sound could come from her. "How clever of you, Captain Know-All. Over the years, gentlemen have offered me every excuse on record to explain their reluctance to court me. I have been responsible for more dead great aunts, horses with the colic, broken buggy axles and even cases of the measles than any other woman in Boston. But this is a first." She heard herself babbling, but she feared that if she stopped, she would waver. She would weep. She might even blurt out the truth. "I can honestly say that you're the first to declare yourself ineligible on the basis of your own personal qualities—or lack thereof. I congratulate you. That was very original."

He stood. "Christ, Isadora. I'm not like the others. You know damned well I'm not."

She forced herself to wave her hand in a dismissive gesture. "It really doesn't matter. I'm told gentlemen have amorous encounters all the time. You're no different. Surely your lack of moral character is not worth dwelling on when there is so much work to do." Doggedly she opened the folio and glanced at the papers. She could not see a word—they all melted together in a blur of unshed tears.

He grasped a shroud, freshets of wind plucking at his hair and shirt. She kept waiting for him to leave, but he didn't. He simply stood there. She made a show of leafing through the papers.

Finally Ryan spoke. "About that day—if anything, that is, if you should find yourself with child, I'll make things right, I swear it." Then he turned and walked away.

Her hands dropped inadvertently to her middle. *A baby.* The very idea filled her with terror and excitement. But at the heart of her wonder lay a deep sadness.

Didn't he understand? Nothing would ever be right again.

Journey stared pointedly at the cup in Ryan's hand. "It won't help, you know."

Ryan leaned against the wheel. He didn't need to steer, for the helm was lashed in place. The sails had been set for days on the starboard tack; with the present steady winds, they'd make landfall in record time.

"What makes you think I'm looking for help?" he asked peevishly.

Journey chuckled in that deep, knowing way of his.

"That's your third cup of rum since Isadora came out on deck."

"Really? I hadn't noticed. When did she come out on deck?"

Laughing harder, Journey took the cup from him. "Oh, you got it bad, don't you?" He drank the rum with an exaggerated swallow. "So what you going to do about it?"

Ryan parked one hip on the rail, folded his arms and scowled up at the foredeck. The men were giving Isadora dancing lessons. They had already introduced her to sailors' jigs and schottisches; this evening they'd moved on to ballroom dancing.

While Luigi and Chips played a broken-sounding waltz on mouth organ and fiddle, Ralph Izard led Isadora through the steps. The others clapped the one-two-three rhythm with their hands or drank from their tin cups with little fingers daintily crooked out.

Isadora's bare feet pattered with increasing assurance on the bare wood of the deck. She wore a simple skirt and blouse and had one of Gerald's bandannas tied jauntily around her head. Her cheeks glowed in the amber sunset, and above the airy music, her laughter flowed like a banner of silk.

Watching her, Ryan felt a powerful jolt of desire, curiously tempered by a rush of tenderness. Before his very eyes he had watched her turn from a prune-lipped spinster who distrusted the world to a laughing young woman with a lust for life. Her transformation fascinated him.

"Where you reckon Izard learned that fancy-ass dancing?" Journey asked.

Ryan kept his eyes on the waltzing couple. "He grew up the son of a New York shipping tycoon. Had a gentleman's education, but he had a falling-out with his family and went to sea." Ryan was relieved when Journey didn't ask the reason for the rift. The chief mate had outraged his family by taking an African wife.

The waltz ended, and Isadora pantomimed the breathless pleasure of a debutante, fluttering a fan the Doctor had fashioned of chicken feathers.

"Why'd you quit courting her?" Journey asked.

Ryan looked at him sharply. He'd hoped to keep his unwise affair with her a secret. He'd hoped the lunacy of falling in love with her would escape Journey's notice.

"I never should have courted her to begin with." He paced across the cockpit as Isadora and the men formed the lines of an elegant country reel. "I didn't actually." He turned to Journey with his hands spread in helpless bafflement. "We just...happened."

A huge grin spread across Journey's face. "That's the way love works, honey. It just...happens." He mocked Ryan's befuddlement.

"You're a big help. I'm trying to forget her."

"And if you think you can, you're dumber than a box of hair."

"I have to forget. In a few weeks, she'll be back with her family and I'll be off on another voyage. Look at her now. The local swains will be falling all over each other in Boston trying to court her." Saying it made him want to roar with frustration.

"Maybe," Journey said. "But the one she wants is you."

"She doesn't know what the hell she wants. The way her family raised her—I don't even think she knows what romantic love is."

"Then show her. Teach her."

"To what end?" Ryan plowed his splayed fingers through his hair. "What would it serve?"

"It'd make her believe."

Ryan stopped pacing and looked at his friend. Journey had always possessed a deep and ancient wisdom that Ryan trusted.

"Believe what?"

Journey toyed with the small leather pouch around his neck, the talisman from his wife. "That someone can love her. How would she know? Other than that grand aunt she talks about, no one ever did."

"That's insane."

"More insane than bickering with each other for the next four thousand miles?" Without waiting for an answer, Journey took the cup and went below.

Ryan stood alone, watching the progress of the dancing lesson and trying to talk himself out of what he was about to do. Why the hell should he trouble himself to instruct Isadora Peabody in the lessons of love? Why should it be his responsibility to show this difficult, fascinating, intelligent, confounding creature about love? Let her think it was all glory and sunshine. It wasn't his job to show her love had its dark side, too, its moments of fear so all-consuming and dizzying that the whole world listed on its axis like a ship in mountainous swells.

That was what had caught Ryan unawares. The agony of love. The soaring joy so quickly followed by a pounding fear, almost a horror.

When he was young, his father had given him a vial of explosives they were using to blast some of the distant fields to make them level. Ryan had been instructed to carry the fragile glass container, afraid for his very life if he dropped it.

Ryan remembered that feeling now, that mingling of elation and terror. Elation that he had been chosen for a task of such importance, countered madly by the terror of the consequence of failure.

He looked across the decks at Isadora and felt the same thing, only ten times worse.

Swearing between his teeth, he leaped up a companion ladder, ignoring a wave of rum-induced dizziness as he ducked beneath the taut shrouds and strode to the foredeck. The dancing lessons had progressed to a minuet, so badly rendered by Luigi and Chips that it was barely recognizable. With mock solemnity, Mr. Izard and Isadora paraded through the steps. Her face was so suffused with enjoyment that the darkness lifted from Ryan's heart. An errant shaft of dying sunlight touched her.

In that moment, Ryan was struck with a realization. He wanted her to be happy. He was amazed at how much he wanted that. Another insane consequence of loving her. He wanted her happiness more than he wanted his next breath of air. It was bizarre, surreal almost, to have such powerful feelings. He didn't want her to feel hurt or fear or uncertainty. It was exactly as Journey had implied. Love wasn't a selfish thing. It was the kindest, most generous impulse a man could have.

He felt curiously liberated as he stepped up on deck. Heads turned toward him; a few eyebrows raised. Though he had established himself as a skipper of few formalities, he rarely mingled with the crew during their evening skylarking.

As if he had entered a formal cotillion ball, he tapped Izard on the shoulder. "May I cut in?"

"Aye, sir." Izard surrendered his partner.

The musicians continued their tortured rendition of the minuet as Ryan smiled down into Isadora's wary face. "From now on, I want you to save the minuet for me," he said, exaggerating his Virginia drawl. He drew her close, feeling her hips press against his, a move Izard hadn't dared to attempt. As quick to learn in this as in all things, Isadora followed the steps, and before long they had conquered the deck.

She looked up at him, clearly pleased by the novelty of having a partner who was taller than she. The expression on her face told Ryan everything he needed to know. His cause was good.

That night he began a pattern of behavior designed to please her, to make her forget she was ever the awkward, socially inept spinster of Beacon Hill. He made it his purpose to prove to her that she was worthy of every consideration. He made it his purpose to prepare her to return to her Boston world, to meet it with confidence, not timidity. To expect courtesy from men, not derision. To speak her mind, not stifle it.

He lent her his favorite books. One day when it was particularly balmy out, he climbed to the topmast and sang her a ballad while the crewmen harmonized the refrain. When Isadora made it known she couldn't bear the idea of butchering the ship's chickens, he ordered them spared.

Her happiness bloomed in those weeks of the voyage

north. And if sometimes her smiling regard was tinged with confusion, Ryan didn't mind. Nor did he attempt to explain. That was the surprising truth about his love for her. He didn't mind giving it away.

Twenty-One

"Home" is any four walls
that enclose the right person.

—Helen Rowland

Mockjack Bay, Virginia,
March 1852

"Land ho!" came the shout from the main-topmast.

Isadora, who had yelled the observation with all her might, grinned across at Gerald Craven, who clung to the jibboom. "I've always wanted to say that," she confessed.

"You sounded like an old salt," Gerald assured her.

"I *am* an old salt." She looked in rueful bemusement at her plain kersey skirt—no petticoats—hiked up between her legs to form pantaloons. Sunshine had bronzed her skin to a rich hue that would have her mother bustling her into a bath of milk and rosewater. Her hair had disintegrated into a mass of hopeless golden brown curls held out of the way with a leather tie. The crew of the *Swan* accepted her this way, perhaps even preferred it, so she rarely thought about her mode of dress.

The voyage from Rio had been uneventful but far from tedious. In the early weeks she'd stayed busy working through masses of paperwork generated by all the transactions Ryan had made on behalf of Abel Easterbrook. It soon became apparent to Isadora and the rest of the crew that the voyage had been enormously successful. No one would desert when they called at Virginia; all would complete the trip home in order to earn a full share.

Anticipation of a lucrative payout raised everyone's spirits. Yet the prospect of landfall disconcerted Isadora. On the high seas, she enjoyed a peculiar sense of liberation. The men of the *Silver Swan* didn't judge her by the way she looked or dressed. Day by day she had slipped deeper and deeper into her role—friend, teacher, helpmeet, listener, learner. One day she forgot to don a certain set of petticoats; the next she left them off deliberately. By the time she spied the misty green hills of Virginia, she had taken to wearing her simplest skirt and blouse; more often than not she remained barefoot and bareheaded as she went about her duties.

For reasons she could not fathom, Ryan went out of his way to entertain her, to amuse her and to fulfill even her most capricious wishes. When she became enchanted by a school of dolphins, he ordered the crew to change tack to give her a better look, even though it took them off course. When she wanted to help with tarring down the mast, he rigged her a canvas seat on pulleys and called encouragement as she painted in the sun with one of the men lowering her away.

Yet for all the fun of his antics, the quiet times haunted her. There were moments when she would stumble upon him unexpectedly in the galley or the chart room and she'd freeze, overcome by memories of the rain forest. She had been certain, afterward, that nothing would ever be the same.

And she had been right.

When he turned and looked at her, she remembered the way he'd eyed her when he'd led her out of the lagoon and told her she resembled a goddess. If her gaze should happen to drop to his hands, she would recall the sensation of those hands caressing her. When he spoke, she heard the low timbre of his voice as he said, "Hold on to me, and I'll show you."

She remembered that day as one remembers a particularly vivid dream. Wrapped in rainbow mist, the memory dwelt apart from the rest of her life. It was an elusive jewel she could see shimmering in the distance but could never quite touch. On that one day of her life, she had been someone entirely different from Isadora Peabody of Beacon Hill. She had been nameless, a forest nymph who was beautiful for the first time in her life, naked and unashamed like Eve before the fall. She had felt passion and inspired it in a remarkable man. For one glorious day she'd been a stranger to herself.

All these thoughts would tumble through her heart and mind each time she encountered Ryan. But since their last conversation about that day, when all her uncertainties and bitterness and confusion had bubbled to the surface, they hadn't spoken of it again.

During those discomfiting encounters, she could not guess at his thoughts. His face was an impenetrable mask.

And so by mutual, tacit agreement they had declared the rain forest interlude an aberration. For all practical purposes, the afternoon had never happened. And perhaps it hadn't. Perhaps it had happened to two entirely different people, people who didn't exist anymore.

Now as she climbed down to the quarterdeck, she nearly ran into Ryan.

"Excuse me," he said, stiffly formal. "I heard a cry of landfall."

"That would be me," she said.

"Oh."

Stubbornly she refused to give way even though he clearly wanted to get past her. She was sick of being ignored, sick of denying what had happened. "Being invisible was always an advantage in Boston, but I assure you, it is not on a ship."

"Invisible? I don't know what you mean."

"You look through me, not at me."

"I apologize. I meant no insult."

His flat, polite manner infuriated her. She knew it was reckless, but she wanted to push him. "I think you've set about deliberately to confuse me."

He scowled. "Trust me, I've more important things to do."

"Then why are you being so polite and cordial?"

"So you can learn what it's like."

"All you're teaching me is that kindness is a false veneer."

"Oh? Would you rather I treat you as Chad Easterbrook treated you?"

"That," she said, "is none of your affair." She couldn't believe how much her feelings for Chad had changed on this voyage. She had set sail cherishing a dream of him. In a few short months, he had become a distant and faintly absurd memory.

The men scrambled about their duties, making ready for landfall. Ryan handed her the spyglass and pointed.

"That's Mockjack Bay."

She peered through the glass, focusing the lens on the distant green shores. A half dozen masts clustered at the port, anchored offshore. Misshapen islands and long fingers of land reached into the water, then rose to blue-tinged hills corrugated by endless, rippling fields. Like spun-sugar palaces, houses and outbuildings crowned each rolling rise of land.

"It looks lovely there," she said.

"I reckon it is. But I spent my youth looking out to sea." He pointed to a more distant location. "See that house with the columns? That's Bonterre, the home of our closest neighbors. Family called the Beaumonts."

She could tell even from a distance that Bonterre was a huge estate. "It's hard to conceive of the scale. New England farms are so small in comparison."

He nodded. "The Beaumonts are the biggest land-owners in the county. My half brother Hunter married Lacey Beaumont a few years back."

She sighed, her imagination caught by the thought of the nuptials taking place at the fairy-tale palace in the distance. She wondered about Ryan's past, his family, what it had been like growing up here. It was pleasant, also, to have a civil conversation with him. Perhaps friendship was not out of the question. Perhaps.

"Was the wedding terribly lavish?" she asked.

"I wouldn't know. I was too busy earning demerits at Harvard. Last time I saw Lacey, she was in pigtails and pinafores. She always did have an eye for Hunter, though. Ever since we were kids."

Isadora tried to guess how he felt about his half brother. But his expression was neutral, his tone casual. She could determine nothing.

"Journey's wife and little ones live at Bonterre," he said.

"Will Journey be able to see them?"

His mouth thinned, and his gaze flickered away. "I don't know."

"But you're practically family. You're related to the Beaumonts by marriage."

"It gets more complicated by the moment." He heaved a sigh. The sea rushed away as the bark angled into the bay. "The wedding between Hunter and Lacey was more like a territorial alliance than a marriage." He shaded his eyes and gazed toward shore. The bark had crossed the bar into Chesapeake and her leeward side offered a closer view of the shorefront estates. A dangerous hissing sound came from between Ryan's teeth.

"What is it?" Isadora asked.

"Albion." He grabbed the spyglass from her and peered through it. "Something's wrong."

"I don't understand."

"The fields are fallow. They haven't been planted."

"That's customary, isn't it? Leaving sections unplanted to restore richness to the soil?"

"Not for all the fields. Not for more than a season."

"What do you suppose the trouble is?"

"I don't know, but I reckon I'll find out."

Twenty-Two

❧❧❧

They have stabbed themselves for freedom—
jumped into the waves for freedom—fought like
very tigers for freedom! But they have been
hung, and burned, and shot—and their tyrants
have been their historians!

—Lydia Maria Child,
*An Appeal on Behalf of That Class of
Americans Called Africans* (1833)

"I'm bankrupt, little brother." Hunter Calhoun's words slurred together, melded by the combined effects of too much whiskey and too little sleep. Slow as cold treacle, he rose from his winged armchair and went to the sideboard to slosh more sour mash into his tumbler.

Ryan sat in the parlor of Albion, trying to hide his shock. It had been years since he'd been back, but he remembered the place well enough to note the drastic changes. The marble mantelpiece, once gleaming, now bore yellowish stains and thick streaks of soot. The Irish

crystal vases and lamp chimneys were black with ne-
glect. The French pianoforte was gone; three dimples in
the wood floor marked the spot where the valuable in-
strument used to stand. No servants or maids bustled
about with their dusters and brooms. No delicious smells
emanated from the kitchen. No singing came from the
compound or the tobacco fields.

"What the hell happened?" Ryan asked, studying
Hunter.

His elder brother had always been a mythic figure to
Ryan. Blond and handsome, an athlete who excelled at
every gentlemanly pursuit from fox hunting to ballroom
dancing, he'd been the man his father had raised him to
be. A true son of the South.

Now Hunter's complexion was ashen, his eyes hopeless. He rolled an unlit cigar between his thumb and
forefinger. "You could say it's a legacy from our dear,
departed father." With an unsteady hand, Hunter lit the
cigar, puffed on it once, then let it dangle forgotten from
his hand draped over the threadbare arm of his chair.

"I don't understand. He left you everything—"

"And you felt so put upon because he cut you out of
his will." Hunter hurled the cigar into the cold hearth.
"You should count your blessings, Ryan. 'Cause you
don't want what he left me with." Hunter made a vague
gesture in the direction of the estate offices across the
hall. "About twenty years' worth of unpaid debts."

Ryan's blood chilled when Hunter told him the
amount. It was difficult even to conceive of that much
money. He had grown up taking it for granted—the luxury, the freedom from want. Now he understood that it

was all an illusion, an illusion built on a broken man's dreams.

"Why didn't you know about this?" he asked his half brother. "Why didn't my mother know?"

"He never spoke of his failure to me. Why should he? You were always off with Journey, and then you were up in Cambridge playing Yankee radical. As for your mother, she paid no attention." Hunter's voice held no contempt. "Father always did deal with problems that way—shoving them aside. Sending them away." He picked up his chipped mug and took a drink of his whiskey. "Selling them down the river."

Remembrance flickered in Ryan's mind. "That was years ago. Do you still think about what happened?"

Hunter gave a sarcastic snort and encompassed the room with a sharp gesture. "Do you see anything better to think about?"

Ryan shrugged awkwardly. "It seems so long ago."

"Didn't mean to bark at you." Hunter swirled his drink. "I guess you were pretty young when it all happened. How old were you? Thirteen? Fourteen?"

"Yes. All I remember is that the slave girl's name was Seraphim, and she was a laundress." He pictured a slender girl in a tattered apron, an ebony curl tumbling down her brow as she bent over her steaming laundry cauldrons. "I recollect a lot of shouting from Father, too. Journey and I were hiding under the stairs when he found out and went looking for you." Ryan glanced at the twisted staircase, hung with cobwebs. "Now that I'm older, I'm surprised he took on so about you having a love affair with a slave woman."

It was one of the things Ryan hated the most about slavery. "So why did Father get so mad?"

A bitter laugh escaped Hunter. "I broke the rules, little brother. I fell in love with her. And that, of course, was unforgivable. It violated the principle that keeps the slave system in place. It acknowledges that a slave is human, that she could be beautiful in the eyes of a man, that she's worthy of love."

Ryan stared at his brother in shock. That was it, then. Now, drunk and broke, Hunter was revealing the defining event of his life. His failed love dwelt at the heart of the darkness in his eyes.

"I suppose you remember how Father ended it between us, too," Hunter said.

"I do. The son of a bitch sent her to auction." The memories washed over him. He heard her pitiful screams as the slave traders carried her off to the dock and put her on a ship bound for the market in Savannah. He remembered the sound of a gunshot, and people running frantically, expecting to find Hunter with his head blown off.

He'd shot his father's prize garden statue, a monument of Jared Calhoun on a horse. Then, without saying a word, Hunter had saddled a horse and taken off for the University of Virginia.

Some years later he'd married Lacey Beaumont, the daughter of their neighbors to the north. They had two children, Belinda and Theodore.

"Where's your wife, Hunter?" Ryan asked quietly.

"At Bonterre. With the children." Hunter stared at his big hands. "Damn it, Ryan. God damn it to hell. I miss my kids."

And so does Journey, said a voice in Ryan's mind. He had been counting on the goodwill of the Beaumonts. But what sort of goodwill would they extend to a Calhoun who had failed their daughter? Now what the hell was he going to do?

At that moment, the door creaked eerily. Ryan twisted around in his chair, but saw no one. "Ghosts, big brother?"

Hunter got up and looked behind the door. "Blue," he said, his voice harsh. His face went ashen as he said, "How long have you been here, son?"

"Don't know, Daddy," came a small voice.

"Lord, but I've missed you." He scooped up the small boy and hugged him close. Hunter squeezed his eyes shut and inhaled deeply. "I've missed you so much, Blue."

Ryan hurried over to them, hoping to distract the lad from the conversation he'd overheard. Most of it probably went over the tyke's head, but it would do the already troubled kid no good at all to hear that his father had once loved a slave girl.

The boy squirmed out of Hunter's arms and regarded Ryan with big eyes. He had the sort of cherublike features that would make middle-aged ladies want to pinch his cheeks and kiss him on his freckled nose, poor kid.

"Hey there, Theodore," Ryan said.

"My name's Blue."

"Hey there, Blue. I bet you don't know who I am."

"Sure I do. You're my damnyankee Uncle Ryan."

"So I'm a damn Yankee, am I?"

"'S what Pappy Beaumont says."

That didn't bode well, Ryan thought. "So how come your daddy calls you Blue?"

"Everybody calls me Blue. On account of the rhyme." He peeked shyly at Hunter. "When I was real real small, Daddy told me I'd always be his little boy Blue."

Hunter pinched the bridge of his nose, trying to gain control of himself. "Does your mama know you're here?"

Blue stabbed the toe of his boot at the floor. "I sneaked out. I hate it there, Papa. Mammy Georgia boxes my ears, and they make me eat oatmeal without any syrup and they give me mustard greens for supper." He made a wretched face. "And I have to stay inside all day."

"How would you like to come outside?" Ryan said, glancing at Hunter. "I'll show you my old lookout tower and you can climb up and take a look at my ship."

"Let's go!" Blue sped out the door.

Wading through knee-high grass, the three of them crossed the lawn and walked down to the landing. Tall salt grass choked the area around the creaky dock, but the old loblolly pine, once a haven for Ryan and Journey, still stood tall and straight as the mast of a clipper ship.

Ryan boosted the boy into the tree. "Take hold of those rungs there and climb on up to that platform. Journey and I spent a whole summer putting it together." He smiled, remembering the soft night air and the dreams he'd once had.

"I see her!" Blue called out, scrambling to the split hickory platform.

"That's the *Silver Swan*. My very own command." From this distance, he couldn't see anything but the silhouette of the ship. He'd come ashore alone, leaving Journey nervous and pacing the decks, Isadora sending him dubious, unreadable looks and the men showing their impatience to return to Boston and collect their pay. Everyone on that ship depended on him. He felt the pressure like a constant headache. And Hunter's problems didn't make his task any easier.

"How are things between you and the Beaumonts?" he asked his brother.

Hunter gave a humorless bark of laughter. "This is the South, little brother. There's no greater shame than being poor."

"So everyone's gone? The servants, the workers, the overseer?"

"Everything. All our people. You'll be pleased to know I freed them rather than handing them over to the slave trader to pay off Father's debts. Joshua lives here still, because he and his wife were so old. I gave him and Willa the overseer's house. Nancy still lives where she always did. She went blind a few years ago. Willa looks after her."

"So what's going to happen with you and Lacey? To Albion?"

"With luck, it'll burn to the ground."

Ryan kept his eye on Blue, high on the viewing platform. "I'm serious, Hunter. You have a family to think of. Joshua and Willa and Nancy are your family, too. Are you going to let them starve?"

"Of course I won't let them starve, damn it." With more speed than Ryan would have expected him capable of, Hunter picked up a rock and threw it. Even after two glasses of whiskey, he had perfect aim, hitting a tree trunk with the rock at fifty feet. He'd always been a crack shot, much to the detriment of that marble statue. "I have a meeting with the officers of Dominion Bank in Richmond next month. If I'm lucky, they'll advance me a loan to start up again."

"But you have no laborers."

Hunter laughed again. He'd always had a marvelous laugh, and it was marvelous still, though edged with desperation now. He held out his big, pale hands to the light and splayed his fingers. "Little brother, these hands have held the reins of the finest horseflesh in Virginia. They've cradled bottles of wine worth more than some men earn in a lifetime. They've been dealt hands of cards that won or lost a small fortune. And they've loved more women than I'll ever admit to. The one thing they've never done is a day of hard, honest labor." He turned them palms up, studied them as if they belonged to someone else. "Right now, they're the only thing I can truly claim as mine. So I suppose I'd better get used to the idea of doing the work myself."

"There's too much to do."

"Your confidence warms my heart, brother."

"I'm being realistic."

"Since when do you care, Ryan?"

"You're my brother. You're family." He shaded his eyes and motioned for Blue to climb down.

"Then *you* lend me the money to make a new start," Hunter said. "I was thinking Irish racehorses—"

"I don't have that kind of money." *I have another use for my money.* Ryan let the idea slide away on a morass of regret. "After I settle…some things here and discharge my cargo in Boston, I'll come home for a while, help you get back on your feet."

Hunter stared out at the bay, nodded absently. Blue dropped to the ground beside him and loyally took his hand.

"I'd best be going," Ryan said, his heart leaden with the knowledge of what lay ahead. "I have to return to my ship to fetch…something before I visit the Beaumonts."

Hunter stiffened. "Why would you want to visit the Beaumonts?"

Ryan had a strange urge to unburden himself to Hunter. He and his brother had never been close, yet for some reason Ryan wanted to tell him. He couldn't, though. He and Hunter lived in different worlds. "Lacey's my sister-in-law. And I've never met my niece."

Hunter gave a bitter snort of laughter. "Give my love to my darling wife."

A sharp oath broke the quiet of the anchored ship. Isadora, who had been listening to Timothy Datty read from *Two Years Before the Mast,* looked up from her deck chair. On the aft deck, Ryan and Journey stood face-to-face.

"Never heard Mr. Journey cuss like that," Timothy observed. "Guess the skipper's business ashore didn't go well."

She remembered the expression on Ryan's face when he'd seen the fallow fields of Albion. "I imagine you're right."

Journey turned sharply away from Ryan and stalked to the rail, holding himself with stiff dignity as he faced the shore. At his sides, his fists clenched and unclenched. Ryan said something with a note of impatience in his voice that quickly crescendoed to anger; then he disappeared into his quarters.

Timothy set the book aside. Isadora's first impulse was to go to Journey, but she hesitated, making her way instead to the captain's cabin. She rapped on the door.

"It's Isadora."

A pause. Then Ryan said, "You might as well come in."

When she saw what lay on the table before him, she gasped. "That's the specie from the ship's till."

"Astute of you to notice," he said.

She refused to flinch at his sarcasm. "I thought only Mr. Easterbrook could open the safe."

"Well, you thought wrong, sugar."

She walked forward and pressed her palms on the table. This was not the Ryan Calhoun she had come to know. This man was driven and angry, uncommunicative and vaguely threatening. But Isadora had changed, too. She wasn't afraid of him.

"Tell me what's troubling you."

"My brother's broke. The farm's a ruin."

She sat down on the curved bench next to the table. "You can't give him this money."

"Christ, what do you take me for?"

"I don't know," she said honestly. "Why don't you explain yourself?"

He helped himself to a cup of port wine from the

silver-clad decanter on the table. When he offered some to Isadora, she shook her head. "Tell me."

"I need to buy three slaves," he said, his voice barely audible. "It's a promise I made a long time ago."

Shock sucked the air from her lungs. She felt her eyes widen and then, in a rush of understanding, she relaxed against the back of the tufted bench. "You mean Journey's wife, don't you? His wife and children."

He didn't speak; he didn't have to. She could read the truth on his face, and it made her want to leap up and launch herself at him, smothering him with kisses. All along she had thought him selfishly ambitious. At last she understood why.

She didn't go to him, of course. She couldn't, not now.

"So you see the dilemma, don't you? I'm compelled to steal from my employer—and therefore from my own men—in order to keep a promise I made to Journey."

"Isn't there any other way? Couldn't you make a promissory note to—what was the man's name?"

"Beaumont. And the answer's no. Calhoun credit isn't much good in these parts lately." Ryan's chest expanded in a deep breath.

"And if you don't take the money?"

"We leave here without Journey's wife and kids. I won't do that."

She felt a tug at the conviction in his voice. It was rare indeed to find a man who was that committed, that loyal. It was a new and thrilling thing to her. And she said, meaning every word, "I know a way to accomplish this."

He looked up and his eyes narrowed. "What?"

"Hand me the bo'sun's whistle."

Frowning, he took the silver whistle from around his neck. "I don't see—"

"Of course you don't," she said in exasperation. "Wait here."

She went out on deck, sounding the whistle. Ryan followed, propping his hip on a spirit barrel and regarding her with unconcealed skepticism. The crew gathered, clearly intrigued when they saw who had summoned them. Men, she thought. Sometimes they had bilge for brains.

She surveyed the circle of faces—harsh and bewhiskered, scoured by sun and wind, and realized with a lurch of her heart that in one voyage she had come to know these men better than she knew the members of her own family. Journey hung back, toying anxiously with the pendant around his neck. He had been solemn and thoughtful the past few days, and he was off his rations. Now she knew why. Terror and hope were consuming him.

"I think," she said, "you probably all know our purpose in making port here."

"We're to fetch Journey's wife and babies," Timothy said steadily, "so they can be together as God and nature intended."

She wanted to hug him for his simple, straightforward wisdom. If people in the South held the lad's view, the abomination of slavery would not exist.

"'Tis only right we tolerate the delay," Gerald stated with a firm nod in Journey's direction.

"We are all agreed, then?" she asked.

Click rubbed his jaw speculatively. "Depends on what we're agreed to."

"I shall get right to it, then, for you are used to plain speaking. Captain Calhoun is in need of several thousand dollars for this transaction, and the only available source is the ship's specie."

"A hanging offense, laying hands on that," said Chips.

"Piracy," added Luigi.

"At the very least, we'll be stripped of our seamen's papers if we're caught," Izard stated.

"This was supposed to be my last voyage," William Click said. "I've been saving up for a little farm."

"I've got a family to feed," Gerald reminded everyone.

"If I don't pay my debts, I'll land in jail for sure." The Doctor stared mournfully down at his hands.

"This wasn't part of the deal." Chips sounded belligerent. "I signed on for full share."

Isadora drew herself up, looking at each man in turn. "You are each free to determine what you can afford to do. Do you understand the meaning of that? You are *free* to decide." She paused, feeling them waver. "Journey's wife is not." She fixed each man with a hard look. "I shall repay you myself out of my dowry money."

"You can't do that," Gerald objected. "What will you bring to your husband when you marry?"

The laughter that bubbled up in her throat was painful. It was hard to believe that at one time, all she had dreamed of was marrying Chad Easterbrook. What a pitiful, self-deluded creature she had been. Ryan Calhoun had broken her heart, that was true. But he had also opened her eyes.

She felt his gaze upon her now, and dared to meet that chilly stare. This man had forever laid waste to her hopelessly romantic dreams. She should be grateful to him, but at the moment the hurt pressing against her chest left no room for gratitude.

"Believe me," she said, "slavery is a far greater evil than my spinsterhood."

Ryan turned away, planting his hands at his waist and staring at the reedy shoreline in the distance.

"What say you, gentlemen?" she asked, pretending not to notice his disgust. "Are you with your shipmate on this?" While she watched and waited, she held her breath, a hard knot in her throat.

The Doctor shuffled forward. "I never did bear the yoke of slavery," he said to Journey. "But I am an African, too, and your brother in spirit. Debt or no debt, I'll throw in my share."

Journey shut his eyes, his face flooding with relief.

"Take it off our sailors' bills," Gerald said. "Whatever you need." He fixed Mr. Click with a flinty eyed stare. "Ain't that right?"

"Our sh-shares are huge on this trip," Timothy added. "And Miss Isadora will make good on her promise."

"Never said I wouldn't throw in my lot." Click nodded his head in Journey's direction. "Whatever it takes, that's what we got to offer."

Journey made a choking sound, then turned away briefly. When he turned back, he could only mouth the words "Thank you."

Isadora beamed at them all, letting the knot in her throat unfurl. "I'll go get the ledger books."

"What if it doesn't work?" Izard murmured as he stood at the rail beside Isadora. They watched Ryan sculling for shore in a launch.

"It will," she stated. "All the figures summed up perfectly—"

"I fear money's not the problem."

She turned to study him. The chief mate was a puzzling man, quiet and somber, yet with a sturdy core of decency everyone respected, and an undeniable intelligence that made her listen when he spoke up. "So what, in your estimation, is the problem?"

"Perhaps I should have spoken sooner. I don't believe Beaumont will take the money. He won't accept any sum for the wench and her babies."

"How do you know so much about this?"

He hesitated, then said, "My late wife had African blood."

She gaped at him in wonder. "Mr. Izard—"

"Trust me, I know."

"Then why didn't you say anything earlier?"

"Would you have listened? Would anyone?" He spread his arms. "You might get to keep your dowry after all."

"That is not funny." She started to pace, her teeth worrying her lower lip. "Something has to be done, then. Something bold. Something audacious. Something that will work."

Izard was silent for a long time. "Miss Isadora, what

are the chances you could charm the stockings off an old Southern gent?''

She laughed. ''I couldn't charm the peel off a banana, for heaven's sake.''

''Not even if three lives depended on it?''

Her amusement faded. Self-doubt, her age-old companion, shadowed her thoughts. But then she glanced at the foredeck and spied Journey silhouetted against the late afternoon sky. He cut a lonely figure, tall and slender against the backdrop of the fiery clouds.

Ain't never seen my baby girl.

Isadora straightened her shoulders. ''I think, Mr. Izard, that I am about to become charming.''

Ryan had expected a chilly reception at Bonterre, but the outright hostility of Hugh Beaumont took him by surprise. The moment he walked up the horseshoe-shaped drive, a houseboy went running, and Beaumont himself appeared on the gleaming white porch, flanked by soaring columns.

He had changed little from Ryan's boyhood recollection. He'd always been a tall, ramrod straight widower with long hair and a waxed moustache with handles wide enough for birds to perch on. He wore well-cut clothes of stark black and snow-white, a marked contrast to Ryan's canary yellow shirt and peacock blue jacket. Maybe he should have listened to Journey and worn more somber colors, but it was too late now.

''Mr. Beaumont,'' he said, ''it's a pleasure to see you.'' Ryan mounted the porch steps and stuck out his hand.

Beaumont ignored it. "I take no pleasure in this meeting. And no Calhoun is welcome in my house."

Ryan flashed his best smile. "We're off to a fine start, then, aren't we? A dandy start. All right, sir. Suppose we forget I'm a Calhoun. I've come to make a business transaction with you, pure and simple. And then I'll be on my way."

The waxed moustache twitched. "What sort of business?"

"I'm interested in acquiring some slaves." Ryan nearly gagged on the words. "The wench called Delilah and her young ones."

Beaumont tilted back his head and roared with laughter. "I guess they didn't teach you much up there at Harvard College. Else you'd know damned well I'm on to you. You're interested in Delilah because you took her man away, set the buck free." His laughter stopped. "Don't you see, boy? If you'd left well enough alone, that family'd be together."

Ryan used all of his self-control to keep from trying to pound common sense into Beaumont's head. "Sir, I'm prepared to pay—"

"Uncle Ryan! Uncle Ryan!" Blue came tumbling across the lawn, a little tousle-haired moppet in tow. "Hey Uncle Ryan! What you doing here? Are you going to stay for supper?" He unleashed a steady stream of questions as he led the little girl up the steps to the porch. "Can we go look at your boat again? You want to help me build a tree house?"

"Whoa, there, son," Ryan said, smiling as he went down on one knee. "This your sister?"

"Uh-huh. Belinda. She's three."

"Well, hey there, three-year-old Belinda." Ryan winked at her. She stuck one finger in her mouth. Through a tumble of yellow curls, she peered at him shyly with eyes as blue as painted china. "I'm your uncle Ry—"

"Children, come inside this instant," said a nervous-sounding voice from the door.

Ryan straightened up quickly. "Lacey, it's good to see you again."

"I'm sure I can't say the same," she stated, then creaked open the screen door. Looking subdued but resentful, Blue and Belinda went to her side. Petite and beautiful, her hands moving in flutters of agitation, she kept her eyes averted from Ryan. "Father, I trust you won't be long? It's nearly the children's bedtime."

He nodded. With visible relief, Lacey let the door slap shut.

Evening was coming on, a long flat lowering of the light over the bay. On the road that passed in front of the main house, a horse whinnied, and somewhere unseen in the distance, a deep voice sang a spiritual hymn. As always in the mysterious tidewater region, beauty and brutality were present in equal measures.

Beaumont said, "I won't do business with you, Calhoun. Is that clear?"

Ryan drew a deep breath. "I'll pay you double what they're worth."

Beaumont smiled. "It's not a matter of money, but one of principle. Allowing this sort of thing would upset the natural balance of things. I can't simply sell a family into freedom. That would be irresponsible of me."

Ryan loosed a bark of incredulous laughter. "Good God, man, do you hear what you are saying?"

Beaumont drew himself up. "Sir, *you* are the one who is having trouble hearing. I'll do no business with you. The wench and her babies are not for sale at any price." He made a loud exhalation of disgust. "Your entire family is a disgrace."

Ryan's hand clenched into a fist. With a will, he kept it at his side. At least, he thought furiously, he would have no need of the ship's money. But now he'd have to find another way to bring Journey's wife north with them.

"Goodbye, Mr. Beaumont," Ryan said formally. "I shall give your regards to my brother."

"Sir, your brother knows exactly where he stands in my regard."

"Of that, I have no doubt."

"Pardon me. I believe I have another visitor." Beaumont brushed past Ryan and walked down the steps.

Ryan turned to see a tall black-clad woman in a plumed hat and beaded veil hurrying across the lawn. His mouth dried as he recognized her. Hell's bells. Why had Izard allowed Isadora to come ashore? This could mean nothing but trouble. It could mean he'd hang even sooner than he feared. "What the devil—"

"Do you know her?" Beaumont demanded, watching with interest.

Ryan couldn't imagine what she was up to. He was out of options with Beaumont, so perhaps he had best wait and see. Isadora had her faults, but stupidity was not one of them. He gave a noncommittal shrug and waited for her to approach.

"*There* you are, Ryan Calhoun," she declared in a remarkable Virginia accent. "I wondered where you'd run off to." Before he could reply she made a dainty curtsy for Beaumont. "Sir, please pardon this terrible intrusion."

"No trouble at all, ma'am." He paused, clearly expecting Ryan to make the introductions.

Isadora spoke before he had a chance. She put out a hand gloved in black lace. "Isa—Isabel Swann, of the...the Hipsucket Swanns. Up in Spotsylvania County, don't you know. I've been promised a berth to Boston aboard Captain Calhoun's ship. I was so afraid he had left without me."

Hugh, ever the know-it-all, smiled with gentlemanly politeness. "I see. Hugh Beaumont, at your service."

Behind the veil, she gave off an air of mysterious allure. "And I fear we must ask it of you," she said. "Your service, that is."

"Oh?"

She drew herself up stiffly. Censure seemed to radiate from behind the veil. "I came looking for Mr. Calhoun—we have been expecting him, you see—when our clarence became mired out on the road. Do you think some of your people could lend us a hand?"

Trying to figure out the angle of her ruse, Ryan marveled at Isadora's poised, calm, elegant performance. How different this beguiling creature was from the awkward girl who had first bumbled her way onto his ship.

"Your carriage is mired?" Beaumont asked.

"I fear so." She aimed a censorious finger at Ryan. "It is all your fault for wandering willy-nilly about the countryside. Mr. Beaumont, if we could please get some help.''

''Certainly, madam. I'll order my overseer to bring you a band of men,'' Beaumont said.

''Thank you ever so much. We shall need a good number. We are quite deeply mired.''

Where the hell had she learned that melting Southern accent? Ryan wondered.

''And Mr. Beaumont, one more favor.'' She leaned forward, put a hand on his sleeve and spoke in an intimate fashion that made Ryan bristle. ''I have a confession to make as well. For years I've heard of a magnificent place called Bonterre. Now I'm enjoying my chance to see it.''

And suddenly Ryan grasped her mad plan. Transporting escaped slaves was a crime. She and everyone involved would become fugitives with a price on their heads.

And—God help them all—he was going to let her.

''Oh, Mr. Beaumont, you do go on,'' Isadora said with laughter in her voice. ''I won't ever want to leave if you don't stop being so charming.''

Strolling by her side in the falling dark, Hugh Beaumont straightened his cravat. ''On the contrary, Miss Swann. *You* are the charmer, not I.''

''Sir, my head shall explode from its swelling,'' she protested.

Ryan gave a derisive snort.

Beaumont ignored him. ''I have fallen completely under your spell.''

She knew a moment of utter incredulity. The idea that

a man, any man, might find her charming was beyond her comprehension. An astonishing novelty. Was she *really* being charming? Was this all there was to it?

She was amazed by the skills necessity could inspire. There was a time when Isadora hadn't had a bold bone in her body; now it seemed that everything depended on her being bold.

She laughed again, amused by how easy it was to flirt and mimic the ways of a Southern social butterfly. "I insist that you stop it now, sir. My poor heart cannot take such flattery."

"And God forbid," Ryan muttered, trudging along behind them, "that your heart should suffer damage from flattery."

Isadora chuckled silkily. Ye powers, was he jealous? Surely not at a time like this. He had to know how desperate the situation was. She had not discussed the plan with him. Watching from the side of the roadway, where they'd half sunk Hunter's clarence in sticky black mud, she and the others had waited in the vain hope that perhaps Beaumont would sell the slaves to Ryan. When he had come out of the house alone, they knew they would have to set their plan in motion.

A stoop-shouldered man arrived at the head of a work crew. By the light of three torches, Isadora could see they were Africans. She tried surreptitiously to get Ryan's attention. He could ruin everything. When his gaze met hers, he aimed a fierce stare at her. "Miss...Swann."

She braced herself. "Yes?"

"I hope you don't expect me to roll up my sleeves

and unmire the clarence." He flicked his thumb and forefinger fussily at his wrist.

She thought she might explode with relief. He seemed to be going along with her masquerade. It was quite a thing, to trust and be trusted by him on faith alone.

They reached the mired carriage, a clarence hitched to Hunter's only remaining horse, a tired nag she hoped Beaumont wouldn't recognize in the uncertain torchlight. Ralph and Luigi had done an excellent job sinking the rear wheels in the soft mud of the salt marsh that bordered the road.

The "mishap" had occurred near a dozen or so split-log cabins arranged haphazardly around a common area of bare earth.

"Stand back, sirs, there you are." Ralph motioned for Mr. Beaumont and Ryan to step away. "Don't want to splash mud all over you."

A number of Hugh Beaumont's "people" had come to help. Odd how he called them people yet treated them like livestock. One man, probably the overseer, whistled and shouted orders.

Ralph Izard gave Isadora the briefest of nods, then cut his gaze away, the signal to carry on with their plan. She waved a handkerchief in front of her face. "Oh, my heavens," she said breathlessly. "All of a sudden I feel quite faint."

Beaumont put a supporting hand beneath her elbow. "Shall I help you back to the house?"

"That's not necessary." She tried to seem mortified. "It is a complaint of a very *female* nature."

That stopped any further speculation on his part. Ryan

pursed his lips as if holding in mirth and turned his attention to the mired coach.

"I shall find a place to rest over here." Her heart pounded as she approached the slave compound. A woman standing by the well and another by the big open-air cookfire stared at her. What a horror she must look to them—a white woman coming uninvited into their midst. Chickens scratched and poked in the beaten-earth yard, and children played a game with sticks and rocks. They were no different from any children, trying to snatch the last moments of the day as twilight fell, yet in too short a time, they would lose that innocent abandon.

Isadora felt as if she had entered a new and alien world, a place closed to a woman like her. A self-protective and savage air hung about the slave women. She guessed that they cultivated this frightening facade, for a white woman walking into their midst could mean nothing good. She was familiar with the antislavery tracts published in Boston, but nothing she had read had prepared her for this direct experience of the squalor and hostility that pervaded the compound.

She despaired of being able to identify Delilah among these silent, suspicious, homespun-clad women. Her every instinct told her to flee, to hide, to shrink away from a place she clearly didn't belong. Then she reminded herself of her purpose. Journey was waiting aboard the *Swan* for his wife and children. She couldn't let him down. Besides, there had been a time when she hadn't belonged on shipboard either, but she had become more at home there than in a drawing room on Beacon Hill.

Holding her head high, she went to the well. How did a Southern lady ask a slave for a drink of water? she wondered wildly. Taking a deep breath, she said, "Please, I'd like a cup of water."

"Yes'm." Without meeting Isadora's eyes, the woman pressed on the well sweep and brought up a bucket.

As Isadora drank the slightly brackish water from a tin cup, her veil kept getting in the way. A scrawny cat streaked across the dirt yard, and a small barefooted girl raced after it, giggling and oblivious to the tension of the women.

"Celeste," someone called, "you get yourself back here, right now!"

Isadora tried not to appear interested in the young woman in a threadbare dress. Isadora was glad for the darkness and the veil, because she felt a glorious smile coming on. Celeste was the name of Journey's younger daughter.

Setting down her cup, she stepped into the child's path and leaned down. "Celeste," she said gently, "Your mama's calling you." She held out her gloved hand. "Come. I'll take you to her."

The child fell as still as a pillar of salt, her eyes big. Isadora cursed herself for not realizing that a stranger with a veiled face was as frightening as a ghost. Celeste sucked in a deep breath and formed her mouth into an O, preparing to let loose with a scream.

Isadora saw her plan falling to pieces. The child's hysteria would draw Mr. Beaumont's attention, and all would be lost.

But before Celeste screamed, Delilah arrived, grabbing her hand and yanking her away from Isadora. The child clung to her mother's skirts, regarding Isadora with horror.

"Delilah," Isadora whispered, keeping her eyes straight ahead. "Please, don't run off. I have something for you."

"I best be going, ma'am," Delilah said, backing away. Her older child held fast to her hand. "It's time to get my babies to sleep."

It was all Isadora could do to keep from grabbing for her. She prayed no one would hear as she said, "I have something from Journey."

A soft intake of breath was her only reaction. "Yes'm," she said, very quietly.

A couple of the other women drew cautiously near. Isadora felt surrounded. Dear heaven, she was so close, yet how could she converse with Delilah now?

"Mistress needs to set a spell," Delilah said calmly. "That's all. Just needs to set a spell."

She led her toward a mud-chinked cabin. To Isadora's relief, the others stepped out of their way.

She sat on a crooked bench outside the cabin. Through the open door, she detected a faint glow from a rude stove with a teapot steaming atop it. The bed was a plank, the pillow a stick of wood, the bedding a coarse blanket.

Out on the road, the men were still busy whistling and hawing at the horse and trying to heave up the mired coach, but she knew she only had moments. She pulled something from her glove and pressed it into Delilah's hand.

"From Journey," she whispered. It was the love knot,

fashioned from a lock of Delilah's hair, on a leather strap.

Delilah's rough, slender fingers closed around the amulet. "Lord be praised," she said, so faintly that her children clutched at her.

"He's worn it around his neck ever since the day he left you," Isadora said. "We haven't much time. If you wish to leave this place tonight, I and the men with me will help."

Delilah's white-rimmed eyes shone in the flickering light with terror and hope. And—God be praised—trust. The love-knot from Journey had convinced her. "Yes'm."

As quickly as she could, Isadora explained the plan. "There is no time to think this over," she cautioned. "But the risks are clear. You don't have to go."

"I know the risks," Delilah said.

Isadora heard the conviction in her words. Delilah knew what was at stake better than Isadora ever would. In spite of her suffering, Delilah had the soft, womanly knowledge of her own humanity. She had birthed two babies and loved a man who was only half alive without her. Choosing between a lifetime of servitude and the threat of capture and punishment could not be easy for a woman with two tiny children. But Delilah had obviously made her decision. "I sorrowed a thousand nights for that man," she said. "I'm through with sorrowing."

"Then you know what to do." Isadora stood, already moving away, not wanting to betray a particular interest in Delilah. She fanned herself vigorously and hoped Mr. Izard would notice, for that was the signal to move on to the next step.

The tense moments drew out unbearably. With a great rocking motion and a squishing of mud, with a chorus of male grunts and "heave-hos," the carriage finally lurched up out of the mud. The horse, exhausted, gave a whinny and hung its head.

Isadora could hear the beating of her own heart in her ears, could feel the pulse of fear in her throat. She tried not to break into a cold sweat when she saw a quick flare of fire on the roof of one of the cabins. A woman screeched, and people ran toward the well. Luigi had touched a torch to the roof, creating mass confusion.

Meanwhile, Isadora walked quickly toward the coach, forgotten now in the excitement over the fire. Beside her, Delilah kept to the shadows, a child on each hip. No one seemed to notice as they went behind the coach. "Under the blankets, just there," Isadora whispered.

Shushing one of the girls, who had started to whimper, Delilah complied. Isadora prayed the darkness and shouts and confusion had covered the maneuver. She waited patiently as the flames were doused. It didn't take long, for the fire had no time to spread.

"Mr. Beaumont," she called, "are things always this exciting around here?"

"Happily, no. I much prefer the genteel excitement of a visitor like yourself." He bent gallantly over her hand, but when he straightened up, he looked at the clarence and frowned. "Isn't that an Albion coach?"

"Oh, heavenly days, I wouldn't say so. I hired it in Fairfield," Isadora said breezily. "The driver and footman as well." As Hugh took a step toward the rig, she moved in front of him. "And now I really must be go-

ing. But thank you ever so kindly. You have no idea
how much you've given me tonight.''

She curtsied, and he bowed dramatically. ''Miss
Swann, you are a bright star in an otherwise dreary evening.''

''And you, sir, are a gentleman beyond compare.
Come along, Mr. Calhoun,'' she said to Ryan. Dear
heaven, she sounded exactly like Lily. She prayed she
had Lily's dignity as she went to the coach and allowed
Luigi to hand her up.

She dared not let herself worry about what Ryan
thought of this charade. Gathering her skirts with great
care, she seated herself as he got in behind her. Then
the rig plunged into darkness, away from Bonterre forever.

Or so she hoped.

Weighing anchor in the dead of night was not the
smartest thing Ryan had ever done as skipper, but thanks
to Isadora's maneuver, he had no choice. He should be
furious, but he couldn't get the grin off his face. He
couldn't stop thinking about Journey's reunion with his
family.

It had been pure magic. A moment he would savor
for the rest of his days. Abandoning the carriage a mile
from Bonterre, Ralph and Luigi had conducted their passengers to an inlet where Chips awaited in a bumboat.
Rowing with all their might, they'd reached the *Swan* at
moonrise. Delilah and the children, who had huddled in
terrified silence the entire time, had spied Journey pacing
the decks.

Ryan would never forget the look on Dee's face when

she recognized her husband by the light of a binnacle lamp. She had looked up from her seat in the boat, and Journey had looked down from the ship's deck. Like a supplicant in church, she had lifted her gaze aloft, tightening her arms around her little girls and staring at Journey while the tears poured down her cheeks.

Isadora had wept unabashedly into her sleeve when Journey met Delilah at the boarding ladder. He'd held his girls in his arms and then, with a cry of joy so powerful it sounded like pain, he fell to his knees in gratitude, wrapping his arms around his wife's waist. He pressed his cheek to her stomach and sobbed. Every sailor aboard, men who had been hardened by the sea and inured to emotion, began to weep, Ryan included. Even William Click rubbed at his eyes and honked into his bandanna.

Now, hours later, they had set sail in the dark, hoping to avoid the shoals Ryan knew like the back of his hand. The moon had begun to set, and its light created a silver stream on the glassy surface of the water. At the mouth of Chesapeake Bay, a fair wind filled the sails.

Ryan turned back to view Virginia. The dark hills rose to the starry sky, a dazzling display of beauty in crystal-studded black velvet.

Virginia. It was a place in his heart. And there it would stay. He could never return now.

He felt...strange. This was a moment of triumph, to be sure. For years he'd awaited this reunion. On some level his life had been moving toward this moment since the day he'd left his father's house in disgrace. This was the culmination of everything he'd wanted, everything he'd worked for, everything he believed in. His heart should be full.

Yet something was missing. Something more. Something he needed in order to feel complete.

The burgeoning wind whispered a name through his mind. He felt a chill, a rising of the hairs on the back of his neck. Not now, he admonished himself. Especially not now. They were a ship of fugitives now, a band of outlaws. He was in no position to offer a future to anyone.

His goal was clear-cut. He had to get Isadora to Boston, leave her safe in the bosom of her family and convey Journey to Canada. That must be his focus, his purpose. Anything more was asking for trouble.

"Ryan?"

At the sound of her soft voice, he nearly let go of the wheel. "It's late," he said gruffly. "You should be sleeping."

"How can I sleep after what we did?" She moved with a spritely gait, her eyes sparkling in the moonlight. She drew energy from the very air around her. How different she was from the pasty-faced, disapproving schoolmarm who had come aboard so long ago. Now she wore plain clothes, her hair unbound, her bare foot pressed casually against the rail. She looked so incredibly alluring to him that he nearly groaned aloud.

"What a fine day this was," she said.

He grew irritated at the elation in her voice. "You turned us all into criminals."

"Don't sound so disapproving. It's what you wanted, isn't it?"

"I wanted Journey and Delilah together again, yes,"

he admitted. ''But I was hoping to do it without turning pirate.''

''Slavery is criminal.''

''Not in the eyes of the law.'' Ryan felt the shock of an ugly truth. This day was not his. This victory was not his. She had taken both from him. Deep down, he felt outdone by her.

Part Four

The Swan

Then, quite suddenly, he lifted his wings. They swept through the air much more strongly than before, and their powerful strokes carried him far. Before he quite knew what was happening, he found himself in a great garden where apple trees bloomed. The lilacs filled the air with sweet scent and hung in clusters from long, green branches that bent over a winding stream. Oh, but it was lovely here in the freshness of spring!

But what did he see there, mirrored in the clear stream? He beheld his own image, and it was no longer the reflection of a clumsy, dirty, gray bird, ugly and offensive.

He himself was a swan!

—Hans Christian Andersen,
The Ugly Duckling (1843)

Twenty-Three

—∞∞∞—

And this is good old Boston,
The home of the bean and the cod,
Where the Lowells talk to the Cabots
And the Cabots talk only to God.

—John Collins Bossidy,
    Toast, at the Holy Cross Alumni Dinner

Boston, April 1852

A sleek harbor launch slid away from the *Swan*, its inhabitants jubilant, their animated chatter carrying across the harbor waters. Ryan stood at the rail and watched it go. He had sent Izard and Click ashore with instructions to report their arrival to the harbor authorities. They also had secret instructions to commission a stout Dutch-built schooner for a swift, clandestine trip to Canada. The transaction would beggar Ryan despite the lucrative voyage, but he didn't care. His goal was to get Journey and his family safe away, to a place they could live free.

Within moments, another launch arrived. Apprised of the arrival of the bark, Abel Easterbrook had sent his factor and clerk out for a preliminary report. Ryan squinted into the cloud-darkened distance, recognizing with an unpleasant jolt that a third man was with the company officials. Chad Easterbrook.

Ryan glanced about to see where Isadora had gone. She was nowhere to be seen; she was probably in her berth, organizing her belongings for her homecoming. He wondered what she would do when she saw Chad. Was he still the object of her naive, dogged devotion? Would she regret her wild interlude on the *Swan*?

Everyone had orders to keep Delilah and the children out of sight. The Fugitive Slave Law was in full force; they wouldn't be taking any foolish chances. By now, Beaumont would have notified the authorities and furnished a detailed description of Journey's wife and children.

With a lordly air, Abel's son boarded and came strolling across the deck. Predictably, he nearly stumbled on a coil of rope. Recovering his composure, he said, "Welcome home, Captain Calhoun. We didn't expect you so soon. Do you have the affidavits for the cargo?"

"Everything's in order." Ryan presented the transactions he'd made in Rio. Seeing Isadora's painstakingly neat figures, he felt a stab of tenderness and gratitude. She had been an asset to the enterprise, something he never would have predicted when they'd set sail.

Chad glanced at some of the papers. Clearly he didn't comprehend all the figures, but the factor adjusted his spectacles and gave a low whistle. "Well-done, Skipper," he said. "Well-done, indeed."

Almost grudgingly, Chad held out a handwritten message on heavy card stock. "There's a dancing party at the house tonight. My father wishes for you to attend."

Ryan grinned, taking the invitation. "I mustn't disappoint him, then."

Chad cleared his throat. "My father will send a coach. Will there be anything else?" he asked the factor.

"Not today. Tomorrow we'll bring her to a berth and begin discharging cargo."

Ryan kept a cordial smile in place as they prepared to leave. Best to get the windbag ashore as quickly as possible. As Chad put one foot on the ladder, the ship's cat emerged from beneath an upended jolly boat and went strolling lazily down the deck. He looked at it, then widened his eyes in disbelief as three-year-old Celeste, giggling, scrambled up through a hatch to chase the cat.

Everyone froze except the plump, laughing child and the harried cat.

"An unauthorized passenger, Skipper?" Chad asked, narrowing his eyes at Ryan.

"No, indeed," he lied smoothly. "You'll find everything in order in the ship's manifest. Knowing what a dedicated humanitarian your father is, we adopted an orphaned child."

As casually as possible, the Doctor scooped up the little girl, crooning to her as he took her down to the galley.

"An orphan, you say?"

Ryan put his face very close to Chad's. "Aye, sir. That's exactly what I say."

Chad departed. Ryan couldn't tell whether or not he'd accepted the explanation. Judging by the rate his heart was clattering against his rib cage, the lie had been obvious. But the day was getting on, Chad would probably forget all about the incident and if the weather held, Ryan would sail for Canada at dawn. He let out a long breath, feeling his heartbeat slow to normal.

"Was that Mr. Easterbrook's factor?" Isadora asked, coming up behind him.

"Yes. Chad was with them."

"Heavens be, Chad?"

"The very one. Why didn't you come out to greet him?"

She looked crestfallen. "I didn't know he'd come. I was below, helping Delilah get the children's things together."

Ryan studied her, trying to read beyond the crestfallen look. Already she seemed different, growing as somber as the stormy weather coming in from the east. He missed the other Isadora, the one who threw herself into the voyage with a sense of adventure, the one who had emerged on deck, barelegged and laughing, to reef sail or haul in line like the ablest of salts.

He handed her the invitation. "Abel is having a reception tonight. A dancing party, actually."

He didn't look at her, but could feel her staring. "Do you think I should go?" she asked.

It infuriated him that Chad had not thought to mention her by name when issuing the invitation. "Of course. I'm certain your family will be there."

"Then surely I should go," she said. "You'll be there, won't you?"

"I'll come later. I have to get Journey and Delilah situated."

"It's Canada for them, then?"

He nodded but didn't elaborate further, didn't want to burden her with the risky plan he knew he had to carry out.

"They can never come back," she said quietly.

"Not unless slavery is abolished."

"*Until* it's abolished, you mean."

"Things are getting worse, not better. Since Congress passed the Fugitive Slave Law, everyone suspects everyone else. It's neighbor against neighbor these days."

She touched his hand lightly, so lightly. "You'll miss him, won't you?"

Like I'd miss my right arm if I cut it off. But he didn't say it aloud.

Thunder rumbled in from the east. The ominous bank of clouds rolled nearer. A storm. Just what he didn't need.

"You'd best get ready for the Easterbrook reception. I'll take you over myself in the launch."

She hesitated, and he made the mistake of looking into her eyes. Damn, but she tugged at his heart, made him wish he could sweep her away, take her to some far-off place and make love to her, make a child with her and spend the rest of his life loving her.

"Ryan," she said. "I wish—"

"Just go," he said, his voice lashing out, making her flinch. "Go and get ready for the reception."

"Yes, sir," she snapped. "I shall do that."

A clap of thunder punctuated her speech as she walked away from him. He forced himself to stay rooted, but his heart wouldn't let her go. He needed her. God, just one more time. He needed her one more time.

Isadora crouched in the hip bath in the cramped cabin that had been her quarters for so many weeks. She fought back a crippling sense of apprehension. *Home.* She had come home to Boston.

She'd bathed with soap and fresh water. Now that they'd reached port, they didn't have to conserve. She used copious amounts of silky clean water as her nervous thoughts churned.

She should not feel disturbed by the idea of being back. This was where she belonged. She should be looking forward to seeing her family again, to her room and her books, to the life she'd always lived.

Yet how could she possibly fit back into her former world? The idea of facing her family and Chad terrified her. The notion of returning to the place where life had been so cruel to her was unthinkable.

With a heavy heart, she opened her trunk and took out the familiar black bombazine gown. She donned a chemise and corset and petticoats, feeling her spirits compress with every layer.

Even the garments themselves seemed to droop mournfully. Formerly her favorite gown, the black dress now hung on her like a half-empty potato sack. Gone were the taut lines, the crisp pleats that used to adorn the outfit so handsomely.

Blowing out a huff of exasperation, she took up a hairbrush and tried to bring some semblance of order to her hair. Instead, she caught herself dreaming. Dreaming of the day Ryan had chopped off her hair, and she'd stormed at him, and then he'd touched her cheek and somehow made it all right.

Though she had no mirror, she could feel the sun-streaked curls going wild. Where were her combs? She hadn't used them in ages.

Hearing a knock at the door, she said, "Come in," barely lifting her head as Ryan stood in the doorway.

"Isadora."

Ye powers. No one said her name like that, in that slow, intimate, Southern fashion.

"Yes?"

"You're supposed to be dressing for a party, not a funeral."

She brushed her hand at the thick black fabric of her skirt. "This is my best dress."

"I wasn't talking about the dress, sugar-pie, though now that you mention it, that frock's a mite somber. I was talking about the expression on your face. You look as though someone's died."

She managed a thin smile. "I was thinking how simple life is on shipboard. We all know our roles. It would be so much easier if I could stay here."

He chuckled. She tried to summon indignation, but somehow when Ryan laughed at her, she had the urge to join him. He held out his hand. "Isadora, come here."

"I am here. This cabin is too small for me to be anywhere else."

He laughed again and took her hand. "I mean here. I want to show you something."

She stumbled after him, following him out into the companionway, up the narrow ladder and to the stern deck. He pulled her through the door to his cabin.

"If there is more paperwork to be done, I wish you would have told me earlier," she said with some exasperation. "I haven't my ledger book or—"

"Isadora."

She nearly melted at the way he said her name. "Yes?"

"This is not about paperwork."

"Then...what?" But she looked into his eyes and she knew. She knew, and her heart leaped while the breath caught in her throat.

"It's about this," he said and took her in his arms.

She felt a rush like the wind moving over her, enveloping her, and she realized that she wanted this, had wanted it for so long that she could no longer remember what it was like not to want it. He kissed her, and all the familiar longed-for sensations washed over her, reminding her of that magical day in the rain forest when he had changed the color of her world.

Only this time was different, deeper, better, more meaningful, because they had not made themselves silly on hemp leaves. They knew exactly what they were doing.

"Ryan," she whispered against his mouth.

"Forget it," he said. "I'm not stopping this time."

"I wasn't going to tell you to stop."

Triumph glinted in his eyes as he bent to kiss her again. And this time he didn't stop at a kiss. His hands, those deft seaman's hands, made short work of buttons and ties and stays, discarding her clothes on the floor. Though it was overcast and stormy outside, the stateroom glowed with soft light through the stern windows. And here she stood in nothing but her shift. She did not even have the excuse of inebriation to explain her lack of self-consciousness or moral indignation.

Yet it never occurred to her to find this objectionable. The first time she'd come aboard this ship she'd found Ryan with a woman, yet the memory didn't bother her. Nothing bothered her.

She wanted to be with him, to cling to him as if to the final vestiges of the voyage that had ended. It seemed inconceivable that they would part, yet they had to. He offered her nothing but this moment in time, this intimate embrace, and she accepted them both gladly, knowing she could live for years on these memories.

He took her by the hand and brought her to the bunk, pressing her against the pillows and kissing her thoroughly, hard and crushingly as if to imprint his mark on her. Then he stood and through half-lidded eyes she watched him undress, admiring the sleek, long muscles in his legs and the breadth of his chest, the frank maleness that she knew a true lady would not stare at. She made a small, involuntary sound and lifted her arms to him, impatient for his touch. He plucked at the laces of her shift and drew it apart, baring her breasts and kissing them tenderly, slowly, drawing a cry of near-pain from her, then soothing her with slow touches that circled down, down to her center and stroked her until she felt such a fierce rise of ecstasy she was certain she'd scream and alert the crew. He lifted himself, moved his hips so that they touched, and smiled down at her.

Slowly, by tantalizing inches, he sank into her, and in shameless response, she lifted her hips to him.

Neither of them spoke; they said what needed to be said with lips and hands and the long, slow embrace of deep passion. It went on endlessly; it was over too soon. She wanted his lovemaking to last forever, yet she was impatient to feel the explosion inside, to make certain the other time hadn't been an aberration. Ryan surrounded her, engulfed her and she finally began to understand what it meant to be one with a man. For surely in this shattering moment in time they were one body, one heart, one mind, driving toward a completion they both needed as much as they needed the next breath of air.

In the rain forest she thought she had glimpsed paradise. She had imagined she'd found a piece of heaven but that it was rare, never to be seen or felt again. Now, in Ryan's arms, with cloudy daylight showering over them and her thoughts as clear as the glass panes in the stern windows, she felt it again, only everything was stronger, brighter, more meaningful.

This time the experience was not blurred by a narcotic fog. Her passion crested in a burst of pleasure that left her mindless. She simply lay there, a creature of air and light, glorying in the feel of him inside her, and nearly exploding again when she felt his release.

He lowered himself against her, his breath warm on her neck, saying her name over and over again in whispers.

She closed her eyes and drifted, smiling secretively.

"What is that smile for?" he asked at last, pressing his lips to her temple.

"It wasn't a fluke."

"What wasn't a fluke?"

"The...um...the moment of pleasure."

He pulled away, chuckling, and lay at her side, his

hand tracing loose, idle patterns over her naked breasts and belly. "You thought the first time was a fluke."

"I had no point of reference, you see. And then there was the matter of the hemp cigars, so I thought perhaps they were the cause of all that, um, pleasure."

"Love, no drug can have the narcotic effect—" he leaned down and kissed her breasts, each in turn "—as physical intimacy with the right person."

"How do you know which is the right person?"

"You don't. Not at first, at least. It happens."

"And you would know."

"Yes. I would know."

"Oh, Ryan—"

"You have to understand, I couldn't let you return to Boston in widow's weeds."

She clung to him. "Why do you bring this up now?"

"I thought you might be wondering why I brought you in here and took off all your clothes." He changed the subject smoothly.

"Because they looked like widow's weeds."

"Because...you're not that person anymore. You're not the Isadora Peabody who came aboard so wrapped in sadness, so timid, afraid of your own shadow. You've traveled the globe. You've had adventures."

"I've had adventures," she said, "I've had you." Her throat felt sore with words unsaid. "Ryan—"

"Hush." He pressed a finger to her lips. "You've got a party to go to."

She glumly eyed her dress and underthings crumpled on the floor.

"Not that," he said, getting up and putting on his trousers and shirt. "I have a better idea."

"But—"

"Hush," he said again. "So long as we're aboard this ship, I'm the skipper. You'll do as I say." He dressed hurriedly in trousers and shirt, then bowed gracefully, holding out his hand. "Come here, Miss Peabody."

She felt wicked rather than awkward as she left the bed and went to the washstand. The water in the basin was tepid but fresh, and with a grave sense of purpose he insisted on bathing her, using the minty soap made in the kitchen of his aunt's house. He took his time, lathering and rinsing her, pausing to kiss her in places that she should forbid him to touch, but instead she opened herself to him. He'd put a spell on her, and she was powerless to object to anything he chose to do to her, with her, for her. Trusting him utterly, she let herself be totally manipulated by him, and the washing became a sensual adventure that left her almost weeping with pleasure.

Afterward he draped a flannel robe around her, then went to the door, murmuring something to one of the men on deck. A few minutes later, Ryan opened the door and dragged in a packing crate from the hold. Using a pry bar, he opened the stout wooden box.

"Raiding your stores already," Isadora said in mock disapproval.

"It's for an honorable cause," he assured her. "My mother sent this as a gift for you."

She tilted her head to read the lettering stenciled on the side. "*Seta fina*—fine silks from Italy."

"There's a case of paints and scent and lacquer, too."

"What on earth would I do with that?"

"We'll figure it out."

With the grave purpose of a Paris couturier, he picked out a rich peacock turquoise gown with fiery scarlet trim. "My mother claims this will flatter your coloring," he said. "Do you like it?"

She laughed because he looked absurd holding it against him, yet she felt drawn to the dazzling iridescent color and the shocking cut of the dress. Then a memory flashed through her—the day she'd dressed in white for the croquet party and Thankful had ridiculed her.

She cast her gaze down. A handsome gown would not transform a frog into a princess. "I would not be comfortable wearing that."

"Trust me," he said. "You'll be comfortable."

And then she recalled what he had said to her—that she was a different person. Perhaps even the sort of person who could wear a shockingly vibrant gown to a staid Beacon Hill dancing party.

"Ryan, I don't know—"

He cut her off with a long kiss that evoked echoes of the pleasure they had shared. "Don't tell me," he said, "a woman can kiss like that and then wear black."

He insisted on putting the gown on her, kicking aside her stays. "The iron maiden again. I'm feeding it to the sharks." He allowed her only one petticoat no matter what she said. Then he made her put on a pair of silk stockings so sheer she could see through the fabric.

It felt good, sinfully good, to experience the whisper of silk against her skin. The dress was snug but not tight, enveloping her like a kind embrace. She loved the slippery smoothness of the costly fabric.

After a long time of fussing and fumbling with the

gown, Ryan stood back and regarded her with a critical eye. "This is beyond me. I need some help."

She flushed scarlet, certain he was making sport of her, but in total earnestness he went to the door and whistled, calling out to various members of the crew. Standing outside the door, he held a murmured conference with the men. Long, horrible moments passed. She stood trapped like a startled doe with nowhere to hide. And then the most extraordinary thing happened.

They all came. Every man aboard, as well as Delilah. Like the daintiest of handmaidens, each man on the crew contributed to dressing her up. They comported themselves like acolytes in a ceremony, paying homage.

Journey brought a pair of embroidered dancing slippers from the crate and slid them on her feet. Gerald Craven, calling on his skill as the resident tattoo artist, used kohl and carmine to highlight her eyes and lips. Luigi, the sail maker, brought out his needle and thread to nip in the dress at the waist where it hung a little too loose. The Doctor presented her with a necklace of abalone shells that glowed with the opalescence of a full moon. Even Chips contributed a surprising item—an atomizer of rare hibiscus scent. Delilah took great delight in lacquering her fingernails while the wide-eyed children looked on. Last of all, with deep concentration, Timothy Datty did her hair.

Isadora took it all in with the stunned inertia of a weary Cinderella. They were fairy godmothers in rugged sailors' garb, and as she came to understand what they were doing, she felt a hard, painful lump in her throat.

"You all planned this, didn't you?" she said thickly.

"'Deed we did," the Doctor said proudly. "Can't

send you back into the world without doing something special for our own Isadora.''

"Don't forget to point your toe when you curtsy," Gerald advised, pantomiming the gesture.

"And hold your little finger out when you drink your tea." Journey demonstrated with a cup.

"It's the least we can do, seeing as how you did so much for us," Timothy added, patting a mother-of-pearl comb into place.

"So much," she said, confused. "I don't know what you mean."

Ryan stood back, smiling at her like some sort of benevolent god. "You touched every one of us, Isadora, in your own way."

"Whoa there." Journey handed her a wispy lace-edged handkerchief. "Don't go crying on us now. You'll ruin Gerald's work."

She shut her eyes and pressed her rouged lips together, taking a deep breath. It didn't help, not much, but because Gerald looked so proud and expectant, she dared not let tears smudge the kohl. "You are," she said, her gaze sweeping the crowded stateroom, "the first true friends I've ever had." She tried to dispel the tension by brushing out the silky folds of her skirts. "But heavens be, what in the world is Boston going to think of me?"

"Why don't you see for yourself?" Chips nodded to Luigi, who brought in a crate marked Fragile. Using the pry bar, they took out a fine gilt cheval glass.

As they set it up, Isadora realized she hadn't seen a mirror in months. Ryan's shaving mirror was so tiny it only showed part of the face. She was almost afraid to take a peek, for she had never enjoyed seeing the unhappy reflection of her gawky, large self.

But the crew seemed so proud, she didn't want to disappoint them. She waited, shoulders straight and chin held high in the new way she had learned to carry herself. They positioned the tall mirror and turned it toward her. Then, for the first time since leaving Boston, she confronted herself in a full-length looking glass. What she saw stunned her speechless.

She was looking at a stranger.

A beautiful stranger.

The ugly duckling had become a swan.

She wasn't pudgy and pale, but fit and strong, thanks to the Doctor's galley rations and an active life on shipboard. A mass of sun-gilt curls framed her astonished, almost elegant-looking face. Sun and wind had turned her pallor to a vivid gold hue, unconventional yet curiously attractive. The daring dress and dancing shoes completed the picture of a bold beauty, unknowingly transformed in ways that she knew went far deeper than looks alone. She realized that it was not so much her looks but her very deepest inner self that had changed.

Completing the voyage, coming to know these men and especially Ryan, had given her the self-confidence she'd always lacked, and that confidence showed in her proud posture and upright carriage. Her dealings in Rio had taught her to meet the most intimidating eye without flinching; her late nights on the midships deck and at Rose's villa had given her the poise to dance with the handsomest of men without feeling inferior; her masquerade in Virginia had taught her that anything was possible if only she dared to believe herself worthy.

Ryan and the crew—her own personal charm school—had given her this.

Isadora couldn't help herself. She burst into tears.

"Don't," they all begged at once, but she couldn't stop. She embraced each man in his turn, and finally Journey and Delilah, soaking first one handkerchief and then another.

"You are all so very dear to me," she said. She indicated the sad, lovely vision in the mirror. "Your friendship has made me into someone I was never able to be before."

Delilah bathed her face with a cool cloth and Gerald repaired the makeup.

"It's time to go," Ryan said, taking her hand.

As if in a dream, she went out on deck and they were lowered away in a launch. Ryan himself manned the oars, pulling them smoothly and cleanly through the waters of Boston harbor. She twisted around to look back at them. They all lined the rails of the *Silver Swan*, and with the sails reefed and the storm brewing on the distant horizon, there was a drama and poignancy in the moment that almost brought on more tears.

"Don't," Ryan said, reading her mind. "I haven't got Gerald's hand with the makeup, so don't start crying again."

She turned to face him. "I won't."

She watched him row, and with the powerful rhythm of his strokes, every moment of their time together flashed before her eyes. The night she'd met him, like a drunken Bacchus on his throne, a woman draped across his lap. Casually handsome in the garden at her father's house, getting a glimpse of her discontented life. On the deck of the ship, issuing orders and laughing as the wind filled the sails. And finally, she thought of how close they had been, how intimate, and how she should be ashamed but could not for the life of her summon shame at what they had done, what they had been to one another.

Too soon, they reached the city dock and he helped her out. The solid ground seemed to list beneath her feet and she leaned against him, catching his scent of wind and sea. He supported her with one arm while signaling to the Easterbrook coach with its crested bridled horses. The doors were painted with the familiar company emblem—the silver swan on a field of blue.

"Have fun at the ball tonight, princess," he told her with a wink. "You do know how to have fun, don't you?"

She smiled, feeling a blush steal up to her cheeks. "I do now. You'll come to the reception later, won't you?"

"Later." He touched her beneath the chin. The bustle of workmen, fishermen, distillers and laborers at the harbor faded into the background. She didn't care who saw them, didn't care what they thought. "I promise."

"Ryan?"

"Yes?"

"Can I ask you something?"

"Anything."

"Why—after that day at the waterfall—why did you keep your distance from me? Why couldn't we be...close, as we were today?"

He laughed, yet his mirth held dark tones of irony. "You really don't know, do you?"

"Know what?"

"You really don't understand."

"Understand what?"

He bent slightly and kissed her. "Isadora. I fell in love with you that day."

For several moments she was too stunned to speak. The raucous cries of seagulls pounded like thunder in her ears. "Don't tease me. It's cruel."

"I'm not teasing." He regarded her steadily, and deep in his eyes she saw an abiding affection that she wanted to close into her heart and keep forever.

"Why didn't you tell me?"

"What would have been the point?" He kissed her again, then he turned and walked her to the buggy, handing her up to the coachman. "Make your way carefully," he instructed. "She is precious cargo."

And that was how she left him. Standing on the wharf, a quickening wind plucking at his hair and shirt, his hand at his waist and hip cocked to one side. She had the horrid, irrational notion that she would never see him again, even though he'd promised he would come to the reception.

A scream built in her chest, but she couldn't let it out, for if she did, everything inside her would follow and she would be empty, with nothing, not even memories, to help her survive.

Twenty-Four

❧❧❧

Whereto answering, the sea,
Delaying not, hurrying not,
Whispered me through the night, and very
    plainly before daybreak,
Lisped to me the low and delicious word death.

—Walt Whitman,
Out of the Cradle Endlessly Rocking

"Here we are, miss." The driver opened the door of the coach and set down a battered wooden step stool. "And I hope you have a fine evening."

Isadora thanked him absently but made no move to exit the vehicle. She stared at the ornate entranceway of the Easterbrook mansion. Marble steps, flanked by tall urns, led up to double doors that had been flung wide to accommodate the press of people who flowed into the foyer. Gaslight glowed in the early evening, creating a soft warmth that surrounded the elegant crowd.

Dancers swirled past the tall bowed windows in a bouquet of color and music. She wondered if she would see her family at the party. Arabella would be married now.

Getting married used to be the beginning and end of all Isadora's dreams. But now she was not so certain. Now she realized that the key to happiness had less to do with setting up housekeeping with an appropriate spouse and more, far more, to do with finding someone who gave one confidence and peace and passion, gifts so rich she had no words for them.

"Miss?" the coachman prompted. He cleared his throat and held out his leather-gloved hand.

"Yes," she murmured, allowing him to help her down. A brisk wind, heavy with rain, gusted along Beacon Street, blowing her feather-light skirts. She walked slowly up the stairs to the door, suddenly conscious that she looked nothing like the other guests. She wore a vivid-colored gown cut in a style that Boston would hardly recognize; her hair was a mass of loose curls rather than the customary Psyche knot with its streamers; days in the sun and wind had ruined the snowy pallor the other ladies strove for.

Isadora smiled. She had never fit in before and she was accustomed to this feeling. Yet unlike before, she didn't wish to be invisible. She wanted everyone to see her, wanted to do honor to the gifts Ryan and the crew had given her.

With her head held high and her smile fixed in place, she stepped into the foyer and greeted her hosts.

"Mr. and Mrs. Easterbrook, it's so good to see you again." She felt the frank heat of dozens of stares fixed upon her. The former Isadora would have melted into a puddle of nerves to find herself the object of such avid attention. But the present Isadora merely smiled wider as she dipped into a polite and graceful curtsy.

She knew it was graceful. Mr. Izard had drilled her on the skill for weeks. Thanks to the unlikely kindness of a band of rough sailors, she now knew how to dance and comport herself like a queen if she chose to.

Abel and his wife exchanged a swift glance. "And you, too, my dear. Welcome to our home. Please, come in and meet ev—"

"Pardon me," said a deep and familiar voice. "I don't believe we've been introduced."

Isadora stood very still, savoring the sound of a voice she used to live for. She turned to see Chad Easterbrook bowing, reaching for her hand. And she laughed, because she realized he truly *didn't* know who she was.

"On the contrary," she said, her laughter gaining even more attention from dancers and passersby. "We have indeed been introduced. Fie on you, sir."

"Then dance with me," Chad said, giving her a look that all but devoured her, "and allow me a chance to recover my memory."

Amazing, she thought as he led her out to the dance floor and joined a lively reel done in two lines. Were people truly that deceived by looks? The most dramatic changes had occurred within. Yet they shone from without.

More inquisitive stares followed her through the reel. For the first time in her life, Isadora knew what it felt like to be the object of male admiration. Foster Candy tried to whisper a compliment to her as they faced each other across the lines of the reel. His younger brother nearly tripped over his feet because he was looking at

Isadora rather than watching where he was going. Chad almost came to blows with Foster as they debated which one of them deserved the privilege of fetching her a cup of punch.

She also experienced, for the first time, the envy of females. Lydia Haven looked daggers at her, and other young ladies had a furious conference about her behind their fans.

This, Isadora discovered, was far less pleasurable. She didn't want to make anyone uncomfortable. She simply wanted to enjoy herself in company, something she'd never been able to do.

Until Ryan showed her how.

Ryan.

She cast a glance at the door. Where was he, anyway? She missed him. She was still in shock over their last conversation.

I fell in love with you that day.

The words sang in her ears, drowning out the music until she danced strictly by rote, a puppet unaware of the actual steps. He'd fallen in love with her. Ryan. Her exasperating, glorious, wild, dangerous, troubled, exuberant, unconventional sea captain.

She couldn't wait to see him.

"We'd best wait till the storm passes," Ryan said, facing the ugly low brow of storm clouds moving in from the northeast. He and Journey stood on the deck of the schooner Izard had managed to commission. Its owner clearly had more greed than pride in his ship. The double-masted vessel, though sleek for fast oceangoing, suffered from rot and had a decided list to the starboard side.

"I don't think we should wait," Journey said, handing him a long brass spyglass. "Have a look at that skiff."

"The revenue man," Ryan said.

"They're heading straight for the *Swan*."

He might be correct, Ryan reasoned, judging by the set of the jib. But there were a lot of boats in the harbor.

"The crew will stall them. Hold them off if it comes to that."

"That Easterbrook character got a look at Celeste," Journey said, his voice low and taut with anxiety. "Damn it, Ryan. Did we come this far just to get caught?"

"The weather's ugly." Ryan's gut churned with indecision. "No one but a fool would weigh anchor in this."

"A fool or a fugitive," Journey replied.

The skiff drew closer to the *Swan* and Ryan had another look. What he saw through the crosshairs of the round brass eye made up his mind for him. "They're carrying armed police."

He and Journey shared a look that needed no words. They had no choice. They had to leave.

"Are Dee and the girls all right below?"

"Yeah."

They didn't even pause to weigh anchor; they cut the cables and ran. While the schooner pitched up and over the growing storm swells and the wind howled through the rigging, Ryan thought of Isadora. He had promised to go to the party. He had broken the first promise he'd ever made her. Surely that was proof she was better off without him.

What was she doing now? Was she smiling her dazzling smile, holding court before a group of adoring swains?

He liked to think he had a hand in making her dreams come true.

And had he been wrong to tell her he loved her? He didn't know. But he was glad he'd told the truth. It might be the only honest thing he could ever give her.

The sense of wonder glowing inside Isadora grew stronger each time she thought of Ryan's declaration. She became anxious for him to arrive. But he didn't. Instead, more guests showed up, the current dance ended, and in the heartbeat lull after the smattering of applause, she looked for Ryan again.

"I hope you'll allow me to call on you," Chad Easterbrook said, coming to stand beside her, a proprietary hand at her waist.

It should be, Isadora thought, a dream come true to hear all of this. Hadn't she wished for years that Chad would notice her, would want to be with her? Yet now she regarded his storybook-prince face, his perfect clothes, and she realized that he had been an illusion, as unreal as an illustration in a children's book. She hadn't loved Chad; she'd loved the *idea* of Chad. He'd stood for those things she'd lacked—good looks, poise, social popularity. Yet now that she possessed those qualities, she realized they weren't at all the panacea she'd thought them to be.

"You'd not object, then?" Chad said anxiously, not at all attuned to her mood. "If I were to call on you?"

"Why would I object?" she murmured distractedly. She couldn't keep from looking at the door. A howl of wind rattled the glass panes in the sidelights. Lightning flashed, filling the foyer with an angry blue glow.

A few minutes later, more guests arrived, but Ryan wasn't among them. Still, Isadora was happy to see the newcomers. She stood beside Chad, smiling as they approached.

A woman's voice said, "Dora? Dear lord, it's Isadora!" and pandemonium broke loose.

"Is...Isadora?" Chad's jaw dropped.

Isadora turned to embrace her sister Arabella, who had been so voluble in her surprise. "Oh, Belle, it's so good to see you," she said, hugging her, feeling their skirts whisper together, then standing back as Arabella held her at arm's length and stared incredulously.

"I don't believe my eyes," Arabella said, her face shining with wonder. "Look at you, Dora. You're absolutely gorgeous!"

Isadora laughed, knowing it wasn't so, not in the way Arabella meant but touched nonetheless that her sister had marked the change. Within seconds, while everyone around them buzzed with the news, her other sister and brothers came to greet her, followed by their parents. Chad stood back, silent, flabbergasted, as everyone spoke at once.

"When did you return?" "What on earth did you do to your hair?" "Where are your spectacles?" "Is this the style in Rio de Janeiro?" "Can you show me that new dance step?"

Isadora tried to answer as many questions as she could, aware of a growing audience at the fringes of the family group. "I have ever so much to tell you," she said. "I feel as if I've been gone for years rather than months."

Her parents beamed with pride. "We're pleased to have you home. We've missed you," her mother said.

And Isadora understood that at last, at long last, she had done something to please her mother. She should have felt satisfied, but instead she was merely puzzled. Why was it so easy to win approval when she looked nice and danced well?

Despite her pleasure at being with her family, she couldn't keep from darting nervous glances at the front door.

"Are you expecting someone?" her brother Bronson asked.

"Captain Calhoun," she said. "I thought he would have arrived by now. This voyage has been such a triumph for him—"

"Didn't you know?" Abel asked, stepping forward, his brow creased. "He won't be calling on us. His chief mate sent word—Calhoun had to send his regrets."

By morning, Isadora Dudley Peabody had become the toast of Boston. At one time, the lauded distinction would have meant the world to her. But now she realized how shallow it was to want something that depended on the opinions and standards of others and had nothing to do with her alone.

Early in the morning she sat up in bed, goggle-eyed and slightly disoriented. She blinked, looking around, taking in the thick flocked wallpaper and the Heppel-white desk in the corner, the highboy and the French doors with their velvet draperies. Belatedly she recognized her own bedroom in her father's house.

Home. She was home again.

And she felt like the stranger she had always been in this house.

She remembered the party last night, dancing until her feet ached and her throat was raw from talking and laughing, and knew that this was the way popular girls awakened every morning after a party. Pretty and popular. The things she had always wanted to be. At least, until Ryan had shown her that such qualities didn't matter.

She got up and washed at the washstand and cleaned her teeth. Opening the parcel from the *Silver Swan,* she discovered more of the elegantly cut dresses Lily had given her, and she put one on, limiting herself to a single petticoat. She was trying to put some order to her hair when a knock sounded at the door.

"Come in," she called.

Thankful, the maid, came bustling in with a tray. "Here's your tea, miss, and a whole bunch of cards and letters."

"Thank you. Set them on the side table." Isadora smiled distractedly. She kept thinking about the night before, the night all her dreams should have come true but had not.

Thankful lingered in the doorway, eyeing Isadora with ill-concealed curiosity and...something else. Admiration. Yes, the maid who had laughed at her, made sport of her in backstairs whispers, was suddenly fascinated with her transformation.

"That will be all for now, Thankful." Isadora poured herself a cup of tea and sipped it as she looked through the cards and notes. Invitations. A huge pile of them. Dancing parties, soirées, reading parties, intellectual debates, picnics, gaming nights, drives to the country. Every sort of social event she had ever dreamed of. Everything she had yearned for now lay before her on a silver platter.

The trouble was, she didn't want this kind of life anymore.

The realization washed over her, and she dropped the letters. Dear God. She'd spent years wanting something that didn't even matter.

Last night's celebration had seemed empty and meaningless without Ryan. The former insecure Isadora emerged briefly, wondering if he regretted his blurted declaration of love and was now avoiding her.

No. The new Isadora remembered the look in his eyes when he said it, and she trusted that look. Against all odds, the most exciting man in the world loved her. She should have guessed it long before. She should have seen it slowly happening, should have seen through his teasing. He had told her he loved her in countless ways, perhaps beginning with the singular act of cruelly throwing her spectacles overboard.

She'd been too thickheaded to realize what his actions meant. "Stupid," she said under her breath. "Stupid, stupid, stupid." Everything she wanted had been within her grasp—aboard the *Swan.* In Ryan Calhoun's arms. But she had been so fixated on coming back to Beacon

Hill, on conquering Chad Easterbrook and impressing those who had made fun of her, that she had been blind to what really mattered.

Ryan mattered. Ryan, and the way she was with him. The way she loved him.

"Ye powers," she said, yanking on a shawl, jamming on a hat. "I do love him."

Terror and joy rushed through her as she raced down the stairs, nearly overturning the tray in the foyer that was fast filling up with a new batch of invitations. "I'm going out, Mother," she called, tugging open the front door without waiting for an answer.

She must have been a peculiar sight, racing down the wet brick streets of Beacon Hill toward the waterfront, her hat trailing down her back on its ribbons and her skirt hiked almost to her knees. Nursemaids pushing prams stopped to stare. Gardeners straightened from their tasks, and inquisitive faces peeked out of coach windows.

Isadora didn't care; she barely noticed. It was only a short distance along the rainwashed streets, yet she had never covered it on foot. She was amazed to find that it took her only minutes to reach the waterfront. The one thought in her mind was Ryan. She had to find him, tell him...what?

That she loved him?

What would have been the point? he'd asked her only the day before. Did he mean there was no point because he didn't think she could love him? Or because there was another reason they should not be in love?

No matter. She knew now, knew with a certainty that mocked her for not recognizing it sooner. Why hadn't she understood, when he'd held her, kissed her, made love to her, that it was love she was feeling?

Because life had taught her to mistrust her own feelings, to obey convention and rules. Ryan had taught her otherwise. Nearly laughing or weeping with the knowledge, she barely noticed when it began to drizzle again. Through the thickening cold mist, she spied the familiar topgallant of the *Swan* and hurried toward it.

Harbor pilots had brought the bark into its berth and stevedores swarmed over the wharves and decks, discharging cargo. Isadora spotted Timothy Datty and waved at him, cupping her hands around her mouth. "I need to see Captain Calhoun," she called.

From a distance, Timothy's posture seemed to change. Was it a trick of the light, or did his face pale, his shoulders hunch?

Then she saw it. A sodden black ribbon suspended from a yardarm.

Isadora forced herself to back up and stand under a canvas awning as she waited for Datty to come down the gangplank. She heard the drumming of rain on the awning, the mournful cry of a gull, the whinny of a drayman's horse. Timothy stopped to hail a fisherman in oilskin slicks, spoke briefly to the man, then approached her.

She didn't want to hear it, whatever awful thing he was about to say to her. She wanted to clap her hands over her ears, but that would be wrong, that would be cowardly, and if she had learned anything from Ryan it was courage.

She went toward Timothy, meeting him halfway between the awning and the ship. She stood in the rain, in the gray, dripping chill that surrounded the wharf, feeling each droplet on her face, feeling the water drip down her temples and not caring that she was getting drenched.

"Where is Captain Calhoun?" Her voice didn't waver, didn't betray the dread that had started inside her the moment she'd seen the black ribbon through the curtain of rain.

"There was t-trouble last night," Timothy said, breathing fast with nervousness. "Please, Miss Isadora, come in out of the rain."

"Say it, Timothy," she said. "Quickly."

She noticed, with a dull thud of hopelessness, that the other crewmen were slowly coming toward her, hats in their hands, gazes cast down.

"The harbor guard boarded us last night. Said they'd heard we had fugitive slaves, said w-we was to surrender them immediately."

"Ryan would never surrender." She caught a sob in her throat and held it off, determined to hear what had happened with a stoicism that did honor to Ryan's bravery.

"We held off the guard as best we could," Ralph Izard said. "There were words, but no one came to blows." He cleared his throat. "There was nothing to find, anyway. The skipper and Journey, they'd already put Delilah and the little ones aboard the schooner."

Isadora closed her eyes. "They put out to sea, didn't they? They set sail right into the storm."

"They didn't have much choice. The guard gave chase—they had a skiff and a longboat—but only to the mouth of the harbor. Then they fell back." Izard squeezed his soggy hat in his hands. "The storm drove them back."

"And the schooner?" Isadora asked.

Silence. It roared at her from a void.

Timothy's shoulders shook with unrestrained sobs. The Doctor snuffled loudly, and William Click put his hand on the cook's arm. Gerald, Luigi and Chips stood around, wringing their hands helplessly. Without their skipper they foundered like a rudderless ship.

Izard gestured at the fishermen, who were busy off-loading their catch of codfish. "The crew of the *Gail* sighted them off George's Bank and tried to give aid, but the swells were too big."

"It wasn't any kind of weather for sailing," Chips said, his voice thin with horror.

"They saw the schooner go down," Izard said as gently as he could.

Isadora heard a terrible roaring in her ears, more awful than the roar of the sea in a storm. "But surely—please God, surely—they escaped in launches."

"No, miss." His long, mournful face was gray with suffering. "There were no survivors."

In the deepest part of her, something shattered. Something died.

Timothy reached for her hand but she didn't take it. She was made of glass; the slightest touch would cause her to fly to pieces.

I should weep, she thought. I should start to weep now and never stop. But it wasn't that simple. The magnitude of her loss was too immense for weeping.

An eerie calm settled over her as she turned away from the crew of the *Swan*.

"Where are they?" she asked. "Where are...the bodies?" The calm pressed upon her, smothering, choking her.

"Miss Isadora, they went down with the ship. There was no saving them in a storm like that. Please, miss, come to the galley. The Doctor will make some tea...."

She ignored the pleading voice, ignored the murmurs of sympathy, ignored everything but the cruel thunder of the ocean in her ears. Blood no longer ran in her veins. It was ice, pure ice, as cold as the ballast that had weighted the *Silver Swan* on its mythical voyage to paradise.

Twenty-Five

~~~∽♋∽~~~

A positive engagement to marry a certain person at a certain time, at all haps and hazards, I have always considered the most ridiculous thing on earth.

—Jane Welsh Carlyle
(1825)

Boston, June 1852

Being invisible used to have its advantages. Isadora Dudley Peabody wished people would stop staring at her. She wished, with all of her heart, that the gleaming ballroom floor would open up and swallow her. It wouldn't surprise anyone if the event occurred. Disappearing in the middle of a crowded room was bold indeed, and Isadora Peabody had lately earned a reputation for boldness.

Being bold, defiant even, was the only way she could

get from one day to the next without shattering into a million pieces. After that rainy morning on the wharf, she had closed herself into a cocoon, refusing to eat, unwilling to sleep, unable to cry. Those first few days after the loss at sea would remain a blur to her.

The authorities had come to question her about the slaves hiding aboard the *Swan*. She had looked them in the eye and declared that she knew nothing, absolutely nothing, about the fugitives.

There was a token search for the missing schooner. The shores were combed for flotsam and—God forbid—bodies. But none were found. Ryan and Journey and his family had disappeared off the face of the earth as if they had never existed. Isadora had forced herself to post a letter to Lily, but the effort had sucked everything out of her. She was empty.

The crew of the *Swan* had all gone their own ways, drifting apart like ice flows in the spring thaw.

Isadora hadn't spoken. Had barely moved. Her parents called in a physician, and she had surrendered to his ministrations until he grew exasperated with her lack of response.

The fool. Couldn't he understand that his patient was dead?

She had died, as horribly and as completely as Ryan had in the great cold briny deep. But, to her annoyance, she kept breathing. Her body kept functioning. She could not will it to stop.

The tragedy surprised no one. Ryan Calhoun was well-known for flouting protocol, he and his African business partner, the two of them so utterly unconventional that it seemed the world wasn't ready for them yet. Perhaps that was why they couldn't survive.

Was Journey better off, she wondered, with his wife and children in the deep hereafter? Was it better to be united in death than separated in life?

Isadora had yearned for death. She'd tried to will herself to surrender to the darkness, yet life for her persisted no matter what. Then, a fortnight ago, she had come to a realization that had thrust her decidedly back among the living.

She had dragged herself from bed, more sick with nausea than she had ever been on shipboard, and while she'd hung retching over the wash basin she had realized what the matter was.

She was expecting Ryan's child.

The knowledge had undammed the tide of her emotions. Long-suppressed grief lifted its shackles, and the shock of feeling sent her, sobbing, to her knees. She'd wept as she had not been able to weep before, letting out all the love, all the aching, shining, unspoken love she'd felt for Ryan. He was dead, and she was going to have his baby.

She carried the secret knowledge inside her, trying to discover a way to bear the feelings of anguish and joy. The one thing she did not feel was shame. They would all expect it of her, once the scandal broke, but even then she knew she could not be ashamed of what she had done with Ryan Calhoun, what she had felt for him, what she had given him. And what he had given her.

The most painful issue to face was that she'd never told him. She had not recognized that the passion and tenderness and excitement she felt for Ryan all added up to love. She'd been so involved in herself and her life in Boston that she had failed to see what was right in front of her. The man she loved was Ryan. She was amazed that she had been able to look at him and not see the truth.

Until Ryan, she had never learned to recognize love, to trust it. Because love in her family was not something given freely and unconditionally, but was a commodity that depended on a very specific protocol and set of values. Whatever virtues she possessed meant nothing unless they came in a lovely, refined package.

Ryan had been so different. He loved *her*. Not the idea of her. Not her status, her family, her looks, her fortune. But her, pure and simple. The idea was so new and alien to her that she hadn't grasped it until too late.

The discovery of her condition had sent her into an emotional maelstrom from which she almost didn't emerge. Once again, the physician was called, this time trying to quiet her hysterical weeping. But in the end it was not medicine, but love that saved her. The universe was trying to tell her something. She might not be able to forgive herself for failing to tell Ryan she loved him, but a larger force was at work. The baby was a statement that what she'd shared with Ryan was special and magical, it was something that not even death could take from her.

To deny life to the baby, to hold herself off from the world because of her grief, was unacceptable. It was time, she'd decided at last, to rejoin the living.

Her first order of business was to take up the cause against the institution responsible for destroying Ryan and Journey and his family. She had started attending rallies, going deeper and deeper into the middle of a core of radical abolitionists who would stop at nothing in order to end slavery.

Thus she found herself at her parents' ball, garbed in a silly costume for a masquerade, trying to pretend she wanted to be here.

In truth she had a secret purpose. She had contacted the Boston Abolition Society. When her parents found out, they would be appalled, of course, for slavery was one of those things they did not approve of but would never have the poor taste to make an issue of.

Isadora intended to do more than make an issue of it. She had learned, through one of the Abolition Society meetings, of a ship outfitted expressly to facilitate the escape of slaves. A virtual ghost ship. No one knew its name, its skipper and crew, or its home port. It was probably a rumor, some people said, but the ship was known to sweep into Southern ports in the dead of night, load itself with slaves and sail to the safety of Canada so swiftly that no pursuit could overtake it.

Isadora thought the legend a romantic idea, even if it wasn't true. And if it was, she intended to dedicate her life to supporting the endeavor.

She had received a cryptic message tonight, saying that an important contact would be made at the masquerade. Intrigued, she had donned a costume and delighted her parents by making an appearance.

Restless with her thoughts and trying to avoid the prying stares of the guests, she pressed herself back in a half-domed alcove window—but still she heard them.

"She's the black sheep of the family in more ways than one," whispered a gossipy voice Isadora was not supposed to hear. "She is so different from the rest of the Peabodys. She's tan as a savage, and her brothers and sisters are all fair as the springtime."

Couldn't they find someone else to talk about?

"But she's so handsome, so striking. It's a wonder no one noticed that before," came the reply. "They say she could have anyone she wants for a husband, but she's turned so strange lately...."

Isadora left the alcove, unwilling to hear any more. The startled speakers—two of her mother's friends— made a great show of fluttering their fans and clearing their throats and appearing totally innocent.

As always, she would pretend she hadn't heard. She would greet her parents' friends cordially. She would stiffly dance with the hopeful men who used to duck when they saw her coming, but lately lined up to partner her.

The pain and humiliation she used to feel at being snubbed at these affairs seemed so trivial now. For she had known the highest heights of joy and the deepest depths of despair. Enclosed in a sort of strange numbness, she endured.

True, the day would come when she would have to reveal the truth about her condition. All of Beacon Hill would buzz with the story of the Peabodys' wayward daughter and her reckless Southern sea captain. She had already determined that she would disappear with the child before scandal could touch it. Perhaps, like the ghost ship that ferried ex-slaves to freedom, a ship would come for her, sweep her away to some far-off land where it was safe to raise a child in the sunlight of approval and love. She owed that much to Ryan. She owed that much to the love they had shared.

Preoccupied with these thoughts, she favored several gentlemen with a dance. They were mostly her brothers' friends from Harvard, costumed as cavaliers and vampires and knights in tin armor. Chad Easterbrook, garbed in the toga of a Greek god, claimed the long waltz, intent on monopolizing her. At the end of the dance he steered her through the French doors to the verandah. They walked down three marble steps to the central fountain in the back, a carp eternally spitting into a huge seashell basin. In the chilly darkness he took her hand in his.

Heavens be. Surely *he* was not her contact.

"It is so very good to see you up and about again," he said, gazing at her hungrily from beneath the silver filigree circlet he wore around his tumbling black curls. "I've done nothing but think about you since you returned from your voyage."

"I hope you're exaggerating," Isadora said wryly, "else I would think you quite empty in the head."

He laughed as if she were joking. "I tell you, it's true. Isadora, I have dared to flatter myself into believing that at one time you showed me great favor."

She saw no point in lying. "Chad, there was a time when you were all I dreamed of—"

"I knew that." He pulled her close, his arms tightening around her.

She realized then that he'd known all along about her worship of him. He had known, and he had chosen to ignore her. It was one thing for him to be oblivious of her ardor; quite another to know of it and coldly disregard it.

Suddenly she wanted to be away from him. "Chad—"

"Isadora, let me finish. You've surely guessed my intentions by now. I want to marry you. We'll be—"

"Please, Chad, I—"

"No, listen. You are the most fascinating creature I've ever known, and I can't possibly ever be worthy of you, but I shall try. Already father has made me full officer in the company. He was quite impressed by my role in deflecting the scandal away from the *Swan*."

A chill eddied over her. "I don't know what you mean. What scandal?"

"We nearly lost our reputation thanks to that unlamented scoundrel, Ryan Calhoun. When the *Swan* first came into harbor, I guessed correctly that she was transporting fugitive slaves. I acted quickly and saved the company from embarrassment, not to mention heavy fines."

She wrenched away from him. "It was you, then. You alerted the authorities about Journey's family."

"It's the law," he said. "I would have been guilty of conspiracy if I'd failed to report my suspicions. And remember, our shipping company does business in the South. We can't afford to lose the cotton and tobacco cargos."

She was tempted to stand her ground, to lash him with a lecture on the rights of man and spout the rhetoric she had learned at her abolition meetings. But she knew it was no use. The man hadn't the wit to recognize another's humanity. Another's intelligence. Most especially in a black man, and certainly not in a woman like her.

She stepped back and looked him in the eye.

"I never knew you until now, Chad. It appears I liked you better when I didn't know you."

"What—"

"Pardon me."

He grabbed her arm, his brow descending like an ominous storm cloud. "Do I understand this correctly? You're refusing me?"

"You always were a clever sort," she said, glaring at the hand still gripping her arm. "Please let go of me now."

"Oh, I don't think so. Do you think you can refuse me? You're not so respectable now that you've been on a ship with a crew of seadogs and escaped slaves."

Ah. Someone finally had the nerve to speak the truth to her face. She knew then that she had not come through unscathed.

"I found their company far more pleasing than anything I've found in Boston," she retorted.

"Which proves your lack of judgment. I knew Calhoun was scum from the moment he entered Harvard, him with his idiotic Virginia drawl and the cheap women he consorted with."

"I'm pleased to tell you, I am one of those 'cheap women.' Do you still want me?"

"I fear I have no choice, since your disgrace happened aboard my vessel."

"But why would you, the mighty Chad Easterbrook, want such a social pariah?"

His face clouded, then grew naked with desire. "Marrying you now would be beneath me, but I could raise you up. You are unique among women, but I expect you to be damned grateful to me for the rest of your days.''

Isadora had forgotten the name of the particular punch she used. Either a roundhouse or a sidewinder; at one time Gerald Craven had taught her the terms. But she did recall, with satisfying swiftness, the precise use of the punch. Her arm, still muscular from her travails on the ship, came around with great force, her fist smashing into Chad Easterbrook's face.

He lost his grip on her, arms paddling the air before he staggered against the rim of the fountain.

She placed her hands on his shoulders and heaved him in.

Hands on hips, she looked down at the cursing, sputtering ruin of her childhood god. ''Oh, Chad, you're all wet. And your pretty costume is stained with moss. Whatever are people going to say?''

Twenty-Six

The Owl and the Pussy-Cat went to sea
In a beautiful pea-green boat.
They took some money, and plenty of honey
Wrapped up in a five-pound note...
They dined on mince, and slices of quince,
Which they ate with a runcible spoon;
And hand in hand, on the edge of the sand,
They danced by the light of the moon, the moon,
 the moon,
They danced by the light of the moon.

—Edward Lear
The Owl and the Pussy-Cat

Isadora hurried across the ballroom, hoping she could leave unobtrusively. As she edged toward the entranceway of the ballroom and paused beneath the carved federal walnut arch, memories flooded her. Less than a year ago, another Isadora had stood at this very spot, trying to slip out of a party she wasn't enjoying.

She had wished to escape that night, as well. But what she had wanted to do was escape her own life.

Now, although the scene was eerily the same, she knew she was here to *live* that life. The gilt cherub mirror hung in the foyer. The graceful Boston fern flourished in a pot with four legs. She had destroyed it the last time. As if the mishap had never happened, it had been replaced.

One step, then another. Invisible. She was invisible; she could fly like a bird, slither like a snake. Though once awkward, she was now lithe and graceful, fleet of foot, causing no more stir than a breeze as she disappeared into nothingness, into freedom—

She barely noticed a commotion at the door. She heard a scraping sound and turned in time to see more guests arriving. A masked and snarling pirate burst into the house.

"Ye powers," she whispered, jolted by the look of him. Her preoccupation with Ryan had made him a phantom in her heart. She was losing her mind, surely.

The pirate had tangled the end of his tattered scarf around one of the legs of the fern pot. Laughing heartily, the pirate gave the scarf a tug.

Time seemed to slow, and Isadora saw the whole sequence as if through a wall of water. The scarf went taut, upending the large plant. The alabaster pot shattered against the marble floor.

The abrupt movement and the explosion of noise caused everyone to freeze for precisely three seconds. Then the masked pirate faced the onlookers and said, "Oops."

Dear God, that was no phantom. He was real.

The band of growling pirates surged into the foyer, pretending to menace people with rusty sabers and antique pistols, but for Isadora, the world stayed frozen.

She saw nothing but the tall man in the tattered red scarf. Heard nothing but the echo of familiar laughter.

Ryan.

Her heart spoke his name when her mouth was too astonished to make a sound.

Ryan.

Alive, he was alive, a vibrant and laughing contradiction to the grim reports of his death.

Sheer joy made her knees nearly buckle. She pressed her hand to her mouth, trying her best to keep in the sobs while the tears flowed down her face. Vaguely, she became aware of her family gathering around, watching her with concern as the masked and jubilant pirates made their merry way through the crowd. She recognized Chips's bald head, Timothy Datty's slender darting form and Izard and the Doctor and Gerald and Luigi and even the surly Click, all of them shrieking with glee as they committed robbery. The guests, thinking it was entertainment, gave up their belongings without a murmur.

She noticed all this through a blur of tears, noticed it even though she didn't take her eyes off Ryan. He threw back his head and released a piratical stream of full-throated laughter, and then, as the other guests joined in the spirit of the "attack," he came toward her.

More swiftly than the wind itself, he crossed the foyer and swept her up into his strong arms so that her feet left the floor. "Avast there, wench! Did you think you could escape me?" Angling a path through the crowd, he carried her out into the night, where a fresh wind, salted by the sea, skirled up from Boston harbor.

He stopped walking and kissed her, a rough open-mouthed kiss that filled her with the taste of him, and at last he was real to her, no dream, no ghost come back from the dead, but Ryan...her Ryan.

Still clinging to his neck, she slid down so that her feet touched the ground. "I thought...we all thought...you'd died in the storm. What of Journey and Delilah and the children?"

"They're working on an apple farm in Canada. We had to stage the accident at sea in order to throw off our pursuers."

"Why did you let me think you were dead?" she whispered. "Why did you let me grieve?"

"I didn't mean to hurt you, love. I came as soon as I could."

She shut her eyes and pressed herself against him, savoring the miracle of his return. God, his smell—the wind and the sea and just...just Ryan.

"I have something to tell you," she whispered.

"Oh, Christ. The scurvy barnacle did it, didn't he? Chad Easterbrook asked you to marry him."

"As a matter of fact, he did, but—"

"Damn it. *Damn it.* I knew I'd be too late. I'll challenge the scum to a duel, blow his empty head off—"

"Ryan. I said he *asked* me. I didn't say what my reply was."

He stared at her, a cautious joy lighting his face. "You mean...?"

She felt the wind cool the wetness of tears on her cheeks. "How could I consider him, when I'll always hold you in my heart? I thought I'd find everything I needed to know in books, but I learned love from you, Ryan. I love you.''

When he kissed her again, she was certain she could taste his joy, could see it in his eyes when he lifted his mouth from hers and said, "So what was it you wanted to tell me?''

She took his hand and covered it with her own, bringing it down to cup her stomach. "Remember when you said if I found myself with child, you'd make it right?''

He swallowed hard, and his voice held a rough catch of emotion. Like the dawning sun, his face lit with knowing. "I remember. I…promised.''

"Then I think you're going to have to make good on that promise.''

He froze in a moment of complete incredulity. Then, throwing back his head, he let loose with a shout of triumph and swept her up into his arms once again. "Say your prayers, wench,'' he said in his mock-pirate snarl, his broad strides hastening along the brick walkway. "You're mine now, all mine!''

And as he carried her down to the harbor, she buried her head against his shoulder, laughing and weeping with all the fullness of her love. "Ah, Ryan. Didn't you know? I always have been.''

Afterword

~~~

Dear Reader:

Although it was unusual for a well-born young lady to be so active in both commerce and in a political cause, it was certainly not unheard of in Boston. The 1850s in particular were a period of unprecedented social consciousness, and I like to think Ryan and Isadora personify the devotion and faith it takes to commit fully to a cause—no matter what the risk.

Often when I finish a book, I'm eager to move on to the next story. But in this case I was haunted by Ryan's brother, Hunter Calhoun, so much so that he has taken on a life of his own and has become the main character in my next book, *The Horsemaster's Daughter*.

Hunter's situation, I regret to say, has gone from bad to worse. Devastated by loss and driven to the brink of bankruptcy, this Virginia gentleman struggles to create a better, safer world for his children. His fortunes rest with a very special Irish thoroughbred, but his prospects are dashed when the stallion arrives from Ireland a crazed beast, hopelessly traumatized by the sea voyage. Everyone advises Hunter to shoot the poor creature. In desperation, he turns to the strange, fey and secretive Eliza Flyte, who lives alone on a storm-battered barrier island, where she was raised in isolation by her learned father.

She is drawn to Hunter out of compassion for a damaged horse, but finds herself swept into the heart of his broken family. Gentling the horse becomes the least of her tasks as she learns her true purpose—to bring light into the darkness of Hunter's life, to restore the love of his troubled children and to take her place in a world that once shunned her.

* * * * *

Please watch for
THE HORSEMASTER'S DAUGHTER
in November of 1999.
Until then, happy reading.

Warmly,
Susan Wiggs
P.O. Box 4469
Rolling Bay, WA
98061-0469

Knowing the truth could be more than
she bargained for...

MORE THAN YOU KNOW

HELEN R. MYERS

A man who had everything to live for was dead.
And his baby had disappeared into thin air.

Nicole Loring was determined to find out what happened to her brother and nephew. With nowhere else
to turn, she enlisted the help of the last man she
should trust, a highly respected police detective who
was behaving suspiciously....

On sale mid-April 1999
wherever paperbacks are sold!

MIRA®

Look us up on-line at: http://www.mirabooks.com   MHRM504